KU-618-982

The Woman Who Died a Lot

'I think it's an episode of *The Dukes of Hazzard*.'

Jasper Fforde

The Woman Who Died a Lot

HODDER &
STOUGHTON

First published in Great Britain in 2012 by Hodder & Stoughton
An Hachette UK company

1

All characters in this publication are fictitious and any resemblance to real persons, living or dead is purely coincidental.

A CIP catalogue record for this title is available from the British Library

Hardback ISBN 9780340963111
Trade Paperback ISBN 9780340963128
Ebook ISBN 9781444709339

Typeset in Bembo by Palimpsest Book Production Limited, Falkirk, Stirlingshire

Printed and bound by Clays Ltd, St Ives plc

Hodder & Stoughton policy is to use papers that are natural, renewable and recyclable products and made from wood grown in sustainable forests. The logging and manufacturing processes are expected to conform to the environmental regulations of the country of origin.

To all the librarians
that have ever been
ever will be
are now
this book is respectfully dedicated

Also by Jasper Fforde

The Thursday Next Series

The Eyre Affair

Lost in a Good Book

The Well of Lost Plots

Something Rotten

First Among Sequels

~~The Great Samuel Pepys Fiasco~~

One of Our Thursdays is Missing

The Nursery Crime Series

The Big Over Easy

The Fourth Bear

The Last Dragonslayer Series

The Last Dragonslayer

The Song of the Quarkbeast

Shades of Grey

Author's Note:

This book has been bundled with **Special Features** including: *The Making of* . . . wordamentary, deleted scenes, alternative endings and much more.

To access all these free bonus features, log on to: **www.jasperfforde.com/features.html** and follow the onscreen instructions.

Contents

1.	*Monday: Swindon*	*1*
2.	*Monday: Phoebe Smalls*	*11*
3.	*Monday: SpecOps*	*19*
4.	*Monday: Shrink to Fit*	*27*
5.	*Monday: Braxton Hicks*	*39*
6.	*Monday: TK Maxx*	*49*
7.	*Monday: Tuesday*	*59*
8.	*Monday: Friday*	*69*
9.	*Monday: The Madeupion*	*77*
10.	*Monday: The Wingco*	*85*
11.	*Monday: Evening*	*89*
12.	*Tuesday: Library*	*95*
13.	*A Penguin*	*112*
14.	*Tuesday: Next Thursday*	*113*
15.	*Tuesday: I'm back*	*123*
16.	*Tuesday: The Finis*	*129*
17.	*Tuesday: Tuesday*	*133*
18.	*Tuesday: The Sisterhood*	*141*
19.	*Tuesday: Smalls*	*157*
20.	*Tuesday: Home*	*165*
21.	*Tuesday: The Destiny-Aware*	*177*
22.	*Wednesday: Library*	*187*
23.	*Wednesday: Goliath*	*197*

24. *Wednesday: Adelphi* 205
25. *Wednesday: Blyton* 217
26. *Wednesday: Smote Solutions* 225
27. *Wednesday: Wroughton* 233
28. *Wednesday: Kemble Timepark* 241
29. *Wednesday: The Manchild* 251
30. *Wednesday: Dodo Buffer* 263
31 *Thursday: Budget* 271
32. *Thursday: Finisterre* 287
33. *Thursday: MadCon 2004* 293
34. *Thursday: Gavin Watkins* 301
35. *Thursday: Evening* 309
36. *Thursday: Aornis* 315
37. *Friday: Morning* 335
38. *Friday: The Righteous Man* 347
39. *Friday: The Smiting* 357
40. *Friday: Destiny* 367
41. *Monday: End* 377
Acknowledgements 383

I

Monday: Swindon

> 'The Special Operations Network was formed in 1928 to handle policing duties considered too specialised to be tackled by the regular force. Despite considerable success in the many varied areas of expertise in which SpecOps operated, all but three of the thirty-six divisions were disbanded in the winter of 1991/92, allegedly because of budgetary cutbacks. By 2004 it was realised that this was a bad move, and plans were drawn up to reinstigate the service.'
>
> Millon de Floss – *A Short History of SpecOps*

Everything comes to an end. A good bottle of wine, a summer's day, a long-running sitcom, one's life, and eventually our species. The question for many of us is not that everything *will* come to an end, but *when*, and can we do anything vaguely useful until it does?

In the case of a good bottle of wine, probably not much – although the very act of consumption might make one believe otherwise. A well-lazed summer's day should not expect too much of itself either, and sitcoms never die. They simply move to a zombie-like existence in repeat heaven. Of the remaining two – the end of one's life and that of our species – regular subscribers to my exploits will recall that I had seen myself die a few years back, and given my past record, it would be probable that much useful work would be done between then and now. As to the end of our species, the possibility of annihilation was quite real, well documented, and went by the unimaginative title of Asteroid HR-6984. Whether the human race managed to figure out a worthwhile function for itself in the thirty-seven years until possible collision was dependent upon your level of optimism.

But it wasn't all bad news. In fact, owing to a foible of human nature that denies us the ability to focus on more than one threat at a time, the asteroid was barely news at all. HR-6984's inconvenient lack of urgency and current likelihood of only around 34 per cent had relegated it well past such front-page news as the Stupidity Surplus and the current round of fiery cleansings by an angry deity, and instead saw the hurtling lump of space debris consigned to pop culture damnation on page twelve: sandwiched somewhere between guinea-pig accessorising and the apparently relevant eating habits of non-celebrities.

My take on it was this: a 34 per cent chance of something happening was also a 66 per cent chance it *wouldn't* happen, and given the rocky road our species had travelled to get here in the first place, these were considerably better odds than we'd seen so far. As for finding a collective purpose for ourselves in what might potentially be the last thirty-seven years of our existence, I was always struck by the paradox that while *collective* purpose might be at best unknowable and at worst irrelevant, *individual* purpose was of considerable importance.

But I'm getting ahead of myself. The events described here occurred during a busier-than-usual week in the late summer of 2004. A week that began with a trip into Swindon in order to find a job, and ended with a pillar of cleansing fire descending from the heavens, a rethink on the Wessex Library Services operating budget and my son shooting Gavin Watkins dead. The last one was a serious downer – especially for Gavin. It's a long story, and with a few twists and turns that take a bit of figuring. What the hell. We'll just run the story in real time as it happened, and worry about the logic afterwards.

So there we were: my husband Landen and I, sitting in the comfort of a Skyrail car, gliding effortlessly above the North Wessex countryside on the Newbury–Hungerford–Swindon monorail. We'd boarded at Aldbourne, where we now lived, and the car was almost empty. We weren't talking about Asteroid HR-6984, nor the Stupidity Surplus or Landen's latest book: *Dogs Who Wonder Why Their Owners Think They Know When They Are Coming Home Because We Dogs Don't Really but Agree It Might Appear as if We Do.* We weren't even talking about other issues of the day, such as pissed-off deities, Phoebe Smalls, the movie of *Bonzo the Wonder Hound*, synthetic Thursdays or the ongoing 'Brains kept alive in jars' ethical debate in *New Splicer* magazine. No, we were talking about our daughter Jenny, and why I needed a tattoo to remind me she was somewhat less than I imagined, or indeed, every bit as I imagined.

'I never thought I'd get a second,' I said, staring at the scarlet rawness on the back of my hand.

'I'm amazed you even got the first,' said Landen.

'It was on a drunken night in Sevastopol,' I replied wistfully, 'a week off the troopship and still without an ounce of combat experience, or sense.'

'Happy days,' said Landen, 'to have experienced the camaraderie before the loss.'

He gave me a half-smile and I knew precisely what he meant. Before the *ziiip* of a round heralded a near-miss, the Crimea seemed like nothing more than a bit of a lark.

'The brigade tattoo was one of those bonding moments,' I said, 'like agreeing to box Corporal Dwight for a kilo of best Beluga caviar.'

He chuckled.

'You were mad. Dwight was a *serious* bruiser.'

'I know that *now*,' I replied, 'but give me credit for the attempt.'

Lance Corporal Betty 'Basher' Dwight remained unbeaten in twenty-seven kick-boxing bouts, thirteen of them against men. She was to become a loyal companion and friend but not beyond my eighteen months of active service. Basher stayed in the Crimea, and I don't mean to open a bar or something.

That first tattoo had been inked the night of my fight with Dwight and had actually been quite useful. Clearly not *that* drunk, I'd asked them to add my blood and tissue grouping to the brigade motif, a simple act that saved my life at least twice. The boxing bout was not so successful. I hit the canvas ten seconds into the third round after a truly punishing first and second – my nose is still a bit bent, even today – and the unit had to go without caviar on their blinis for a month.

My second tattoo was done only two weeks ago, just after I'd turned fifty-four. It was of a purely practical nature and, unlike the first, which was etched unobtrusively on my upper arm, was on the back of my hand for all to see, *especially* me. It was at my family's request, too – an attempt to remind myself that my second daughter Jenny wasn't real at all, but a troublesome Mindworm foisted on to me by a vengeful adversary.

'Did it have to go on my hand?' I said to Landen as the Skyrail car docked at Clary-Lamarr, Swindon's main TravelHub.

'It has to be somewhere you'll have a chance of seeing it. The constant reminding might help you get over her.'

I stared at it again in order to keep the thoughts in my head as long as possible. Now we were talking about Jenny's non-existence everything seemed fine, but I knew also that these moments were fleeting. In a few moments all knowledge of the Mindworm would be gone and I'd be fretting over Jenny again. Where she was, how she was, and why the teachers called Landen when I came to school to pick her up.

'Do you think it will?'

'I'm hoping *yes* but thinking *no*,' replied Landen in a typically stoical manner. 'The only person who can fix your Jenny problem is the person who infected you with the Mindworm: Aornis.'

This might seem strange until you realise that Aornis is a mnemonomorph – someone who can manipulate memories. She could rob a bank and no one would remember she'd been there. And trying to capture someone who can manipulate memories is like trying to sweep a partial vacuum into a bell jar using only a yard broom. But we could make enquiries about her, and that was another reason we were in Swindon.

I grunted resignedly and then, after a short and oddly treacly pause, wondered what I was grunting resignedly *about*.

We drifted down the escalators from the south entrance of Clary-Lamarr and stepped on to the large concourse outside, which was dominated by the thirty-foot-high bronze statue of Lola Vavoom. We had missed the rush hour and only latecomers and shoppers were walking out of the TravelHub.

'What were we just talking about?' I asked.

'Stuff,' replied Landen vaguely, taking a deep breath. 'You know, I'm not sure I'm going to get used to living out of town. To me, grass is simply a transitional phase in turning sunlight into milk.'

'You're changing the subject,' I replied suspiciously.

'I do that sometimes.'

'You do, don't you?'

But Landen was right. He wasn't really a country dweller.

'After a few months you'll be wondering how you lived anywhere else.'

'Perhaps.'

We'd moved out of Swindon four months before, not long after I'd been discharged from hospital. The main reason was that our daughter Tuesday needed more room to experiment, but an equally good reason was security. I had more enemies than was considered healthy for the peaceful family life I had half-promised myself, and a country home was more easily defended – from enemies either side of the printed page.

'I think the City Council are taking the threat of a smiting a bit lightly, don't you?' I asked, as aside from a few billboards outlining the possibility that the Almighty would lay the centre of Swindon to waste in an all-consuming fire next Friday, little seemed to be going on.

'Joffy said the cathedral received a leaflet slipped under the west door,' murmured Landen. 'It was called: *Vengeful Cleansing by a Wrathful Deity and You*.'

'Helpful?'

'Not really. A few tips for a safe evacuation when the order is given – covering the windows with brown paper, hiding under tables, mumbling – that sort of thing. I'm not sure they're taking the threat seriously.'

'It was serious enough for Oswestry,' I replied, recalling the first of the nine random smitings that had been undertaken around the globe by a clearly disgruntled deity, eager to show his wayward creations the error of their ways.

'Perhaps so, but that was the first time and no one believed it would happen. If they'd evacuated the town, all would have been fine – and only the buildings destroyed.'

'I suppose so. Did they ever decide whether it was ethical for those turned to pillars of salt to be ground up for use as winter road grit?'

'I don't know. Probably not.'

He looked at his watch.

'What time are you meeting with Braxton?'

'As soon as I've had the psychological evaluation.'

'I thought you'd have to be a bit nuts to want to run SO-27,' mused Landen.

'Undoubtedly,' I replied, 'but it's not so much a question of how mad applicants for the job might be, but the *style* of madness. Obsessive drive is probably good, speaking in tongues and shouting at the walls less so.'

'Do you think Phoebe Smalls has the requisite loopiness to get the job?'

Detective Smalls, it should be noted, was the only other person who could realistically lead the re-formed Literary Detectives division. She was good, but then so was I.

I thought for a moment.

'Perhaps. She applied for the job, after all – no one would do that unless a little bit odd.'

'She's not got your experience,' said Landen. 'Running SO-27 isn't for tenderfoots.'

'But she's got the *youth*,' I replied, 'and her health.'

'Phoebe Smalls might look a sound bet on paper,' he replied, 'but when weird comes knocking, grey hairs count. Braxton knows this. Besides, the boss need never leave the office. Leave the running around to the young pups.'

He smiled at me, but he knew I wasn't happy. I was yet to walk without a stick, or pain. My broken femur had knitted badly in the two weeks before I was found following my accident, and it had to be broken and reset with pins, which is never satisfactory. I wasn't particularly worried; running is overrated anyway, and sport only makes you sweaty and smug and wears out the knees. Besides, Landen had been missing his leg above the knee for longer than he hadn't, and he was fine. In fact, since he had a left limp and I had a right one, if we walked side by side it apparently looked quite comical. I told Tuesday we were her 'cute cripple parents' and she retorted that 'cripple' wasn't *really* a polite term, and I told her that since my leg got mashed I could define myself in any way I chose. In answer to *that*, she huffed, glared and then pouted, as teenagers are apt to do.

'You're right,' Landen had remarked when I told him. He'd lost his leg to a landmine in the Crimea almost three decades before, and referred to himself as either a 'deconstructed bipedalist', or more simply 'a man unjustly overcharged for socks'.

'Will you be okay?' he asked.

'I'm fine,' I told him, 'with a stick to lean on and four Dizuperadol patches.'

'Four?' said Landen. 'You shouldn't have more then three.'

'It's the only thing that seems to have any lasting effect. Slow and constant release – double thickness, too.'

I'd recently moved to the more effective stick-on patches rather than Dizuperadol taken orally. The patches seemed to work for longer, and I'd been prescribed the double-strength ones: sometimes it felt like I had a waffle stuck to my bum. They were effective, but there were side effects.

'How's the vision?' asked Landen.

'In focus more often than it's not. And that's good, right?'

'A Zen dog dreams of a medium-sized bone.'

'Actually, there is one thing you could do. Can you put my mobile phone in my right pocket so I can get it out?'

Landen did as I asked. I'd been working on the grip of my left hand, but it was slow going. The damage to my hand had been caused by the taxi's indicator stalk as it passed through my forearm during the taxi's sudden stop in the swamp, and caused all sorts of mayhem on the way. The stalk broke off when it hit my jaw. These days I used it as a tea stirrer. The stalk that is, not my jaw.

'I'll meet you in TK Maxx around two,' said Landen, giving me an affectionate nuzzle, 'and don't be too mean with the shrink, will you? They've got feelings too.'

'I'll play nice. What's the password this time?'

For a few years now, Goliath had been sending synthetic Thursdays out into the world to try to get information from people who would speak only to me – Landen being an obvious example. They had also tried to gain access to my house, the SpecOps records department and even blag a free membership at a health farm. The copies were initially crude, but had made steady and sustained advances in sophistication since first appearing eighteen months before. The Mk IV and Vs wouldn't have fooled anyone, but the Mark VIs were impressive and had been able to crack single code words, which was why we used the more cloak-and-daggerish sentences and responses.

'What about if I say: "No cookies at the hunt, sir!" and then you reply with: "It's not a cookie, it's a Newton"?'

'Sounds random enough.'

So with the passwords committed to memory, we limped off in opposite directions. I turned once to take a look at him, and he did the same, and we smiled a simple smile of understanding. Parting for us was generally sweet sorrow, as past experience had taught us there was a fair possibility we might not see one another for a while, if at all – a state of affairs for which I took full responsibility. Sadly, a lifetime in law enforcement tends not to create a bunch of grateful villains happy that you have shown them the error of their ways, but a lot of disgruntled ne'er-do-wells eager for payback.

I hobbled across the pedestrian walkway and passed beneath the shadow of Swindon's centrally located anti-smiting tower, the primary defence against God's planned cleansings of the sinful. I stopped to stare for a moment at the two hundred foot tower. It looked like an electricity pylon topped with a domed metallic mushroom, the burnished copper sheathing glowing in the sun. Even though the many towers dotted about the country were *mechanically* complete, there were still several hurdles to overcome. The software controlling the 8.2 million independently controlled lasers inside the dome had yet to be fine-tuned, and until it was, the defence shield remained non-operational.

Perhaps the reason the City Council weren't so bothered about Swindon's smiting was because they'd convinced themselves the tower would be running in good time to deflect the Wrath of the Almighty in four days' time. I didn't think it would, and with good reason – I knew the genius behind the technology, and despite much midnight oil, the Anti-Smiting Defence Shield remained firmly on the theoretical side of reality.

I hurried on, passed the Thistle hotel to my right, and presently found myself outside the front entrance of the Wessex Special Operations Headquarters.

2

Monday: Phoebe Smalls

> 'The SpecOps division most associated with Thursday Next was SO-27, the Literary Detectives. It was their job to protect the citizenry against literary fraud, overenthusiastic interpretations of protected plays, and the illegal trade in bogus Shakespeareana. Miss Next joined the Swindon branch in 1985 not long before the adventure that came to be known as *The Eyre Affair.* She worked there on and off in various capacities until disbandment in 1991, and was always suspected of continuing her job under the radar in the years since.'
>
> Millon de Floss – *The Thursday Next Chronicles*

The offices had survived almost completely unchanged since most of the Special Operations Network was disbanded thirteen years before. The building was of a sensible design from the forties, and the worn wood and eroded stonework contained more memories than any other place in my life, with the possible exception of the Jurisfiction offices at Norland Park. I pushed open the heavy doors and walked into the lobby. High above me a glazed ceiling let in a directionless grey light and, by the look of it, some rainwater. The paintwork was peeling, and there was the ever-present smell of damp carpets and boiled cabbage – or, if you prefer, boiled carpets and damp cabbage.

The lobby had a few officers milling about, which reflected the fact that the Special Operations Network had not been *completely* disbanded. There were six SpecOps divisions remaining out of the thirty or so who once worked here. SO-6 and SO-9 had been merged and looked after National Security and Diplomatic

Protection. SO-1 policed the network itself and SO-5 were a super-judiciary search/destroy unit – I'd worked for them myself when we'd hunted down Acheron Hades. The Tax Office was SO-28, and the Cheese Enforcement Agency were SO-31.

This left only SO-3, whom we had called 'The Odd Squad'. They looked after dimensional travel issues, which were so disagreeably complex and mind-bogglingly strange we were all glad to have nothing to do with them. Suffice to say there were a shade over six thousand entirely separate dimensions within the League of Alternative Realities – a tiny fraction of the total but you didn't get to join the League until you'd figured out how to move across, something that now seemed so blindingly obvious it's astonishing we couldn't see it before. Our own dimension was coded ID-11 and was the only League member with diphtheria, David Hasselhoff and the French, which amused the rest of the multiverse no end. It wasn't all bad news as we were also the only one with bicycles, dogs and music, which put us in a robust trading position. SO-3 mostly dealt with trade issues like this; early trades were Brompton folding bicycles to HC-110 in return for escalators, and Dalmatians to X-TOL for fax machines. A more recent deal was the complete works of Bartok in exchange for a chain of grocery stores peculiar to D-76, which featured cheaper groceries. The chain was called Aldi, which explained the low cost and why you can't ever recognise the brands.

As I stood there for a moment, lost in thought, three operatives walked past in civvies. I could tell they were Odd Squad because they wore their left thumbs on the wrong side of the hand. No one knew quite *why* but we suspected it was similar to a hazing or a rite of passage, like my bout with Basher Dwight. The story goes that newbies at SO-3 get sent to mirror dimension E-6 to get partially reversed, but have to be careful – stay a second too long and you'd have ears on backwards or genitals in the small of your back. Mind you, it was less permanent than a tattoo – stay for *just* the right length of time in E-6 and you'd go all the way round and revert to normal. None ever did. You carried two right hands for life as a badge of honour, and *solidarity*.

By way of comparison, hazing at the now-defunct time travelling elite known as the Chronoguard was just as frightening but a lot more spectacular: a sixty-five-million-year backjump to ground zero during the KT Extinction Event. The losers jumped out as the meteor struck, but the bold and proud waited for the shock wave. If you returned with grit in your hair and the smell of terrified Hadrosaur about you, well, you'd not be buying the first round for a while.

I limped across the lobby to the main desk. A slim young woman had her back to me as I approached, but she turned as soon as I limped up to the desk.

'Detective Next?' she said, giving me a broad smile and holding out her hand. 'It's a huge honour.'

She was taller than me by a few inches, slender and attractive. Her long dark hair was unflecked by grey and tied in a loose ponytail. She had fine features and smiled with easy confidence. She was also young – barely thirty – and I'd heard that she spoke three languages and had graduated with a double first in English literature from Oxford. I also knew that she'd been a cop since graduation, made detective in only three years and been awarded Swindon's highest award for bravery, the Dorcan Star. It was well deserved – she took a bullet through the ear defending the mayor against Elgin separatists. This was Phoebe Smalls.

'Detective Smalls,' I said, shaking the proffered hand, 'you've been making quite a name for yourself.'

'I looked to your career for inspiration,' she said. 'Everything I've ever done was because you did it first.'

'I never lost an ear on the mayor's account,' I told her, indicating the ragged thing on the side of her head.

'Pardon?'

'I said: "I never lost—"'

'Just kidding. I can hear perfectly.'

She looked down at my walking stick.

'I heard you took all this in pursuit of the law,' she said. 'I only tackled the separatists because I knew you would. Ever since I was a little girl I wanted to be just like Thursday Next – only more so.'

She gave me the steely gaze of the supremely ambitious, and my hackles, which had already risen, rose farther.

'Like me only more so? How's that meant to work?'

'Go farther, achieve more, fail less.'

'Oh yes?' I replied. 'And how's that working out for you so far?'

'I'm already taller.'

'But not older.'

'I'm working on that daily. I think you should be flattered – someone who wants to be a better version of you. I think we should have a longer meeting,' she added, 'to have a chat. Find out the areas in which there could be improvement.'

'That's the point about failure,' I said. 'It's an intrinsic part of success. You win some, then you lose some. But with experience and luck, you learn to lose less as the years go on.'

Smalls nodded in agreement.

'Like in sports,' she said, 'it all boils down to lose/save ratios. I've been studying your stats, Thursday. You've got a career lives lost/saved ratio of 32:1 over sixty-two encounters, and a solve ratio of sixty-two per cent. That places you at number twenty-eight in the global tables.'

'Is that a fact?' I said.

'Yes,' she replied eagerly, 'it's all *very* scientific.'

'There's nothing scientific in tackling a crazed lunatic coming at you with an axe,' I said. 'How did you do in the league table?'

'Okay so far. But if I'm to improve my ratio I need to know where you failed, and how I might do better. In that way I can make your mistakes the mistakes I would have made but now won't. It's for the good of the citizenry we protect, Miss Next. I'm not in this for the glory, as I'm sure neither were you.'

'Neither *was* I?'

'Sorry,' she said, 'I wasn't suggesting that your career was effectively over.'

But she just had. I sighed. I didn't want to fight her. She was good, it was undeniable. Just a bit, well, intense – and obsessed with figures.

There was a pause.

'So,' I said, 'would you like to be my second-in-command when Braxton offers me the SO-27 job?'

'Generous, if a little misguided,' she replied with a smile. 'As far as I can see I'm the only viable candidate.'

'Not *quite* correct,' I replied with a smile. 'Braxton values experience above all.'

She looked at my stick and my leg, and then back at my face.

'Yes, I'm fully confident that Commander Hicks will come to the correct decision. I'd still like us to be friends, Thursday. Together we have much to offer the service. Youth, vitality, vigour . . . and experience. See you around.'

And she left me there in an empty pause in which I was thinking up a pithy rejoinder. I *did* think of one, but her back had already turned and it was too late to be anything but a lame attempt to get the final word.

'Detective Smalls is the Gold Standard in law enforcement,' said the officer at the main desk as he watched her slender figure walk elegantly to the exit. 'Can I help?'

I told him I was here for a psychiatric evaluation and showed him my ID. He recognised the name and raised an eyebrow.

'Welcome back, Detective Next. When I said Smalls was the Gold Standard my comment may have been taken out of context. I really meant that she met the high gold standard set by *your* reputation.'

'You're a terrible creep, Sergeant.'

'Thank you, ma'am.'

'Is the shrink in his usual room?'

'They moved him to the first floor,' said the officer, 'Room 101. Another high-ranker is with him at the moment. We had Officer Stoker in this morning – before dawn, for some reason.'

This was better news. Spike was a good friend and, like me, had also lost his job during the SpecOps disbandment.

'He's up for the SO-17 Divisional Chief's job?'

'Apparently, although as he himself says: "Who else would be dumb-arsed enough to take it?"'

'There might be some truth in that,' I mused. Spike's work with the semi-dead, ethereal horrors, demons, bogles and vampires wasn't everyone's cup of tea. In fact, aside from Spike himself with my occasional assistance, it wasn't *anyone*'s cup of tea. His old division of SO-17 were known colloquially as 'Suckers and Biters', but they dealt with anything of a nominally undead or horrific nature. Despite the cuts, Officer 'Spike' Stoker had managed to keep the phantasm containment facilities and deep refrigeration units going in the sub-basements, but only after he demonstrated *precisely* why there was a good reason. The councillor who was eager to make the cuts rashly took up Spike's offer of a tour. She was struck dumb for six months. Only a fool looked into anything below the fifth sub-basement.

'May I ask a question, Detective?' said the sergeant.

'Go on.'

'Why are they resurrecting SpecOps?'

'I have no idea. First floor, did you say?'

'Room 101. Don't be too harsh with Dr Chumley. He's our third shrink in as many years. The last one was taken away in an ambulance. They don't make them like they used to. Let me give you a visitor's pass.'

3

Monday: SpecOps

> 'The recent smitings undertaken around the globe have taken many theological analysts by surprise, as this level of apparent interest in mankind's affairs by the Almighty had not been seen since biblical times. The reason for the sudden reversion to Old Testamentism has spawned a thousand debates on late-night chat shows, none of which has so far provided a coherent answer. Traditionalists stated that it was simply vengeance for sinful behaviour, but of the eight confirmed smitings around the planet, only two locations could be described as "sinful", leading scholars to muse on what being sinful might actually mean in the twenty-first century.'
>
> Eugene Plugg – *God, the New Interventionist*

I took the lift to the first floor, and trod along the familiar corridors. The SO-27 staff had taken other jobs or retired when the Literary Detectives unit was disbanded. Victor Analogy had gone one farther and was currently embracing his new-found eternity from a sunny corner of Wanborough cemetery. I'd lost contact with most. Herr Bight had returned to Germany, where he came out in spectacular fashion as a fantasy author, much to the shock of his classically educated parents. The Forty brothers ran an antiquarian bookshop in Hay-on-Wye, but Jim Finisterre was still local – he was the head of the prestigious Really Ancient Texts department at the locally sponsored Swindon All You Can Eat at Fatso's Drink Not Included Library. Even Bowden Cable, my one-time partner and closest work colleague, had found that running Acme Carpets suited his health better. The worst that could happen was laying an Axminster over someone's budgie or handing out a refund.

Room 101, I discovered, was sparsely furnished. There was a small desk at which sat a receptionist, and against the wall was a row of hard chairs. On a coffee table were much-thumbed copies of *SpecOps Gazette*, and on the wall were posters suggesting various help groups that overstressed SpecOps officers could attend. One was for an Odd Squad support group for those diagnosed with 'Dimensional Fatigue', and another for SpecOps accountants, which offered assistance for those who had become dangerously overstimulated by calculating tax exemptions for year-averaged pension deductibles.

I gave my name to the receptionist and she asked me to take a seat. I said I'd stand since I could maintain at least a pretence of good health if no one saw me try to get up, but after she said 'Are you sure?' and I'd walked round the office twice, I opted to sit on the windowsill, which was higher and afforded an easier transit to my feet. You learn to adapt.

Once comfortably perched I looked around, having been in the office a number of times. This had once been the reception for the ChronoGuard, the division that had policed time travel, defending the Standard History Eventline from the rapacious plundering of the temporally mischievous.

Unlike most of the other SpecOps divisions, the ChronoGuard had not been disbanded because of budgetary difficulties. They had been shut down when it was found that the Retro Deficit Engineering principle couldn't be applied to time travel technology. The Deficit concept was simple: use a technology *now* in the almost certain knowledge that it will be invented in the future. Nanotechnology works this way, as does the Gravitube, thermos flasks, Tachyon Data Streaming and the wheel. The reason the concept as applied to time travel had *once* worked but now didn't was simple: a courageous time traveller by the name of 'Flipper' O'Malley had upstreamed his way to where time eventually ended, and discovered that during that unthinkably vast swathe of time, no one actually got round to inventing time travel. So with the technology now unsupported by the Retro Deficit Engineering principle, there was nothing for it but to spool down the C-90 Fluxgates and decommission the Time Engines.

This was a serious blow for the three thousand Timeworkers who suddenly found that the glittering career they should have had was no longer going to happen. It was bad news for the human race, too, whose potential extinction by asteroid HR-6984 in thirty-seven years' time had once been averted by an ingenious flexing of the Eventline, an act that lowered the potential Armageddon to a manageable 1.8 per cent and not the alarming 34 per cent it was at present. 'Flipper' O'Malley had chosen a bad time to declare time travel impossible. And if all *that* makes no sense at all, then welcome to the time industry.

'Wasn't the wallpaper from the seventies just now?' I asked as the room wobbled for a moment and suddenly became a more modern pastel shade.

'It was a backflash,' said the receptionist, 'the residual effect of the offices once being ChronoGuard. There'll be another in a few moments. They usually come in pairs.'

There was another ripple and her modern dress was replaced by one from the fifties.

'Always in pairs,' she said without looking up. She was about twenty, doing her nails a garish blue and eating a packet of Maltesers. Up until a few moments ago she had bleached hair. She looked better in the more reserved style of the fifties, but interestingly, she seemed utterly indifferent to the sudden change, so I ventured a theory.

'You would have been ChronoGuard, wouldn't you?'

She gazed up at me with large intelligent eyes. The grammatical inference of my question showed I understood the complexities of the service.

'I would have had a successful career in the Timestream,' she replied with a sad smile, 'but the way things stand at the moment I marry a guy named Biff I don't much like, have two unremarkable kids and then get hit by a car in 2041, aged fifty-five.'

'I'm sorry to hear that,' I said, musing on the misguided wisdom that allowed ex-potential employees to have both their original and new lives summarised in a paragraph or two. It was dubbed the 'Letter of Destiny', and was apparently part of the Federated Union of Timeworkers severance package. The unions were powerful, but had achingly slow bureaucracy. Despite the Time Engines being shut down over two years previously, the 'Letters of Destiny' were only just falling through people's mailboxes. To many, it was a complete surprise, and met with mixed feelings. *Yes*, it was good to know you might have been a hero at ChronoGuard, and *yes*, it was good to know that you make it to fifty-one without losing your mind or your hair, but *no*, perhaps you could do without knowing that your wife/husband is going to sleep with your best friend and enjoy it more, and *no*, it's not healthy to know that you're going to have an arm torn off by a gorilla in six hours and there's nothing you can do about it.

'You would have known my son,' I said, 'Friday Next.'

'Ooh,' she said, eyes opening a bit wider at the mention of his name. 'I'd have left my husband for him. We'd spend a sweaty weekend consummating our affair in his late-Pleistocene weekend retreat.'

This was news to me, and I wasn't happy knowing my son might once – in an alternative future – be sleeping with another man's wife. There was the ethical question of second homes, too.

'I never knew he would've had a holiday home in the late Pleistocene.'

'One Interglacial back so with good weather, nothing too bitey, and only twelve thousand years ago, so easy access for Friday afternoons – the Time Engines would have got really clogged as soon as work ended.'

'If you *must* have a second home, best have it somewhere where it doesn't inflate house prices,' I mused. 'Have you met him in this timeline?'

'No; I only got my Letters of Destiny last week.'

'Are you okay about it?' I asked, as my son Friday has also been summarised recently, and was being a bit more reticent about how it turned out for him.

'I'm fine about it,' she said cheerily. 'Before, I suspected I might not amount to anything, and now I know I won't, so at least it takes away the wearisome burden of delusive hope.'

'Very . . . philosophical of you.'

She thought for a moment.

'Will you tell Friday Shazza says: "It would have been *seriously* good"?'

My son and father would both have been in the ChronoGuard if the Engines hadn't been switched off, so the seemingly pointless discussions on the might-have-been were not *exactly* relevant, but certainly of interest.

I told her I'd pass on her message and she gave a half-smile before returning to her nails and bag of Maltesers.

The door to Dr Chumley's office opened and a short, heavy-set man walked out. He had prominent brow ridges, dark eyes and a broad nose. He wore a well-tailored suit woven from three different colours of baler twine, and his head was topped by a shock of unruly hair that had violently resisted all attempts to be combed. When he moved he had the side-to-side gait of a sailor, and the smell of woodsmoke and hot mud moved with him. This was not at all unusual. He was a re-sequenced Neanderthal named Stiggins, and soon to be, I assumed, divisional head of SO-13, the department that policed all unextincted creatures. Not just the legal ones like mammoths, dodos, sabre-toothed tigers and himself, but also all the ones that were illegal – Diatrymas, to list an example never far from the news, and a host of chimeras – creatures that had sprung not from the random machinations of evolution, but from garden-shed laboratories of meddling hobby geneticists who should have known better.

'Hullo, Stig.'

He gave a snorty grunt of pleasure and we hugged and smelled each other – once in the armpit, once in the hair, as was the Neanderthal custom.

'Co-op generic shampoo,' he said with a grimace, the Thal version of a smile, 'but stored in a Pantene container.'

'I like the shape of the bottle.'

'Us, too. Bacon and eggs for breakfast with arabica coffee, pushy-down, not bubble bubble. Toast with jam. Raspberry. You travel Skyrail, sit next to someone too much Bodmin aftershave, and I smell much-much painkiller, Dizuperadol patches, two per cheek.' He took another deep breath. 'But no oofy-oofy with husband. Not for weeks. Not like you. Problems?'

'I'm still a bit mashed,' I replied with a smile, well used to Neanderthal ways, which were dazzlingly direct and unencumbered by the complex peculiarities of human etiquette, 'but thanks for the concern.'

'Oofy-oofy very important.'

'I'll second that,' I said with a sigh. 'I'd *like* to but have no *desire* to. How are Felicity and the boys?'

'We are all well, thank you. Mrs Stiggins is ripe at present and the boys passed their Flint-Plus with distinction.'

'You must send them our congratulations.'

'We shall. And your own childer, Thursday?'

'They're well, mostly. Friday still doesn't have a purpose since his future was erased, and Tuesday is going to be the keynote speaker at the annual Mad Inventors Convention on Thursday. Jenny keeps herself to herself most of the time. When do you restart SO-13?'

'We start now. But work no different to past thirteen years. Just legal, and paid – end to beetle soup, leaky roof and sixteen-mile walk to work. Afford bus.'

And he gave enough grunty laugh.

'But why?' he added.

'Why what?'

'Why SpecOps back? Something change?'

'I don't know,' I confessed. 'I'm seeing Braxton later. I'll ask him.'

'Detective Next?' said the receptionist, having finally decided to answer the plaintively wailing intercom. 'Dr Chumley will see you now.'

I wished Stig good day, and walked past the receptionist, who had reverted to her bleached hair and modern dress. I took a deep breath, knocked on the door, and when I heard a muffled 'Enter!' walked in.

4

Monday: Shrink to Fit

'The somewhat bizarre nature of SpecOps work and the high level of stress-related retirements led SpecOps management to undertake a top-down psychological overhaul as early as 1952, when a stringent psychological appraisal of all personnel revealed that few, if any, were completely free of work-related mental issues. Before the entire service was retired it was discovered that a control sample of ordinary citizens were probably just as mad as those in SpecOps, and that the "ordinary" classification was simply set unrealistically high. Once adjusted accordingly, the matter was resolved to the satisfaction of everyone.'

Dr Franz Egg – *'The effect of SpecOps work on the human psyche, its possible consequences for a healthy life and comments upon needlessly long titles to academic reports'*

Dr Chumley had his back to me when I entered, and seemed to be leaning on the filing cabinet for support while his back moved in that way it does when people are silently sobbing.

'Are you okay?' I asked.

'Never better,' he replied, his voice with a forced quietness – like when someone steps on your toe with a baby asleep near by. 'Are you here to talk about issues regarding your work as a serving SpecOps officer?'

'No,' I replied, 'I'm here for a psychiatric evaluation at Commander Braxton Hicks's behest.'

'Thank God for that,' he said with obvious relief. 'I thought I'd have to listen to the crazy antics of some deranged operative who should have been straitjacketed long ago.'

He paused for a second.

'I just said that out loud, didn't I?'

'I'm afraid so.'

'*Damn*. I'm Dr Newton Chumley by the way.'

'Detective Thursday Next,' I said, shaking his hand.

He placed a file in the cabinet, then took out a buff folder. It was big, and Dr Chumley heaved it to the desk with a thump. He was a young man, probably not long since graduated, but the work was already having an effect. His eyes were red, and he had a noticeable tremor.

'You have no idea what I have to go through,' he said, offering me a seat before sitting himself. 'It's intolerable, I tell you, intolerable.'

He rested his face in his hands.

'Early this morning,' he said quietly through his fingers, 'I had someone who had killed a zombie with a sharpened spade.'

'That would be Spike,' I replied brightly, having joined him on a few of these expeditions myself.

'And doesn't anything about that seem remotely unusual to you?'

I reflected for a moment.

'Not really . . . Wait—'

'Yes?'

'Spike *usually* favours a semi-auto twelve-gauge. He must have been out of cartridges and used whatever was to hand. It's one of his many talents. *Adaptability*.'

'Very . . . laudable,' murmured Dr Chumley, and lapsed once more into quiet despondency.

'Actually,' I added in order to fill the silence, 'technically speaking zombies are already dead, so you can't kill them – just disable the diseased part of the cortex that gives them locomotion and an insatiable thirst for human flesh.'

'I *so* didn't want to know that,' said Chumley, staring at me, 'and will now have to do my very best to forget it. But I have a feeling the thought will remain, and fester in my subconscious until it bubbles to the surface as a fully fledged neurosis a dozen years from now, when I begin to have an inexplicable aversion to buttons and hedgehogs.'

He took a deep breath, calmed himself and then opened the bulging file, which I noted had my name on the cover. I'd forgotten how much stuff I'd done.

He indicated the closed door. 'Do you know Officer Stiggins?'

'Yes, very well.'

'He uses "we" when he means "I". Is that an affectation?'

'Neanderthals are hardwired Marxist,' I told him, 'and have no concept of the personal pronoun. He would die tomorrow without fear or worry if he felt it would better serve his community.'

'Are you saying Karl Marx was a Neanderthal?'

'He *was* exceptionally hairy,' I remarked reflectively, 'but no, I don't think so.'

'You know what's really strange?'

'You could once buy lion cubs at Harrods?' I replied helpfully. 'That's pretty strange.'

'Not as strange as this: of everyone I've interviewed, Officer Stiggins is the most normal. Sensible, thoughtful and utterly without ego. *That's* strange, given that he's the only one who's not human.'

'Have you met Officer Simpkin?' I asked.

'Yes – charming lady.'

'She's not human.'

He frowned.

'What is she, then?'

'Perhaps it's better you don't know,' I replied, considering Chumley's delicate mental state.

'In that you are correct, and I thank you for it.'

He looked at my file for a moment, read the good conduct

report and then the summary. He stopped after a minute or two and grimaced.

'Did you really kill Acheron Hades with a silver mullet?'

'I think you'll find it says "bullet".'

'Oh yes,' he said, peering closer, 'that makes a lot more sense.'

'Acheron's sister wasn't best pleased that I did,' I said. 'In fact—'

'Can I stop you there?' said Chumley abruptly. 'I'd be happier not knowing who Acheron's sister is. My job is to give Commander Hicks an appraisal of your psychological well-being. Now, do you have any delusions, hallucinations, unresolved and deep-seated personal issues, inexplicable phobias or any other related aberrations that might negatively impact your working efficiency?'

'I don't . . . think so.'

'Thank heavens,' he said with a contented sigh as he produced a small book of certificates. 'I'm going to mark you NUT-1 on the internationally recognised but tactlessly named scale of psychological normality: "Disgustingly healthy and level-headed". There, that was easy. I can have a break until my twelve o'clock – she had to kill a man with her thumb, and now can't tie her shoelaces or change her mind without losing her temper. Well, nice meeting you. Close the door on your way out. Cheerio.'

But I didn't get up. No one I knew in SpecOps had been given a clean mental bill of health for decades. In fact, it struck me now that it was possibly a disadvantage. After all, who would ever do the stuff we did without being a little bit nuts? Victor Analogy had run SO-27 for twenty-six years and was never ranked higher than a NUT-4: 'Prone to strange and sustained delusional outbursts, but otherwise normal in all respects'. I had respected Analogy a great deal, but even I felt slightly ill at ease when he confided in me with all seriousness that he was pregnant with an elephant, foisted on him by an over-amorous server at Greggs.

'Actually,' I began, 'I think someone might be trying to kill me.'

Chumley stopped what he was doing and stared at me over the top of his spectacles.

'Oh no,' he said, 'I'm not falling for that. First you say you're fine, then you say you're not. We call it "Hamlet Syndrome" – an attempt to get your own way by feigning insanity, generally by saying what comes into your head and dithering a lot. Mind you,' he added thoughtfully, 'it works a lot better if you're a prince.'

'I'm not kidding,' I replied, 'Goliath are out to cause me harm.'

I stared at him earnestly and he narrowed his eyes. It was true, too – the Goliath Corporation and I had not seen eye to eye for the past two decades. They no longer controlled SpecOps, but had run the police force ever since the entire service was put out to private tender.

'In my experience that's hardly evidence of delusion,' he said. 'Goliath are out to get lots of people. Being wary of multinationals shouldn't be paranoia, and more a case of standard operating procedure.'

Goliath weren't universally loved, but since they employed almost a fifth of England's workforce, no one was keen to rock the boat. Few ever dared to speak out against the behemoth.

'So,' he said, pen poised above the 'signature' part of the certificate, 'what form does this harm take? Assassination?'

'I'm too valuable to assassinate,' I told him. 'They're more interested in attempting to access information by *impersonation*. There are people who might talk only to me about information that Goliath are after.'

'They'd have to be good impersonators to fool people who know you well.'

I thought for a moment. I wanted to aim for what Analogy had been given: a NUT-4. Anything saner and I was probably too normal, and anything more insane and I'd be disqualified. I wondered what Phoebe Smalls had been given. She was utterly sane – but smart, too, so I'd have to assume that she knew the system as well as me. She'd probably go for the same. It would be a delicate task to not just feign madness, but just the right *level* of madness. I leaned forward.

'It's not the sort of impersonators you imagine. The Goliath Corporation have made considerable advances in the manufacture of *Homo syntheticus*,' I told him, 'and for a few years now they've been manufacturing Thursdays who try to pass themselves off as me – six times that we know of.'

'Did you take these synthetics to the police?'

'The police are run by Goliath. I have a feeling we'd be wasting our time.'

'I see. And where are those synthetics now?'

I stared at him thoughtfully. Although *Homo syntheticus* were wholly artificial, they *appeared* sentient. If they were shown to be legally equivalent to Neanderthals, we could be convicted of murder. If they were deemed illegally spliced chimeras, we were in no trouble at all – and could even claim a bounty by presenting an eyelid as proof. I decided to play it safe.

'I have no idea of their precise whereabouts.'

He stared at me for a moment, attempting to gauge whether this idea could be real, or a complex delusion.

'Okay,' he said, 'I'm going to make you a NUT-2: "Generally sane". Seven Thursdays? Interesting.'

It was a step in the right direction, but it wasn't enough.

'There weren't seven,' I said quickly, 'there were ten.'

'*Ten?*'

I counted them out on my fingers.

'Six synthetics, two fictional Thursdays, me, and my gran, who wasn't *actually* my gran – just a version of me that I *thought* was my gran, hiding in our present rather than hers. She had to spend the last twenty years of her life in gingham and read the ten most boring classics.'

'I'm sure there's a good reason why.'

'Because she – me – changed the ending of *Jane Eyre*. It was an Illegal Narrative Flexation; they would have liked to have let me off, but the law is the law. Oh, perhaps I should have added that for much of my career I've worked for Jurisfiction. It's a sort of policing agency in the BookWorld, the realm that exists beyond the other side of the printed page.'

'You've been there?'

'Many times. I can read my way across, or at least, I could before the accident. My mentor was Miss Havisham, who was terrific so long as you didn't mention the wedding, and Emperor Zhark, who is a barrel of laughs when he's not subjugating entire star systems in his tyrannical and inadequately explained quest for galactic domination.'

'Really?'

'Yes. Remember how two weeks went missing out of Samuel Pepys' diary a few years back? That was me having an off-day.'

I continued in this vein for a while, outlining various adventures I'd had in the BookWorld. I talked about the ongoing metaphor shortage, Speedy Muffler, the witheringly tiresome internal politics at the Council of Genres, about ImaginoTransference engines, Ultraword, Commander Bradshaw's gorilla wife Melanie and the first time I was attacked by grammasites. I ended with an account of the reason for my current physical state during an assassination attempt in a quiet corner of the Thriller genre, and how Red Herring was responsible.

'Was Red Herring a red herring?' asked Chumley in some confusion.

'No,' I replied reflectively, 'but his name was. By calling Red Herring Red Herring, it made people think that he couldn't be a red herring as it was too obvious, so his name – Red Herring – then became the red herring when we found out he wasn't a red herring. Simple, yes?'

'No.'

'I agree it's complicated,' I said with a shrug. 'Working in fiction does gives one a somewhat tenuous hold on reality, but it's not the hold that's tenuous – it's the *reality*: which reality, whose reality, does it matter anyway – and will there be cake.'

'And was there?'

'Was there what?'

'Cake.'

'Generally speaking, yes.'

Dr Chumley rubbed his temples.

'I think I preferred Spike's sharpened spade earlier. At least that had a sort of uncomplicated creeping menace about it. The BookWorld? It's all *very* confusing.'

'I've spent most of my life confused,' I replied. 'You get used to it after a while. There's a lot to be said for merely having a hazy idea of what's going on but generally reaching the right outcome by following broad policy outlines. In fact, I've a sneaky suspicion that it's the *only* way of getting things done. Once the horror and unpredictability of unintended consequences get a hold, even the most well intentioned and noblest of plans generally descend to mayhem, confusion and despair.'

'I see,' said Dr Chumley, tearing off another certificate and scrunching it up. 'I'm going to lower you to a NUT-3: "Mildly aberrant behaviour with occasional long stretches of lucidity".'

It still wasn't enough.

'So the whole BookWorld thing doesn't make me nuts?' I asked, semi-sarcastically.

'We do try to avoid that particular word when making a diagnosis in our profession,' said Dr Chumley with a sigh, 'but sometimes I wonder if the human race aren't collectively as mad as a sack of doorknobs. Where does that put me and my profession? Trying to sort out the real nut-jobs from the partial nut-jobs? Or just in a state of muddled damage limitation?'

He took another deep breath and slumped face down on the table.

'Don't tell anyone I told you that. We're really just meant to nod and say things like "Ah-ha" and "Go on" and "How does that make you feel?" It would have helped me a lot more if Spike had told me he baked novelty cakes rather than killed the undead. And no, it doesn't make you nuts – as you suggest, it might actually be true.'

Damn. He partially believed me.

'Before I worked here,' he said with a sigh, 'I would certainly have thought you dangerously delusional, but the SpecOps standards of reality are pretty broad. Here's an example: I had Captain Henshaw of the Odd Squad in here yesterday. But it wasn't *our* Captain Henshaw, it was Captain Henshaw^{F76+}, apparently on an important trade delegation from Reality^{F76+} where everything is pretty much identical to here – only everyone has two heads.'

'That's a bigger and more bizarre claim than the BookWorld.'

'Not really, because Henshaw^{F76+} actually *had* two heads.'

'Did he argue with himself? I always wondered about that.'

'Quite a lot actually – that's why he came to see me. But there they were. Two heads. So you see, what you say might actually be true. Might not be. But might. There you have it. NUT-3.'

It wasn't going well. I needed to lose that extra ranking. NUT-4 or nothing.

'I have something else I need to share,' I said.

'Yes?' replied Dr Chumley from where he was still resting face down on the table.

'Yes. I . . . think I'm pregnant with an elephant.'

'An elephant?' he asked, sitting up.

'Yes – foisted on me by an over-amorous server at Greggs.'

He shook his head sadly.

'Now I know you're trying to pull a fast one. *Everyone* uses the

"Pregnant with an elephant" gambit to be down-ranked. I think Victor Analogy used it first.'

He smiled triumphantly and pulled the pad of certificates towards himself again.

'You're a NUT-3, my girl, and nothing you can say will change my mind.'

'What about the fact that I think my mother was a snail named Andrew?'

'NUT-3,' he said firmly, and continued to write.

'That I have a dodo named Pickwick who is the oldest in existence?'

'Perfectly plausible,' he replied.

'How about the fact that my son would have been given the job of ChronoGuard Director General owing to his expert handling of asteroid HR-6984 that hasn't happened?'

Dr Chumley looked up at me and smiled.

'Listen,' he said, 'if you give me any more of that "Pretending to be mad" act I'll disregard all that BookWorld stuff and you'll be upgraded back to a NUT-2.'

Blast. Foiled.

'Okay, then,' I said, and sat quietly while Dr Chumley filled out the form. I was just wondering – in vain – what else I could do to mitigate the fact that I might not be mad enough to run SpecOps when I noticed that the previous certificate had Detective Smalls' name on it, and by expertly reading upside down – a skill that I'd recommend to anyone working in a wheezing bureaucracy – I saw that she had indeed been listed as NUT-4. She must have thought up something *really* wacky. Smart, young, driven, insane – the SpecOps job was almost hers. I was just thinking about whether I could function under Smalls' leadership when Dr Chumley stopped and stared at me.

'Why do you have: "Jenny is a Mindworm" written on the back of your hand?'

'I don't.'

'You do.'

I looked down and he was right – there it was. I frowned for a moment as I tried to remember who had written it, and when. I licked my fingers and rubbed pointlessly at the writing – it was a tattoo, but one I couldn't remember getting. I felt confused, angry, and my eyes moistened as I realised what was going on. The daughter Jenny I remembered – the twelve-year-old with the infectious laugh and freckled nose who had taken twenty-two hours of labour to push out – wasn't real at all. She didn't fall off a wall when she was eight years old, and didn't have nightmares about foxes in her bedroom. Never had. Never would. As the realisation dawned I felt a sudden and overwhelming stab of grief – loss and bereavement that gave way to anger, then a sense of sad realisation that I went through this many times a day and that Landen, the kids and I had agreed that the tattoo was for the best. I knew too with a falling heart that this moment of clarity would be fleeting, and my eyes filled with tears.

'Acheron Hades' little sister,' I told him as reason momentarily filtered into my head. 'She gave me a Mindworm before going down for life. We're making enquiries at TK Maxx as to what happened to her. We're hoping the tattoo will remind me often enough to break it. As it stands at the moment, I can forget I have the Mindworm almost mid-sentence.'

'Does it affect your work?'

'Does what affect my work?'

'The Mindworm.'

'What Mindworm?' I asked, unsure of who he was referring to. 'Has Aornis been up to her tricks again?'

'You're joking, right?' he asked.

'What would I joke about?' I asked, truthfully enough. 'You're here to rate me at Braxton's request – hardly the time to piss about.'

Dr Chumley took a deep breath, scrunched up the certificate for the third time, and started to fill it in again.

'NUT-4,' he said resignedly.

'I'm grateful,' I said, 'but what made you change your mind?'

'Any more from you, my girl,' he said through gritted teeth, 'and you'll be a NUT-5 so fast it will make your head spin.'

'Remember to remember me to your son,' said Shazza as I walked back through Dr Chumley's waiting room.

'I haven't forgotten I'm to remember,' I said with a smile, and departed, clutching my prized NUT-4 certificate. I was now officially 'Prone to strange and sustained delusional outbursts, but otherwise normal in all respects', and it felt *good*.

5

Monday: Braxton Hicks

> 'The Toast Marketing Board is a wholly owned subsidiary of Goliath Foodstuffs, Inc., and was an attempt by the Corporation to raise sales in their Jam, Butter, Toaster and Bread divisions by promoting the consumption of toast. One of Goliath's more resounding successes, the worldwide consumption has risen by almost 3,200 per cent, partially in response to an aggressive advertising campaign, and numerous celebrity endorsements.'
>
> Fiona Pipette – *A Brief History of Toast*

I returned my visitor's pass, then walked the short distance to the Brunel Centre and the nearest Yo! Toast outlet. Braxton hadn't yet arrived so I took a seat at the counter and ordered a mocha and a marmalade on white from a very intense waitress who had clearly been thoroughly indoctrinated by the hyper-efficient Yo! Toast training.

'Butter or margarine?' she demanded.

'Butter.'

'Thin or thick cut?'

'Thick.'

'Orange or lime?'

'Orange.'

'Right,' she said, and hurried off.

I sat for a moment in silence contemplating the morning's events. I wanted the SO-27 headship badly. It wasn't for the prestige and it certainly wasn't for the cash, and probably wasn't *totally* because I didn't want Phoebe Smalls to get it. Landen had suggested it was because I had to have something to positively define myself, and although family were great and good and wonderful, I needed something more. He was probably right. For many years Jurisfiction had been life's marker, but since I discovered that owing to my injuries I could no longer make the transfictional jump, my career in the BookWorld was at least temporarily curtailed.

Landen had suggested some sort of retirement, but I wasn't ready for that. Pruning and gardening and stamp collecting and taking dodos for long rambling walks weren't really my thing. Dealing with bad guys, now *that* was my thing.

My toast arrived and I took a bite. It was excellent. Perfectly toasted, a hint of al dente about the crust, and a tangy blast of marmalade on an aftertaste of melted butter. It wasn't difficult to see why toast had become the faddy buzz food of the noughties, with TV chefs falling over themselves to write entire books dripping with pretentious toast recipes – and a legion of critics who claimed that food chains like Yo! Toast were paying their staff too much, and criticised the lack of unsaturated fat and salt on the menu.

'Next?'

I looked up. It was Regional Commander Braxton Hicks, long-serving head of the SpecOps departments in Wessex, and also on the board of at least five other Swindon-based organisations. He had a non-executive post on the City Council, had been involved in the awarding of contracts to build St Zvlkx's new cathedral, was a director of the Wessex All You Can Eat at Fatso's Drinks Not Included Library Services, and held posts at Cheeseaholics Anonymous and the Campaign for Less Ludicrously Dressed Teenagers.

I knew him best in terms of SpecOps. He'd been working there long before the service was partially disbanded, and had been my boss during the whole *Eyre Affair* gig almost nineteen years before.

The fact that he had survived so long was down to a mixture of affability, the ability to delegate, and efficiency – mostly the latter. He *loved* his budgets. It was why he was so much in demand. Despite his penny-pinching ways and often odd ideas, I had grown to like him enormously, and he tended to look upon me as the daughter he'd wished he had, and not the one he did have, who was a bit of a tramp. In fact, Braxton wasn't having much luck with his son Herbert, either – he was currently in prison for armed robbery.

'Don't get up, old girl,' he said as he sat at the counter next to me. 'How's the leg? Smarts a bit, I shouldn't wonder. Once had a spiral fracture of the femur m'self. Skydiving for my seventieth, courtesy of Mrs Hicks, who never tires of attempting to cash in on my life policy. Didn't stop me running a half-marathon afterwards, which was odd, since I never could before.'

Despite being now well into his seventies, Braxton had lost none of his vigour, either from his tall and somewhat gangly frame, nor his moustache, which was still a luxuriant red.

'I'm okay, sir – a bit busted up but I'll get over it. Physio helps enormously.'

He stared at me for a moment.

'They nearly succeeded, didn't they?'

'Yes, sir.'

'Never been the victim of an assassination attempt myself, y'know. Never upset enough people.'

'You upset a lot of people, sir.'

'Agreed, but usually only SpecOps agents when in defence of my budget. Now, how does this work? I've never been into Yo! Toast before.'

I explained that you could either have the highly skilled toasti-chef make you something special, or just simply choose something as it came round on the conveyor.

'Hmm,' he said, helping himself to a couple of rounds of white with peanut butter as it moved past, 'never thought toast would catch on – not as a restaurant, anyway. Did you hear that a topless toast bar is about to open in the Old Town?'

'Tooters, it's going to be called. My daughter Tuesday is picketing the opening night.'

'Good for her. How's she getting on with the Shield?'

'Coming along . . . okay.'

'In time for Swindon's scheduled smiting at the end of the week?'

'We're *hoping* so, but Anti-Smiting Defence Shields aren't exactly standard physics. And besides, Tuesday only guaranteed a solution in eight years and for thirty billion pounds – it's been barely three, and she's only twenty-seven per cent over budget.'

Braxton nodded sagely.

'May I ask a question, sir?'

'Of course.'

'Do you know anything about the plan for evacuation on Friday? It's not like anyone in the City Council seems that troubled.'

'They are, believe me. With the whole of the financial district and the cathedral up for destruction, they've been hunting about for another plan. The price of cathedrals is simply shocking these days, and insurance is impossible, as you know.'

'The "Act of God" clause?'

'Right. You know Councillor Bunty Fairweather?'

'Very well.'

'She's in charge of Smiting Avoidance as well as Fiscal Planning, so you should talk to her. I hear whispers of a "grand plan" to save Swindon from His wrath.'

'Any idea what? Just in case Tuesday doesn't manage to get the Defence Shield working?'

'I'm afraid not. All a bit hush-hush. I can make enquiries, though.'

I thanked him for this. From past experience, a smiting could take out an area half a mile in diameter right in the middle of the city – easily evacuated. But that being the case, something had surely been planned by now. Perhaps the council had more confidence in Tuesday than I did.

'And your son?' asked Braxton, who was big on family. We rarely met without comparing our relative fortunes. 'Is he coming to terms with his non-career move at SO-12?'

'Slowly. Knowing you were once going to save the planet seven hundred and fifty-six times but now won't do it even once takes some adjusting. He'll be okay when he discovers a new function for himself.'

'What about house, car, wife and babies? Not *strikingly* original but as functions go, it has the benefit of long tradition.'

'Perhaps.'

'My daughter could do with a stable hand on her tiller,' said Braxton. 'High-spirited lass, is Imogen. Perhaps we should get them on a date or something. Coffee, please . . .'

He was talking to the waitress.

'. . . and let me try a sardine and moon-dried banana on caraway seed closed with reduced butter and coleslaw and shredded trumpet on the side.'

'You do know the shredded trumpet is only for decoration?' said the waitress.

'I'd assumed it was,' said Braxton with a smile.

The waitress nodded and departed.

'So,' I said, 'we all want to know why SpecOps is being reinstated.'

Braxton looked at me for some moments.

'No one will confirm this,' he said at last, 'but what we think is this: it was an act of supreme folly to disband the SpecOps divisions, and arguably an even bigger act of folly to reinstate them.'

'I'm not sure I agree,' I replied, 'it seems rather sensible to me.'

'Financially speaking,' said Braxton, 'it's *insane*. It's like building a cathedral, then tearing it down so you can build another just like it. Reinstatement of the service after disbandment is not *just* an act of folly, but a hugely expensive one. And the more wasteful of public funds it can become, the better.'

'This is linked to the Stupidity Surplus?'

'So it seems,' said Braxton in a grim tone. 'It looks like SpecOps is expected to help make up the shortfall.'

The problem was this: Prime Minister Redmond van de Poste and the ruling Commonsense Party had been discharging their duties in such a dangerously competent fashion over the past decade that the nation's stupidity – usually discharged on a harmless drip-feed of minor bungling – had now risen far beyond the capacity of the nation to dispose of in a safe and sensible fashion. The Stupidity Surplus was so high, in fact, that three years ago Van de Poste had sanctioned the hideously expensive anti-smiting shields, in order to guard against the damaging – yet unlikely – wrath of an angry God, eager to cleanse mankind of sin. It was hoped that building a chain of anti-smiting shields at massive expense would lower the Stupidity Surplus and bring the country back towards the safer realms of woolly-headed complacency.

Unfortunately for Van de Poste and to many people's surprise, the Almighty had decided to reveal himself, and in a spate of Old Testamentism not seen for over two millennia, began to punish mankind for his many transgressions. Damage to people and property aside, this had the unintended consequence of making the anti-smiting shield de facto sensible, a state of affairs that required a new and increasingly expensive outlet for the nation's burgeoning Stupidity Surplus.

The opposition Prevailingwind Party led by Alfredo Traficcone were calling for a needlessly expensive and wholly unnecessary foreign war to mop up the surplus, an act that de Poste declaimed as 'one mind-numbingly idiotic step too far'. To appease voters and

Parliament de Poste poured millions into a doomed plan to rust-proof the Menai bridge by boiling it in wine, then spent an equally large amount in a vain attempt to fill St Paul's Cathedral with ping-pong balls, on the rather vague premise that it might be 'fun'. While these ideas were indeed dumb, they did not properly address the issue nor the size of the burgeoning Stupidity Surplus, so Van de Poste must have looked around for an expensive decision to reverse – and decided to reinstate SpecOps.

'We have a new mission statement,' said Braxton. 'Before, SpecOps was meant to help the police deal with "situations outside normal duties". Now, we have to do the same but to generally overspend, change our minds about expensive technical upgrades, commission a plan to regionalise SpecOps with expensive state-of-the-art control rooms that we will never use, and inflate the workforce far beyond the realm of prudent management. And it is from within this new culture of waste and mismanagement that we think de Poste hopes to achieve his Stupidity Surplus reduction target.'

'Does that sit okay with you?' I asked, knowing that Braxton and his tight budgeting had been part of the fabric here in Swindon for longer than anyone could remember.

'I am simply a servant of the state,' he said simply. 'If they want me to save money, I save money. If they want me to waste it, I waste it. But it's not that easy, because to discharge the Stupidity Surplus most transparently, I have to think up *insanely* moronic ways of frittering money away – simply pouring cash into a pit and setting fire to it doesn't work. The FSA would see through that sort of scam straight away.'

The FSA were the Fatuous Services Authority, the government department created to oversee the safe discharge of the Stupidity Surplus. Some would argue that it was the FSA's good management and unimpeachably honest adherence to sound business practices that got us into this mess, but anyone can attribute blame with the benefit of hindsight.

'How's the reinstatement of the service going for you so far?' I asked.

'Not too bad,' replied Braxton thoughtfully. 'We decided to rebrand SpecOps at great expense to bring it all up to date. We designed new logos, uniforms, notepaper and stuff with SpecOps' new name: EnSquidnia.'

'I don't like it.'

'No, it's a stupid name, and the focus group hated it, so we changed it back to SpecOps. That small debacle alone wasted almost three million of taxpayers' money.'

'I can see you're taking the Stupidity Surplus Reduction Programme with the seriousness it deserves.'

'I do my best. Now, how did things go with Dr Chumley?'

'He gave me a NUT-4.'

'That's awkward,' said Braxton. 'The position I had in mind would require a NUT-2, but we could probably make an exception.'

'Ah,' I replied, surprised yet somewhat relieved that Phoebe Smalls had also overcooked the goose in the insanity department. 'Has the entry requirement been changed since Victor was heading up the department?'

Braxton looked at me with a frown.

'I don't recall Victor Analogy ever being Chief Librarian.'

I suddenly had an odd feeling. I had assumed Braxton's interest in me was SpecOps related, but he was involved in a lot more than just the Special Operations Network. I wasn't up for the SO-27 at all. I cursed my own arrogance, and felt seriously stupid for going so far as to offer the deputy's job to Phoebe.

'You . . . want me to run the Swindon *library*?' I asked, trying not to make my disappointment show.

'Good Lord no!' said Braxton with a laugh. 'I want you to be head of the entire Wessex All You Can Eat at Fatso's Drink Not Included Library Services. Annual budget of £156 million, salary is seventy-two K plus the most up-to-date Vauxhall KP-3 automobile, a dental plan, free lunches and a generous stationery allowance.'

I said nothing for a while.

'I know,' said Braxton, 'tempting, isn't it? I thought you'd be shocked into silence by the generosity. Just the thing to ease you into a slower pace, eh?'

'I'm not sure I need a slower pace, sir. I was hoping for something more . . . SpecOps related.'

My disappointment would not have been hard to divine, and the smile dropped from Braxton's face.

'Oh Lord,' he said, covering his mouth with his hand in embarrassment. 'Did I give the impression I wanted you to head up SO-27? I apologise if I did.'

I thought for a moment. He hadn't, actually. I had simply assumed it, probably as a result of a little too much delusive hope.

'No, sir, it was my error.'

'Gosh,' he said as another thought struck him, 'you must have worked hard to convince Dr Chumley to give you a NUT-4 classification. You didn't use the old "pregnant with an elephant" gambit, did you?'

'Of course not. That would have been ridiculous.'

We both fell silent for a few moments.

'Listen here,' he said, 'can I be honest with you, Thursday?'

'I'm going to say *yes* when I should probably say *no*.'

'We all slow down. Sometimes through age, and sometimes through . . . *circumstance*. I'm seventy-six next June, and I'm out two weeks before then. I still have much to offer, but, well, sooner or later I'm going to make a humongous mistake – the sort that kills people – and I don't want to be here when I do.'

He thought for a moment of the impossibility of the last statement.

'You understand what I mean?'

'Yes,' I replied, 'but I'm only fifty-four.'

'But in that time you've had a lot of mileage. The head of Wessex Libraries is a cushy number, and this is why I want you in at the top: I'd like you to liaise closely with Divisional Commander Smalls, who will be re-establishing the Literary Detectives over the next few weeks.'

I took a deep breath, and Braxton continued:

'It's time to move on and out, Thursday. Phoebe is a good choice. Qualified, fearless, smart, nuts – and good with stats. I want you two to get along. It'll be better for you, her, and the service. Now, how about it?'

'I'll . . . have to discuss it with Landen.'

'I expect nothing less,' he said as his order arrived. 'By Jove, this looks good.'

We ate while Braxton talked at some length about his daughter's latest drunken escapades, and how this was a huge worry to Mrs Hicks. But I wasn't really listening. Somehow I didn't really think a career of saying 'shh!' and stamping return dates was really my thing. I could go freelance at the drop of a hat, and join any private detective agency on the planet with a single phone call. But if I *did* join the Wessex All You Can Eat at Fatso's Drink Not Included Library Services, I was still in a government agency, and in the loop, ready to step in when Phoebe fell flat on her small and very perfect nose.

Within half an hour I had thanked Braxton for his time and limped out of Yo! Toast.

6

Monday: TK Maxx

> 'Many people still think that TK Maxx is an outlet for last season's designer clothes, bought in bulk. The same people still think IKEA is there to sell flatpack furniture and Pet Depot's primary interest is DIY. They're not, and never were – and after the 2004 scandal regarding the SpecOps involvement with Lidl and Aldi, their position within the retail landscape might be slightly more precarious.'
>
> Millon de Floss – *A Longer History of SpecOps*

I walked through the Brunel Centre with a sense of disappointment mixed with the realisation that until my health improved, things were going to be very different. I couldn't do what I wanted to do, which led me to the inevitable conclusion that I couldn't be who I wanted to be. My purpose was suddenly blunted, and I didn't like it.

I arrived at the Swindon branch of TK Maxx at a little after two. I knew as well as anyone that the store hadn't been deliberately set up as a bargain store for end-of-line designer garments, but as a high-security facility for the imprisonment of dangerous criminals. Swindon's most celebrated convict had been Oswald Danforth, whose punishment was to be trapped in an endlessly recurring eight-minute loop of time. In his case, while his girlfriend Trudi tried on a camisole. She never knew about the loop, of course – but Danforth did. That's why it was called TK Maxx: *Temporal-K, Maximum Xecurity*. It had been run by the ChronoGuard. The official title was 'Closed Loop Temporal Field Containment' but SO-12 simply called it being 'in the loop'. It was cruel and unusual, sure, but it was cheap, and required no guards, food or healthcare.

Or at least, that had been the case. There were no prisoners now – not since the ChronoGuard had been disbanded and all their technology decommissioned.

I found Landen staring at the frying pans on the second floor, wondering, as he usually did, whether they were more expensive than at the Co-op, and if so, what the point was of selling them.

'Hey,' I said.

'Hey,' he replied, putting back a cheese grater before adding: 'No cookies at the hunt, sir.'

'What?'

'The password?'

'Oh. "It's not a cookie, it's a . . ." *Shit*. Hang on.'

As I stood there trying to remember the last word I saw Landen's hand move to his pocket. Not usually an issue, only I knew he kept a COP357 there, a small pistol that packed enough power to punch holes in . . . well, almost anything.

'*Newton*,' I said with a stupid smile, 'it was a Newton. "It's not a cookie, it's a Newton".'

Landen breathed a sigh of relief and took his hand out of his pocket.

'Don't do that,' he said, 'it just makes me jumpy.'

'Sorry.'

'How did it go?'

'Pretty shittily.'

I told Landen all about Braxton's offer, and how Phoebe Smalls would be heading up the Literary Detectives office, and how I felt that everything was just falling down around my ears because of the blasted accident. I may even have mentioned something about 'unfairness' or 'a waste of good experience' before I'd gone on to a Level 2 Rant at that point, the sort where you raise your voice in public and sound like an idiot, but without realising it. I paused at the end, expecting him to agree, but he didn't. He simply stared at me with an expression of benign conciliation.

'Look,' I said, 'I'm kind of looking for agreement here.'

He took a deep breath.

'Listen, Thursday, I'm your biggest fan. I'm your husband, lover, best friend, confidant, back-rubber, bridge partner. You've even got one of my kidneys. I have invested in Thursday futures my entire life and not regretted it for one moment. I'm the last person to stand in the way of anything you want to do and would follow you anywhere. But even I think you should be taking it easy. They damn near killed you and, well, I think you've done enough for the moment. You deserve some downtime. We *all* deserve some downtime. A change of pace.'

Landen had been on at me since I turned fifty to slow down. The accident had made it easier for him. Before he was a man in love. Now he was a man with a mission to protect the one he loved. And he was making it hard to ignore him. But I tried anyway.

'What are we here for, anyway?' I asked. 'None of us shop at TK Maxx.'

'Aornis Hades,' he said, 'we need to find her.'

'Any particular reason?'

'Because SO-5 have failed, and finding Aornis is the only way to get rid of the Mindworm.'

'What Mindworm?'

'The one she gave to . . . someone we know.'

'Have we talked about it?'

'Often. That's part of the Mindworm.'

'Ah.'

I followed Landen to the manager's office. The assistant manager rose to shake our hands. He was an earnest, helpful young man, part of the retailing industry's 'fast track' scheme to have people at a regional sales level in as little as twenty-six years. He said his name was Jimmy-G, and that he'd read our request, and was keen to help. We explained to him that we wanted to see the security camera footage for the day that Aornis was released, and he said he had to clear *that* with Head Office, so went out of the room to make the call.

'So let's suppose I slowed down,' I said. 'What would I do?'

'As Braxton suggests: become Chief Librarian.'

'*Aside* from that.'

'You could open a restaurant. You do really good Sunday roasts.'

'A restaurant that only opens one day a week is destined to fail,' I pointed out.

'Then that's our unique selling point – Sunday lunches . . . on *weekdays*.'

'You've got it all planned out, haven't you?'

'No, I'm making it up as I go along.'

'A restaurateur?'

'Okay, maybe not. But your career path has only been heading in one direction for a while now, and biggest fan or not, I don't want to lose you.'

'And I don't want to be lost.'

'Then tell Braxton you've changed your mind. That you'll take the job.'

And at that moment, the assistant manager walked back in.

'That's all cleared with Head Office,' he said with a smile. 'If it were anyone but you, Detective Next, we'd not entertain the idea. In fact, helping you now makes me feel I'm doing what I *should* be doing. I received my Letter of Destiny last week. I would have been running all the enloopment facilities for SO-12 after I was retired from field duty when a jump to the sixteenth century dumped me in the forty-fifth owing to a Gimbal Lock precession error on the Fluxgates.'

'What does that mean?'

'I've *absolutely* no idea. I didn't get the ChronoGuard career. I got the retailing one. Ask me about monthly sales figures, dismissal procedures and weekend comparison stats and I'm your man. This way.'

He led us through to the security office, which was of a larger than normal size. On the main console were several smaller monitors that surrounded a central, larger one, and they all looked a bit dusty. In fact, the room all looked very disused, and several cardboard boxes of wire hangers and security tags were lying on the floor.

'No one has used this place since they switched off the Enloopment Engines two years ago,' said Jimmy-G. 'Before my time, I might add.'

After the facility was shut down, the prisoners had been transferred to conventional prisons, but Aornis Hades was different. With a rap sheet that included extortion, blackmail, illegal thought crimes, theft, torture and murder, her sentence was commuted to quadruple life with added life. She was transferred out, but that was the last anyone heard of her. Quite where she was transferred to, who transferred her and whether she ever got there was anyone's guess. It was why Looping was so perfect for her. No one to memory-manipulate.

The assistant manager threw several switches and after we waited a few minutes for the valves to warm up, the central monitor sprang into life. Jimmy-G punched in the date and rough time, and a broad image of the interior of the shop appeared.

'Here,' said Jimmy-G, 'it's easier if you do it. If you want to change cameras, use this switch here; to shuttle back and forth it's this knob here.'

We found her by the checkout, a well-dressed young lady with a sour expression and with her features partially hidden beneath a large floppy hat. It was definitely her, though – the Hades chin and nose were unmistakable. Either side of her were two prison guards, the first of whom was holding Aornis by the arm, and the second of whom was holding a clipboard.

'Can you get his badge?' I asked, and Landen zoomed in further.

'Quinn,' he said as I scribbled it down on a notepad, 'and the second is Highsmith.'

'Anything else?'

'Wait,' said Landen, zooming and shifting so he could read a clipboard that was tucked under Highsmith's arm.

'It looks like *Tesco*,' muttered Landen, staring at the indistinct lettering. 'That can't be right.'

'Aornis liked shopping.'

'In Abercrombie and Fitch, she did,' said Landen, 'not Tesco's.'

'I can give you a hard copy,' said Jimmy-G, and he printed one which was just the same: hazy and indistinct, but this time on paper instead of a screen.

We searched some more, but the only other picture of Aornis and the two guards was as they were leaving the facility two minutes later. We stood up and thanked the assistant manager as we walked out.

'Glad to be of help,' he said, shaking our hands and giving us some discount vouchers. 'Tell your son Jimmy-G would have been proud working under him. If I had. Which I won't.'

'You would have known him?' I asked, intrigued that I'd met two people who were ex-potential ChronoGuard in one day.

'Yes; he helped me find a new job when the service wanted to retire me after my accident. He would have been a good friend. Will you ask him to come to my Destiny-Aware Support Group meeting tomorrow? I'm setting it up for ex-potential ChronoGuard who have received their life summaries, and Friday would be very welcome. We need guidance, and he would have been there for us time and time again. And might again. For the first time. You know. Anyway, it's at the sports centre at eight.'

'I don't think he'll want to come.'

'If he's anything like the person I'm told he might have turned out to be, he'd say no but come anyway.'

'I agree. I'll tell him.'

We walked out of TK Maxx and sat on a bench to compare notes.

'Quinn and Highsmith,' I said. 'We can get Millon to look them up.'

'They were travelling by road,' said Landen, staring at several other images that Jimmy-G had printed out. 'Those are car keys, and that's a road atlas.'

'So not local. Are you sure it says Tesco's?'

'You have a look, Clever-clogs.'

'You know my vision is mildly blurred.'

'That's not my fault.'

'Well, it's certainly not mine.'

'Am I interrupting something?'

It was Phoebe Smalls.

'Nothing at all,' I said. 'Phoebe Smalls, this is my husband, Landen. Landen, meet the new head of SO-27.'

'You seem quite young,' said Landen.

'It's due to my age,' said Phoebe, and Landen laughed, and I glared at him.

'What do you think that says?' said Landen, handing the picture to Phoebe before I could stop him. I glared at him again, and he mouthed: 'What?'

'Tresco,' said Phoebe, handing the picture back, 'the prison island off the coast of Cornwall. That's my guess.'

'That's *exactly* what we thought,' I said hurriedly, 'but it's always best to get a second opinion.'

'Oh?' said Phoebe.

'Congratulations on your appointment to SO-27,' said Landen. 'We just heard. Who are you considering as your second-in-command?'

I looked at him. He was using his 'I'm so really up to something' voice.

'Landen—?'

'That's *exactly* why I'm here,' said Phoebe. 'Earlier, you generously asked me to work with you, and I thought I would return the compliment. I want *you* to be my deputy at SO-27, Thursday. My number two. My *rock*. What do you say?'

'That's a very kind offer,' I said, 'and although SpecOps is in my blood and I would dearly love to accept . . . I've just accepted the job of Chief Librarian from Braxton.'

'Ah,' she said, 'now that's a shame.'

'Yes, it is, isn't it?'

I rose from the bench with considerably less elegance than I had hoped.

'Good luck with the job,' I told her. 'I expect our paths will cross pretty soon.'

'I'll look forward to it.'

We exchanged farewells and walked off. I didn't speak until we were heading back towards Clary-Lamarr.

'I hate that Phoebe Smalls.'

'Don't be so cross, Thursday,' said Landen, stifling a smile. 'She seemed rather nice. Kind of like you.'

'She's *nothing* like me.'

But she was, of course. Just younger. Once we were back in the Skyrail car heading home, Landen passed me his mobile and I called Braxton to accept the Chief Librarian job.

'Bollocks,' I said as soon as I had snapped the mobile shut.

'Now what?'

'The Tesco/Tresco thing. Before my accident I would have made that connection instantly. I used to be sharper.'

'It's the Dizuperadol. I said you should stick to just three patches.'

'I know. I hate the stuff, but without it I can barely function.'

Landen laid his hand affectionately on my thigh, and I let my head fall on to his shoulder. We sat like that for several minutes. I wasn't going to tell him I had upped my patch dosage to six.

'Landen?'

'Yes?'

'Aornis gave the Mindworm to me, didn't she?'

'Yes,' said Landen quietly. 'Damaging, annoying, and potentially destructive of personality and family. And since those memories are as much part of her as you, there's only one way we're going to be able to get rid of them.' He patted the pocket where I knew he kept his pistol. 'We're going to deal with the Aornis situation once and for all.'

I looked into Landen's eyes for a long time. He was deadly serious.

'Is the BookWorld the Mindworm?'

'No, that's real enough.'

'The whole Granny Next thing?'

'No.'

'I'm not me at all but someone else?'

'No.'

'Then what?'

'Look at your hand.'

So I did, and I was confused, and angry. And not for the first time today, apparently.

7

Monday: Tuesday

> 'Although a "Divinely Induced Destructive Event" is highly tangible, the warnings of that same event remain tiresomely obscure. Even after the Almighty's revealment to his creations, the time and place of a pillar of all-cleansing fire is revealed only to a State Registered Meek – usually in the form of a vision, or some other inexplicable sign. Following a rash of false vision claims, the Lord agreed that a secret code word should be given so a genuine divine apparition could be differentiated from, say, a dream.'
>
> Charles Fang – *Mankind and the Modern Smiting*

We stepped off the Skyrail at Aldbourne and picked up our car from the station car park. It hummed quietly up to the house, and after a brief pause as we punched in our security number on the keypad, the gates swung open and we drove in.

We drove straight into the garage and parked the car. The Wing Commander was standing at the door waiting for us.

'Password?' he asked.

We always felt happier arriving before darkness fell. Less risk of someone or something slipping past security.

'My postilion has been struck by lightning,' recited Landen.

'No ring goes like a Ringo goes,' returned the Wing Commander.

The passwords over, the Wingco took our coats and led the way into the house.

'I trust the day went well?' he asked.

'Pretty good,' I replied as we walked into the kitchen. 'You're looking at the new head of Wessex Libraries.'

'Congratulations,' said the Wingco. 'What did you find out about Aornis?'

I handed him the names of the guards and the date and time at which she probably would have arrived at Land's End International, the usual last stopping-off place before convicts were flown to the small cluster of islands twenty or so miles off Land's End.

'See what you can find out – the time she arrived at Tresco Supermax, ideally. If she didn't, we can work backwards from there. Did you get the hotpot on?'

'It went on at five.'

The Wing Commander's place in the household had been of huge benefit over the past couple of years, the last few months especially. His full name was Wing Commander Cornelius Scampton-Tappett, and he was a stereotypical wartime RAF officer. Very English, very stiff-upper-lip, and very young – barely twenty-five, but with the demeanour of one who had seen and experienced much, and all of it harrowing. He was utterly steadfast, fearless and loyal. He sported a large mutton-chop moustache and wore the blue uniform of an RAF officer, except when he went out, when he wore an Irvin flying jacket. His four greatest laments were that he no longer had a bomber of any description, nor the spiffing chaps to fly it, that he would as likely as not never take tea with Vera Lynn now she was president, and that the war wasn't still on. It hadn't been, in fact, for over fifty years, and if Scampton-Tappett's appearance, eternal youth and general demeanour caused a few raised eyebrows, it was because he was entirely fictional. I had bought him in a BookWorld salvage yard to pep up one of Landen's books. That didn't really work out for a number of reasons, so he now acted as family bodyguard and general assistant – as well as conducting vital research and development work for the BookWorld.

'How's Jenny?' I asked.

'Unchanged since this morning,' he replied, glancing at Landen, 'but she ate some lunch, so I think the flu is easing.'

'I'll go and see her,' I said.

'I'll go,' said Landen, and walked off towards the stairs before I could argue.

'Any progress today?' I asked.

'Not much,' replied the Wingco. 'I've interviewed two dozen ICFs since I've been here, three of which have subsequently vanished. None of them has ever managed to transmit anything back to me – it's like the Dark Reading Matter is a heavy black curtain that only allows movement one way.'

The Wingco's research work involved finding some evidence of the disputed Dark Reading Matter. Theoretical storyologists had calculated that the readable BookWorld makes up only 22 per cent of visible reading matter – the remainder is thought to be the unobservable remnants of long-lost books, forgotten oral tradition and ideas locked in writers' heads when they died. A way to enter the Dark Reading Matter was keenly sought as it might offer a vast number of new ideas, plots and characters as well as a better understanding of the very nature of human imagination, and why STORY exists at all.

Naturally, wagging tongues insisted that the real reason the Council of Genres were interested in the Dark Reading Matter was for the potential yield of raw metaphor – something that was in dwindling supply in the BookWorld, and often the cause of disputes. But the bottom line was this: every single explorer had vanished without trace, and the DRM remained stubbornly theoretical.

'So no headway at all?' I asked.

'None, but it's still early days. Research into ICFs offers the strongest thread I've encountered so far.'

An ICF was an 'Imaginary Childhood Friend', those pretend

friends one sometimes has when a child. Contrary to popular belief, they don't go away when no longer required; they simply wander the earth until their host dies. They share a common element of DNA with fictional people like the Wingco in that they are constructs of the human mind – living stories, if you like. Because of this, they are quite visible to fictional people, and on occasion to us as something normally dismissed as 'ghosts' or a 'trick of the light', an area in which the Wingco was at present directing his efforts. And when he wasn't doing that or looking after us, he liked to tinker with a small bomber he was building – purely for sentimental purposes.

'I say,' said the Wingco, 'I hate to mention something as vulgar as money, but could I ask Tuesday to lend me a few quid? A bargain's come up.'

'What is it?'

'Nothing much – just a Rolls-Royce Merlin aircraft engine. A pair, actually.'

'Everyone needs a hobby,' I said with a shrug. 'I have no objection.'

Tuesday was the one with the money in the household, as the licensing rights from her many inventions brought in a considerable income. She was the reason we could afford the move to a huge Georgian house, with extensive grounds and outbuildings to match. She used the old library as a laboratory, and that was where I headed next. There was a cross-sounding 'What?' as I knocked on the door, but I walked in anyway.

The room was large, airy, and boasted an ornate plaster ceiling. The floor space was covered with workbenches piled high with interesting devices in various stages of completion. In one corner there was an experimental Anti-Smiting Field Generator, and an Inverse Teleport device that would only take you to places you didn't want to go. Tuesday had recently turned her attentions to domestic appliances, and had developed a 'Nuclear Aga' that ran off a non-radioactive isotope of Nextrium. To increase the heat, all one did was remove a graphite rod from the middle of the circular pellet of ^{253}NX underneath each hotplate. The stove had not yet made it to the marketplace because a test model broke a graphite rod on demonstration, and the suits from Aga then had to watch in dismay as the cooker melted in front of their eyes.

There was a large blackboard in the middle of the room where Tuesday often jotted down ideas, and scribbled on the board today was an ingenious way in which jellyfish could be dramatically improved, as well as some early conceptual work on an attempt to understand the Reality Distortion Field. On a worktop near by lay a machine that could assemble itself into a machine that would be able to dissemble itself, the practical applications of which were somewhat obscure. The room looked like Uncle Mycroft's laboratory, in short, and it was from my father's side of the family that Tuesday had got her intellect. Sadly for Mycroft and Polly – who were *both* geniuses – their sons Orville and Wilbur had turned out to have something resembling low-quality putty between their ears.

'Oh, it's you,' muttered Tuesday grumpily, looking momentarily up from her workbench. 'How's the leg?'

'Still painful. Back from school early?'

'Mr Davies said the school was grateful for my valuable insights, but there were only so many exciting concepts they could cope with in a day. So he gave me the rest of the day off – after I'd done the school accounts and figured out a way to heat the school for free. So I did. And here I am.'

I put on my stern look.

'Your father and I don't insist you go to school for the education,' I implored, and Tuesday put down her soldering iron and removed some papers from a chair so I could sit down.

'I know that,' she said in a huffy manner, 'but having to mix with dimwits is *hideously* boring. Great-Uncle Mycroft put it best when he said that for a genius this planet is excruciatingly dull, only made briefly more illuminating when another genius happens along.'

'Maybe so,' I replied, 'but if you're to have even the *hope* of achieving a meaningful human relationship or learn to discourse usefully with us – the dimwits – you're going to have to suffer the slings and agonies, bruises, defeats, betrayals and compromises that all the other sixteen-year-olds have to suffer. I'm serious about this.'

'I *am* taking it seriously,' she said, rolling her eyes. 'Before I left school this morning I stole Linda Blott's eraser, teased Mary Jones about her dad being in prison, got caught writing "Mrs Henderson's got a fat arse" on the loo door, was given double detention, then showed my boobs to Gavin Watkins for 50p behind the bike sheds.'

'Tuesday!'

'Oh, puh-lease,' she muttered sarcastically, 'are you *really* going to tell me you never showed your boobs to anyone at school for cash?'

'I might have done,' I replied, 'but that was completely different.'

'How was it completely different?'

'Mostly because Flossie Buxton dared me to. She was more into that sort of thing. Still is, actually. And . . .'

'. . . and what?'

'I charged a pound.'

'Holy strumpets,' said Tuesday, making a quick mental calculation, 'that's the equivalent of – let's see – over £22.75 in today's money. Did you ever consider a career as a stripper? It was going pretty well for you.'

'No I didn't, and yes, I know what we said, but please, no more flashing. It's . . . *undignified*.'

I was actually relieved that she was taking the social side of being a sixteen-year-old seriously. She might be a super-genius, but we wanted her to be a real person, too – even if that meant her being a bit grumpy, sometimes uncommunicative and on occasion demonstrating ill-judgement with boys.

'Okay, no more flashing,' she said.

'And *especially* not to Gavin Watkins.'

'I think he's cute.'

'Cute? He's a foul-mouthed little creep.'

Tuesday giggled. She was pulling my leg.

'No flashing, promise,' she said. 'Boy, your face!'

'Very funny,' I said. 'What are you doing to Pickers?'

I had turned my attention to her workbench, and in particular our pet dodo, Pickwick, whom I had personally sequenced almost twenty-six years before, when the home-cloning fad was in full spate. She was a valuable V1.2 – without wings, as all the early ones were – and unique in that she was not just the oldest dodo in existence, but also sequenced before the mandatory auto-senescence laws were brought in. Barring a major extinction event and the cat next door, she would outlive everything.

'Ah, yes,' said Tuesday, turning to stare at Pickwick, who was sitting patiently on the workbench. She was wearing a small bronze domed cap on her head that was about the size of half a tennis ball, from which trailed a jumble of brightly coloured wires.

'After rejiggling her DNA until her feathers grew back, I got to wondering in what other ways she might be improved.'

'I'm not sure Pickwick needs improving,' I said somewhat dubiously, since Pickwick had been with me for so long it was almost impossible to recall a time when she wasn't wandering around the house, plocking randomly and bumping into furniture. 'I'd miss her glorious pointlessness if it were taken away.'

'Okay, well, maybe,' said Tuesday, 'but I found that re-engineered dodo brains have neural pathways that are particularly easy to map. That copper helmet thingy she's wearing is an avian encephalograph.

By reading the electrical brain activity I'm attempting to discover what's going on in her head.'

'I'm not sure you'll find very much,' I said, for despite my affection for the small bird, I was under no illusion about the level of her intelligence.

'In that you might be mistaken,' said Tuesday, 'for with my newly invented Encephalovision I can decode and then visualise her brain patterns. Watch.'

Tuesday turned on a highly modified TV, tuned it in carefully and, after a while, strange shapes flickered and danced on the screen.

'What we're looking at,' said Tuesday with a grin, 'is what Pickwick is actually *thinking*.'

I tried to make some sense of the shapes on the screen.

'What's that?' I asked.

'Either a small ottoman or a large marshmallow,' said Tuesday. 'That blurry thing down there is the cat next door, this is a supper dish, that's you and me, and that folder in the corner is all her system files. I'm not sure, but I think she's running on software modified from that used to run domestic appliances. Washing machines, toasters, food mixers and so forth.'

'That might explain why she caused such a fuss when we got rid of the old Hoovermatic. What do you think that is?'

I pointed to an image on the screen that looked like a large red car leaping through the air.

'I think it's an episode of *The Dukes of Hazzard*.'

'She used to like watching that,' I said. 'Never thought it went in, though. Just a simple question: is there any useful purpose in knowing what a dodo is thinking?'

'Not at all; it's simply part of wider research on a neural expansifier that increases the synaptic pathways in the brain. Aside from repairing traumatic damage and reversing the effects of dementia, it can potentially make dumb people smart.'

'I'm trying hard but I'm not sure I can think of a more useful invention.'

'I think so too – but it's a long way from testing on humans. This is just a crude device to test proof of concept. This afternoon I successfully increased Pickwick's intelligence by a factor of a hundred.'

This was astonishing indeed. I stared at Pickwick, whose small black eyes stared back at me, and she cocked her head on one side.

'Hello, Pickwick,' I said.

'Plock,' said Pickwick. I took a marshmallow from my pocket, showed it to the dodo, hid it in my left palm in full view of her and then displayed both fists to her.

'Where's the marshmallow?'

Pickwick stared at both my hands, then at me, then at Tuesday. She blinked twice and scratched the side of her head with her claw.

'Hm,' I said, 'she doesn't seem much different to me.'

'I admit it's not a blazing success,' agreed Tuesday, 'but I think the problem lies in Pickwick. Because her intelligence is on a par with a dishwasher's, making her brain a hundred times the size makes no appreciable difference. D'you think I should have made it a *thousand* times smarter than it was?'

'I think you should leave her alone. Having almost no brain doesn't seem to have stopped her enjoying a long and successful life.'

'I suppose so,' agreed Tuesday, switching off the machine.

'How's the keynote speech for MadCon on Thursday?'

'Going pretty well,' she replied, patting a pile of much-corrected papers lying on the desk next to her. 'I'm just not sure whether I should open directly with my algorithm that can predict the movement of hyperactive cats, discuss the possibilities of the Encephalovision Entertainment System where we beam the thoughts of vain idiots straight into the nation's homes, or go straight to the Madeupion Field Theory by which I hope to power up the anti-smiting shields.'

I thought for a moment. Although I didn't have a clue *how* her ideas worked, I knew what they did – kind of – and could understand their importance.

'The work on predicting the chaotic was your breakout paper,' I said, 'so you should allude to that, I think. I'm not sure about the anti-smiting device; after all, we've yet to see it work. What about your pioneering work on finding a way by which you can tickle yourself? That was pretty groundbreaking.'

'You're right,' she said. 'It still needs work, but once self-tickling is possible, the home entertainment and psychotherapy industries can take a running jump. I've already had a call from Cosmos Pictures asking if I wouldn't consider dropping the research in exchange for a signed picture of Buck Stallion and a walk-on part in *Bonzo – the Movie*.'

'Meeting Bonzo could be cool,' I said, as the long-running TV series was very much a cultural icon, 'but to be honest, being asked to do the keynote speech at MadCon is probably more about saying a few jokes and getting the delegates in a good mood than delivering a doctoral thesis.'

'You're right. I could do the joke about the three paradigm shifts at the races. That always brings the house down. Will Dad come?'

'He wouldn't miss it for the world, although one of us should stay here to keep an eye on Jenny.'

'The Wingco can look after her,' replied Tuesday. 'They get on very well together. You know how he likes to talk about the power of the imagination, and how it has the potential to make things real.'

'Only too well,' I replied. 'Dinner at seven, Sweetpea.'

8

Monday: Friday

> 'The danger from Asteroid 6984 was first noted in 1855 when calculations showed this to be the same asteroid that was observed in both 1793 and 1731, and that it was missing the Earth by the astronomical equivalent of a coat of paint every sixty-two years. Observations during the last fly-past in 1979 proved what scientists had already feared: that the Isle of Wight-sized lump of debris was travelling at over 42,000 mph, and would one day strike Earth. The question of whether it would or not in 2041 was calculated by the International Asteroid Risk Likelihood Calculation Committee to be "around 34%".'
>
> Dr S. A. Orbiter – *The Earthcrossers*

'I spoke to Braxton Hicks today,' I said as Friday and I went into the dining room to lay the table. 'He tells me his daughter Imogen is looking for a "steady hand on the tiller". I said I'd mention it to you.'

'I don't need my mother to set me up on dates,' he retorted. 'Besides, Mimi is totally bonkers. She surfed on the roof of a speeding car between junctions thirteen and fourteen of the M4. How insane do you have to be to do something like that? If she'd slipped she'd have killed herself instantly.'

'You need a careful driver and soft-sole shoes,' I replied thoughtfully.

Friday looked at me with horror.

'You didn't?'

'I did. The flush of youth.'

'Does Dad know about this?'

'I think he was driving.'

'For God's sake, Mother,' he said in an exasperated tone, 'is there nothing dumb, daft or dangerous that you haven't tried at some point?'

I thought for a moment.

'I've never tried oysters. They can be quite dangerous.'

Friday shook his head sadly. To most of his and Tuesday's friends I was considered about the coolest parent one could have, but to Tuesday and Friday I was simply embarrassing.

'So . . . how many are we for supper?' asked Friday, counting out the cutlery.

'Joffy and Miles are in town and want to speak to your sister about the Defence Shield. All of us, of course, but maybe not Polly or Gran. Grandad will be coming.'

'Do you think he will want to talk endlessly about the good old never-happened days at the ChronoGuard?'

'Probably. Try and steer him on to plumbing. Which reminds me, Jimmy-G and Shazza both wanted to be remembered to you. Shazza said: "It would have been *seriously* good". And she raised her eyebrows in that sort of way when she said "seriously".'

'Sharon "Steggo" deWitt,' he murmured with a smile. 'She would have been known as "The scourge of the Upper Jurassic".'

'Curiosity dictates that I enquire why.'

'It was a popular place for timejackers to hang out. The Epochal Badlands, we would have called them. A jump into the Upper Jurassic was usually a safe escape. Not for deWitt. Twenty million years and she knew each hour like the back of her hand. She was the one who tracked down "Fingers" Lomax, hiding out after the Helium Heist of '09. Or at least, she would have.'

'She said you were going to have a weekend retreat in the late Pleistocene.'

'I was going to have a lot of things. She and I would have been very close, so I got some of her deleted future in my own Letter of Destiny. How will she turn out now?'

'Not great,' I replied, handing him the forks. 'Two unremarkable kids, a husband she doesn't like – and then gets hit by a car in 2041.'

'Same year as me,' mused Friday.

I stopped folding the napkins.

'You never told me you only make it to fifty-five.'

'Bummer, isn't it?' said Friday with a shrug. 'Thirty-seven years to go and counting.'

I stared at him for a while, and felt a heavy feeling of grief in my heart. It was over three decades away, so I didn't feel the *loss* quite yet, just the notion that I was going to outlive him. And that wasn't how it was meant to happen.

'But there's an upside,' he added.

'There is?'

'Sure. I miss HR-6984 slamming into the Earth by three days.'

'That might not happen.'

'I'll never know whether it does or it doesn't.'

'What else happens to you?'

'My future's my own, Mum.'

'Okay, okay,' I said quickly, since we'd covered this ground before, 'forget I asked. Have you thought any more about university or a career?'

'No.'

I thought for a moment.

'You know your sister needs a lab assistant she can trust,' I said, 'and she'll pay you well. There's a career there ready and waiting.'

'Mum, Tuesday's work is Tuesday's work. My life lies along a different path. I was going to be important – I was going to do wonderful things. I would have been head of the ChronoGuard and saved an aggregate seventy-six billion lives. Shazza and I would have made love on the veranda of my place in the Pleistocene while the mastodons bellowed at one another across the valley. I would have been there at Mahatma Winston Smith Al-Wazeed's historic speech to the citizens of the World State at Europolis in 3419, and listened to his last words as he lay dying in my arms, and then implemented them. But now I don't. All gone. Not going to happen. Mum, *I don't have any function*. No kids, no wife, no achievements, nothing. I die aged fifty-five, my life essentially . . . wasted.'

There was silence for a moment. We stopped laying the table and I gave him a hug. One of those strong mum-hugs that always do some good, no matter how bad things happen to be.

'Listen,' I said, 'you don't know for certain there are no good times. They didn't give you a full view of the future, did they?'

'No,' he said, 'it's always a summary. A side of A4 on what we *would* have done, and the same again of what we *will*. An entire life compressed into barely five hundred words.'

'Right,' I said, 'so you don't know for *certain* you won't a have a few boffo laughs and some good times, now, do you?'

'What's going on?' asked Landen, who happened to be walking past the open door of the dining room.

'Friday's lost his life function,' I said.

'He looks fairly alive to me.'

'No, no, his purpose. His *raison d'être*.'

'Everyone has a function,' said Landen, walking in to lay a comforting hand on his son's shoulder, 'even if they don't know what it is. Some of us are lucky enough to have a clear function. I wasn't sure what mine was for a while, until I realised it was to support your mother – and make sure you and Tuesday survived into adulthood.'

'Don't forget Jenny,' I said.

'Yeah, her too. Yours might not be obvious right now or even known – but it's there. Everyone has a function. A small role to play in the bigger picture.'

Friday detached himself from my arms and continued to lay the table.

'You're wrong, both of you. Here's the thing: my life didn't even warrant a full sheet of A4. This coming Friday at 2.02 and four seconds I murder someone. I'm in custody by the evening. In three months' time I'm sentenced to twenty-two years in hokey. Fifteen years into my sentence I stab Danny "The Horse" Bomperini to death in the prison laundry. It was self-defence but the courts don't see it that way. My sentence is extended. I finally get out on 1 February 2041. A few days later I'm found in the car park of Sainsbury's. It looks like they used a baseball bat, and they never find who did it.'

There was silence. It explained the sullen mood he'd been in ever since his future had arrived from the Federated Union of Timeworkers.

'My money's on the Bomperini family,' said Landen thoughtfully. 'Payback for offing the Horse, y'know.'

'Landen!' I scolded. 'This is serious shit we're talking here.'

'I beg to differ, wifey darling,' he replied emphatically, 'it's not. You can change it. The Standard History Eventline's not fixed. If we've learned anything over the past two decades, it's precisely that. Yes, it follows a general course that remains the same, but detail can be changed. We've all altered the future – and the past, on occasion – and so can he.'

'I could do,' replied Friday, 'but I have this strange feeling that I won't. That I'll let it go ahead.'

There was a pause.

'Do you know *who* you're going to murder on Friday?'

'Yes. It's . . . Gavin Watkins.'

'Gavin Watkins?'

'Do you know him?' asked Landen.

'A boy in Tuesday's year,' I replied, 'not very pleasant. He paid 50p to see her boobs.'

'I might have to kill him myself,' said Landen. 'Does that have something to do with it?'

'I don't think so,' said Friday with a shrug, 'but I'm amazed she didn't hold out for at least a pound.'

'Market forces,' I observed. 'We've already established that the boob-flashing market isn't what it used to be. But we can warn the Watkins. Have him taken into custody or something.'

'I've got four days,' said Friday, 'so we might learn some more before it happens. Who else did you say sent their regards to me?'

'Jimmy-G at TK Maxx,' I replied. 'He's setting up a Destiny-Aware support group for those who have been summarised, and wanted to know if you would attend? Eight p.m. at the sports centre tomorrow.'

'I'm not really into support groups,' he grumbled. 'Are we going to get this table laid or not?'

So we did, and chatted of lighter things, such as Friday's part-time job at Pet Depot, and whether his fellow workers actively pursued a policy of looking busy when customers needed assistance.

'It's the first thing we learn,' he said, 'but you have to remember that most customers are as dumb as pig shit and couldn't find the floor if they fell on it, so there's a sound reason behind it.'

Once the table was laid Friday went off to tinker with his motorbike, and Landen and I managed to have a few words in the kitchen together. Friday's future looked bleak, but Landen was right – we'd changed the timeline before, and could do it again.

'What do you think Gavin Watkins will do to make Friday murder him, just supposing he does?' asked Landen.

'What *could* a sixteen-year-old do?' I replied.

We thought for a moment.

'Do we intervene?' said Landen.

'We can *try*,' I said, 'but the Eventline can be a tricky beast. Push it too hard and it will push back – and almost *guarantee* that you complete the event you were trying to avoid.'

'It's annoying,' said Landen.

'What is?'

'I thought we'd seen the back of all this time travel nonsense.'

'Even when it's not there,' I murmured, 'it still is.'

'Like forgotten dreams,' said Landen.

9

Monday: The Madeupion

> 'Thursday's father was a retired ChronoGuard operative, whose nebulous state of semi-existence was finally resolved when the Time Engines at Kemble were shut down. As part of the downstream erasure that there had ever been a time industry, his career had been replaced with something immeasurably more mundane. He was, and now had always been, a plumber. Only one with no name, which made paying by cheque somewhat tricky, and word-of-mouth recommendations almost impossible. But despite his new past, he also kept the old one. Few of us are so lucky as to draw experience from two lives.'
>
> Millon de Floss – *Thursday Next: A Biography*

As it turned out, we were eight for dinner. Landen and myself, obviously, and Friday and Tuesday, equally obviously. My brother Joffy and partner Miles also made it, as did my dad. Mum and Polly, more inseparable as the years went by, were going to listen to the live studio recording of *Avoid the Question Time*. The Wing Commander would always sit down to talk but he never ate as he didn't need to, being fictional. Jenny would have been there – for the starter at any rate – but still had the 'flu, so was confined to her room.

But Friday was right. My father *did* want to talk about matters ChronoGuard.

'Get your future in the post?' he asked, sitting down next to his grandson.

'Last week.'

'Any good?'

'It'll be . . . challenging.'

My father had also worked in the time industry, but unlike Friday, who now no longer had the future he was going to have, my father no longer had the past to which he was entitled. ChronoGuard agents who were active during the shutdown were offered a replacement past career to replace their theoretically unsustainable ones, and most chose something in the arts, sciences or politics. My father, ever the maverick, had opted for a fifty-seven-year career in plumbing. The reason, he stated, was so his new memories would have him at home as much as possible, to better reminisce about his family. This worked well for him, but not for us – we retained only those memories of his first career as a time-travelling knight errant. As far as we were concerned he'd turned up the day after the Time Engines were shut down, full of fond memories of us that we couldn't remember, but he *could* – sort of like having an aged parent with a bad memory, only the other way round.

'Challenging is good,' said Dad. 'I used to take your mother and her brothers on long hiking holidays in Scotland. Now *that* was challenging. Do you remember that time when we got lost on Ben Nevis, Thursday, and had to be rescued by several men in beards, all of whom smelled of pipe tobacco and Kendal Mint Cake?'

'No.'

'I saw a few posters up in town about the smiting,' said Landen. 'The City Council don't seem to be taking it very seriously. Are you sure it's still on?'

Joffy and Miles exchanged nervous glances.

'It's on, all right. When He announced the smiting to a State Registered Meek in a lonely petrol station in the small hours, He had the Meek write it down so he wouldn't forget, and then went and told another Meek, just in case. After that, He reiterated His plans in the pips of a cucumber, and burned them into the side of Haytor on Dartmoor.'

'He's kind of done with ambiguity, hasn't He?' I said.

'Pretty much,' replied Joffy. 'Since His revealment He's kind of ditched the idea of subtle signs or obscure clues. Burning His intentions into granite is a lot more direct, and certainly makes people take notice, although the Dartmoor Parks Authority were none too pleased. But there it was: Swindon will be hit with a Grade III Smiting, on Friday at midday.'

We all fell silent. It kind of sounded more ominous coming from Joffy, even if a Grade III was not the worst. More to do with cleansing fire, and none of the mass murder, lava and pillar of salt stuff.

'Why Swindon, anyway?' asked Friday. 'In the National Sinful City stakes, Swindon sits only fifty-seventh.'

'The cleansings aren't always just about sin,' said Joffy quietly. 'Sometimes it's about unimaginative architecture, poor restaurants or even an overly aggressive parking fine regime. This time it's none of those. I think He aims to hit Swindon because He knows it's my home town and wants to make a point.'

'What sort of point?'

'I'm not sure. It's all very mysterious.'

Joffy was my eldest and only surviving brother, and was Supreme Head of the Church of the Global Standard Deity, a sort of homogeneity of faiths that hoped to bring peace and prosperity, consensus, harmony, tolerance of diversity and social inclusion to all His creations. Joffy had decided many years before that the problem with religion wasn't religion itself, but its flagrant misuse as an absolutist argument against narrow tribal agendas. Joffy argued – as had many before him – that one religion would be a much better idea. But instead of going on a murderous ideological rampage to bend others to his will, he used arguments of such clarity and reasoned debate that even the most hardened nut-jobs finally came over to his way of thinking. It had taken him and his network of fearless 'Unifiers' only thirty years to accomplish, something that was a staggering achievement that most would agree 'could only possibly exist in fiction', if they hadn't seen it with their own eyes.

The other big plus of Global Religious Unification was collective bargaining powers. Before, dialogue with the Almighty was unclear and centred around unworthiness and mumbling inside large buildings, but following unification the GSD was in a strong position to ask clear and unambiguous questions of the Almighty, such as: 'What, precisely, is the point of all this?'

Unfortunately, this angered His Mightiness as theological unity was emphatically *not* part of His plan, and a series of cleansings had taken place around the globe – mostly as a warning to His creations that messing with the Big Guy's Ultimate and Very Important and Unknowable Plan was not going to be tolerated.

'We're in talks with the Almighty to bring Him to the negotiating table,' said Joffy, 'but we're not prepared to talk until He agrees to stop incinerating the unrighteous in an all-consuming pillar of fire.'

'Maybe He doesn't have a plan and there is no answer,' said Landen. 'Perhaps that's why He appeared to all those different religious leaders with subtly different messages – in order to divide mankind and keep us from adopting a united front to demand an answer to the question of existence.'

'Even if there is no answer to the riddle of existence and we are all random packets of replicating cell structure in a dying universe devoid of meaning,' added Miles, 'we have a right to know that. Five thousand years of prayer, conflict, self-sacrifice and being tested daily must count for *something*.'

'I always thought His plan for mankind was: "Let's just muddle through and see what happens",' said Friday, 'and historically speaking, it's a sound one – it's worked on thousands of occasions.'

'There must be more to the ultimate meaning and purpose of

existence than muddling through,' said Tuesday with disdain. 'Otherwise there's *no* reason for the eternal quest for knowledge, and *every* reason for celebrity biographies and daytime soaps.'

'So religion *could* trump science after all,' said Miles with a smile. 'That'll be a turn-up for the books.'

'Mind you,' added my father, 'at least you forced Him into revealing His existence.'

'That *was* unexpected,' admitted Joffy, 'and very welcome – the billion or so former atheists now on board really boosted the membership and bargaining powers.'

'Didn't Dawkins shoot himself when he found out?'

'Yes,' replied Miles sadly, 'a great shame. He would have been *excellent* GSD bishop material. Single minded, a good orator, and eyebrows that were pretty much perfect.'

'So why destroy Swindon just to annoy you?' I asked. 'It doesn't sound like a very responsible use of resources.'

'I think it's probably more to do with setting the tone of our first meeting. We've been trying to get Him to the negotiating table to thrash out our grievances, and I think He just wants to show who's boss, and to set the tone for the meeting – like when criminal overlords have their hideouts in hollowed-out volcanoes. Highly impractical and the heating bill's astronomical, but good for the overall *ambience*.'

'And when might this meeting take place?' asked Tuesday.

'A fortnight, perhaps,' said Miles. 'Winged messengers can be pretty vague.'

'Would you put in a good word for Polly?' asked my father. 'Her sciatica is playing up again.'

'I'll be honest with you,' said Joffy. 'The agenda has 1.2 billion items on it, and it'll be most likely lunch before we even get round to item one on the agenda: "What, precisely, is the point of all this?"'

We all thought about this for a moment.

'Tuesday,' added Joffy in a quiet voice, 'just how close are we to success with the Anti-Smiting Defence Shield?'

We all looked at Tuesday. This, we knew, was pretty much the reason Joffy and Miles were here – to see whether she could overcome the many technological hurdles in time to avert Swindon's partial destruction.

Tuesday pulled a face.

'We're having a few . . . teething troubles,' she said, 'but they're mostly of a mathematical nature. I simply need to find the upper and lower limits of the constant U_c.'

'Is there an easier way for you to explain it?' asked Miles. 'It's kind of important. If we can't get the Defence Shield up, we're going to have to reluctantly agree to a back-up plan.'

'Okay,' said Tuesday. Like many scientists she had become obsessed with the science itself, and not its intended purpose. She took a deep breath, got up and drew a schematic of an anti-smiting tower on the wall with a felt pen.

'Field research has indicated that a Wrath-inflicted Deity Groundburst is a five- or six-second burst of high-energy particles concentrated in a circular pattern with a blast radius of about half a mile. The high-energy particles arrive so fast and with such energy that there is no material we know of that can withstand the bombardment. A defence shield made of tungsten, steel, concrete – useless. Which is why we must meet energy with mass.'

'We get that bit,' said Joffy, since all this had been repeated on the Toad News Network Science Channel quite a lot over the past year, 'but how does your system actually work?'

Tuesday smiled.

'I got the idea from a ninja movie.'

I looked at Landen.

'Have you been letting Tuesday watch ninja movies?'

'One or two,' he replied sheepishly, '*after* she did her homework.'

'Humph,' I replied.

'In the movie,' continued Tuesday enthusiastically, 'there was a ninja who could move so fast he could run through a rainstorm without getting wet. And I got to thinking that if a ninja could do that, then *conversely* he could just as easily move through the same rainstorm and get absolutely sodden – and if there were several ninjas, they might be able to stop *all* the raindrops actually reaching the ground.'

'Okay,' I said slowly, 'I'm getting the analogy.'

'Right. So what I have to do is to meet each charged particle with the ultra-dense nucleus of a lead^{187} atom. The particle is halted and drained off as thermal energy to be turned to electrical energy using a steam turbine. Part of this energy is used to power the shield, and the rest is fed back into the national grid. The feed-in tariff is so good these days we hope to be able to recoup all our production costs within about twenty-three smitings. Joffy, do you think you can convince the Almighty to schedule His cleansings to coincide with peak demands of power? Everyone pops on the kettle at half-time during the Superhoop.'

'I'm not sure the Lord takes account of sporting events when deciding on a bit of smiting.'

'And the shield has to work first,' added Landen.

'Yes, there is that,' replied Tuesday thoughtfully. 'Anyway, the problem is being able to predict the position of each charged particle in the column of all-cleansing fire and then have a lead^{187} nucleus ready and waiting for it *precisely* underneath. To put it in practical terms it would be like attempting to predict where in Hertfordshire an acorn would fall, and have another acorn waiting underneath it.'

'I should imagine that's almost impossible.'

She smiled.

'Predicting random events is possible if you examine the effect a subatomic particle named the Madeupion has on the arrow of time near the event. For a trillion trillionth of a second *before* the event, cause and effect entangle. And if in that short period we can disentangle the effect from the cause we can see an event before it has happened – and do something about it.'

She wrote an equation on the wall and rapped her knuckles against it.

'And that's the problem. Attempting to find an upper and lower limit for my Madeupion Unentanglement Constant or U_c. Too high and we're not seeing far enough back, too low and we get to see the event after it's happened. I've brought the limits down to between 6.3 and 6.8 quintillionths of a second, but it's still too large. To the fleeting existence of a Madeupion, the U_c is like the Jurassic – only without the dinosaurs.'

Tuesday stared at her scribbles on the wall for a while.

'It's just that maths isn't my strong point,' said Tuesday with a sigh, 'and we're not actually sure the Madeupion exists. It just seems a good theory to explain déjà vu, intuition and the ability of ninjas to dodge bullets. Ninjas are far more important to science than anyone realises. If we could capture one to study, I think most of science's biggest puzzles might be resolved.'

'So where does that leave us?' asked Joffy.

'We might crack the U_c problem in ten minutes,' replied Tuesday, 'or it may *never* be cracked.'

We all fell silent for a few moments.

'Pudding, anyone? Tuesday, would you do the plates?'

10

Monday: The Wingco

> 'The book from which the Wingco hailed was a typical tale of wartime derring-do. He and his crew had hidden themselves when England fell in 1942, and then, after a series of adventures, stole a bomber at Coventry and headed towards London to bomb the occupying force's High Command. But the book was abandoned as they started their first run from Putney Bridge, so they never got to find out if they were victorious or not. "It's frustrating," the Wingco said when asked, "to not know whether one's purpose is fulfilled. You humans must get it all the time."'
>
> Thursday Next – *private journals*

'Can I ask a personal question?' asked Miles of the Wing Commander once we all had started on the trifle, which was excellent.

'Of course,' said the Wingco affably, 'ask away.'

'Are you really fictional?'

My career in the BookWorld had not been common knowledge until the attempted assassination, and after that there didn't seem a lot of point in hiding it. I think most of the family knew anyway – Landen in particular – and while the BookWorld was truly bizarre as only fiction can be, the inclusion of evidence in the guise of the Wing Commander changed my experiences from being the product of an overactive imagination to something quite remarkable.

'Mind, body and socks,' replied the Wingco cheerfully, 'and I don't mean that metaphorically. Because I never disrobe in my book, my mind and body are truly at oneness with my socks – look.'

He pulled up his trouser leg to reveal two inches of grey

RAF-issue sock which merged seamlessly into his skin. The sock was actually *part* of him.

'That's kind of weird,' said Miles.

'It's a lot more convenient than dressing every morning. My clothes never need washing or pressing either. Permanent trouser creases for all eternity. Levi's would love to learn the secret of *that*.'

'Do you have organs and stuff?' asked Tuesday, now that the Wingco seemed to be in the answering vein. 'I mean, are you actually *alive*?'

'I'm as real as my author made me or the readers want me to be. I don't have blood or tissue or organs or anything, nor do I age or feel pain. I can't reproduce, but out here I do have free will and a form of autonomy, so in that respect, very much alive.'

'Can you die?' asked Joffy.

'Erasure or deletion has always been a very real danger for a character, and even more so for me. I may look fairly robust to you, but I'm on the BookWorld's "Critically Endangered" list.'

'How so?' asked Miles.

'Because I'm only in single-copy manuscript form. If the manuscript were to be destroyed by a house fire, mould or snails, myself and my flight crew – Septic, Jammy, Snuffy and all the others – would simply vanish.'

'You must go *somewhere*,' said Joffy thoughtfully. 'I'm not convinced the spirit can be simply extinguished.'

'I agree – and that's really what I'm here for,' said the Wingco, segueing seamlessly into his research project. 'Since the observable BookWorld makes up less than twenty-two per cent of the theoretical quantity of Reading Matter, we think there is an unseen region of STORY that we call Dark Reading Matter. I'll go there when my book finally rots away to nothing. But what I'll find, no one knows – it's a one-way trip.'

'We have a similar concept,' remarked Joffy.

'So where is your manuscript?' asked Miles.

'I wish we knew.'

'It might be stuck in an attic somewhere,' I added, since we'd looked for it on several occasions, 'or at the back of a desk drawer, fallen down the back of a filing cabinet – who knows? All we'd need is ten minutes with a photocopier and the Wingco would merely be "Vulnerable". A limited print run of ten and he'd be on Vanity Island and "At little risk of endangerment".'

'What if you're landfill?' asked Tuesday. 'Anaerobic digestion could take *years*.'

'Would you make some coffee, please, Friday?' I said quickly, in order to change the subject. The Wingco had thought of that too, and the landfill theory was good and bad news. Good in that he could last for a century or more with few ill effects and perfectly safe – but bad in that the inevitable breakdown of the manuscript would be painfully protracted as the story fell apart word for word. I'd seen it happen, and it wasn't pretty.

'Back in 1996, I headed up Jurisfiction's "Manuscript Retrieval Squad",' I said. 'I spent almost a year doing little but tracking down Critically Endangered manuscripts. Did I tell you about how I found what came to known as "The Hemingway Hoard"?'

'Many times,' said Tuesday, getting up to help Friday with the things.

I thought I wouldn't bore anyone else, so we changed the subject to my mother and my aunt Polly, who seemed to get even less and less dignified as they worked their way through their eighth decade together.

'She doesn't listen to me at all,' said Dad sullenly. 'You know those "personal injury" travelling booths where dumb people who feign accidents go to grub for cash?'

Joffy said that he did.

'They had one up at the Brunel Centre. A display with a table and some chairs. Your mother pretended to fall over it, then claimed she'd broken her hip and told them she wanted to make a claim – against them.'

'How did it work out?'

'There were three *other* personal injury salesmen there, and they all started fighting to represent her. I had to call the police when it came to blows. During the melee, she crept away giggling and said that watching personal injury lawyers punching one another had an inexplicable joy to it.'

'At least it keeps her from playing dominoes at the day centre.'

'She's always been feisty,' said Dad with a warm smile. 'Do you remember that trip to the Atlas mountains when your mother tried to smuggle a live goat across the border, wrapped up in a carpet?'

'No,' I said.

'Joffy?'

'No.'

'Damn,' said my father, 'all those memories, and none of them shared.'

11

Monday: Evening

> 'The sound cannon was one of Tuesday's notable inventions, a device that used a low-frequency/high-amplitude resampling of Van Halen's "Eruption" to cause momentary unconsciousness. The device had not actually been designed as an intruder deterrent, but was one of Tuesday's attempts to adapt hard rock for domestic use in the kitchen – she had been attempting to use Led Zeppelin's "I Can't Quit You Baby" to whisk egg whites when she over-modulated the bass and punched a two-foot-wide hole in the fridge.'
>
> Gordon von Squid – *Tuesday Next – The Early Notions*

We had coffee in the living room. Tuesday went off to jot down an idea she'd had about a device to make yourself aware when sleeping so you'd enjoy it more, and Friday just wandered off. Joffy, Landen, Miles and I talked for a while until Joffy's assistant called at the door to say that it was time for him to leave. He had to take the Gravitube to Dubai for a meeting in the morning.

'It was good to see you,' I said, giving him a hug.

'And you,' he replied. 'My time is not my own these days. I'll be back in Swindon for the smiting on Friday. If there's anything you can do to help Tuesday find a way to make the anti-smiting tower operational, I'd be grateful.'

I hugged Miles, too, and they were soon gone, the five-car motorcade vanishing off into the darkness.

'I wouldn't have Joffy's job for anything,' said Landen as we watched them go. 'Trying to demand the answer to the question of existence from an all-knowing omniscient Supreme Being takes negotiating to a whole new level.'

Once the outer gates had shut, the Wingco went to check on security arrangements. There was a high-perimeter fence all the way around the house with razor wire and proximity alarms linked to searchlights and sound cannon, and aside from the odd false alarm, it all seemed to function quite well. Once the Wingco had checked all was well I walked through the quiet house, and found Landen in the office, where he was trying to stay ahead of the paperwork generated by Tuesday's many patent licensing deals. We had a business manager and a team of lawyers, but Landen liked to read through most things so he knew what was going on.

'Hispano-Fiat are interested in bringing Tuesday's Micro Kinetic Battery system to market in under six years.'

'I'm not surprised. Has she agreed to it?'

'With the usual non-military rider. Do you want some chocolate? I've got a bar hidden at the back of the fridge.'

'Go on, then.'

I got up and went through to the kitchen, where the fridge door had been left open, something that Friday tended to do these days. I also noticed that he had made himself a sandwich and left it half eaten on the kitchen table. I put it in a Tupperware box, found the bar of chocolate, and walked back to Landen's office.

'Did Joffy tell you what the "alternative plan" to the anti-smiting shield was?'

'He only mentioned there was one – no details. Who were you talking to?'

'No one.'

'And why do you have a cut above your eye?'

I touched my hand to my eyebrow and looked at the blood on my fingertips with confusion.

'I don't know.'

He looked at me for a moment, then put the papers down and went into the kitchen. I heard him say something to somebody, and then heard a crash as some pots and pans fell to the floor, so shuffled through to join him. I found him gazing into the cupboard where we kept the tins. He turned around and looked at me, mildly confused.

'What did I come in here for?'

'You thought you heard me talking to someone.'

He looked around.

'I did?'

'Yes. But then I heard *you* talking to someone.'

The door swung shut and it made us both jump.

'A breeze?'

Landen and I both *quimped* – our word for limping quickly – to the hall, expecting to see the front door open, but it was securely bolted.

'Who were you shouting at?' asked Tuesday, popping her head out from the library.

'Were we shouting?'

'Sure – sort of like telling someone to get the *effing* hell out of the house.'

Landen and I looked at one another.

'It wasn't us,' I said.

'It *sounded* like you. Intruder!' said Tuesday and ran past us and up the hallway to the converted butler's pantry that was now our security nerve centre. By the time we'd caught up she had finished a sweep of the perimeter and was now running a systems diagnostic.

'Nothing has crossed the boundary,' she said, checking all the monitors. 'Last exit point was Grandad.'

'What's going on?' said Friday, walking in from the stables.

'Not sure. Been out on your motorbike?'

'Why do you say that?'

'You smell of hot exhaust.'

'I do?' he said, sniffing at his clothes. 'No, I've been in the garage.'

'Then why do you have grass stuck to your trousers?' asked Tuesday.

Friday looked at his knees – which did indeed have blades of grass and mud stuck to them.

We all stared at one another stupidly. A mild sense of occasional confusion was not unusual, especially recently. Every now and then a small tremor of uncertainty spread around the household like a rash.

'I think we all need to take a breather,' announced Landen. 'We can't be jumping like idiots every time a mouse farts. We're all safe and—'

He stopped in mid-speech as a worried look crossed his face. I sighed inwardly. He'd be mentioning Jenny next.

'I need to check Jenny is okay.'

'I'll go,' I told him, and took the stairs to the first floor. I didn't go to the room that we pretended was Jenny's in order to spare Landen the torment of Aornis's Mindworm, but instead to the Wingco's.

I knocked quietly as I could hear him talking, and when he bade me enter, I walked in.

There was no one in the room except the Wingco and two empty chairs facing him. I knew who would be in one, but wasn't sure of the other. I nodded in the direction of the second empty chair.

'It's a blue monkey named Mr Snuffles,' explained the Wingco, 'an Imaginary Childhood Friend I'm interviewing. Their owner has been given two weeks to live, and we're trying to figure out a way to communicate once Mr Snuffles moves into the Dark Reading Matter. Is there a problem?'

'Nothing. I said I'd look in and see if Jenny was all right for Landen.'

The Wingco looked momentarily confused.

'For *Landen*?'

'Yes.'

There was an odd pause. I felt a draught on the side of my face, and the clock, which had been striking when I walked in, now read five past the hour.

'Ah yes,' said the Wingco, 'tell Landen Jenny is fine.'

He nodded towards one of the empty chairs. Jenny, as a figment of Landen's imagination, was technically the same as an Imaginary Childhood Friend. And that being so, the Wingco was able to see her. He described her as 'amusing and charming, but with a streak of melancholy'. It made the whole 'Jenny is not real' issue a mite confusing, but if you considered that the only person who could see her wasn't real either, it helped.

I thanked the Wingco and left him to Mr Snuffles.

Aornis's ability to alter memories was tiresome, and the Mindworm she had given Landen gave me especial reason to despise her. Still, at least after looking at the security images at TK Maxx we had something to work on. We'd find Aornis, no matter where she was hiding. And being a mnemonomorph, she could be hiding just about anywhere.

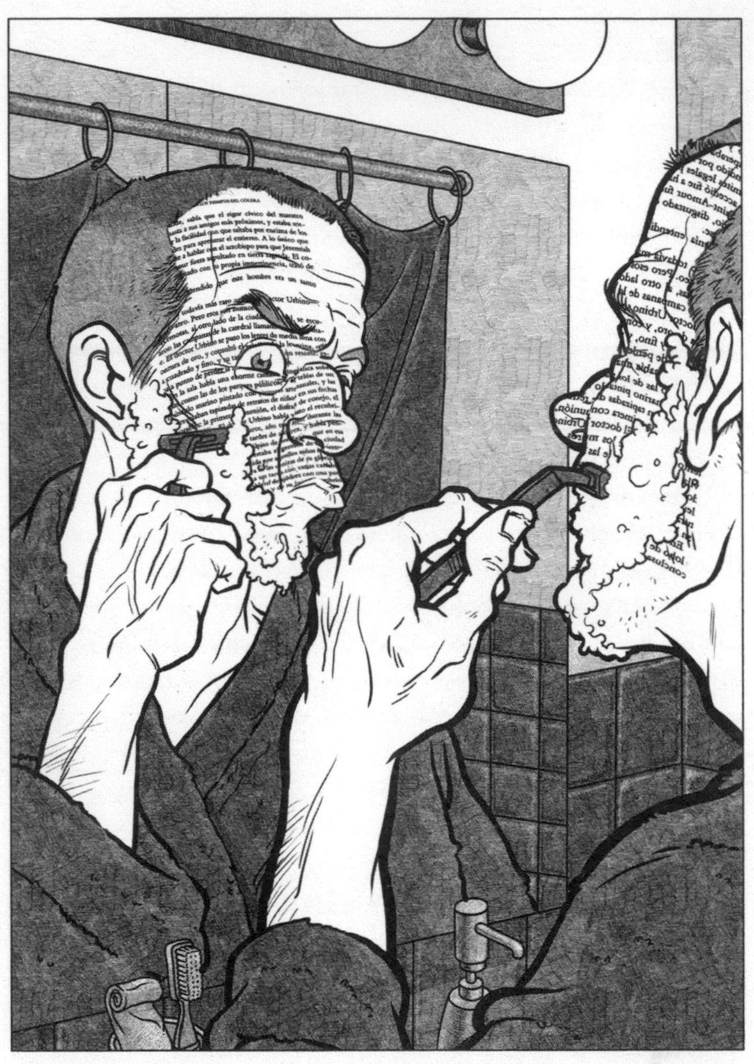

'It made him look a bit severe, but at least gave him something to read while shaving.'

12

Tuesday: Library

> 'The SLS was the Special Library Service, the elite forces charged with protecting the nation's literary heritage, either in libraries or in transit. They had taken over many of SO-27's duties when they were disbanded, and their commitment was never in question. All of them had sworn to "take a bullet" in order to protect their charges, and an average of three a year did. The SLS were the most respected law enforcement group in the nation, and often featured in movies and their own TV series. Recruitment was never an issue.'
>
> Mobie Drake – *Librarians – Heroes of the New Generation*

It was one of those crisp late summer mornings, when a drop in the air temperature gives the air a sharpness like ice on a beer glass, and the leaves, which had clung desperately to the trees throughout the late summer, were now beginning to fall upon the ground. I'd missed all this in the BookWorld, for although we had mornings which matched the description, you didn't really witness them – just the description. In fact, residents of the BookWorld would comment on a beautiful morning in that sort of odd meta-language they often used: 'What a beautifully described morning!'

Friday was working the early shift for the rest of the week so was gone by the time we came down, and Tuesday was, as usual, not keen to go school.

'We've discussed this before,' I said in my mildly-firm-mum voice, 'you're going to have a normal childhood whether you like it or not.'

She pulled a face.

'I have some work to do on the Defence Shield.'

'You'll go to school, my girl – even if only for the morning. Just remember not to take the dopey teenage thing too far.'

'No flashing?'

'Right,' I said, 'and *especially* not to Gavin Watkins.'

She gave a loud *hurrumph* and without another word got down from the breakfast table and stomped upstairs to get ready for school.

'Do you think we're doing the right thing?' asked Landen, sitting down at the table.

'I don't know,' I replied, staring after Tuesday. 'Whatever we do it'll probably turn out to be wrong.'

'Hurt yourself?' he asked.

'Where?'

'On your face. It looks like someone thumped you.'

'I assure you they didn't,' I replied, although I had noticed it myself, as well as several skinned knuckles and two broken fingernails that I had no memory of doing.

'And that bandage?' he asked, pointing to my wrapped hand.

'Oh, that was a burn,' I replied hastily, 'on a saucepan.'

I poured some more coffee. I hadn't burned myself, of course, I had simply covered up the tattoo on the back of my hand that read 'Jenny is a Mindworm' so that Landen didn't see it and go off on a furious rant. What was confusing to me was that *I* was the one with the warning tattoo – it would have made more sense on Landen's hand.

'I'd better make sure Jenny is ready for school,' he said, rising.

'She's ready,' I said, 'and . . . just doing her homework. I'll ensure Tuesday looks after her on the bus in.'

I repeated the instructions to Tuesday in case Landen was within earshot, and Tuesday acted out her part by saying something to Jenny. I let Tuesday out of the security gate, made sure she was safely on to the school bus then came back inside.

The Wingco was in the kitchen when I got back.

'Was that Imaginary Childhood Friend of any use?' I asked.

'Mr Snuffles? Not really,' admitted the Wingco. 'The trouble with ICFs is that they are invented by children, so don't have a large vocabulary or a sophisticated worldview. It's an ongoing problem – most of the time we talk about sibling rivalry, the price of sweeties and how repulsive spinach is. Still, I'll keep at it. Oh, I managed to get some information.'

'And?'

'Tresco Supermax were tricky to begin with, but I said I was working for you, and eventually got through to Records.'

'And?'

'Aornis never arrived. They raised the alarm when the prisoner was two hours overdue. The police were called, then SO-5, and that was it.'

'Okay,' I said, pinning a large map of southern England on the kitchen wall and drawing a red circle around Swindon with a felt pen, 'she left here at 1.15 p.m. on 3 July 2002 and was being driven towards Cornwall, but she never made it. Have you called Land's End International? She would have been flown out of there to Tresco.'

'I've got the operations manager calling me back.'

'Anything on Highsmith and Quinn, the guards?' I asked.

The Wingco consulted his notes.

'Quinn died six months ago in a car accident when she ran a red light into the path of a bus. Highsmith quit the Prison Service after losing Aornis. They were chosen for Aornis duty as they were both completely deaf.'

'They think she used speech to manipulate memories?'

'Apparently.'

'They know *nothing* about her,' I said with a sigh.

The Wingco handed me a Post-it with Highsmith's address on it, and I thanked him.

'Someone named John Duffy called,' he added.

'Yes?'

'He's your personal assistant at the library, and wanted to know when you would be starting work. Apparently they have a lot of "pressing issues".'

'So do I.'

We took the car into Swindon and spoke to Highsmith, who was tidying up his allotment now it was the end of the growing season. Only his speech gave us any clue to his disability – he'd been deaf for so long he had adapted almost perfectly. He was keen to assist us, especially when I told him I could get him Joffy's autograph, but he was of little help.

'The last thing I remember was leaving Swindon with Aornis in the back of the van.'

'By motorway, to Land's End?'

'Right. I think I remember turning off the M4 and on to the M5, but I couldn't swear to it. Next thing I know I'm sitting on a bench at Carlisle railway station five days later with £40,000 in cash, eight kilos of bootleg Camembert in the car and a wife waiting for me in Wrexham.'

'You explained all this to SO-5?'

'Many times. Quinn was the same, only she "came to" a day sooner than me, upside down in a Mercedes she had bought for cash two hours previously. There was an iguana on the back seat and the boot was full of rabbits.'

I exchanged looks with Landen. One of Aornis's little memory tricks was to make you think you were someone you weren't, then send you off to cause mayhem on the five-day non-recall bender. We thanked Highsmith, who told us that on the plus side he now had a very lovely wife and two-year-old daughter – and when no one claimed the cheese, he was allowed to keep it.

'That was a waste of a morning,' said Landen, once we had dropped into Yo! Toast for a coffee and a bowl of crusty toastettes.

'Perhaps,' I mused, thinking of the tattoo on my hand. I needed to ask Swindon's lone tattooist at Image Ink if she knew why I'd had it done on me rather than Landen, but I wanted to do it on my own – he didn't need to have a panic.

'I'm going to walk up to the library,' I said, 'to have a look at my new office.'

'I'll come with you.'

'No, no,' I said hurriedly, 'I'd like to do this on my own. I won't be long. New password?'

'How about me saying: "Nothing should disturb . . ." and then you finish it by saying: ". . . that condor moment"?'

'Condor moment. Very random. Got it.'

We agreed to meet in Shabitat in an hour as they were having a closing-down sale, and I walked out of the Brunel Centre. I looped up and around Commercial Road, then, once I was halfway up, remembered that I was meant to be visiting the tattooist. I was closer to the library by now, so elected to visit her on my way back, and arrived outside the library ten minutes later, my leg feeling sore and tired. It was just over a mile, and it was the first time I'd done a walk that long. Before the accident I could have run it in a couple of minutes.

The Swindon All You Can Eat at Fatso's Drink Not Included Library was a large, glassy and very angular building sixteen storeys high at the corner of Emlyn and Commercial. Libraries had always been a priority for the Commonsense Party, along with training, educational standards, national exercise programmes and preschool assistance for mothers, and the sleek and brightly coloured building was only two years old.

I announced myself to the receptionist, who went into a panicky lather, dialled a number with shaky hands and announced '*She's here!*' breathlessly down the line. While we waited she simply stared at me, transfixed.

'Nice building,' I said by way of conversation.

'Yes it is, isn't it? Gosh, we love it here and we're so glad it's you finally we might be able to get something done around here especially sorting out the budget ha-ha-ha you'll speak to the council won't you I have a daughter I need to pay through school she has only one leg and can't . . .'

And she fainted clean away, having failed to take a breath.

'She does that a lot,' said a voice behind me, 'it's nothing to worry about.'

I turned to see a slightly built man who had the upright manner of someone in the military, and was perfectly presented in a neat pinstripe suit.

'Welcome to the Wessex All You Can Eat at Fatso's Drinks Not Included Library Services,' he said. 'I'm John Duffy, your personal assistant. Everyone calls me Duffy.'

I knew him by sight and reputation, although we'd never met. He was a decorated ex-Special Library Service operative, invalided out after a riot gun exploded in the Guildford Wicks Aircraft Supplies Try Us First Library. It was during a demonstration by Shakespeare followers, incensed that the Town Council had downgraded Will from 'Poet Saint' to 'Eternal Bard'. The explosion sent a copy of *Love in the Time of Cholera* slamming into his face with such force that it blinded him in one eye and transferred the text of the book permanently into his cheek and forehead. It made him look a bit severe, but at least gave him something to read while shaving.

'Your reputation precedes you,' I said. 'Glad to make your acquaintance.'

He nodded politely.

'May I show you around?'

'Thank you,' I replied, gazing around at the magnificently bizarre building, an odd mix of randomly shaped modernism with large voids, oddly shaped glass panels, bright colours and soaring internal verticals. 'It's quite something, isn't it?'

'Designed by Will Alsop just before he went sane,' replied Duffy. 'We were very lucky. I understand you know Colonel Wexler, who heads up the SLS?'

A lean woman with a face pinched by hard workouts walked forward to greet me. She was in her mid-fifties, did not look well disposed to joy in any form, and was wearing the standard SLS combat fatigues, replete with the distinctive camouflage pattern of book spines for blending into library spaces. When I was at SpecOps she was at the Search/Destroy division of SO-5, and you didn't get to join them until you'd killed eight people with a gun, four with a blunt instrument or two with your hands – it was a sliding-scale sort of thing. Wexler's appointment to the SLS was enough to precipitate a 32 per cent drop in late returns.

'Welcome to Wessex Library Services,' she said in a voice that sounded like a twelve-mile run washed down with two raw eggs, 'and good to see you again.'

We shook hands.

'You too, Mel. Husband well?'

'Dead.'

'I'm very sorry to hear that.'

She shrugged.

'I killed the man who did it with my thumbs,' she said. 'I've not washed this one since.'

She showed me a grubby-looking thumb.

Duffy quickly intervened with an embarrassed cough.

'Colonel Wexler offers her full support, don't you, Colonel?'

'Of course,' she said in a hollow tone. 'What sort of leadership can we expect from you? Decisive and bold, or faltering and ambivalent?'

'The first, I hope.'

'Good,' said Colonel Wexler, visibly pleased. 'The previous Chief Librarian refused to sanction dawn raids to retrieve overdue books. But that will change under you, yes?'

'I'll be giving it all due consideration,' I said, meaning that I'd do no such thing.

'That's a start,' she said. 'I'd also like you to review the rules regarding spine bending and turning over the corners of pages. If we let simple things like that slide without punishment, we could open the floodgates to poor reading etiquette and a downward spiral to the collapse of civilisation.'

'Good idea,' I said. 'Will you memo your ideas to me?'

She said she would, and we shook hands again and moved off.

'She's certifiably insane, isn't she?' I asked once we were out of earshot.

'I'm afraid so,' replied Duffy, 'but loyal to a fault. She and the rest of the SLS would die protecting any book in the library – with the possible exception of those bloody awful Emperor Zhark novels and anything written by Daphne Farquitt.'

'That's good to know.'

We walked into the main Fiction lending floor. It was light and airy and there were racks and racks of books and very little computer space, which I liked the look of. The second floor was more of the same, but was for 'Non-fiction and General Interest'.

'This is where we relax,' said Duffy as we toured the luxurious staff recreation room complete with ping-pong table, a meditation Zen Room for chilling out and a Michelin-starred chef to make lunch.

'Nice recreation room,' I said with a nod. 'The only thing missing is a string quartet.'

'They're here on Monday mornings, to ease in the work week. Let me show you to your office.'

'. . . the distinctive camouflage pattern of book spines for blending into library spaces.'

We took the elevator to the fourteenth floor and walked across the swirly-patterned carpet to my office. The room was large and square in plan, with a ceiling that sloped down from the windows. Two sides of the office were glazed and were on the corner of the building where they faced the glassy towers of Swindon's financial district and would thus afford me a spectacular view of the smiting, should it come to pass. Another wall was covered by a bookcase and three videoconferencing screens, in front of which were two sofas and a coffee table for more informal meetings. The final wall contained two doors. One led into Duffy's office and the assistants, and the other to the waiting room. The office was spacious, modern and very corporate. In an instant I didn't feel as if I belonged here. Dingy basements smelling of photocopier toner and old coffee suited me better.

'This is your desk,' said Duffy.

In a bit of a daze, I sat down on a plush armchair and looked around. I was parked behind a desk that seemed like an acre of finely polished walnut. There was a large exchange phone with a separate button for every library in Wessex, and next to this was a single, old-fashioned red telephone, without a dial – just a single button with 'NP' etched on to it.

'That's the emergency hotline to Nancy at the World League of Librarians,' explained Duffy. 'She'll be on the first tube from Seattle if you call her. But make sure it's a real emergency,' he added. 'If Nancy is dragged all this way for nothing you'll be in *big* trouble.'

'I'll remember that.'

'Do you want a light day or a heavy day tomorrow?'

'Better make it a light one.'

'Very well.' He pressed the intercom button and leaned down to speak.

'Geraldine, would you bring in the light schedule, please?'

'I'll tell you what I *will* do,' I said as we waited for Geraldine.

'What's that?' said Duffy.

'I'm going to change the name of the library service. All that "Fatso's all you can eat" stuff is nonsense.'

Duffy raised an eyebrow.

'That's what the last Chief Librarian said. He didn't like Fatso's and told them he was going to instigate a compulsory sponsorship buyback.'

'How did he get on?'

'The engine was still running when they found his car on the Lambourn Downs. His wallet and mobile phone were on the passenger seat. There was a discount voucher from Fatso's for kids to eat free under the wiper, but that might have been a coincidence. Of the Chief Librarian, no trace. I should forget them. If you want something controversial to do on your first week, then announce biometric data for library cards. Identity theft is a big issue with people eager to take out more than six books at one time.'

'How about we up it to seven?'

Duffy gave a polite cough. Clearly, I had a lot to learn about libraries.

An assistant of not more than twenty and dressed in a bottle-green suit entered the room and walked nervously up to the desk.

'This is Geraldine,' said Duffy, 'the assistant's assistant to the assistant personal assistant of my own personal assistant's assistant.'

'Hello, Geraldine.'

'Hello, Chief Librarian,' she said nervously. 'Have you really killed seven people?'

'I tend to try and dwell on the people I've saved,' I replied.

'Oh,' she said, obviously intrigued by the notion of an ex-literary detective running the library service, 'of course.'

'How many assistants do I have?' I asked, turning back to Duffy.

'Including me, three.'

'Three? Given Geraldine's job title? How is *that* possible?'

'They have multiple jobs. Geraldine, apart from being the assistant's assistant to the assistant personal assistant of my own personal assistant's assistant, is also my own personal assistant's assistant's assistant.'

'No,' said Geraldine, 'that's Lucy. I'm not only your assistant's assistant's sub-assistant, but also the assistant to the assistant to your personal assistant's assistant.'

'Wait,' I said, thinking hard, 'that must make you your own assistant.'

'Yes; I had to fire myself yesterday. Luckily I was also *above* the assistant who fired me, so I could reinstate myself. Will there be anything else, Chief Librarian?'

There wasn't, so she bobbed politely and withdrew.

I looked at the schedule she had deposited on my desk, which was packed full of meetings, budgetary discussions, two staff disciplinary hearings, and several forums with Swindon's readers' groups.

'How does the heavy schedule differ from this one?'

'The same – only it's on blue paper and instead of lunch you get two more meetings: the first is a pep talk to the many frustrated citizens who *weren't* selected last year to train as librarians, and will have to console themselves with mundane careers as doctors, lawyers and lion-tamers.'

'And the second meeting?'

'A "round table" with the Swindon Society of Bowdlerisers. They're anxious that "certain passages" be removed from "certain books" in order that they can "shine with greater lustre" and be made more suitable for family audiences.'

'Which books in particular?'

Duffy handed me a list.

'*Wanda Does Wantage*?' I read. 'There'd be nothing left except nine prepositions, six colons and a noun.'

'I think that's the point.'

I handed the list back.

'Tell me,' I said, 'did the previous Chief Librarian *really* vanish without trace?'

'Not entirely,' said Duffy, passing me a photograph of a concrete monorail support somewhere on the Wantage branch line. 'We were sent this.'

I stared at the photograph.

'Did you tell the police?'

'They said it was nothing and that people get sent pictures of concrete monorail supports all the time.'

'Do they?'

'No, not really. Can I schedule the budget meeting for Thursday morning first thing? The City Council want to reassign some of our financial resources.'

'Any particular reason?'

'We've got generous funding not just because it's sensible and right and true and just and proper, but because we've been doing all SO-27's work for the past thirteen years. But now Detective Smalls is taking over the Literary Detectives, much of our budget will be reassigned to her.'

'Is this important?'

'Funding's about the most important thing there is.'

'I suppose you should, then.'

I stared at the huge number meetings I still had to attend on my schedule.

'I've got an idea,' I said, 'I'll just turn up tomorrow morning and start having meetings until my brain turns to jelly, then we'll stop and I'll hide for a bit, then do some more while thinking of other things, then forget it all by the evening and we'll do pretty much the same thing again the day after – and rely on subordinates and assistants to deal with actually running the place.'

'Thank goodness for that,' said Duffy with a sigh of relief. 'I was worried you had no experience of running a large public department.'

There was a knock at the door and a tall, fastidious-looking man appeared.

'Am I disturbing anything?'

It was James Finisterre.

'Jim!'

We embraced and he held my hands in his.

'Great to have you on board. We need some safe hands in the boardroom. Duffy looking after you well?'

'He has been exemplary.'

Finisterre had been one of our back-room boys at SO-27, one of the dependable boffins who rarely did fieldwork but could answer almost any literary question you might care to ask. His particular expertise was the nineteenth-century novel, but he was fully competent to professorial standard in almost all fields of literature, whether it be Sumerian laundry lists or the very latest Armitage Shanks Prize winner. He spent his life immersed in books to the cost of everything else, even personal relationships. 'Friends,' he once said, 'are probably great, but I have forty thousand friends of my own already, and each of them needs my attention.'

I thanked Duffy for his time, then followed Finisterre to the elevators.

'Surprised to see you here,' he said. 'I heard you were in the frame for heading up SO-27?'

'Overrated,' I replied. 'Phoebe Smalls got it. She'll be good.'

'I'm sure she will. How long do you give her before she's either killed in the line of duty or resigns a quivering wreck? A week?'

'A lot longer than *that*, I should imagine.'

'I'm not so sure. As soon as she opens for business we're dumping thirteen years of unsolved caseload at her feet. Up until this morning there was no one to take responsibility for the wholesale theft and bootlegging, copyright infringement and larceny. We logged reports, but didn't do anything. It's been a bibliothief's smorgasbord for the past decade. Why do you think the library is so heavily armed?'

'It's that bad?'

'You've been out of the loop for a while, haven't you?'

I stared at him.

'I've been working more on the . . . *supply side* of the literary world.'

'Really? Well, Braxton was doing you a seriously big favour not giving you that job. Any idea how much of our budget is being transferred to SO-27?'

'Duffy says quite a lot. I'll speak to Braxton.'

'Good luck with that. Want to see what I do here?'

I nodded, and we descended in the lift towards the basement.

We stepped out into a small lobby with a single armoured door and an armed guard sitting behind a window of bullet-proof glass. Finisterre licked his finger and held it in the DNA reader aperture. There was a puff of air and the light turned green. I did the same. The door clicked open and we stepped inside.

'Welcome to the Antiquarian section,' said Finisterre, leading me along shiny white corridors. 'The Swindon All You Can Eat at Fatso's Drink Not Included Library isn't just a central lending library, but a repository of all the important documents currently in the County of Wessex's possession.'

He indicated a row of historic documents displayed in a glass display cabinet that stretched down the corridor.

'That's our copy of the Magna Carta,' he said walking slowly past the treasures, 'and this is a rare first edition of the *Principia Mathematica* dedicated "To dearest Googly-bear love Newt".' He moved to another glass case. 'This is St Zvlkx's original list of

Revealments, and over here, a unique treasure of Shakespeareana – a blindingly rare First Folio Advanced Reader's Copy, still with the front page marked "not for sale or quotation".'

We walked into a larger room in which a dozen conservators were working their way over a series of vellum parchments folded into books with flaking leather covers.

'This one's from the eleventh century,' said Finisterre, showing me a volume that looked like a prayer book, 'and we've two dozen or so from the ninth. Religious texts, mostly, but we're hoping for a few treasures.'

'In Wessex?' I asked, for the county was not noted for its stock of tenth-century manuscripts.

'We've your brother to thank. Now that religious orders are transferring their theological allegiances to the Global Standard Deity, they've thrown open their collections for scrutiny, and to be honest, no pun intended – it's a godsend. We're seeing stuff that we never thought existed. This one here,' he said, pointing to a badly water-damaged tome, 'is Gerald of Wales' book of recipes. It confirmed what nutritionists have long suspected: firstly, that celebrity chefs were as popular in the twelfth century as they are now, and secondly, that Welsh cuisine has not improved at all since then, and may even have got worse.'

He pointed to another, equally worn book.

'Over here is an account of a night out in Copenhagen in 1182 with Saxo Grammaticus – boy, do the Danes know how to party.'

'You're copying all these, yes?' I asked, for an original and unique work was at grave risk of literary extinction if anything happened to it.

'First thing we do,' he said, leading me into another room where each book was meticulously scanned once the conservators had decided they were robust enough.

'This is cutting-edge stuff, Thursday. Unique codices, right here in my lap – and we don't have to be shot at to study them. Well, not much, anyway.'

'I can't argue with that.'

He looked at the trolleys full of old books.

'The Sisterhood are opening their Salisbury collection for initial appraisal this afternoon,' he added. 'Do you want to come along?'

I stared at him. By the Sisterhood he meant the Blessed Ladies of the Lobster, one of the most numerous, long lived and secretive of Wessex's religious orders. A lot of time and effort had been expended in defending their library against would-be thieves, eager to get their hands on a collection that was rumoured to have unique treasures of almost incalculable value.

'What a question,' I replied. 'Absolutely.'

'I'll pick you up at your house at three,' he said, 'and bring identification. The Sisters can be a bit trigger happy with anyone they don't know. I arrived unannounced last week and had to dodge a rocket-propelled grenade.'

'Employing mercenaries, are they?'

'No. The Lobsterhood have often been described as pious, but rarely seen as restrained.'

14

Tuesday: Next Thursday

> 'The dismantling of SO-27 had some peculiar and unforeseen consequences, not least the legalising of lethal force within libraries: "for the maintenance of the collections and public order". Originally intended as a deterrent to thieves, the legislation quickly became known as the "Shush Law", when overenthusiastic librarians invoked a "violent intervention" for loud talking. Libraries have never been quieter, and theft and vandalism dropped by 72%.'
>
> Mobie Drake – *Librarians – Heroes of the New Generation*

I was searched before leaving the library – no one was exempt. The stealing and selling of rare antiquarian books were still big business, and the library weren't taking any chances. They had recently shot dead a thief who had attempted to steal one of the library's first editions of *Dialogue Concerning the Two Chief World Systems*. Luckily for the librarian who fired the shot, the potential thief had been shot *within* the library boundary, allowing the killing to be categorised as 'Justifiable Lethal Force by a State Registered Librarian in the course of their duties', an incident that required only a few forms to be filled in. As it says on the T-shirts: 'I don't scare easily – I'm a librarian,' which was the polite version of the original: 'Don't give me any of your shit – I'm a librarian'.

I took the longer way back towards the Brunel Centre and was just passing the Swindon branch of Booktastic when I remembered I had walked that way *specifically* to drop in at the tattooist's, and had forgotten again. It was a half-mile back, and I could drop in when I drove past later. It was probably the Dizuperadol making me forgetful.

On a whim I walked into Booktastic to check on whether my books were still core stock. I took the lift to the third floor and was relieved to find they were. Not relief for *personal* me, but for *written* me inside the books, to whom I owed a huge debt of gratitude – a debt I hoped to repay by keeping her well read. I had changed my tune over the fictionalised account of my life, now being broadly in favour rather than wishing it were quietly remaindered or, better still, pulped. I placed the books cover out at eye level, noted that there was another in the series, told a browsing couple that the books were probably 'worth a look if you've nothing better to do,' then heard the cathedral clock begin to chime midday.

Soon after, I trotted down from the third floor at Booktastic and made my way towards Shabitat, where Landen was hoping to buy one of their huge trademark 'Flipdate' clocks. I found him in the glassware section. The trouble about having a huge house was that it was easier to double or treble up on things than carry them from the kitchen to the dining room and back again, which meant we needed three of everything.

'You can get an entire set of glassware for only fifty quid,' said Landen, looking at me for a moment before digging out his mobile.

'It's ugly,' I said.

'Ah, yes,' replied Landen, dialling a number, 'but before it was expensive and ugly, and now it's cheap and ugly. So everything's changed.'

'Has it?'

'Sure. What was your new office like?'

'Pretty cool.'

'Describe it to me.'

'Windows . . . a door, and a phone. A large red one. A hotline.' I narrowed my eyes as I tried to remember what else I had seen.

'I bumped into Jim Finisterre. Who are you calling?'

'Stig.'

'What do you want to talk to him about?'

'Just a job we have to do. All three of us.'

'Can I know?'

'It's a surprise.'

'I like surprises.'

'Stig?' said Landen. 'It's Landen. We need you.' He paused for a moment and looked at me. 'We're in Shabitat, glassware section . . . yes, I know they're ugly. See you soon.'

He snapped the mobile shut and looked at me with his head on one side. There was a brief silence. Not one of those companionable silences that are quite enjoyable, but an empty, cold silence, of people soon to be strangers. And that was when I had a peculiar feeling. One I hadn't had for a while.

'Landen?'

'Yes?'

I leaned closer and lowered my voice.

'I want to make love to you.'

'What, here?'

'Well, no – we could find a hotel. I've not felt it this strong since well before the accident – probably that holiday in Greece when you'd lost ten pounds and we had dinner at Arturo's. On our own. No kids.'

Landen said nothing, and stared at me. I frowned. It wasn't a bad feeling – quite the opposite, of course. But it was *unusual*, and that worried me. Even following the accident I still wanted him in a 'that would be nice if I wasn't feeling so shit' sort of way, but this was like being a teenager again – that sort of lusty yearning that is born of fresh discovery, and young hearts bursting to be free.

'Say something,' I said.

'What do you want me to say?'

'Anything. "Me too" would be good for starters, rapidly followed by "Does the Finis Hotel rent rooms by the hour?" to which the answer is: "Yes, notorious for it".'

Landen gave me a weary half-smile.

'If I were to say: "Nothing should disturb . . ."' he asked, 'what would you say in reply?'

'Nothing should disturb us . . . in the Finis?'

'No, it's a password. The one we swapped on parting less than two hours ago.'

'Oh yes. Nothing should disturb . . . that . . . No. I can't remember.'

'And why do you think that might be?'

He said it in a sarcastic manner that he would never have used on me. Not unless we were having a serious, balls-out, door-slamming 'I don't know why I sodding married you' row. But then, the penny dropped and I looked down. I wasn't holding a walking stick, felt no pain and I was standing upright, without a stoop. No wonder Landen could tell I wasn't the real one straight away. I hadn't walked this well for a while.

'Shit,' I muttered, 'I've been replaced', and I looked stupidly around to see whether the real me might be somewhere close by. I wasn't, so I looked back at Landen, who raised an eyebrow.

'This is a novel approach,' he said, 'a synthetic aware that it *is* a synthetic?'

'Wait, wait,' I said, knowing only too well what we did with synthetics, 'this is different. I'm me. I'm conscious, I have some of the real me's memories. Maybe not all of them, but some, and enough.'

'You *say* you have,' said Landen, placing his hand in the pocket where he kept his pistol, 'but that's what you're *programmed* to think. Try and make a run for it and I'll drop you where you stand. The first time we killed one of you it was hard to explain – until the second one turned up.'

'That's what Stig's coming to do, isn't it?'

'As Divisional Chief of SO-13, he's legally empowered to destroy unlicensed non-evolutionary life-forms, and that's what you are, my friend. But before we get to that, what do you want? Why do Goliath want to replace my wife with one of their own?'

'I don't know. Or at least, if I *do* know, it's not readily apparent to me. You'd really kill me?'

'Without a second thought. Still want to make love to me?'

'In an odd kind of way, yes,' I said, shifting my weight from one foot to the other. 'But listen, if this *is* me and I am Thursday but weirdly in another body, you might actually kill me for real. And that might be it. This could be the final vessel for my consciousness.'

'Fascinating,' remarked Landen. 'You must be a Mark VII or something. None of the others were so articulate.'

'Or knew they were a synthetic?'

'Right. But first things first: what did you do with the real Thursday? It'll save a lot of time.'

'I don't know.'

'You must know. They *always* know.'

'No, I really don't. I have no recollection of being activated.'

'So you say,' said Landen suspiciously.

'No – to me, I'm me.'

'In that case, think back to what you *can* remember. I want my wife back.'

'Okay, okay. I was still in pain and had a stick when I left the library. It can only be between there and here.'

'Did you stop anywhere?'

I paused, deep in thought, trying to figure out when Real Me stopped being Real Me and started being Synthetic Me.

'Nope,' I said, 'nothing.'

'It good likeness,' said Stig, who had just arrived, 'but why made no attempt to stoop and limp like real Thursday?'

'It's much more impressive than that,' said Landen, referring to me as though I were the latest model of car or something. 'It's trying to tell me it has the real Thursday's consciousness and partial memory.'

Stig peered closer at me.

'The craftsmanship different to others. More hurried. It thinks it is her?'

'It *is* me inside, Stig,' I said. 'We met yesterday at the SpecOps office.'

'Anyone could know that. What did we speak of?'

I tried to think of the conversation I'd had with him.

'It's kind of hazy,' I admitted, 'like the handover between Real Me and Synthetic Me isn't complete. It's like when you wake up and you're not sure who you are or where you are, or even your own name – you know, how rock legends spend the first two hours of each day.'

'That sounds more like Thursday,' said Stig.

'Yes,' replied Landen, 'none of them ever had a sense of humour before.'

'*Shit*,' I said.

'What?' asked Landen.

'I can remember more of the password. Nothing should disturb that *condor* . . . something. And Stig, we talked about what I'd been doing that morning, and something about shampoo being in a different bottle.'

'Did that happen?' asked Landen.

'Yes.'

'And the shrink's name was . . . *Dr Chumley*,' I said as memories came seeping through, 'and he gave me a NUT-4 because I was hoping to run SO-27. Shazza said to say to Friday that it would have been *seriously* good.'

'Is that true?' asked Stig.

Landen nodded and I stared at the pair of them. They looked, well, *spooked*. None of the other synthetics had been anything like this.

'What all this mean?' Stig asked Landen.

'I don't know.'

'I can feel the memories filter in, like I'm waking up to a new body,' I said. 'It feels good, too – like I've never felt before. Ask me a question.'

'What's 3,598 multiplied by 9?'

'32,382,' I replied without pausing. 'Do you want to hear about every single monarch of England before the 1st Republic? I can give you precise dates of when they ruled, the names of their consorts and an estimation of their weight with a 2.3 per cent margin for error. Give me a piece of paper.'

Landen passed me a receipt from his pocket, and in a brief flurry of dexterity, it was an elegant origami swan.

'I can do this, too.'

I picked up a glass vase and tossed it in the air. I closed my eyes, waited until I thought it should be coming back down and caught it in midair. I opened my eyes again.

'It's like being Wonderwoman,' I said, 'only without the stupid costume. DON'T look up.'

'Why not?' asked Landen, not unreasonably.

'There's a ninja assassin hiding in the rafters. But don't worry, there's no danger to us. He's been there for six weeks already – probably waiting for a Romanian who can't keep his mouth shut.'

'You saw him?'

'I *heard* him. And one of his eyelashes just landed on your shoulder. Want to see me juggle?'

Landen and Stig stared at me. As my old memories filtered through to their new home, I could recall that no synthetic Thursday had ever acted this way. This one seemed from where I was standing not just as good as a human, but *better*. I could have taken on Landen and Stig there and then if I'd wanted to. But so far as I could tell, I was still Thursday. And Thursdays don't beat up their husbands and best friends.

'Would you excuse me one moment?' I said. 'I have to find me.'

Without waiting for an answer I ran out of the glassware department with Stig struggling to keep up. I ran out of the store, accelerated fast down the concourse and felt a surge of raw elation as my legs ran like they had never run before. I was stronger, smarter, fitter and faster – and if this one had never had children, my stomach was probably joyously flat, too. I skidded to a halt outside Booktastic and paused for a moment, hardly out of breath.

I was still thinking when Stig arrived a few moments later.

'You fast,' he said, '*really* fast.'

'When I left here I *didn't* have my stick with me,' I said, 'and I ran down the stairs. But I remember swearing over the lack of a handrail as I went in – and also slapped another patch on my arse in the loo. So I must have been the previous me then.'

'*Booktastic* big,' said Stig, 'why you enter?'

'Probably putting the *Thursday Next Chronicles* face out – I've done it before.'

I ran up to Speculative Fiction on the third floor, again with Stig labouring behind. I found my way to the *Next Chronicles*, but found no one there, not even hidden behind the sofas. We started to search the recesses of the bookshop, as it was fairly labyrinthine; it wasn't unusual to be lost in its twisting corridors; once, a Henry James fanatic was locked in for the entire weekend.

'What's going on?' asked Landen as he lumbered out of the elevator, panting.

'I remember now that she's in the stockroom,' I said, pushing the door from its hinges. We found a pale figure of a woman in her underwear hidden behind a pallet of Colwyn Baye's latest book.

She looked terrible. One leg was thinner than the other and badly scarred, and her skin was a pasty shade, the colour of hospital inpatients. She was unconscious. I'd forgotten how tired and old I looked. Landen checked the unconscious me for vital signs.

'Alive?' asked Stig.

'Very much so – just unconscious.'

Landen slapped me around the face. First softly, then harder. This didn't seem to have much effect, so he pinched me – twice. Nothing.

'Any ideas?' asked Landen.

'The upload takes less than half an hour,' I said, not knowing how I knew, 'it's a neural bandwidth issue. And it's almost complete.'

I was now getting the deep subconscious stuff. The memories of childhood, the time our hamster ate its young – I was only eight. *Never* forgot that. Then other stuff started to come in, too, stuff I thought I'd forgotten. Arguments with Anton, long before he died in the Crimea, and my mother crying for her husband, the first time he died. But through it all, there was one thing that was strong in the front of my mind – this wasn't me. It was subtly different in ways impossible to explain. It was wonderful, but disturbing, too.

'I know what we have to do,' I said quietly, 'but first, I have to prove to you that this was really me.'

I took out a pen and scribbled a note on the back of my old Skyrail ticket. I took a step forward, and placed it in Landen's trouser pocket. I hugged him, placed my cheek to his and whispered in his ear.

'I love you. Now do it.'

15

Tuesday: I'm back

'Chimeras took many forms. Many of them hideous, and all dangerous. The hobby geneticists of twenty years ago who made odd-looking pets in a garden shed had transformed into a younger elite who called themselves Gene Hackmen. They'd make anything for kicks and giggles, and generally did. Famously, FunBoy-6 built a centaur from spare parts. It was a good effort and galloped elegantly, although having the cerebral cortex of a pig, it was prone to oinking. Stig had dispatched the creature without mercy. The Hackmen hated Stig, and he hated them. And that from a Neanderthal, who thought that Hate, like Greed or Envy, was the emotion of a species doomed to failure.'

Ronald Crick – *Hobby Geneticists, the new Dr Frankensteins*

My eyes flickered open and Stig and Landen's familiar faces swum into view. My leg had a dull throb of pain from the hip to the knee and I was cold – but then I was lying on concrete in only my underwear. It felt uncomfortable and pleasant all in one. I was broken, but I was me.

'It smells of cat's piss down here,' I said, 'and Landen: nothing should disturb that condor moment.'

I saw Landen let out a gasp of relief and brush away some tears.

'Thank the GSD,' he said. 'I thought you were gone for good.'

'Not at all – the worst that would have happened to me was cramp, thirst and hunger – and probably the release of waste products, given time. I was simply waiting for the return of my id. My clothes? I'm freezing.'

'You won't want your own back,' said Landen, 'but she must have arrived dressed in something – here.'

He pulled out some quality-looking threads from a carrier bag pushed beneath some Daphne Farquitt boxed sets.

'Chimera,' said Stig to the retail staff, who had popped their heads into the stockroom to see what the gunshot had been about, 'nothing to see.'

'She was different to the rest,' said Landen as he helped me on with the clothes. 'She was actually convinced that she was you – and had tapped into your memories.'

'Landen, she *was* me. I was there. I was inside her. I was becoming her or she was becoming me – or we were becoming each other.'

'That's not possible.'

'Did she seem like me? More than the others, I mean?'

'By a factor of ten. But I don't buy into this whole "transfer of consciousness" shit. It's impossible for a whole bunch of reasons.'

I grasped his forearm.

'The note I scribbled down for you, just before I told you I loved you and you killed me. It says: "Two minds with a single thought, two hearts that beat as one".'

Landen pulled the piece of paper from his pocket and stared at it.

'Okay,' he said, 'I *totally* buy into this whole "transfer of consciousness" shit. But what does it mean? That Goliath are out to replace people with copies of themselves just better and faster and stronger with an increased libido, a good head for figures and origami skills to die for?'

'It looks that way. As to why, I've no idea. But *she* probably did.'

I nodded towards where the body of the new and improved and now very dead Thursday was lying on the floor of the loading bay. A long trail of dark blood was pooling near a stack of remaindered Lola Vavoom conspiracy books.

'We need get her back to lab,' said Stig as he pulled out his mobile phone, 'find out more.'

'No one move,' came a voice.

It was the police. A sergeant I recognised named Kitchen and two constables.

'SO-13,' said Stig, holding up his ID, 'this chimera. Our jurisdiction.'

They stared at one another for a moment. The friction in the air was tangible. SpecOps and the police didn't really get along – mostly because SpecOps had seniority, and the police had a better canteen and a final salary pension.

'SO-13 was disbanded thirteen years ago, Stiggins.'

'From midday today back in business.'

'O-kay, but I'll need confirmation from Commander Hicks.'

'No problem, friend-O. You take charge? Not double-tapped yet. Maybe you take honour.'

Stig drew a twelve-gauge revolver out of his shoulder holster and offered it to the policeman.

The officers looked at one another.

'It's still alive?' asked the sergeant.

'Always best make sure.'

'SO-13 reinstated, you say?'

'From midday.'

'We'll leave it in your capable hands,' remarked Kitchen, and beckoned to the officers to back away.

'You have acted . . . *wisely*,' said Stig as he parked the massive weapon back in his jacket, 'hold perimeter and call when our transport arrive.'

'Yes, sir,' said the sergeant as he saluted smartly, glad to be spared the responsibility of command.

While Stig called his brother-in-law to bring a van to take away the body, I stared at the latest synthetic. She was the seventh we knew of, and the third since my accident. The pre-accident ones had all been killed by the Stiltonista thinking they were me, and of the post-accident batch, one we'd found in the house going through my stuff presumably in order to better emulate me, and the other was arrested when it tried to cash a cheque on my behalf. Both of them had been questioned but could explain little, and were helped into long eternity pleading that they were me – but without being able to answer anything but rudimentary Thursday trivia. Landen and Spike had disposed of them. I think they're in the Savenake forest where the Stiltonista disposed of the earlier ones. None of them had seemed that smart, and none of them – until now – would have fooled anyone. But maybe that wasn't the point. Maybe the early ones were simply testing the water.

The small data plate under her eyelid had simply stated that she was a TN-v7.2. The last one had been a v6.6. There was a serial number, and I jotted it down. We stared at it for a while. It was kind of weird, seeing me lying dead on the ground with half a head. It was a waste of a good body, too. Boy, could she run. And although I'd not had a chance to put it to the test, could have given Landen a seriously good run for his money in the sack.

'Do you have any of her memories?' he asked. 'I mean, she didn't pop into existence here at Booktastic. She must have walked in the door like the rest of us.'

I thought hard. I knew nothing of her being her before she was me being me. My memories were simply of me.

'Nothing.'

'Shame. Stig?'

'Physically, specimen excellent,' he said, 'good muscle tone, firm all over – almost no fat.'

'It was a great body,' I said somewhat wistfully.

'But it made *hastily*,' he said, 'look at legs.'

He showed us an athletic yet hairless leg.

'Stretch marks on the knees and shin?' said Landen, leaning closer and putting on his reading glasses. 'And why is the skin so smooth otherwise?'

'No sweat glands. On a hot day she'd boil.'

'How quickly did they grow her?'

'Our guess ten weeks,' said Stig as he showed us her hands. The fingernails looked long, but they were stuck on. He pulled one off to reveal a real nail below, and only a quarter of the way down the nail-bed. He pointed to the side of the scalp still remaining, which at first glance seemed to have a goodly amount of long hair, which was in fact man-made fibres stuck manually into the scalp.

'Six brushings and no hair left,' he said. He prodded the stomach – which *was* flat, I noted. He then grunted with interest, looked in her throat, rolled the body over and pulled down her trousers and pants.

'No digestive tract. Not designed for longevity.'

A tract wasn't the only thing she – or it – was missing.

'She was going to be seriously frustrated with that libido, too.'

'Not what she designed for,' said Stig, 'see here?'

He pointed to what looked like a thin scar on her upper back. It wasn't, though – it was a flap.

'Umbilical went here,' he said.

He wiped his finger on the flap then smelled it.

'Activated two hours ago, give/take. Not seen this sort of synthetic before. Cheap body.'

'But excellent brain,' added Landen.

'Indeed,' agreed Stig, 'she sent here find out something, do something, see something – perhaps report back, then die.'

'The BookWorld,' I said. 'Goliath have always wanted to get in there. I could easily have read my way in there with this body. Do you think that's what they were up to?'

No one answered because no one knew. Stig peered into the

skull cavity and poked a chubby finger into the remains of the brain stem.

'Dismantle it when back at lab. Shame you shot it through head, Landen. We could have learned more.'

'Note to self,' said Landen sarcastically, 'don't shoot wife through head.'

Landen and I walked out of the bookshop after offering our apologies for the mess, and I told them to send a bill for any damaged books to Braxton Hicks.

'Are you okay?' asked Landen as we hobbled back towards the car.

'I'm fine,' I said, 'I just miss running.'

'You will again,' he said, but I knew, despite the conviction with which he said it, that it was going to take a while.

'Sure,' I said, 'and your leg is going to grow back.'

He said nothing, but squeezed my hand.

'We've got to be home at three,' I said, 'Finisterre is taking me up to the Sisterhood to view the contents of their scriptorium.

'Wait a moment,' I added, 'that synthetic wouldn't have been activated without help, and she was barely two hours old.'

'What are we looking for?' asked Landen. 'A cobwebby basement with ancient electrical equipment and a mad scientist? Or just a *really* large jar?'

'She'd certainly have been sealed in something. Hang on.'

I delved through my pockets – I was wearing her clothes, after all – and found a keycard from the Finis Hotel.

16

Tuesday: The Finis

> 'The Finis Hotel remains not the most luxurious or stylish of Swindon's many hotels, but certainly the most notorious, with the ballroom and rooms host to more attempted coups, murders, formation of political splinter groups and police raids than those of any other establishment. It had become so notorious, in fact, that people came to holiday here simply to witness what management refer to as: "The Finis's diverse clientele and their antics".'
>
> *Swindon Tourist Board Leaflet*

The receptionist greeted me cheerily as we walked into the lobby.

'Welcome back,' she said brightly. 'Did you find what you were looking for?'

'In a manner of speaking. How long am I booked in for?'

'Let's see,' she said, looking at the screen set into the desk, 'two nights.'

'Did I arrive with anyone?'

Her eyes flicked to Landen. We were a recognisable couple in the city, and the Finis prided itself on its discretion.

'I'm a very understanding husband,' said Landen.

The receptionist said that someone named Mr Krantz checked us both in, but we didn't arrive together. I asked for a photocopy of the ID they had copied from him, and she added that she had seen me only once recently – just before midday.

'Is Mr Krantz okay?' she asked anxiously.

'Did he appear unwell?'

'A little. I offered to call a doctor but he said it wasn't necessary. Do you not remember any of this?'

'I've been having memory lapses. Which room am I in?'

'Jacob Z. Krantz,' I read from the copy of his ID as we took the lift to the top floor. 'Ladder number six-seventy-three, based in Goliathopolis.'

Anyone under a thousand was way up high in the upper echelons of the Goliath corporate structure. Last I heard of my old adversary Jack Schitt, he had entered the Goliath Top One Hundred at eighty-eight.

'Krantz is easily high enough to be involved in the Synthetic Human Project,' I murmured thoughtfully. 'We're here.'

The Formby was the largest and most luxurious suite in the hotel, right on the top floor. The room didn't contain a large jar as Landen had suggested, but a human-sized sarcophagus made of Tupperware to ensure freshness. There was a large quantity of cellophane wrapping, an empty wooden crate that had once contained the sarcophagus, and several items of medical equipment. All the towels were sodden and almost everything was covered with splashes of thick fetid-smelling slime, the bathroom especially.

'This has a very military feel about it, don't you think?' said Landen, rummaging among the bric-a-brac.

'I think even an idiot like me could bring one of these to life,' I replied, referring to a pictorial instruction card.

'If Neanderthals were designed by Goliath as experimental medical test vessels,' he said, 'why not a disposable soldier? Volume trumps longevity if you're thinking of a quick conflict.'

'It doesn't explain what a corporate high-flyer like Krantz is doing in Swindon with a synthetic,' I said. 'What are Goliath up to?'

Landen said he had no idea, and then opined that we shouldn't be found here, with which I agreed. We took the elevator back to the lobby but it was too late. The doors to the lift opened to reveal six Goliath operatives, all dressed in the signature dark navy suits and sunglasses of Goliath's Internal Security service. The one in front was holding a clipboard, and he would have been the boss.

We stopped and stared at one another. They knew *who* I was, that much was certain, but I think they were wondering *which* I was. I felt Landen's hand move in the pocket he kept his pistol in. The man with the clipboard took off his sunglasses and looked at Landen. He'd seen him move, too. They'd all be armed. I thought the world of Landen, but didn't see how he could outshoot six highly trained Goliath security officers. I shifted my weight and might have winced. The Goliath agent looked at my stick, then smiled.

'Miss Next,' he said, 'so *very* glad to make your acquaintance, and congratulations on your new appointment. I am Swindon's Goliath representative: Lupton Cornball. Don't laugh. We'll be formally introduced tomorrow at the library, but today, I'd like to talk to you about some stolen property that might make itself available to you.'

They were *definitely* after the synthetic, but Goliath always spoke euphemistically as it afforded them deniability. I wasn't going to play along.

'What sort of property?'

'I'm not at liberty to say.'

'Then how will I know when it has made itself available to me?'

He stared at me for a moment, lost for words. But it told me what I needed to know – if these guys had intended to do us harm we'd both be unconscious in the back of a van by now with flour sacks over our heads.

'We're done,' I said as they parted to let us through. I had often bested the Goliath Corporation in the past, and because of this I had a protocol all to myself. It was numbered 451, and declared that I was not to be approached for any purpose. I had probably cost them a trillion pounds in lost revenue, and they had no desire to lose any more. I was the thorn in the side that you didn't touch – you simply left it alone, and dealt with the pain.

'I love the way you talk to them,' said Landen with a chuckle. 'What's the next step? Look for Mr Krantz?'

'I guess.'

'I hope that's the end of it,' he murmured, 'one sarcophagus, one synthetic.'

'Don't be too sure,' I said, handing him some paperwork I had fished out of the waste-bin. There was a Gravitube ticket all the way from Tarbuck International, the most convenient place to depart from the Island Corporate City-State of Goliathopolis, situated in the middle of the Irish Sea.

'At least we're no longer in doubt the synthetic was from Goliath,' said Landen.

'Yes,' I replied, 'but look at the luggage manifest.'

'Shit,' he muttered, once he'd examined the ticket stub.

'Right,' I replied, '*five* crates came by Gravitube freight. I don't think we've seen the last of synthetic me.'

17

Tuesday: Tuesday

> 'The mandatory hermit requirements for estates larger than eighty acres was one of the many "Inverse Consequences" directives undertaken by the Commonsense Party. The theory was not sound, but that was the point: bearing in mind that well-meaning ideas often had negative unforeseen consequences, it was argued that daft, pointless or downright bizarre ideas might have unforeseen *positive* outcomes. Hence mandatory hermits. Aside from the weekly gruel allowance and the construction of a damp cave, it cost little.'
>
> *The Commonsense Party Inverse Consequence Directive Explained*

Tuesday was already back home when we got there at a little after 1.30. She and the Wingco were in the far paddock with a quarter-size mock-up of the anti-smiting field generator. The Wingco was readying the high-speed camera, and standing around were assorted observers and representatives of various interested parties. Landen and I exchanged new passwords, and while he made a sandwich I took the golf buggy down to see how things were going. The far paddock was the place usually reserved for any of Tuesday's tests, partly because it was a good distance from the house, but mostly because there was a useful screen of mature leylandii to absorb blast damage.

'I thought I told you to go to school this morning,' I said, making sure we were out of earshot of the small crowd.

'Mum, like *duh*, I did go to school. I went into maths class and proved that there actually *is* a highest number, and then helped Derek in the chemistry lab to make a new type of quick-setting PVC substitute from potato starch and an enzyme readily grown on onions. During the break I figured that Janice Lovegrove was up the duff and probably by Scooter Davis, that Debbie Trubshaw is now putting it about in a big way, and that Sian Johnson's new hairstyle was pinched from page nine of the Swindon edition of *Vogue*.'

'Anything regarding Gavin Watkins?' I asked, considering that Friday was meant to murder him on Friday, and had yet to have a motive.

'He didn't offer me any money to see my boobs again.'

'That's good.'

'No, he said he'd give me five pounds for sex.'

'He did *what*!?!' I yelled, outraged. 'You said no, right? I'm going to report him to the headmaster.'

'Mu-u-um! Of *course* I said no. Please don't do that,' she implored, 'I'm already a swot and a teacher's pet and a brainbox and a smart-alec. I don't want to be a snitch as well. Besides, I punched him in the eye.'

'You did?'

'Yes. Quite hard. I may even have detached his retina. I left school after that and got back in time to do a test of the Defence Shield for this bunch of suits.'

'Well, okay,' I said, looking over her shoulder to where they were all milling about, 'who are they anyway?'

'The guys in the macs are from the Ministry of Theistic Defence, and the two in tweeds are from Tobin & Scott, the anti-smiting tower building contractors. The guy in the lab coat is from the Health and Safety Executive and the three on the left are from Swindon City Council.'

I noted that one of the women in the last group was Bunty Fairweather. I needed to talk to her about alternative plans for Swindon if the shield didn't work, but this, I noted, was probably not the time.

'Leave you to it, then.'

But I didn't leave completely. To watch the test I stopped the golf cart above the long steps, where the landscaped water cascade tumbled into the lake, one of the many garden features within the eighty-eight-acre estate.

'Every journey begins with the first step,' came a deep voice that was tinged with wisdom and august pronouncements.

'Hello, Millon,' I said, greeting our ornamental hermit with a friendly nod, 'how's the hermitage?'

'Draughty,' he said simply, 'but the discomfort of one man is but sand upon the beach to the iniquities undertaken by the few, to many.'

'You won't want central heating put in, then?'

'Comfort is the measles of modern man,' he said in a half-hearted manner, 'and only through cheerless discomfort will the mind be clear and unfettered.'

I smiled. My ex-stalker and biographer Millon de Floss had recently volunteered to be our ornamental hermit, part of the Commonsense Party's Inverse Consequences Directive. If we were going to have someone living on the estate who was to wander around aimlessly spouting quasi-philosophical nonsense, we far preferred it to be someone we knew.

'When's the hermit exam?' I asked.

'Next week,' he said nervously. 'How am I sounding?'

'I'll be honest – not great.'

'Really?'

'I'm afraid so.'

'Damn! I was hoping six months of silent contemplation would suddenly imbue me with sage-like intelligence, but all I seem to be able to manage is a strange fungal growth on my shins caused by the damp and lukewarm aphorisms that would scarcely do favour to the back of a matchbox.'

'I don't really get the whole "intellect through isolation" thing,' I said. 'I'm not sure anyone can claim to understand the human condition until they've talked two people out of a fight, smoothed over a best friend's marital break-up or dealt effectively with a teenager's huffy silence.'

'I'd include an appreciation of Tex Avery cartoons in that list,' added Millon sadly, 'along with Gaudi, David Lean's later movies and a minimum of one evening with Emo Philips. But the hermit elders are traditionalists. The City & Guilds Higher Hermiting Certificate is based mostly around Horace, the Old Testament, Descartes and Marx.'

'Groucho or Karl?'

'Harpo. I think it reflects the "silent" aspect.'

'Ah. Couldn't you just smear yourself with mud and excrement and mumble Latin to yourself in a corner?'

'What, now?'

'No, no – during the exam.'

Millon shook his head.

'*Everyone* tries that old chestnut. Instant disqualification.' He nodded towards the far paddock. 'What's Tuesday up to?'

'Another anti-smiting shield test.'

'Will this one work?'

'Hope springs eternal.'

We watched as the observers were shepherded into the concrete viewing bunker while Tuesday made some trifling adjustments to the Defence Shield. It was identical to the full-size versions dotted around the country – a large copper-domed head like a mushroom atop a lattice tower. Above the test rig was the Smiting Simulator, a single electrode twenty feet above the copper dome, suspended from three towers. This was charged to several trillion volts and would discharge on cue in an attempt to simulate the sort of high-power ground burst that was the Almighty's favoured attempt at cleansing.

As we watched, Tuesday walked to the concrete bunker herself, and a few moments later the domed copper hat of the shield began to slowly rotate. It moved faster and faster until small crackles of electricity started to fire off around the edges, and a bluish field began to form in a soft undulating dome that reached beyond the tower and to the ground, like a large umbrella.

'Fingers in ears,' I said, and a second or two later a soft blue flash of lightning descended from the simulator, followed a millisecond later by a loud crack. For a moment I thought the shield had held, but then the spinning copper disintegrated into thousands of fragments, some of which were thrown hundreds of feet in the air. Millon and I ducked behind the golf buggy as the expensive shrapnel fell to the ground around us.

'She'll be disappointed,' I said.

'Always expect a kick in the teeth,' said Millon, 'so that when you get a slap in the chops it seems like a triumph.'

'Listen,' I said, 'what do you know about a Goliath employee named Jacob Krantz?'

Before his days as a hermit, Millon de Floss had been editor of *Conspiracy Theorist* magazine, a position that necessitated a somewhat lower profile these days, as some of his wackier 'exclusives' had turned out to be far truer than expected – much to the displeasure of Goliath, who were implicated in almost every conspiracy you cared to invent.

'Krantz?' said Millon. 'Doesn't ring a bell. Does he have a Ladder number?'

'Six-seventy-three.'

'Wow.'

'Wow indeed. He might be working in the Synthetic Human Division.'

'According to Goliath, there is no Synthetic Human Division. Let me make a few calls.'

He disappeared back into his hermitage and I watched as the observers trailed out of the bunker to stare sadly at the remains of the Defence Shield. They had all been driven away by the time I got down there, and I found Tuesday in the bunker, trying to make sense of the vast amount of telemetry generated by the test.

'I'm sorry, Sweetpea,' I said, 'it must be a huge disappointment.'

She turned to glower at me.

'If you hadn't sent me to school this morning to insist I was a *real* teenager, then I might have made this bloody thing work.'

'Really?'

'No, not really. This is me being angry and you being gullible and sensitive when reacting negatively to my wild accusations.'

Tuesday could be very direct when angry – but also quite honest.

'I can think of three things at once, so school isn't usually a problem,' she said as she calmed. 'I've just got to fine-tune the algorithm to better predict the Madeupion Field. Do it right and we have over twenty gigawatts of free energy and a vexed deity. Get it wrong and we've got seven tons of the most expensive scrap on record.'

'Will you be able to get it finished by Friday?' I asked. 'I'm not keen to see Swindon's downtown disappear in a flash of Blue Wrath.'

'I'll figure it out, Mum,' she said with a sigh. 'You should have seen their faces. That mock-up cost them sixty million to build, and it's the tenth I've destroyed.'

'So you sure you're okay?' I asked as a distinctive thup-thup-thup sound heralded the arrival of a Tiltrotor aircraft.

'I'll be fine,' said Tuesday, as the small craft appeared above the treeline and folded its rotor panels to landing configuration.

'That'll be my ride.'

'Where are you going?'

'The Sisterhood are opening their library for scrutiny.'

'Oooh,' said Tuesday, 'if you see a copy of Archimedes' fifth issue of *Practical Mechanical Theorems*, the one where he outlines how to build a tumble dryer, I'd love a copy.'

18

Tuesday: The Sisterhood

> 'The first Tiltrotor was designed in the early twenties as a novel method of using ducted fans as a propulsion and lifting mechanism. It took thirty years for a powerful enough engine to be introduced, and even then the craft was not a serious proposition until the introduction of a light and powerful nuclear reactor. Of their benefits, vertical take-off and ease of use are their two best, and reactor leaks and the ability to drop out of the sky unannounced their two worst.'
>
> *Jane's Aviation Digest*

The small craft had landed on the front lawn, and Landen was chatting to Finisterre about how the technology had progressed since Tiltrotors were used in the Crimea as spotter aircraft, a role in which they had been less than successful. The joke at the time had been 'How do you get to own a Tiltrotor?' and the answer was: 'Buy an acre of land in the Crimea, and wait.'

'We'd better be going if we're to keep our appointment,' said Finisterre as I arrived. 'The Sisterhood can't abide unpunctuality. Will you bc coming?'

He was talking to Landen, but I already knew he wouldn't ever get in a Tiltrotor again. Although his leg injury had initially been due to a landmine, it was the evac on a medical Tiltrotor that necessitated the partial amputation – the craft crashed owing to a gearbox failure sixteen miles short of the military hospital in Sevastopol, and those jeep-ridden sixteen miles, said Landen, were the most excruciating he had ever known. Still, that had been almost thirty years ago, and Tiltrotor technology had come on in leaps and bounds since then – especially after Mycroft became involved, which explained why they were no longer used militarily. I kissed Landen, we exchanged passwords again and I climbed aboard the small craft as Finisterre spooled up the reactor, and a few minutes later we had left Aldbourne behind us, passed overhead Marlborough and were skimming low across the downs.

'How's your day going?' asked Finisterre.

'Interesting so far,' I replied, and he smiled knowingly.

'Wouldn't want you to get bored.'

'No indeed,' I replied.

We swept past the single induction rail of the Southern Bullet Route and dropped down into the Vale of Pewsey. We flew on in silence for a few minutes until Finisterre called Air Traffic Control for transit permission into the Salisbury Danger Area, and orbited twice around Urchfont while we waited for clearance. I had trained on Salisbury Plain myself in tracked vehicles before being dispatched to the Crimea aged only eighteen. We had been briefed never to stray near the Sisterhood's hundred-acre enclave, and it was hard to claim you didn't know if you had – the convent's tower soared two hundred feet above the plains, and the main Venerating Chamber was the size of an airship hangar.

'We're in,' said Finisterre, and we headed off towards the convent, which even now dominated the landscape, and we were still five miles away. We circled the tower once before coming in for a neat landing near the entrance, and while Finisterre conducted the power-down checks, I stepped clumsily out and looked around.

I had never been here before; few had. The Salisbury Plain order of the Blessed Ladies of the Lobster was the hub from where all other orders received instructions, and to where all funds were sent. The Lobsterhood had been the nation's most populous religious order with over a hundred convents across the land, and although the Global Standard Deity's unifying action had subsumed many of those within the order, a few had held out, Salisbury among them. But all that defiance had come to nought the day that He had revealed Himself and confirmed that, yes, the game was up, there was only One, and all the silly Lobster stuff was indeed transparent nonsense, and all should cower in the presence of Him. The fact that it was a He after all caused a lot of problems with the feminists. But it might have been worse – He could have turned out to have been French, too.

'My name is Sister Megan,' said the greeter-nun who had stepped out to receive us, 'and you are fourteen seconds late. We cannot abide unpunctuality here in the Lobsterhood.'

'We had to orbit for clearance into the zone,' I explained. 'My name is Thursday Next.'

Sister Megan gave a sharp cry and covered her mouth with her hand. I had to get used to this. Joffy's efforts with the GSD had not always been welcomed, and indeed, before the Lord's Revealment, over a billion people wanted him shredded as a heretic.

'Causing trouble already?' asked Finisterre as the greeter-nun ran back inside the lobster-shaped double doors.

'I think it's the connection with my brother. There were many religious orders that found it difficult to accept that they had been idolising clearly demonstrable falsehoods for hundreds of years.'

'Like the notion of the all-redeeming, ever-knowing and oft-nipping "Big Lobster"?'

'One of the more sensible ones,' I replied. 'You'd better do the talking from now on, and refer to me by my married name.'

But it didn't come to that. No sooner had we taken two steps towards the convent than another nun had come running out of the doors firing a small pistol and screaming at the top of her voice that I was a 'procreating girl-dog', but not using those *precise* words. I was used to being called that, of course, but rarely by a nun. She had loosed off two shots by the time she had been adroitly rugger-tackled to the ground by two other nuns, and Finisterre and I, caught out by the sudden violence, had not had time to move a muscle and had simply stood there as one of the shots passed between us at head level with a *zip* and the second passed cleanly through my shoulder bag, penetrating not just my purse and notebook, but also a picture of Landen.

Finisterre and I stared at one another as an unseemly fight developed in front of us, our assailant being finally subdued by two additional nuns, both of whom I suspected might actually be men. The gun was wrested from her hands and she was sat upon while she struggled, howled and screamed the sort of obscenities that would embarrass a docker.

'I'm sorry about that,' said one of the other nuns, who had a cut lip and a wimple now dented and askew, 'but we all joined the order for different reasons and, well, some of us have a lot of repressed anger.'

'Against me?' I asked.

'I'm afraid so. Daisy always swore to kill you the next time you met – that was why she has closeted herself here. To protect herself and you from her rage.'

'Should we take this up with the mother superior?'

'Daisy *is* the mother superior. We'll have to wait until she calms down. By the way, we all think Joffy is remarkable even if he is a man.'

'No one's perfect.'

'Right. And we thank him for pointing out the error of our veneration. We all felt a bit silly to begin with, but when our mistake was plainly spelled out, we were more than happy to change four centuries of loyal tradition.'

'Perhaps I should leave?' I said. 'And let Finisterre speak to Mother Daisy on his own?'

'No, no, no,' replied the nun, 'she'll be fine. She has to calm down and compose herself. Forgiveness, companionship, self-control and not reading in the toilet are but only four of the ninety-seven simple rules we live our life by.'

Mother Daisy was indeed calming down, and after another five minutes the others thought it safe to stop sitting on her and she got to her feet, covered in grass clippings, and a bit bruised. She smoothed her habit, took a deep breath, and approached us both.

'Welcome to the Sisterhood of the Lobsterhood, Salisbury Plain chapter,' she said in a calm and measured manner. 'My name is Mother Daisy. I do apologise for the attempted murder. It is not how we usually welcome distinguished guests. Can you find it in your heart to forgive me?'

'Of course,' I said, suddenly realising who she was and why she tried to kill me, 'think no more of it. May I present Head of Antiquities James Finisterre of the Swindon All You Can Eat at Fatso's Drink Not Included Library?'

She shook his hand.

'Welcome, Mr Finisterre. Your expertise and reputation precede you. Just one question: why did you have to . . . *bring that lying man-stealer with you?!?*'

She had screamed the last line and in an instant had her hands around my throat. We fell over backwards and I felt myself losing consciousness, but in an instant I was gasping for air as the two nuns who looked suspiciously male dragged her from me.

'*Shit,*' I said, sitting up.

'Are you okay?' asked Finisterre.

'Annoyed,' I said, giving him my hand so he could heave me to my feet.

'Yes, I should imagine being attacked by a nun might be annoying.'

'It's not that,' I said, coughing and rubbing my throat, 'it's just that even six months ago I would have been fast and aggressive enough to have *her* on her back before she'd even grabbed me. And earlier?'

'Yes?'

I tapped the centre of my forehead.

'I'd have planted one right here before she got to fire the second shot.'

'I'm very glad you didn't,' said Finisterre with a shudder, 'it might have put the dampeners on getting access to their library.'

'She could have killed us both.'

'Life is short, art is long, Thursday. You and I are passing through history, the contents of this library *are* history.'

He thought for a moment.

'You came to a convent tooled up?'

'I'm *always* tooled up.'

'I'm *so* sorry about that,' said Mother Daisy, who seemed once again to have recovered her composure, 'my only companion from the outside world during nineteen years of isolation has been my personal hatred of Thursday Next. It's kind of like the old me suddenly taking over, and I promised myself that this was how I would act if I ever saw you.'

'I have the same thing but with Tom Stoppard,' I said.

'You'd kill Tom Stoppard?'

'Not at all. I promised myself many years ago that I would throw myself at his feet and scream "I'm not worthy" if I ever met him, so now if we're ever at the same party or something I have to be at pains to avoid him. It would be undignified, you see – for him and me.'

'I can see that,' said Mother Daisy, 'and since I demonstrably can't control myself I have allocated Sister Henrietta as your bodyguard.'

One of the more masculine nuns bobbed politely and took up station beside me.

'Thank you,' I said.

'Don't mention it,' replied Sister Henrietta in a deep voice.

'I'm impressed that the Sisterhood has embraced inclusivity as regards its adherents,' I said as we walked towards the main doors.

'What do you mean?' asked Mother Daisy.

'That you now count men among the Sisterhood.'

She stopped and looked around suspiciously.

'You think there might be men present in our sanctuary?'

'Oh,' I said, suddenly realising that it might be a secret, 'just idle talk from Swindon, I suspect.'

'Hmm. Worth looking into. Sister Henrietta, would you conduct a gender check tomorrow? Nothing intrusive. Just find out if there is anyone who doesn't know the name of Jennifer Gray's character in *Dirty Dancing*.'

'Yes, ma'am,' said Sister Henrietta, staring daggers in my direction as soon as Mother Daisy looked away.

'And what news of Swindon?' asked Mother Daisy. 'We have no radio, no TV, and only *The Toad on Sunday* once a month.'

'There's a new roundabout in the Old Town, Acme Carpets are having another sale, SpecOps is to be reformed – oh, and part of the city is to be wiped from the earth by a cleansing fire on Friday.'

'An Acme Carpets sale?'

'Forty per cent off everything, I heard – with free fitting but you have to pay for the underlay.'

'Worth a look. And a smiting, you say? What level?'

We were now at the reception desk in the lobby. She indicated the visitors' book for me to sign. I noted that the last visitor had been admitted in 1974.

'A Level III,' I said, 'to punish Joffy for his impertinence, we think. That is,' I added, 'unless my daughter Tuesday can perfect her anti-smiting device.'

Mother Daisy reached behind the counter and picked up a length of lead pipe that happened to be there. She made a swipe in my direction.

'*A daughter that should have been mine, you scarlet Jezebel!!*'

I was quicker this time and took a step back. Sister Henrietta was on the ball, too, and had Daisy around the waist and grappled to the floor in less than a second.

'The Sisterhood like to scrap, don't they?' said Finisterre as the pair of them wrestled on the ground with Mother Daisy howling and scratching and biting while Sister Henrietta attempted to calm her down. She did calm, eventually, and once more apologised for her conduct and asked for my forgiveness.

This I gave, although less readily, as one can take just so much nun violence. We moved into the main part of the convent, a large room that served as living space and refectory. To either side of the chamber were smaller cells for the sisters to live in. All about us was the lobster motif that the order lived beneath, a constant reminder of the mildly deluded notion that the world would one day be unified under a single lobster of astonishing intellect, and all ills, sorrow, hunger and thermidor would be banished for ever. Although this might seem peculiar – even when compared to other, equally wild religions – my father had often travelled into the distant future and learned that there *was* indeed a time when the earth was dominated by the arthropods. Two hundred million years away, he said. But any notion that the Sisterhood might be planning for this was doubtful – there would be only six species of mammal on the earth at that time, and none of them with an intellect higher than that of a confused hedgehog.

'How is he?' asked Daisy through half-gritted teeth.

'He's . . . very well,' I said warily, making sure there was a reasonable distance between us. Sister Henrietta had guessed this was over a man, and had placed herself in a position where it would be most easy to intervene.

'A best-selling writer by now, I expect?'

'Not *quite*,' I replied slowly, as Landen's career since winning the coveted Armitage Shanks Literary Prize had been in a somewhat downward trajectory.

'Why?' she asked.

'I guess he was looking after me,' I replied as honestly as I could, 'and the kids.'

'I would never have allowed that if he were *my* husband,' she scolded. 'You should be ashamed of yourself. Has he still got one leg?'

I stared at her.

'It's not likely to have grown back.'

'He . . . he might have lost the other one.'

'He's not that careless.'

'You had children?'

'Two.'

'What sort?'

'One of each.'

'A boy and a girl?'

'No, an ant and a whale.'

She glared at me and a vein in her neck pulsed.

'There's no cause to be snippy.'

'I'll stop being snippy if you stop making inane observations.'

'You were the one who stole my husband at the altar.'

I stared at her for a moment. Before she was Mother Daisy she had been Daisy Mutlar, and had almost ensnared Landen into marriage.

'He didn't love you, he loved me, and technically speaking, he was *never* your husband.'

'Only because of a short, meddling, plain-as-wallpaper delusional ex-girlfriend with relationship issues and a borderline personality disorder.'

'I'm *not* short.'

I could see Sister Henrietta tense, expecting another attack. There wasn't, however, and we moved on through a wide stone arch to the large building that I had seen attached to the tower. It was, as previously stated, enormous – perhaps more than seven hundred feet long and one hundred and twenty feet to the roof. But what I hadn't expected was that the interior would be pretty much hollow, and made of a delicate latticework of wood and steel that seemed to have an air of temporariness about it. Around the periphery of the chamber were workshops, rooms, scaffolding and the evidence of recently abandoned industry. Tools lay about, and large blocks of stone were lying on trolleys half finished. The focus of the centuries-old toil lay in the centre of the room.

'Is that what I think it is?' asked Finisterre.

The sculpture was about the size and shape of a Carrier-class airship, but more flattened, and clearly designed for longevity, not flight. At one end the sculpture had only just been begun with the inner foundations constructed of blocks of limestone, while up near the finished end the limestone had been clad with delicately carved Portland stone, each piece set into position so finely it was difficult to see where each individual block began. The surface was mottled, lumpy, and it was hard not to see what it was – the claw of an enormous rock-hewn lobster.

'Tremble before the might and majesty of the Great Lobster,' breathed Mother Daisy. 'We had planned to build the entire lobster. It would have been over a mile in length and made the pyramids at Cairo look like the work of uninspired amateurs.'

'How long did this take?' asked Finisterre.

'Five centuries. As soon as we were done with the claw we were going to move the building shed to begin on the antenna and feeding mandibles. We estimated the whole thing might have been finished in as little as five thousand years.'

'It seems a shame,' I said, 'after five centuries of toil.'

'Yes,' replied Daisy stoically, 'we'll grind it up and sell it as motorway hardcore. Shame but, well, there you go. This way.'

We arrived at a large steel-belted door. There was a bunch of keys on the rope tied around Daisy's waist, and she paused, waited until Sister Henrietta wasn't watching, then threw a punch in my direction.

I was more wary of her now and expertly sidestepped the blow, although it was so close I felt the air move across my face. She shrugged, cursed me below her breath, then placed a key in the lock. It turned easily and she pushed the door open to reveal a long staircase that led upwards into the gloom. Blast. Stairs.

I think there might have been at least a hundred of them, and they wound slowly upwards for what seemed like an age, while my leg and back throbbed and shouted at me. I told them to move on ahead and was helped eventually by Henrietta, who wasn't Henrietta at all, but an ex-physicist from Manchester named Henry who was trying to find meaning in an otherwise empty existence by pretending to be a nun.

We reached the top of the stone steps in due course, and entered the lowest tier of the libraries. There were books here in abundance, and Finisterre was already looking through the dusty tomes. I pulled one out at random and found an obscure treatise on accountancy dating from the tenth century. Of interest to those obsessed with the history of finance, but no one much else.

'There is an index here,' said Daisy, pointing to a younger book. 'The older stuff is on the top floor.'

'Aeschylus' *The Spirit of Pharos*,' murmured Finisterre, peering through the gazetteer, 'which it is clained is the first ghost story. Have you read it?'

'Sister Georgia translated it for us,' said Daisy, 'it's not *totally* rubbish. The ghosts turn out to be the lighthouse keepers in disguise to keep people from discovering their illegal trade in stolen amphorae.'

'So *that's* where the Scooby-Doo ending originated,' I murmured. 'Scholars have been hunting for the primary source of that for years.'

'It's one of only two known copies anywhere in the world,' said Finisterre, 'although the other copy is fragmentary. But you're right about primary sources: when we discovered the second volume of Aristotle's *Poetics* it ended a lot of academic contention on who devised the format for *Columbo*.'

'There's little new in literature,' I added. 'For many years William Shatner's depiction of Kirk in *Star Trek* was considered unique, until it was discovered that an identical character pops up in Ovid's *Metamorphoses 2: Fat Foreigners Are Funny* all the time.'

'Horace wrote truly *filthy* limericks,' added Mother Daisy. 'We recite them on special occasions. There was a very good one about a young man from Australia who painted his arse like a dahlia. Do you want to hear it?'

'No thanks.'

'Well,' said Finisterre, who was in no doubt as to the unique value of the library, 'I'd like to catalogue all this *in situ*, then take the books to my team of conservators to be copied and—'

He had stopped because there was a sharp report far below in the convent.

'What was that?'

'A shot,' I said, 'but then we *are* in the middle of a firing range.'

'Range fire is softened by distance,' replied Daisy expertly, 'closer ones are a *crack* – and that was a *crack*. Sister Henrietta, close the Scriptorium door and defend the library to the death.'

'We use a similar oath in the Wessex Library Services,' murmured Finisterre. 'Thursday, do you still carry two pistols?'

'One on my right ankle – but you'll have to get it. I can't bend that far – Landen has to put on my socks these days.'

'Isn't he just the perfect husband?' murmured Daisy sarcastically. She was herself searching through the folds of her habit and produced a very ancient-looking Colt.

'How do I fire this thing?' she asked, showing it to me.

'Pull back the hammer, push this lever down,' I said, 'and to fire, squeeze the grip safety and trigger. The bullets come out here.'

'Cow.'

'Moo.'

I drew my own automatic, released the safety and we all stood facing the stairway entrance.

'Is there another way in?' I asked.

'The roof,' said Daisy, 'next floor up. But don't worry – it's bolted from the inside and can't be reached from the ground.'

As she spoke there was a muffled detonation from somewhere far below us. We all looked at one another.

'Word has got about of the treasures within our walls,' said Mother Daisy. 'I fear for my library.'

I thought quickly. If *I* was planning a raid on the library, I would use a diversion and attack from where it was least expected.

'You stay here and open fire at anything that comes up the stairs that isn't in black and white. I'm going to keep an eye on the entrance to the roof.'

I didn't wait for a reply, as sporadic gunfire was now ringing out downstairs along with shouts and cries as the nuns returned fire. I limped up the steps to the next floor, which was a similar room to the one below – made of stone, lined with books and smelling of damp and birds' nests. Above me in the ceiling was a large wooden hatch that was bolted from the inside. I took up station behind a stone pillar and waited. The windows gave little light, and were too narrow to climb through. If an attack was forthcoming, then this was where it would come from.

I raised my pistol in readiness as with eerie predictability the hatch blew inwards with an almighty concussion. I was vaguely conscious of firing off one shot, probably by accident, and the next moment I was lying on my back among shards of wood, earwigs and dust. Ears ringing, I struggled to sit up. I even half-heartedly raised my pistol, only to have it removed from my hand by a smiling face that I recognised. It was Jack Schitt.

We'd crossed swords many times in the past, and I kind of thought we had reached something of a truce when his wife died and I returned her locket to him. In fact, the last I heard he was retired. But the odd thing about this was that Goliath weren't really into violent assaults on libraries – they always favoured stealing stuff by persuasive arguments about 'the greater good', and when that failed, veiled threats, legal action and covertly sneaky behaviour. This wasn't their style, and to be honest, Jack was getting a bit long in the tooth for fieldwork – as was I.

'Shit and bollocks,' I said, more through frustration than anger.

'Language, Thursday.'

Jack dropped the magazine from my pistol, pulled back the slide to eject the unfired round and tossed the empty weapon to the other side of the room. He paused to bolt the door to the lower levels of the scriptorium, and then looked thoughtfully about the room. He didn't look as though he was in much of a hurry.

'We've not even begun to catalogue it yet,' I said, 'I hope you've got some time on your hands.'

He ignored me and moved past the shelves, his fingertips brushing the spines of the books. He wasn't choosing a book by reading the spines; indeed, there was nothing written on many of the spines. It appeared that he was *sensing* the book he was searching for, and after a moment, he stopped, paused, and drew out a volume.

'Goliath stealing antiquarian books?' I said. 'Bit of a come-down, isn't it?'

He had opened the book and answered without looking at me.

'What are you doing here, Next?'

'Playing silly buggers,' I told him, slowly crawling into a position from where I might be able to get to my feet.

'I meant in particular,' he said with a smile, 'not in general.'

There was more gunfire from the floor below. It looked as though the diversionary attack was utterly successful – in that it was diversionary. I got to my feet and staggered across the room to where he had thrown my pistol. He saw what I was doing but didn't seem that put out by it. I picked up the weapon, then looked around to see where he had thrown the clip.

'Over there,' he said, still not looking up from where he was leafing through the book. I moved to the other side of the room to where the clip lay, lying in some dust by the door. I tried to bend over, but when that failed, I grasped the door handle and used that to lower myself.

'You're pretty much trashed, aren't you?' said Jack, tearing two pages out of the book and letting the rest of the volume fall to the ground.

'It's early days,' I said, grunting with the pain and effort. 'Physiotherapy will see me as right as rain in the fullness of time.'

'There aren't enough years left in the universe,' he said, staring at the pages he had torn out, 'the weak will not survive.'

'Personal opinion?' I asked, my fingers just touching the magazine.

'Corporate policy. Crabbe? Would you?'

A foot descended on my hand – a second assailant, one I had not seen. I would have cried out in pain if I hadn't already been in pain.

'Okay, okay,' I said, handing him the pistol, 'let me keep my fingers.'

'It's good news for you that you're Protocol 451,' Crabbe breathed close to my ear. 'It would give me immeasurable pleasure to put an end to the once magnificent Thursday Next.'

'Why don't you tell me what you are looking for? I might be able—'

I had stopped because when I turned back to look at Jack, he had gone.

'Time to go,' said Crabbe. 'I hope we don't meet again – next time I won't be so charitable.'

He took my arm, twisted it until I crumpled in a heap, then walked across to where Jack had been standing. The book was lying on the ground, splayed downwards, pages crumpled against the stone floor.

He reached into his pocket and pulled out a plastic sack, much like an evidence bag. He cracked it open, dropped the two pages Jack had been reading inside, ziplocked it, then broke a large phial that was inside the bag. There was a hissing noise and he shook the bag twice, then dropped it to the ground where it bubbled quietly to itself.

'Really time to go,' he said, and moved to the centre of the room, where the shattered trapdoor was positioned. He fired a flare gun through the aperture and then jumped up, grabbed the parapet, and was out in an instant. I heard his footfalls on the roof as he took several long paces, then a pause, then the high-pitched whine of a fast rope descender. I frowned. Now I'd heard Crabbe's descender I realised that I hadn't heard Jack's.

As the light from the parachute flare flickered red through the narrow window slits, the diversionary gunfire abruptly stopped, and within a few minutes it was calm once more, the only noises those from nuns who had been wounded in the action.

'Shit,' I said, to no one in particular.

19

Tuesday: Smalls

> 'St Zvlkx is the patron saint of Swindon, a choice that owes more to local saint availability than any notable good deeds. The thirteenth-century saint is known today mainly for his likeness on "Zvlkx Brand" bathroom sealant and his long list of Revealments, all of which came true – including his own second coming in 1988. Aside from being the inspiration behind *Catweazle* and murmuring that a "new cathedral might be nice", St Zvlkx did little good work on his return, and was run over by a number twenty-three bus two days later.'
>
> Extract from *Swindon Great Lives* (expanded edition)

Finisterre was unharmed, as was Daisy. The worst off was Sister Henrietta, who had fallen downstairs, and was now nursing a burst kneecap and the embarrassment of being outed as a man. Oddly – although a low profile would doubtless have been beneficial to the gang – no one had been seriously hurt. The pinpoint accuracy the diversionary force had used ensured zero casualties, but they *had* been live rounds – just intended to miss by a narrow margin. The only hits were the result of ricochets. Few were serious, and none life threatening. Even Goliath would have realised that killing nuns is bad PR.

I was investigating the plastic bag and what remained of the torn-out pages when Mother Daisy and Finisterre joined me. The vellum had been reduced to a sticky gloop that had eventually dissolved its way through the plastic bag and on to the stone floor. I pushed a pencil into the smouldering muck and the paint blistered.

'It's Malevolex,' said Finisterre, sniffing the air, 'an organic acid used in the pulping industry to prepare remaindered books for being turned into MDF. When they cracked the phial in the bag the two parts mixed and the book was history.'

I had been staring at the plastic bag for a while. It had been a slick operation.

'They came up here knowing they would destroy these pages,' I said, climbing to my feet. 'They didn't copy them, or even have enough time to read them all.'

'They'd have been *seriously* bored if they did,' said Daisy, handing me the rest of the book. It was entitled: *Trawling around Tewkefbury after darke while piffed and the pleafuref to be found therein.*

'A thirteenth-century racy novel with which early members of the Sisterhood used to entertain themselves,' explained Daisy.

'It's all a bit more proper these days, I take it?' observed James delicately.

'Goodness gracious no!' replied Daisy. 'We're more into Jilly Cooper and Daphne Farquitt. This particular racy codex is a bit, well, unimaginative – unless you like that sort of thing.'

'Who wrote it?' I asked.

'Stephen Shorts of Swine-dome,' said Finisterre. 'You'd know him better as St Zvlkx.'

'Ah!' I said, having come across Swindon's very own saint before. Aside from his 'Revealments', which turned out to be a complex sporting fraud, St Zvlkx wrote only banal books that revolved around drunkenness and womanising. The reasons for his sainthood are somewhat obscure, but knowing St Zvlkx, probably had some basis in blackmail.

Daisy was flicking through the book, trying to find which pages had gone.

'He pulled only one leaf out,' she said, studying the book carefully, 'which lay across the spine, so from two parts of the book. The first part was a report on which tavern in Tewkesbury offered the best opportunity to get totally plastered for a farthing, and the second section – if memory serves – was a lengthy digression on how best to handle the fallout from getting a town elder's wife pregnant, an area in which Zvlkx was something of an expert.'

We stood in silence for a moment. Finisterre aired the thoughts we all shared.

'Why would someone attempt to break into a library guarded by dangerously violent nuns – sorry, no offence meant—'

'None taken.'

'. . . only to read the licentious ramblings of a despicable rogue from the thirteenth century?'

'Goliath are smart,' I said, 'so there would have been a good reason. Perhaps that too was a diversionary measure – do something utterly random and incomprehensible, knowing full well we'd spend hours trying to figure it out. No, we take this as an attempted theft and vandalism. Was this the most valuable book?'

'It was possibly the *least* valuable,' said Daisy. 'Almost every book in this room is worth more. Have a look at this.'

She drew out a volume almost at random and passed it to Finisterre, who stared at it, lower lip trembling.

'*Pliny the Really Very Young's account of being unable to see the eruption of Vesuvius owing to being put to bed early for some bullshit excuse.*'

'We have only fragments of this stuff,' I murmured as Finisterre reverentially placed it back on the shelf. 'Worth ten million?'

'More. *Much* more.'

We looked around at the book-lined chamber.

'We're surrounded by about half a billion pounds' worth of books,' said Daisy. 'Do you think we should consider insurance, and if so, what would be a reasonable excess?'

My ears had stopped ringing by the time Finisterre had called in Colonel Wexler, who arrived with ten of her crack Special Library

Service troops dressed in their 'Antiquarian Book' camouflage of musty browns and water-stained dark reds. Colonel Wexler nodded respectfully as she passed me, and we were about to leave when Detective Phoebe Smalls turned up.

'Smalls, SpecOps 27,' she said to us when she arrived, presumably for Mother Daisy's benefit as we knew who she was. She was in a police Tiltrotor along with half a dozen armed cops.

'Hello, Phoebe,' I said brightly, 'I knew we'd meet again soon. What are you doing here?'

'I'm taking charge,' she announced. 'Why didn't you call this in straight away? I had to find out about the break-in through the grapevine.'

'Is there a grapevine?' asked Finisterre.

'I've *heard* there's one,' I returned with a half-smile.

'Very funny,' said Smalls. 'I want you to turn over the command of your SLS troops to me, and have a full report on my desk by tomorrow morning – after you've given me a debrief on what you know right now.'

'Where are your own people?' I asked, since she had arrived without any SO-27 operatives.

She glared at me.

'We're having recruitment . . . *issues*,' she said quietly. 'I went through the list of reassignment requests. The formation of SO-27 has been on the cards for weeks. Lots of time for officers to ask to join me.'

'There weren't any, were there?'

'Not one,' said Phoebe, 'but we'll resolve that soon enough. Now, this is SO-27 jurisdiction. The debrief, Next.'

'It's our jurisdiction,' I said simply.

'How do you figure that?' she demanded, her mood angrier by the second. 'Scriptorium, theft, thirteenth-century codices – what could be more Literary Detectives about it?'

'We've given the Lobsterhood book collection Wessex Library status,' I said. 'This library and all within comes under our control. The Special Library Service troops are legally empowered to shoot to kill. I can ask SO-27 for assistance, but that's as far as it goes.'

Phoebe Smalls looked at me, then at Mother Daisy, who nodded agreement. Smalls could have carried on with a dopey rant, but she was smart enough to know yelling would be pointless and degrading, and there was a better than good chance I knew what I was doing.

'Very well,' she said at last. 'SO-27 offers every assistance to the library in this matter. But I'd like to be kept in the loop,' she added in a softer tone, 'simply as a professional courtesy.'

'Okay,' I replied, 'here it is: thieves of unknown origin with an unknown motive destroyed a single leaf from a book with marginal value, literary merits or rarity.'

'That's it?'

'That's it. But,' I added, 'there might be a Goliath angle to this, and if someone is monkeying around with thirteenth-century codices for no reason, all antiquarian suppliers, dealers and collectors need to be informed so they can increase security. You can do that better than I.'

'It might not be the first time this has happened,' said Phoebe thoughtfully. 'I'll run through reports of any unexplained vandalism in the lucrative and highly buoyant Seriously Ancient Codex market.'

It wasn't a good idea, it was a *great* idea. So great that I should have been the one making it.

'Goes without saying,' I said, and she flashed me a quizzical look.

'I'm glad to see we can work together,' she said. 'I'll have my staff make it happen. When I get staff. *Shit*. I'll be doing it.'

She paused.

'What sort of Goliath angle?'

'I don't know,' I replied, 'they have lots of angles. It shouldn't be too hard to find two dozen – we can narrow it down from there.'

'Right. May I ask a favour in return?'

'Sure.'

'Would you have a word with Bowden Cable? I need a good deputy and he'd be pretty much perfect.'

'He's very happy working at Acme Carpets,' I said, 'but I'll ask him.'

She nodded, placed her armed police under the command of Colonel Wexler, then departed. If she couldn't get any staff to work for her – SpecOps was always voluntary – then the department could be closed as quickly as it had been reopened. It wouldn't affect Braxton's wasteful budget policy as there were plenty of other SpecOps departments in which to squander money.

Finisterre vented some steam from the condensers before winding the craft up to lift-off power.

'All right back there?'

Sister Megan was with Sister Henrietta, whose kneecap had been placed back in position and then covered with bandages. The blood was already seeping through. We asked for an expedited transit of the Salisbury range and were at the Lola Vavoom Discount Sofa Warehouse See Press For Details Memorial Hospital less than twenty minutes later.

'Are you sure you don't want to be checked over?' asked Finisterre after we had offloaded the recently renamed Brother Henry.

'Bruised and sore but I'll be fine,' I told him. 'Despite being pretty much useless, I actually enjoyed myself.'

'Don't get too used to it. You're Chief Librarian now: less running around waving a pistol and more in charge of policy and procurement, appointments and budget responsibility.'

'I am, aren't I?'

If I had clout, it was time to use it. I called the office to tell Duffy that I needed to see Swindon's Goliath representative in my office first thing in the morning 'as a matter of the utmost urgency'.

Duffy said he would see to it, asked me what time I wanted to be picked up in my car in the morning, and whether I had any 'dietary considerations' regarding lunch. I was going to tell him I didn't need a car, but since I couldn't drive myself, and it wasn't fair to use Landen as a taxi service, I told him 9 a.m. and that I ate most things except okra and marzipan.

'James?' I said as soon as I had rung off.

'Yes?' he replied, scooting low across Liddington Castle as he made the short hop to Aldbourne.

'Why did we find only Crabbe's descender?'

We had been to look at Jack and Crabbe's escape route before Smalls had arrived. The rope was still there, and the descender used by Crabbe – but no sign of Jack's.

'Logic would dictate that he escaped using another method. Not sure how, though – a base jump would be the only other way out, but there was no evidence of a parachute either. Unless you have any bright ideas?'

I didn't, which raised the question: if Jack didn't parachute out and didn't go down the rope, how *did* he escape?

20

Tuesday: Home

> 'From when they first opened, motorway services were always a welcome mix of good food, restful surroundings, clean and spacious hotels and reasonably priced shopping. Some people ventured solely on to the motorway to visit these oases of calm on the bellowing asphalt, and poor food and less-than-exemplary service were simply not tolerated. When Aust Services lost a prestigious Dunlop Star from their rating, the manager, overcome by shame, set himself on fire and threw himself into the River Severn.'
>
> J. Fforde – *Motorway Services and Sarcasm, Unsubtly Used*

'Holy cow!' said Landen when he saw me. 'What happened to you?'

'Remember how Daisy Mutlar said she would devote her life to silent introspection within an obscure religion if she couldn't marry you?'

'We all make threats like that. No one takes them seriously.'

'Daisy was *totally* serious. She's now Mother Daisy over at the Salisbury Lobsterhood.'

'She always did want to be a mother. She did all this to you?'

'Only that one and . . . that one,' I replied, showing him the bruises that had been Daisy-inflicted, 'the rest was Jack Schitt and one of his cronies.'

'I've a feeling you weren't reminiscing about the old days over a glass of wine.'

'Very astute of you.'

We went through to the kitchen, where we exchanged passwords before I sat at the large kitchen table and related all that had happened. While I talked he fetched some TCP and a packet of cotton wool. I had numerous scratches, cuts and abrasions from when the trapdoor was blown open, and I winced as he tended to them. When I'd finished speaking, he stared at me for a while, concerned rather than shocked.

'Trouble really does follow you around, doesn't it? Even when you're just a librarian.'

'There's nothing "just" about being a librarian,' I corrected him, 'and as for Jack Schitt – I've a feeling we've not heard the last of him.'

'It doesn't make much sense him allowing you to see his face and survive, does it?'

'None of it adds up,' I replied with another wince as he picked a wood splinter out of my head. 'How have things been here?'

'The Wingco got through to Land's End International. Quinn, Highsmith and Aornis never got there.'

'It's a long journey from Swindon to Cornwall,' I said, 'they must have stopped for fuel.'

'Millon came up with these,' said Landen, laying some pictures on the table in front of me. They were grainy images from a security camera at a motorway services somewhere.

'What am I looking at?' I asked.

'These were taken at Agutter Services two hours after Aornis and the van left Swindon.'

He pointed to three figures – one, Aornis, being escorted by two others, recognisable as Quinn and Highsmith.

'Okay,' I said, 'a toilet break. Now what?'

He showed me another taken a minute later with Aornis on her own.

'Probably made them forget what they were doing,' said Landen. 'The whole deafness-as-defence must have been totally wrong – she can manipulate memories in quite another way.'

'What happened to her after that?' I asked, and Landen showed me a picture of Aornis, this time getting into an Alfa-Morris Spyder. There was a road sign next to her which indicated she was heading back the way she had come.

'Okay,' I said, 'so she headed back up the motorway. See what Millon can find from the motorway cameras. There can't be many Alfa-Morris Spyders on the roads these days. It's a start, at least.'

'Why are we looking for Aornis again?' asked Landen. 'I'm sure there's a good reason, but I can't remember what it is.'

'One of us has a Mindworm. We have to kill Aornis to get rid of it.'

'Is it me?'

I nodded.

'*Cow*. Wonder what it is? Don't tell me! Will I forget about having one soon enough?'

'Pretty soon, yes.'

'Good.'

He returned his attention to the wood splinters stuck in my neck and shoulder.

'Ow!' I said as he wiped some dirt out of a wound. 'Be careful. How did Tuesday feel about the failure of the Defence Shield?'

'She's taking it well, but something's brewing at the City Council – she overheard them as they made their way out. Since they think it's unlikely the anti-smiting shield will be operational by Friday, they said that "Smote Solutions" will have to be confirmed instead.'

'Is "Smote Solutions" an evacuation plan or something else?'

'Not sure,' he replied, 'but even *with* an evacuation, the entire city centre will still be destroyed in a firestorm. A billion pounds worth of damage, in less time than it takes to prepare a pot noodle – and no insurance owing to the "Act of God" clause. Will you keep still?'

'You're hurting me.'

'I didn't tell you to go out and do fieldwork.'

'I was going to look at some books – it *became* fieldwork. Shit, I need a Dizuperadol patch the size of a face flannel. My leg is screaming at me like a stuck pig.'

'You're not allowed to replace them until seven,' replied Landen, checking his watch.

'You're my doctor now?'

'No, I'm your husband now. And you're meant to have only three, changed every two days. Doctor's orders.'

'Damn the doctor.'

Landen sighed.

'I can run you down to the Lola Vavoom Memorial,' he said. 'You can argue with them instead. They'll say the same – only with medical authority.'

'Never mind,' I muttered.

He glared at me.

'There's no point in grumping at everything and everyone, Thursday.'

I shot him an angry look.

'Oh, and you weren't grumpy, when you lost your leg?'

'Yes, I *was* grumpy. Very grumpy. In fact, I was probably the biggest pain in the arse imaginable. But I had someone to tell me when I was being *too* grumpy for my own good.'

'That's *completely* different.'

'No, it's *completely* the same. You told me not be an arse then, and I'm telling you not to be an arse now.'

I took a deep breath and gave him a hug so my mouth was close to his ear.

'You were grumpier,' I whispered, and he laughed, and threatened to tickle me, so I had to promise I'd be good. I *hate* being tickled.

'You two are so disgustingly fond of one another,' said Millon the Hermit as he shambled in the back door, 'you should try arguing once in a while. Good for marriages, apparently. Holy cow, Thursday, what happened to you?'

'An argument with a trapdoor. How's your hermit exam revision going?'

He narrowed his eyes and waved his hands randomly in the air.

'It is adrift on the sea of time, lost in the endless wastes of human vanity.'

Landen and I looked at one another and nodded.

'Not bad.'

'Thank you. Want to hear what I found out about Krantz?'

Millon did indeed have some news. Jacob Krantz had worked for seventeen years on the Book Project – Goliath's attempt to enter the BookWorld.

'Krantz was one of three scientists who contributed significantly to the transfictional drive on the Austen Rover Transfictional Tour Bus,' said Millon. 'He was Professor of Theoretical Particle English at St Broccoli's in Oxford, so knew how to merge physics and literature. Loved both, they said.'

'And then what?'

'He was moved to the Synthetic Human Division. As soon as synthetics were officially given banned "chimera" status, he was reassigned – but to where, I'm still trying to discover.'

'Why is he in Swindon with a stack of Thursday Next lookalikes?'

'He isn't. He never left. He was found at home in Goliathopolis Sunday morning – *dead*.'

'Murder?'

'Natural causes, it seems. A brain aneurism. He was sixty-eight.'

'Well,' I said, 'there was someone or *something* that looked a lot like him in the Finis Hotel this morning.'

'I'm not disputing that.'

We all fell silent. I tried to figure it out but my brain felt fluffy, so I thanked Millon and invited him to stay for supper, which he said would be a great improvement on the breadless gruel sandwich he had planned. We made some tea and he and Landen chatted about the conspiracy network. Not so much about the imminent smiting, but more long-term stuff like HR-6984's arrival in thirty-seven years. Namely, just what algorithms were being used by the Asteroid Strike Likelihood Committee to account for the 34 per cent likelihood of a strike, and why this might be important. I got bored just as Friday wandered in and started to rummage through the fridge.

'How was work?' I asked.

'S'kay,' he replied, taking random bites from things.

'Any news?'

'Not really.'

'Anything cool happen at Pet Depot?'

'Neh.'

'Something on your mind?'

'Why do you ask?'

'You've just eaten Pickwick's food.'

'Ugh,' he said, and spat it in the bin.

'It's the Destiny-Aware Support Group Meeting,' he said, after swilling his mouth out with water, 'I'm not sure I want to go.'

'It might help to discover why you're going to kill Gavin Watkins on Friday.'

He looked up at me.

'I think that's why I don't want to go.'

'I'll take you. We'll leave at seven thirty.'

He grumpily agreed, gave me a silent hug, and was gone.

I took Tuesday some hot chocolate in her lab, and found the Wingco with her. Despite Tuesday's ongoing work to discover the value of the illusive U_c, she was also committed to helping the Wing Commander with his efforts to try to prove the existence of the Dark Reading Matter.

'What's unique about early dodos is how they functioned with so few lines of code,' explained Tuesday when I asked them what they were doing. 'Whoever first programmed the dodo's brain must have discovered pretty quickly that it was possible to crash a dodo's cortex simply by mild overstimulation. Watching a kitten while eating a cake and walking all at the same time would be enough to do it. And although a reboot would only take five minutes, the rebooted dodo would have forgotten everything it had ever learned, *ever*, which isn't ideal. Rather than redesign the brain, they simply added a buffer to slow down the processing of information.'

I looked at Pickwick, who was sitting on the workbench with an uncomfortable 'if you wanted a guinea pig, why not just buy a blasted guinea pig?' look about her.

'Is that why she often reacts to stuff ten seconds late?'

'*Exactly*. But what's more interesting for the Wingco is that we can pick up the buffered information on a wireless. The annoying static you get between Swindon-KZXY and Rant-AM is actually buffered Dodo thoughts.'

'And this helps the Wingco and his Dark Reading Matter project . . . *how*?'

'Isn't it obvious?'

'Not even the tiniest bit.'

'Watch.'

Tuesday carefully tuned in the Encephalovision through a standard wireless set, but this time *without* it being connected to Pickwick via the avian encephalograph.

'There's nothing there,' I said, which was true, as only random static danced across the screen.

'Patience, Mum. We have to overstimulate her first.'

It was surprisingly easy. While Tuesday showed Pickwick several marshmallows, the Wingco juggled with some oranges and then I, so as not to be simply a casual observer, recited the opening soliloquy to *Richard III*, Pickwick looked at all of us in turn, blinked twice and then stood stock still.

'Ah!' said Tuesday. 'She's buffering. Wait for it.'

We looked at the screen and sure enough, after about ten seconds, there was a fuzzy interpretation of what Pickwick had seen. Juggling, a giant marshmallow and me, walking up and down. There was also more *Dukes of Hazzard*, and her water dish. But then, after ten seconds, it faded. The buffering had ended.

'An *ingenious* discovery,' I murmured slowly, 'but I *still* can't see how this fits into the Dark Reading Matter.'

'We think a dodo's buffered thoughts might be able to transit the Dark Barrier,' said the Wingco, 'so all I need to find is an Imaginary Childhood Friend who is about to pass into the DRM with the death of their host, and get them to take a dodo with them. The dodo gets overstimulated by what it sees, and we read those buffered thoughts on the Encephalovision back home. It's really very straightforward.'

'Is it?' I asked, not unreasonably, and both Tuesday and the Wingco went into a complex explanation of how a thing might be possible, which seemed to revolve around the fact that the ICF and the dodo would fuse into a transient state of semi-fictionalisation that would permeate – at least temporarily – the Dark Barrier in two directions.

'I'm a fool not to have seen it myself,' I said, still not understanding it fully, then added, mildly suspiciously, 'Which dodo?'

'Don't worry, we won't use Pickwick,' said Tuesday. 'There are plenty of other dodos around, and so long as we get one that is pre-V4 with the old-style brain, we'll be laughing.'

'Okay, then,' I said as the security gate buzzer sounded, 'keep me posted.'

It was Stig outside the gate, so I let him in. He had a cup of tea and talked obsessively about the weather for ten minutes, something that, along with tea and kicking balls about, was very Neanderthal, leading some palaeontologists to speculate that Neanderthal behaviour might have somehow crossed over to the English in the distant past.

Millon and Landen came in to listen too, and the reason for Stig's visit was not long in coming.

'That synthetic Thursday we retired,' he said. 'We made . . . discoveries.'

'Such as?'

'She low-budget no-frills model. Nothing designed to last – skeletal, musculature, endocrine system – low-quality engineering. All internal organs not required removed and body cavity stuffed with slow-release glucose compound that looks and smells like nougat. She burn brightly twenty-four hours, then downhill. Within three days it poisoned by own waste products.'

'Unpleasant.'

'They designed to be euthanised after only twenty-four.'

'Okay, what else?'

'Disposable models like these called day players. They used internally at Goliath when extra staff needed daily basis. If lot extra photocopying needed, chit for a day player made to stationery store – extra pair of hands. Makes much much financial sense than a temping agency, and no security issues.'

'It's the reason they can't regulate body heat that well,' added Millon. 'Within an office environment they never needed to.'

'Are they not illegal?' asked Landen. 'Synthetics were banned almost as soon as they were invented.'

'There's a loophole,' said Millon. 'So long as they never leave the Island of Goliathopolis, they're quite legal.'

'Why would they have day players look like me?'

'A company in-joke most likely,' suggested Millon. 'My sources tell me day players have transferable skill adaptations, so you don't have to teach them everyone's names again and where the photocopier paper is stored. The technology might have advanced since then to a full Cognitive Transfer System.'

'Say that again?'

He did, and we pondered over the possibility of what a Cognitive Transfer System might potentially mean. At its most complex, eternal life in a series of hosts, and at its least complex, a way to carry out potentially fatal repairs inside nuclear reactors.

'Krantz,' said Landen softly, 'was probably a day player himself. It would explain why he's down here alive and not up in Goliathopolis dead.'

'When precisely did he die?' I asked.

'Sunday morning.'

I looked at Krantz's Gravitube ticket, the one I'd found in the Formby Suite.

I thought it over for a moment.

'Okay, how about this: he activates his own day player at least an hour before he dies of an aneurism so he achieves full consciousness and memory download, then the day player catches the midday Gravitube to Clary-Lamarr with five unactivated synthetics in Tupperware sarcophagi on his baggage manifest. He checks into the hotel, and then activates the first Thursday this morning.'

'How did he know he was going to have a brain aneurism?' said Millon. 'It's not something you can predict, is it?'

'You have something there.'

'And why is he on holiday in Swindon with five – now four – ersatz Thursdays fresh packed in Tupperware?'

'You have something there, too,' I conceded, 'but what we *do* know is that somewhere in the city is a day player who's been going for two and a half days out of a maximum three. He'll probably be in pain and a bit panicky and will certainly be dead by midnight – but he'll have the answers.'

We all exchanged glances.

'Here's the plan,' said Landen. 'I'll search hotels, Stig can check out boarding houses, and Millon can put his ear to the ground. No one could move that amount of Tupperware around the city without arousing suspicions.'

'I don't know,' said Millon, 'this is Swindon, remember.'

'Agreed,' replied Landen, 'but ask around nonetheless.'

'And me?' I asked.

'You're accompanying Friday to his Destiny-Aware support meeting.'

21

Tuesday: The Destiny-Aware

> 'After many years of employing operatives from only within a couple of hundred years around the end of the twentieth century, the ChronoGuard were forced by increased lobbying from the thirtieth and fortieth centuries to broaden their employment criteria. After threatening to withdraw transit rights through their time periods, the thirtieth and fortieth centuries successfully had the ChronoGuard implement an Equal Temporal Employment Policy. The success of this was short lived, as the service was disbanded a few years later.'
>
> Norman Scrunge, *time industry historian*

Shazza and Jimmy-G had just finished setting out about a hundred chairs when we turned up, and I wondered just how many ex-potential employees might be turning up. Although we knew the ChronoGuard had employed about three thousand, it wasn't known how many came from which era, and indeed, the covering letter attached to the summaries indicated that the Letters of Destiny were only for the Swindon branch of the Timeworkers Union.

'This is Friday,' I said, introducing him to them both. 'Jimmy-G, you would have worked together, and Shazza, you and Friday would have—'

'We know what we would have been. Thank you, Mum.'

They shook hands and looked at one another shyly. In another timeline they would have been lovers and inseparable, but in this one their future was considerably bleaker. Shazza marries a clot named Biff, and Friday spends his life in the slammer. It wasn't the sort of circumstances in which romance could blossom, really – unless found in the pages of a Farquitt novel, in which case all would doubtless turn out well.

'We would have worked together closely,' said Jimmy-G, giving Friday a warm embrace, 'on many exhilarating adventures, apparently.'

'Any idea what?' asked Friday.

'Nothing too specific,' said Jimmy-G, 'just that we would.'

'Mine says the same.'

'And mine,' said Shazza, 'but I like the idea of being known as "the scourge of the Upper Triassic".'

'Is this the ChronoGuard thing?' came a voice from the door. I turned and saw a moody-looking teenager with oily hair and a black eye. He looked as though he had just lost an argument about something, and was plotting payback. More significantly, he was the one who had paid 50p to see Tuesday's boobs and more recently offered her a fiver for sex. He was also due to be murdered on Friday. It was Gavin Watkins.

I didn't want to be judgemental, despite his offer earlier to Tuesday, so used instead that mildly condescending voice you reserve for acquaintances of your children.

'You're a friend of Tuesday's, aren't you?'

'Not really friends,' he replied, 'our relationship is based more on a . . . business footing.'

I narrowed my eyes at his impertinence, my patience rapidly vanishing.

'Is it now? Listen, Gavin, I'm not so sure offering cash for sex is really appropriate behaviour.'

'Why?'

'Because it's disrespectful, insulting and . . . she's not that kind of girl.'

'This is what happened,' he said. 'I asked her if *theoretically* speaking she would sleep with me for £4.3 million, and she said she *theoretically* would, so then I asked her if she'd accept a fiver. So she is *definitely* that kind of girl. All we're doing is discussing the price.'

I stared at him.

'Oh, c'mon,' he added with a sneer, 'are you really going to stand there and tell me you haven't sold yourself at least once? If not for cash, then certainly for influence.'

'You're a nasty piece of work, aren't you?' I said, although privately admitting that he was right. A long time ago, but he was right.

'Apologise, Gavin,' said Friday, who had heard enough, 'you just crossed the line.'

'I wasn't the one who drew the line,' he said in a low, controlled voice, 'and I'm only telling the truth. Both your mother and sister are—'

'Don't say it! I swear to God I'll—'

'You'll what?' said Gavin, taking a step closer so they were almost nose to nose. 'Kill me?'

Friday took a step back, firmly rattled. He *was* going to kill him, but not over name-calling. I hoped.

'Lost your appetite for a fight?' sneered Gavin.

'Okay, okay,' I said, not wanting this to get any more out of hand. 'Time out. Friday, cool it. And Gavin, there's tea and coffee and squash on the side and some biscuits. You can help yourself.'

'Nothing stronger?' he asked.

'You could always not dilute the squash, big guy.'

He grunted and moved off.

'I kill him because he insulted my mother and sister?' said Friday as soon as Gavin was out of earshot. 'No, that's just crazy.'

'You don't kill him until Friday,' I said. 'A lot of time for stuff to happen – or not.'

'Everything all right?' asked Shazza as she walked up.

'Just Gavin.'

'He lives down our street,' said Shazza. 'The corner shop won't let him in because of all the stealing, and I know for a fact that he gets beaten up at school at least once a day simply for being Gavin.'

'Figures.'

I looked at the kids who were entering in ones and twos. All of them were in their late teens.

'Any idea of attendance numbers?'

'It's not packed, I must confess,' said Shazza, looking at the small group, 'but I'm willing to bet he'll take careful note.'

She indicated a middle-aged man in a turban who was standing by the door.

'And he is?'

'Mr Akal Chowdry. He's Swindon's rep for the Asteroid Strike Likelihood Committee.'

'Oh.'

The ASLC relied heavily upon statisticians like Chowdry to compute an Ultimate Risk Factor for HR-6984.

'Any significant data from a meeting of ex-timeworkers,' added Jimmy-G, 'might allow the ASLC to update the Ultimate Risk Factor.'

We were currently at 34 per cent likelihood, and this figure was derived from many sources – astronomical observation, computer modelling, level of divine concern, guesswork and archaeology – *future* archaeology. Artefacts from the future *had* been found, but dating was contentious as it is difficult to say when something was to be invented or built. Of course, something with a date on it beyond 2041 would be conclusive, but the fossil record – both forward and back – is sketchy at best and, so far, nothing like that had turned up.

Three other members walked in. They were all clutching their Letters of Destiny and didn't look too happy. We waited another five minutes, but when no one else turned up, Jimmy-G called the meeting to order.

'I was hoping for more than fifteen,' he began, scanning the small group. 'Perhaps we'll see more as the weeks pass.'

He cleared his throat, and began.

'A fortnight ago the future was the undiscovered country. None of us knew what we would do, or how we would do it. As part of the Union of Federated Timeworkers severance package, we now have a clear idea of what *might* have happened, and what *will*. If anyone here is in any doubt over the truth of these summarisations, I draw your attention to Gerald Speke, who received his papers three days ago. They predicted he would lose an arm to a gorilla in Swindon zoo, and within six hours, he had.'

There was some murmuring at this.

'His name was Bongo,' said Gerald, who was sitting at the back with a large bandage wrapped around his upper body. 'But if I hadn't received the Letter of Destiny, I never would have gone to the zoo to see if there *was* a gorilla.'

'That's how it works,' said Jimmy-G. 'The Letters of Destiny and the effect they have on you are now *included* in your Letter of Destiny. But we're sorry for your loss nonetheless. I suggest we begin with introductions.'

He looked out over the gathering. No one moved.

'I'll start,' said Friday, standing up to face the group. 'I would have been the sixth Director General of the ChronoGuard. My first major feat was in the Armageddon Avoidance Division where I ensured our survival of HR-6984, but I have no idea how. After a long and apparently eventful career, I retire at eighty-two the most decorated ChronoGuard operative ever. Now, it's a bit different. I spend thirty-seven years in prison for murder. Three days after release, on 3 February 2041, I'm beaten to death by persons unknown with a baseball bat up in the Old Town.'

There was a pause, and everyone clapped. Not presumably because they liked what they'd heard, but for his honesty. I was just relieved he hadn't mentioned that Gavin was his victim.

'My name's Sharon deWitt,' said Shazza. 'I would have had a dazzling career in the timestream. I'd be pioneering trans-Palaeozoic jumps by age thirty and a full colonel by forty-two. I'd have retired third-in-command at the ChronoGuard with four citations for bravery and be *Flux* magazine's "Woman for all Time", then comfortably retired in fourteenth-century Florence at age eighty. The way things stand at the moment I'm a receptionist for twenty years, marry a guy I don't much like, have two kids who turn out so-so, and then get hit by a Vauxhall KP-13 at age fifty-five, late one rainy night near the library. They never find the driver.'

There was more applause, and she sat down. There was a longer pause, so Jimmy-G stood up again.

'My name is Jimmy-G, and I would have worked alongside both Shazza and Friday. I would have been Time Engine Policy Director from 2014 until 2032 when a gravity surge in the auxiliary Time Room dumped me in the forty-fifth century. I was stuck there for sixteen years, and upon my return ran the enloopment facilities. These days, I work in retail and have a happy if unexciting life with a fine son. I don't see him graduate, though, since I die in mysterious circumstances in 2040.'

He sat down again, and, heartened by his contribution, the remainder of the ex-potential timeworkers joined in. There was someone who would have worked as part of the Retrosnatch Squad who was unhappily not going to see his sixtieth year owing to a car accident, and a youthful Bendix Scintilla, whose future self we had met a few years back when he was giving a ChronoGuard recruitment talk. He was eighteen, and would now work in engineering until vanishing without trace in Kettering not long before his fifty-fifth birthday. Braxton's son Gordon was also here, to give a much-needed positive take on the proceedings. He was slated to suffer a fatal time aggregation when his gravity suit leaked, first day at cadet school. Now he gets to be fifty-six. He wasn't the only one. A girl named Lauren would have been fed alive to pterosaur infants next April during an assignment in the Cretaceous that went badly wrong, but now succumbs to Gruppling Bongitiasis at age forty-four.

'Go, me!' she announced happily at the end of it.

'I would have suffered a fatal time aggregation,' said another attendee, 'twenty-two years from now. Instead, I die falling from the roof while attempting to adjust the TV aerial – on *exactly* the same day. Whoop-de-do.'

'What was the programme you would be wanting to watch?'

The attendee looked at his summary.

'Er . . . a repeat of *The Very Best of the Adrian Lush Show Repeats Again, Part 7*.'

'*Serious* bummer.'

In this way the room told of their differing destinies, and we offered as many encouraging noises as we could, although the practical help this afforded was questionable.

The last person to speak was Gavin Watkins.

'I might be unique in this room,' he said in a loud, clear voice, 'in that according to my summary, I would not have been a distinguished member of the ChronoGuard. After an early career helping to map the twenty-fifth century, my later career seems to consist mostly of disciplinary hearings and suspensions. Bored and in need of cash owing to an expensive Precambrian tourism habit, I take a hefty bribe in 2028 to undertake an illegal eradication.'

'What sort of bribe?' said someone.

'A Titian – *The Battle of Cadore*.'

'You *hate* Titian,' said someone else. 'And you'd have nowhere to hang it.'

'I change my mind and grow to love him, apparently,' said Gavin, 'and I guess I must have had somewhere to hang it . . . *moron*.'

'Okay, okay,' said Jimmy-G soothingly, 'this won't happen, and what's more, it won't happen twenty-four years from now. Go on, Gavin.'

'Right. Well, I was caught – we all were, of course – and spent two years in an enloopment facility before being released owing to a technicality. Not a great career, but better than what I get now. *Friday Next will murder me in three days' time!*'

There was a sharp intake of breath as he said it, and he glared at Friday.

'Why are you going to kill me, Friday? Because I insulted your mother and sister?'

Friday took a deep breath, and stood up to face Gavin.

'I don't know. I have no *real* motive. But you can stop me. Take a random Tube ride. You can be anywhere on the planet in under six hours. If I can't find you, it won't happen.'

'As soon as my destiny papers arrived my parents put me on the Deep Drop to Sydney,' said Gavin. 'I checked in under a false name to a crappy motel near Dame Edna International. I even hid in the cupboard. My summarisation papers hadn't changed, you were still due to kill me. So I came home. If I was going to be murdered, I'd rather it happened near family and friends.'

'Friends?' said Shazza.

'Family, then. Body repatriations are pricey these days, and they always seem to go astray.'

'I'm not going to kill you,' said Friday.

'You will,' said Gavin, 'and what's more, I know for a fact you won't get away with it.'

'It's Tuesday night,' returned Friday, 'and I've got sixty-six hours to figure out a way to bend the Eventline.'

'Maybe the Eventline did bend,' said Shazza thoughtfully. 'It's possible that once you were in the hotel cupboard your Letter of Destiny changed to say you survived. You probably then wondered why you had flown all that way to hide in a cupboard, but as soon as you returned, so did your death.'

Everyone fell silent at this. Shazza was right. It was entirely possible that the Eventline was vibrating like a rubber band and that what was written on the Letters of Destiny right *now* was not what had been on them even ten seconds ago.

'Okay, then,' said Friday, 'I need to find a way of *permanently* changing our destinies. Right now, things don't look very good.'

There was silence after this, and Jimmy-G thought it a good time to call the group to an end and to meet again the same place next week, unless the smiting went ahead, in which case he'd let everyone know. The small party dispersed without much talk; the proceedings had been pretty joyless. Gavin glared at us both as he filed out and as Jimmy-G walked up to speak to us, I noted Mr Chowdry pulling his mobile phone out of his pocket as he turned to leave.

'That was *seriously* strange,' said Friday as we walked back to the car. Shazza was with us as she and Friday were going to have a drink together to see whether any of their future spark could be pre-ignited, and Jimmy-G was with us because his car was parked next to ours.

'Time travel stuff generally is.'

'No,' said Friday, 'I mean *murderously* seriously strange.'

'In what way?'

'Didn't you notice?' he asked, and when I said I didn't, he counted out the people at the group on his fingers.

'Only three of us die seemingly natural deaths. I'm murdered in 2041, as is Shazza and Bendix, Miranda, Joddy and Sarah. The other six die in "unexplained" deaths, all of them in 2040. Can you see a pattern?'

‘None of us live beyond February 2041,’ said Shazza in a quiet voice.

‘Right,’ said Friday. ‘I’m the last to die – three days *before* HR-6984 is scheduled to strike the Earth. No one lives long enough to be killed by the meteorite that’s hurtling our way.’

‘Does that mean the HR-6984 will *definitely* happen?’ asked Shazza.

‘It means we can’t prove it *won’t*,’ said Friday, ‘since none of us live beyond it.’

‘Why would anyone want to murder someone just before everyone is about to die anyway?’ asked Jimmy-G. ‘It raises vindictiveness to a whole new level.’

They all looked at one another in a confused and dejected manner. It must be like having an itch and not being able to scratch it. Nevertheless, I thought I should be a mother rather than a colleague, so said the first thing that came into my head.

‘Fish and chips, anyone?’

22

Wednesday: Library

> 'The Hotel Bellvue was squeezed disagreeably between the M4, the Swindon Tannery and the city's main electrical substation, hence the name it was popularly known by: the Substation. It was the last place one would book a room, even if hygiene wasn't an issue, and it seemed to exist only to give other hotels a benchmark for failure, and indeed, the Substation had managed to wrestle *Clip-Joint* magazine's coveted "Five Bedbug" rating from its only competitor in the South-East: the equally grimy Bastardos, in Reading.'
>
> Josh Candle – *Ten Places Not to Visit in Wessex*

'Good morning,' said Duffy as I walked into the office. 'Did the car find you okay?'

'Eventually.'

'If you want a different pick-up address we'd appreciate it if you would give us more notice. It helps the Special Library Service ensure your route is safe.'

'I understand,' I said, 'and I'm sorry. I was called to the Substation Hotel this morning. It was – um – family business.'

I wasn't going to tell him we'd discovered Krantz – or what remained of him.

'Mrs Duffy and I spent our honeymoon there. The hum and crackle of the electrical substation was . . . restful.'

'It sounds very romantic.'

'When we want to rekindle that flame,' continued Duffy, 'we leave an orbital sander running in the basement. Hums just like a 500KVA transformer. If we want to hear the crackle of morning dew on the insulators, we have Gizmo play with a cellophane wrapper.'

'I'm so hoping Gizmo is a dog.'

'A pug.'

'Duffy?'

'Yes, ma'am?'

'Do people usually attack the Chief Librarian as they are driven in?'

I was alluding to an incident when someone fired two shots at our vehicle as we pulled off the Magic Roundabout. The vehicle was bullet-proofed, but even so.

'Usually, ma'am. The 720 per cent increase in library loans caused by the government's New Book Duty has caused a three-day delay on library book availability. When the citizens can't get the books they want they often vent their fury at the person in charge.'

This was, sadly, all too true – and not just about loans. Only a month previously, an all-new 007 book had been published by that author with a beard whose name I can never remember. James Bond fundamentalists argued that this was 'A grave and heinous affront to the oeuvre' and warned that if the library stocked it, they would sit outside in silent protest, stroking white cats and thinking fiendish thoughts. And if that had no effect, they would riot. They did, and two people, six cats and three Diana Rigg impersonators lost their lives.

'Do you want to see the Goliath representative first, or shall I make him wait for an hour to show your utter contempt for him and his company?'

This would be Lupton Cornball, who I had met yesterday at the Finis.

'I'll see him first.'

The phone rang. I reached out but Duffy beat me to it.

'Hello?' he said. 'Office of the Chief Librarian.'

He listened for a moment then looked at me.

'I'll ask.'

He put his hand over the mouthpiece.

'Detective Smalls wants to talk to you. She's on the way up.'

'Smalls? Okay, her first, then Goliath. Oh, and I'd like to talk to Councillor Bunty Fairweather. She's in charge of Fiscal Planning and Smite Avoidance Policy. They've an alternative anti-smiting plan cooking, and I want to find out what it is.'

'She's your two o'clock. Shall I push her up to your eleven thirty?'

'Is that straight after Goliath?' I asked, glancing at the clock.

'No, Mrs Jolly Hilly, the insane Enid Blyton fundamentalist is after Goliath. Bunty is after them.'

'Do I have to talk to insane people?'

'You're a librarian now. I'm afraid it's mandatory.'

'Hm. Okay, Smalls first, then Goliath, then Hilly, then Bunty.'

Duffy nodded, made a note on his clipboard and opened the door to admit Phoebe. I smiled agreeably. I didn't much care for her, but we needed to get along.

'Detective Smalls,' I said, getting up to welcome her.

'Chief Librarian Next,' she replied, shaking my hand. I gestured her to the sofas.

'That's a bit of a mouthful,' I said, 'better call me Thursday.'

'Then you must call me Phoebe. You've recovered well from the attack at the Lobsterhood yesterday.'

'I got lucky. One of the hinges from the trapdoor embedded itself in an Aeschylus only inches above my head. Coffee?'

'Thank you.'

Duffy took the cue and moved silently to the coffee machine while Phoebe looked around her.

'This is very plush.'

'Libraries have been monstrously overfunded these past thirteen years,' I said. 'The librarians had to take industrial action when the City Council threatened to have gold taps in the washrooms. Mind you, that will all change. I think you're getting some of our funding.'

'Fifty million that I know of,' she said.

I raised an eyebrow. Fifty million was a third of our budget.

'But we have to fund the Special Library Service out of that,' she added.

This made it a lot easier – Wexler's team was expensive.

'Tell me,' she continued, 'do you think Colonel Wexler is mad?'

'Yes, but in a good way. Got anyone on your staff yet?'

'A few trigger-happy nutters who were too mentally unstable even for SO-5. I told them to sod off – I want to keep gratuitous violence *inside* books, where it belongs.'

'Very wise. Your watch is slow.'

She looked at me oddly and pulled up her sleeve. The watch was a Reverso – the face was hidden. She flipped it over.

'You're right. How did you know?'

'I can hear it tick. And it's ticking slow. Not important. Anything on the "stolen thirteenth century codex" question?'

She pulled out a small pocketbook and turned to a page marked with a rubber band.

'Possibly. Out of the eighty-three reported biblio-thefts over the past month, only two had the same modus operandi. One in Bath, and another in Lancaster. Exactly the same. Torn-out pages, then destroyed, but with the rest of the book left untouched.'

'Both by St Zvlkx?'

'Bingo. The first a gazetteer of taverns in the Oxford area that give credit, and the second a list of credible excuses to give your bishop if he thinks you are misappropriating church funds – neither of them valuable, nor particularly rare.'

'That links the books,' I said, wondering whether Jack Schitt had been there on each occasion. 'What are your thoughts?'

'I did some research into St Zvlkx, and I was struck by a recurring theme in his life.'

'You mean his stealing, debauchery, embezzlement, drunkenness and the total absence of pastoral care or moral rectitude?'

'I was thinking more of his *meanness*. St Zvlkx was notoriously tight fisted. It was said that Augustus IV, the "Bouncing Bishop" of Salisbury, joked that his idea of eternity would be dinner with St Zvlkx and Kevin of Kent, and waiting for one of them to pick up the tab.'

'So?'

'Zvlkx would *never* have used fresh vellum in his books because it would cut into his drinking funds. He probably used second-hand books, dismantled them, scraped the vellum clean and then reused them. It's only a guess, but I think the thief was looking for palimpsests.'

I could see what she was getting at. A palimpsest was the ghostly image of the writing that was still just visible on the reused sheet of vellum. If the writing was from a long-lost book, it would be of inestimable value.

'Good thought,' I murmured.

'There's more.'

She reached into her bag and brought out a thirteenth-century book wrapped in acid-free paper. She placed it on the coffee table and donned a pair of latex gloves to unwrap it.

'This is Lord Volescamper's copy of St Zvlkx's *Book of Revealments*. It wasn't one of the books that was vandalised by our mystery book damagers. I had a look under UV light and I can just see the original text beneath St Zvlkx's prophecies. I'm thinking that *all* St Zvlkx's original works were written on recycled vellum.'

'Any idea of the source book?'

She smiled.

'Let's see how good you are, Chief Librarian.'

She opened the book at a marked page and pushed it across. I looked closely. There was some text written sideways beneath St Zvlkx's second revealment, the one predicting the Spanish Armada, or, as he called it 'The Sail of the Century'.

'It looks like a copy of the Venerable Keith's *Principia Accounticia*,' I murmured, and Phoebe was suitably impressed.

The Venerable Keith had been a contemporary of St Zvlkx's, and also the accountant for the Bishop of Swindon between 1276 and 1294. The *Evadum*, as it was known, explained the new science of utilising loss-making companies to offset tax liability against profit. Monks couldn't hand-copy them fast enough.

'There were lots of copies,' I said, 'which was probably why St Zvlkx could buy them up cheap to scrape clean and rebind in order to peddle his own rubbish.'

'I agree,' said Phoebe, producing another book, this time Zvlkx's treatise on herbal remedies for 'unwonted flaccidity', *A Short Historie of Thyme*.

I stared at the two books. This still didn't tell us why Jack Schitt and Goliath were destroying parts of worthless thirteenth-century books, even if they *did* have palimpsests of almost equally banal titles beneath them. Still, I was seeing the Goliath rep next, so it was possible I could rattle their tree a bit and see what fell out.

'I know,' said Phoebe, sensing my confusion. 'Doesn't make much sense, does it?'

I picked up the phone, punched a button and asked to be put through to Finisterre.

'You're right, it makes no sense at all,' I said to Phoebe. 'But at least we know what they're after. James? Thursday. I've got Detective Smalls here and she's found a link between the vandalisations. *St Zvlkx books*. There have been three including the one at the Lobsterhood. Place the library's copies under armed guard.'

I put the phone down and Smalls got up.

'I hope I've been candid,' she said.

'Very.'

'In that case, perhaps you can tell me who was in the scriptorium yesterday? I think you're not telling me everything you know.'

So I did, which wasn't much, but Jack Schitt's presence clearly implicated Goliath, which she didn't like the sound of. Few people did. Tangling with the Goliath Corporation generally left you in one of two places: inside a wooden box with a grieving family outside, or inside a wooden box under six foot of soil with family wondering where you were. The former was if they didn't hold a grudge. I'd probably be the latter.

'Ready for the Goliath rep?' asked Duffy as soon as Phoebe had left.

My mobile rang. It was Millon.

'Give me two minutes,' I said to Duffy. 'Millon?'

'I'm outside the hotel,' he said, 'and you were right. The Goliath clean-up squad have just left. Took everything in the back of a van.'

Millon had tracked Krantz down to the seedy Substation Hotel at 3 a.m. that morning. He'd found Krantz face down on the floor of Room 27 stone dead, and looking pretty dreadful, even for a corpse at the Substation. A quick examination confirmed what Landen had thought – the corpse wasn't Krantz, but his day player. Next to him was an empty Tupperware sarcophagus, and no sign of any others. He had come here, activated a new day player, waited until he was transferred, then left. The room held few clues. We still had no idea what he was doing. But we did know that Krantz had another couple of days of life left in him, and would be stronger, smarter and fitter. He would be harder to find, too, and when found, harder to tackle. Still, at least we didn't have to worry about reporting any of this to the authorities. The Goliath cleaners would have removed all trace of Krantz, and since they were experts, left intact the crusty mat of human hair, spilled beer and dried body fluids that the Substation impudently referred to as 'carpet'.

I thanked Millon, told him to keep looking for the new Krantz and rang off. I turned back to Duffy.

'Listen, this may sound seriously weird, but I might turn up and not be myself one day, and if that happens, I need you to call my husband on this number and tell him that his wife isn't who she thinks she is.'

'You're wrong.'

'About what?'

'It's not seriously weird, it's *obscenely* weird. How can you not be you, and how am I meant to know anyway?'

'Easily. See this tattoo? It's to remind ourselves that Jenny is a Mindworm. Not mine of course, but my husband's. I'll explain about Aornis one day, and if you're wondering why I have the tattoo on *my* hand and not Landen's, I meant to find out this morning but forgot to drop in to Image Ink . . . again.'

Duffy stared at me, a single eyebrow raised.

'What tattoo?'

'This one—'

But he was right. I didn't have one. *Damn*. Replaced again.

'I *thought* it was weird that I could hear Phoebe's watch ticking slow,' I muttered.

I thought quickly – which fortunately I was now able to do – and worked my movements backwards. I'd struggled to get into the back of the Daimler at the Substation Hotel, so I was real me then. I could remember arriving at the secure entrance at the back of the library, then walking through the building to the front office and up the elevators. The real me was somewhere between those places – in a store cupboard, I hoped, and more comfortable this time. I called Landen and told him what had happened.

'It wasn't unexpected,' he said after a moment or two of reflection. 'Do you want me to come and kill you again?'

'That's very sweet of you, darling, but I need to make sure real me is safe. The password was "Has to be there overnight" after you say "When it absolutely, positively".'

Landen was silent for a moment.

'You didn't have to tell me you'd been replaced, did you?'

'I needed you to know you could trust me.'

'Okay, now I trust you – whatever body you happen to be in.'

'Thank you, Pumpkin. Have the car in the loading bay at lunchtime so we can bundle real me in the back. And Landen?'

'Yes?'

'I'm having those feelings again.'

'There's nothing you can do about them, so just think of something else until we put an end to you and we can have you back.'

'I'm not going to get rid of this me. Not yet.'

There was a long silence from Landen.

'I hope you know what you're doing.'

'I hope so too, but I'm not offering any guarantees.'

'That's my girl.'

He rang off and I turned to Duffy, who had the largest frown I have ever seen etched in the forehead of anyone, before or since.

'Okay,' he said in a resigned manner, '*now* are we ready for the Goliath rep?'

I jumped up and looked in the mirror behind the desk. I looked sickeningly well, and I wanted Lupton to think I was the real, damaged me. He knew about the contents of the Tupperware sarcophagi, and him knowing I was a Thursday day player was the sort of interest I didn't want right now.

'I'm going to need a walking stick, a red felt marker and a box of sticking plasters – and you're going to have to be quick.'

'Certainly, ma'am. But I must say I'm concerned. Your behaviour seems somewhat . . . *erratic*.'

'Ha!' I said with a grin. 'You haven't seen anything yet.'

23

Wednesday: Goliath

> 'All cities had a representative from the Goliath Corporation to guide and lobby for the company's interests, of which it had many. Because Goliath catered for everything from the cradle to the grave, it was hard to find a decision in which the Corporation's representative would not have some sort of opinion. Councils loved them. They were like a trade union, management consultancy, retailers' association and consumer association all in one. You could, in fact, talk to one person about almost everything – except impartiality.'
>
> Milton Tablitt – *A Guide to the Goliath Corporation*

Duffy nodded to the Goliath representative, who entered my office. He was immaculately turned out in a dark blue suit, and carried with him the unmistakable air of supreme confidence that only connection to the planet's dominant corporate enterprise could supply.

'Hullo, Thursday.'

I should have been surprised, but I wasn't. It was Jack Schitt.

'Well, well,' I said, 'do I call you Jack Schitt or Adrian Dorset?'

'Either,' he replied, as the less polite epithet was the name by which he had become known in the ghost-written Thursday books – to guard against lawsuits, apparently. I thought quickly. He would know that I had seen an empty Tupperware box at the Finis, but that would be all he could be sure about. I would have to be careful.

'Most people call me Jack these days. I think it's a form of ironic humour. Can we speak alone?'

I nodded to Duffy, who went out and closed the door behind

him. I heaved myself to my feet in a clumsy manner using the stick Duffy had provided. I could see Jack looking at me with interest. My gait, my hand, on which I had drawn the tattoo with felt tip, and the sticking plasters I had placed on my face – precisely in the places real me had been cut during the fight at the Lobsterhood. I lumbered to the coffee machine and poured him a cup.

'So where's the usual rep?' I asked, offering him a seat on the sofa.

'Representative Cornball is engaged on . . . other duties. I'm taking over for a few days.'

'We're honoured,' I said, setting the coffee down in front of him and then clumsily sitting down myself – a sort of controlled descent for two-thirds of the way, then a drop on to the cushions from there. If he was suspicious, he didn't show it.

'We don't often see any Goliath high-fliers in Swindon,' I added. 'What position are you on the Ladder these days?'

'Ninety-one. The Corporation rewards loyalty.'

'So? Starbucks rewards loyalty – and they're not out to take over the world. Okay, that was a bad example. Tesco's reward loyalty, and they're not out to . . . okay, that's a bad example too. But you know what I mean.'

He stared at me thoughtfully, and his diamond tiepin caught the light. We'd first crossed swords almost twenty years ago, and although there was a deep enmity between us, there was also a certain strained respect. Even though his death would not fill me with any sense of sadness, I would probably feel the loss. Even enemies are part of one. I shifted my position with a wince of faux pain, while at the same time resting my hand close to the butt of my pistol. He picked up on it instantly.

'I'm not here to murder you, dear girl,' he said in a kindly manner. 'Protocol 451 is still very much in force. Now that you're effectively out to grass, we can look forward to a rosy Thursday-free future. We respect you greatly, and mean you no harm.'

I pointed to one of the sticking plasters on my face.

'So what was this all about, then?'

'I have no idea what you're talking about.'

'The Stout Denial technique, eh?'

'If you'd like the Stout Denial with Faux Shock Outrage, you can have that too. If you really want it, I can play the ever-popular "Lawyers to file suit for defamation" gambit as well.'

'I'm no longer SO-27,' I told him, 'I'm a respected member of the establishment running one of the pillars of modern society. Do you really think you'd win a PR war against a bunch of committed librarians?'

He thought about this, but he knew I was right. The libraries were a treasured institution and so central to everyday life that government and commerce rarely did anything that might upset them. Some say they were more powerful than the military, or if not, then certainly quieter. As they say: don't mess with librarians. Only they use a stronger word than 'mess'.

'Okay,' said Jack, looking down for a moment. 'Off the record?'

'Sure.'

'You have my sincere apologies for yesterday. I voluntarily downgraded myself three Ladder numbers as a sign of corporate penance.'

'Oh, stop – you're making me all misty. What's your interest in St Zvlkx? Hardly a search for bargain thirteenth-century bordellos, I'm thinking.'

He leaned forward.

'You just got an apology. You should accept that with good grace, and ponder your good fortune. But I'll let you in on a little secret, too. Protocol 451 is presently under review.'

'Is that some kind of threat?'

'It's a polite warning. This Chief Librarian job is a cushy number. I think you should stick to lending books. You can leave Detective Smalls to deal with Goliath.'

I took a deep breath. It was time to get proactive.

'Let's not bullshit one another,' I said. 'We know you're not interested in Zvlkx codices, but the palimpsests they contain – so what's so special about Venerable Keith's work?'

'I have no idea what you're talking about,' he said with a smile, 'and will strenuously deny any wrongdoing on my part or the Corporation's. I am only here to offer my best wishes to Wessex's new Chief Librarian, explain that Smalls at SO-27 has jurisdiction over booky matters, and to tell you that if there is any way in which we can assist you in the smooth running of the Wessex All You Can Eat at Fatso's Drink Not Included Library Services, you only need to call. That's it. I think we're pretty much done.'

'No, I think we're pretty much just getting started. What's Krantz doing in Swindon?'

'Krantz is a traitor who turned against a benevolent company which had helped and nurtured his career.'

'Krantz *was* a traitor,' I corrected him, 'he died in Goliathopolis on Sunday.'

'You know more than I do,' replied Jack.

'But then Krantz's day player checked into the Finis yesterday morning. What would the Central Genetic Council say if they knew that Goliath had permitted unlicensed non-evolutionary life-forms on the mainland? Last I heard it was a £10 million fine per chimera – plus a long and potentially damaging public inquiry.'

'That is a scurrilous and outrageous suggestion,' replied Jack evenly, 'and is a gross slander upon a company whose only wish is to assist the fine citizens of this nation find fulfilment and prosperity. And besides, such a suggestion would require proof to sustain in court.'

'Lupton might be going around clearing up after you,' I said, 'but we found Krantz's own day player dead in the Substation Hotel this morning. We took pictures of the corpse, a mouth swab, then recorded Mr Cornball leaving once he'd cleaned up the mess.'

Jack stared at me, and his eyebrow twitched.

'Now,' I said, 'let's start again. Why is Goliath interested in valueless palimpsests locked inside St Zvlkx codices?'

'I am shocked and outraged,' he said in the tone of anyone but, 'and deeply concerned that an ex-employee of Goliath should be conducting perverse and outrageous experiments here on the mainland. Day players are rightly classed an abomination, and as soon as you furnish us with all your information, we will vigorously investigate this claim and punish those responsible.'

I rolled my eyes and smiled at him.

'Are you really going to try and pretend you don't know?'

'Don't know what?'

'That you're not in this room at all. The real Jack Schitt's body is comatose in a hotel room somewhere, while your personality gives animation to that host body you've temporarily entered. And don't give me the "Krantz rogue" bullshit. What are you people *really* up to?'

He smiled, pulled my pistol from his waistband and laid it on the table. He had taken it out of my holster two minutes and twenty-six seconds earlier, when he leaned forward to shake my hand. I'd seen him do it, but I wasn't going to blow my cover. He was a Mk VII as well – or even a Mk VIII.

'Guilty as charged,' he said with a laugh. 'How did you figure out I was a day player?'

'Simple,' I replied, 'you've sipped the coffee several times but the quantity in the cup hasn't gone down. You've no oesophagus, so you can't swallow. And your spectacles. They're clear glass. The real Jack is long sighted.'

He picked the pistol off the table and released the safety.

'I'm sorry, Thursday. It pains me to do this, especially as you showed me such compassion over my wife, but corporate matters always come before friendship.'

He pointed the gun at me.

'Here's how it goes: "Police were today called to the offices of the newly appointed Chief Librarian who had been killed by a deranged Goliath representative who blamed her for his wife's death. The Goliath rep then turned the gun on himself." What do you think?'

'I'd certainly agree with the "deranged" bit.'

'Luckily, it's not important what you think. I would have hoped for a less ignominious end for us both – no, wait, for you. I get to wake up in a hotel suite. Your end will be permanent.'

I pretended to give out a long, dispirited breath. He still hadn't figured I was a synthetic. As soon as he shot me, I'd wake up too – but probably somewhere less comfortable, and certainly without room service.

'Well,' I sighed, 'this had to happen sooner or later. I'm amazed I survived so long, to be honest. What about Protocol 451?'

'I lied about that, too. It was rescinded a week ago.'

'And the palimpsests? If I'm going to die, then at least let me know what it was you were doing.'

He leaned in, grabbed my jacket and pulled me closer.

'Krantz was weak and disloyal. He can't help you. Do you know what a Whistleblower is?'

'Someone who feels that they won't compromise their ethical responsibility as regards corporate malfeasance?'

'No, that's what we at Goliath call "a loathsome snitch". A Whistleblower is a small device no bigger than a grain of rice implanted in the *medulla oblongata*, the part of the brain that deals with involuntary functions, like breathing and cardiac control.'

'I know what the medulla does.'

He raised an eyebrow. I was being too calm, so I quickly

engineered a nervous tremor in my leg and adjusted my heart rate up from ninety to one-twenty. If I could have sweated, I would have done that too. But it was subtle enough to allay suspicions.

'This device,' he continued, 'detects the brain waveforms associated with ethical thought, guilt, nervousness and vocalisation – and when they are all running together assumes the recipient is about to blab and explodes, destroying the medulla and extinguishing life functions – and all it ever looks like is an aneurism. Everyone above Ladder number one million gets one. I have one. Even day players of Goliath personnel get one. Krantz knows a lot, but not even his day player can tell you. Neat, eh?'

'Goliath never fail to surprise me. What did Krantz want to tell me? And how does that relate to Zvlkx?'

'It's part of our long-term corporate policy for domination. And the best part of it is that you put us up to it. I'd not imagined how HR-6984 might link with your discussion about—'

But he stopped, laughed and got up from the sofa.

'You're good,' he said, 'real good. The heart rate thing totally had me fooled.'

'What do you mean?' I asked, attempting to retrieve the situation.

But Jack was having none of it. He *knew* I was a synthetic. I sat up straighter and placed my stick to one side.

Jack laughed again and waved a finger at me.

'I can't believe I almost fell for the "tell me the secret plan before you kill me" gambit. But tell me,' he added, 'since we have a few moments to compare notes on wearing a day player, does the increased libido with zero chance of fulfilment get you frustrated?'

'You have to put it to the back of your mind. How're the overheating issues treating you?'

'I generally try to remove layers of clothes *before* there's a problem.'

'Good tip,' I said, 'thanks.'

'Have you come across the faulty knee issue yet?' he asked. 'Get a bad one and they don't last the full twenty-four.'

I told him I'd not been in a body long enough to have seen a problem, and he nodded sagely. I asked him how he knew I wasn't her – simply as a matter of curiosity.

'The real you is almost addicted to Dizuperadol. Your skin and breath should reek of it. Enough talk. See you in the next life.'

He pulled the trigger and it clicked uselessly.

'I dropped out the clip when I figured what you were,' I said, 'and I never keep one up the spout. Not since I shot off Bowden's little toe by accident. Safety first.'

I reached for the .25 Beretta on my ankle only to find it wasn't there. He had taken that too, but more skilfully. He was *definitely* a Mk VIII. I looked up and saw my small automatic pointing back at me.

'As I was saying,' said Jack Schitt with a smile, pulling back the slide to chamber a round, 'see you in the next life.'

They're right. You never do hear the sound of the shot that kills you.

24

Wednesday: Adelphi

> 'Inhabiting a day player was like riding a Segway. They both come easily, but can occasionally catch you unawares once you feel so comfortable with them that you forget they are there. A well-fitting day player is a great joy to use, but I heard later that inhabiting a body not designed for your own use was like driving a car with all the controls reversed.'
>
> Thursday Next – *private journals*

My guess had been correct: she'd put me in a storage cupboard. I was surrounded by cleaning products, buckets, brooms, a chair and table for tea breaks and an industrial floor cleaner. I had been wrapped in a blanket this time and laid on a camping mat, so was at least warm. For the record, waking up from a cognition retransfer is pretty much instantaneous, but the memories I'd formed when a day player took a minute or two to establish themselves.

I pulled myself to my feet using the floor cleaner and noticed that my day player had kindly pinned a pay-as-you-go mobile to my shirt where I couldn't possibly miss it. There was also a key to the storeroom taped to the palm of my right hand. I rubbed my tattoo, just in case, but I didn't really need to – the ache in my leg told me I was well and truly home.

I tried to think clearly through the mild fog of the Dizuperadol. Synthetic Jack had said: 'I get to wake up in a hotel suite', which suggested that his base of operations was in one of the six five-star hotels in the city.

I'd had a quick look around my office before Jack killed my day player, and that gave me a few clues. First, there was the faint aroma of jet fuel in the air, which suggested Dyson International, the airship field to the east of the city – a location that narrowed the choice of hotel down to the Majestic, the Adelphi or the Piper-Astoria. The swing of his jacket suggested a heavy key fob in his suit pocket, and if that was so, then he was in a suite at the Adelphi – the others used keycards.

I unpinned the mobile from my shirt and dialled one of the numbers that synthetic me had considerately left myself on speed dial.

'Phoebe? It's Thursday. I need a favour.'

I outlined what I needed her to do, and heard her sharp intake of breath. She knew she'd be tackling Goliath eventually, but hadn't thought it would be so soon.

'Arresting a Top One Hundred is . . . *problematical*,' replied Phoebe. 'Are you sure you've got something on him?'

'Not yet.'

'Here's the deal,' said Phoebe. 'I'll help you, but if it all goes squiffy, you take the flak.'

'Deal.'

My synthetic had thoughtfully left me some clothes and as soon as I was dressed I unlocked the door and peered outside. I was in a service area somewhere on the ground floor, so grabbed my stick and limped out of the door, but then stopped abruptly as the service elevator opened at the far end of the corridor. It was Jack – with what looked like a body wrapped in a sofa cover across his shoulder. I reversed direction as soon as I saw him and limped as fast as I could back towards the storeroom. The first shot zipped past my head as I ducked inside, and I had only just thrown the lock when a second shot struck the door. After five more shots, without a single one penetrating the heavy wood, I heard the clatter of a dropped pistol and footsteps down the corridor. I opened the door to find I wasn't the only one. Heads were popping cautiously out of offices all the way down the corridor to see what was going on. I picked up the small pistol and traced the route Jack had taken in time to see him driving off in my Daimler, my driver lying on the ground, rubbing his jaw. Within a few seconds I was joined by two Special Library Service troopers.

'Where is he, ma'am?' asked the first.

I told them he was in my Daimler but that he'd be dumping it in less than ten minutes. The trooper nodded and barked some instructions into his walkie-talkie.

I retraced my steps and took the elevator back to the seventeenth. Duffy looked surprised when he saw me.

'You're okay?'

I showed him the tattoo on the back of my hand and pulled off the plaster on my neck to show a dry wound with a single stitch.

'It's me,' I said, '*really* me. What did he tell you?'

'That you had collapsed and he was taking you to the Lola Vavoom Discount Sofa Warehouse See Press For Details Memorial Hospital.'

'Wrapped in a sofa cover?'

'Yes, I thought it a bit strange.'

'He actually gave me one here,' I said, pointing to my forehead. 'Cancel my eleven o'clock and push my eleven thirty back half an hour. If Bunty can't be moved, put her in my two o'clock and bump who was going to be there until tomorrow. Yes?'

Duffy had been writing frantically.

'Right. But I don't think the Blyton fundamentalists will take kindly—'

'Ah-ha!' said a loud voice. 'Chief Librarian!'

I turned to see a middle-aged woman dressed in a tweed suit. She had a shock of grey hair poking from under a matching tweed hat, and a pair of silver pince-nez was attached to her lapel with a chain. She was also holding a large leather handbag and an umbrella, both of which could be lethal in the correct hands – and she looked as if she had the correct hands.

'I have been called away on sudden business,' I told her in the requisite tone, 'I will speak to you in an hour.'

'I shall not be ignored, Chief Librarian Next, 'she replied. 'My name is Mrs Hilly, and I think—'

'I have to be at the Adelphi. Good day.'

And I walked away. But Mrs Hilly wasn't going to take no for an answer, and because I couldn't move faster than her, she was going to be difficult to get rid of.

'I *am* coming with you,' she said, 'to make my opinions known.'

We were in the elevator by now.

'Listen,' I said, 'we will talk, but I need to be at the Adelphi five minutes ago and I'll be lucky to get a cab this time of day.'

'Then it is a good job I happen to have a car parked outside,' she replied. 'We're very upset about the way our Blyton's work has been revised and cut, mangled and rewritten. We will not rest, Miss Next, until her works are *exactly* as the author intended, with all whiffs of xenophobia, sexism and class-ridden references returned.'

'This isn't a library matter, Mrs Hilly,' I explained, 'it's for the publishers to decide.'

'They refuse to listen to us. They have even been so underhand as to issue restraining orders. No, we are petitioning for Class II Protected Book status.'

This was a new angle. If a book was given protected status, it was taken into the care of the League of Libraries, and crucially, no editorial changes would be allowed without express permission – the legislation was modelled on the law which protected old buildings. In fact, they even drafted it using the same text, only substituting the word 'book' for 'building'. It was a pleasingly economic approach to lawmaking, but sadly left a few passages open to interpretation, such as how a 'book might be considered derelict if it had no roof' and 'an owner might be prosecuted for allowing dry rot to develop'.

'We need one Regional Library Authority behind us to endorse our petition,' she said. 'We have chosen Wessex to stand up for what is right, good and fine in children's literature.'

We were outside by now and I noticed that the taxi rank was indeed empty.

'Well, we'll talk later,' I said, then added after having a thought, 'Is your car fast?'

'Very.'

She was right; it was a V8 Austin-Maserati, and it – and she – were *very* fast. Although the Swindon Adelphi was on the far side of the airship field, we were there in record time.

'I hope I'm not frightening you,' she said as we drifted sideways around the Oxford Road roundabout, leaving two strips of hot rubber on the road and a cloud of thick tyre smoke.

'Actually, no,' I replied, 'your driving reminds me of someone I once knew.'

We screeched to a halt outside the Swindon Adelphi, and I hurried inside after telling Mrs Hilly that I would accept a lift back – and would hear all her grievances. I went to the eighteenth floor, where I knew the suites were located, and found Phoebe in the lobby area outside the elevators.

'No armed back-up?' I asked.

'I was countermanded,' replied Phoebe. 'Anyone in the Goliath Top One Hundred is Protocol 684: not to be approached without a signed warrant from the Attorney General.'

This was quite true – Goliath had taken over the running of the police years ago. Phoebe could be here only because she was SpecOps, who were independent.

'I booked myself into Room 1802 down the hall,' she added, 'so as to have deniability in case this all turns nasty. I'm not losing the best job I'm likely to get the day after I'm offered it.'

'But you're here.'

'Yes,' she said with a sigh, 'I'm here.'

I thanked her, then asked which room Jack was booked into.

'The Dyson Suite, under the name of "Jacques Chitt". What do we do?'

'We go in. He said he was returning here and he's a day player, so technically a chimera, and can be destroyed on sight. But be warned: he's a Mk VIII and can think and move three times as fast as us.'

'What if he's *not* a chimera?'

'He is.'

'Yes, okay, but what if he's not? Killing a Goliath Top One Hundred would be a serious career downer.'

'If he's real, we don't kill him.'

'How can we tell?'

'Leave that up to me. But *if* he is the real one, he'll be in a coma, and we take him into custody and wait for him to wake up.'

'O-kay,' said Phoebe doubtfully. 'You can do the talking. I brought you this . . . and this.'

She handed me a navy blue ballistic vest with 'LIBRARIAN' written on the back in white letters. The other item was a revolver. I stared at it stupidly. I hadn't used anything but an automatic in over two decades.

'They never jam,' said Phoebe, pulling out her own weapon, a Webley top-break that looked as though her grandfather might have bequeathed it to her. 'A dodgy Walther gave me this.' She pointed at the ragged remnants of her ear. 'Ready?'

'Ready – but help me off this chair. This vest is heavy.'

Phoebe heaved me to my feet and we paced down the corridor

to the Dyson Suite. But before we could knock on the door it was opened – by Jack Schitt himself, dressed in an Adelphi monogrammed bathrobe. As soon as he saw that we were armed he put his hands in the air, and we all stared at one another. I could feel my finger tighten upon the trigger. If he'd twitched, I would have fired.

But he didn't.

'Hello, Thursday,' he said, 'how have you been?'

'Is he real?' asked Phoebe.

'Easy way to tell,' I replied. 'Day players are budget humans – anything not required for a simple twenty-four-hour existence is eliminated – he won't have an alimentary canal, or genitals.'

'Show us,' said Phoebe.

'I'm sorry?' said Jack.

'Open the bathrobe,' I said, 'and slowly. Phoebe – you look. I'm covering him for any tricky business.'

He stared at us both and very gently complied.

'Well,' said Phoebe, 'that looks a lot like a penis to me.'

I looked, then.

'Yes,' I conceded, 'I think you're right. His day player, that just killed my day player, must have just killed himself – and Jack is back.'

'You're making no sense,' said Jack. 'Can I cover myself up now?'

'Yes.'

'What's going on?' came a voice, and a woman's face hove into view behind Jack. She was also wearing a bathrobe, and covered a bare shoulder when she saw us.

'Keep your hands where I can see them!' yelled Phoebe and the woman wearily complied, as if this sort of thing happened to her a lot, which I knew for a fact it did.

'Is that you, Thursday?' she said.

'Hello, Flossie,' I replied, 'anyone else in the suite?'

'No. And why are you calling him Jack?'

'It's complicated.'

I told Schitt to step back, and while I kept the two of them covered, Phoebe checked the rest of the suite. It was quite large, so took more than just a cursory glance.

'Day players on the mainland?' said Jack with a creditable pretence of shock and outrage in his voice. 'How irresponsible do you think we are?'

'How long have you been back inside this body?' I asked. 'Five minutes?'

'We've been together all morning,' said Flossie, 'and I can assure you that the only body he's been inside during that time is—'

'Thank you, yes, I get the picture, Miss Buxton.'

'Nothing here,' said Phoebe as she returned. 'Just a suitcase and a Gravitube ticket from Karachi. Hey, Thursday, the suites here are *huge*. There's even a snooker room and the minibar has fourteen different types of water.'

'Are you sure? No coffin-sized Tupperware?'

'Well, let me go and look again,' she said sarcastically. 'I just might have missed one of *them*.'

She looked at me with an annoyed glare and I felt a bit, well, stupid.

'Mr Schitt,' Phoebe added, turning to Jack, 'we're *extremely* sorry for this intrusion upon your leisure time. We had a miscommunication but had to act at short notice – hence our lack of preparedness.'

'Polite of you, Officer—?'

'Detective Judith Trask – Swindon PD.'

Phoebe could lie well when she wanted to.

'Polite of you, Officer Trask. But I feel Thursday owes me the bigger apology.'

'I apologise unreservedly,' I said through clenched teeth. Jack was good – real good. He'd have had a Plan 'B' and most probably a Plan 'C', too.

'Then we'll say no more,' he said, staring intently at me without blinking, 'but heed my words: my sources tell me that you were designated NUT-4 in a recent appraisal: "Prone to strange and sustained delusional outbursts". If that is the case, then threatening a Goliath executive and making ridiculous claims about day players while demanding to see my genitals at gunpoint wouldn't go down very well in an official complaint, now, would it?'

'In that,' I said slowly, 'I think we are in complete agreement.'

'If anyone but you had done this, I would use my full powers to ensure the perpetrator was ruined personally and financially, not to mention enmeshed in suicidally wearisome litigation for the rest of their natural life. But I have Protocol 451 to consider and more important matters to deal with, such as an alternative plan to save Swindon owing to your daughter's failings.'

He paused to let this sink in.

'So we'll just forget this ever happened. Am I not magnanimous?'

I glared at him hotly and opened my mouth in order to make things worse. Luckily, Phoebe was there first, told Jack that we would most definitely leave him well alone, that we were terribly sorry for disturbing him, he was *truly* magnanimous, and took me by the arm. The door slammed shut behind us, and we quickly beat a retreat to the elevators.

'Damn,' I muttered as we walked back down the corridor, 'he's got it all sorted out.'

'You've got nothing,' said Phoebe. 'In fact, you've got less than nothing. 'So until you have, we're going to do *exactly* as he says. Who was Flossie, by the way?'

'Flossie Buxton,' I said. 'We were good friends at school. *Very* different career paths. Who's Judith Trask?'

'The first name that popped into my head,' she said with a shrug.

'I always use "Linda Cosgrove" when I'm in a sticky spot,' I said, thinking things over. 'Jack's day player must have died already – or maybe Flossie was a day player. Perhaps we should have checked her, too.'

I stopped walking, but Phoebe took my arm and steered me firmly towards the elevators. She pressed the call button and stared at me.

'Your friend Miss Buxton would doubtless say anything Jack asked her to. I think we were lucky to get away with our jobs.'

'If you want to be a Thursday,' I told her, 'being fired is very much an occupational hazard.'

'I heard that. I also heard a rumour that Goliath had SpecOps disbanded simply to get rid of you. And if that is the case, then you being fired had huge and very negative repercussions for law enforcement in general.'

I'd heard the rumour too.

'That was never proved,' I said. 'Besides – bollocks to them. I do what I do.'

'I've noticed. Asking to see a top Goliath executive's whatnot. I ask you.'

She shook her head at my audacity, and then started to giggle. I joined her at that point and we were so helpless with laughter that we dismissed the first lift and caught the second.

Suitably composed, I told Phoebe what had been going on as we descended to the lobby, and the admission from Jack's day player that they were stealing and destroying palimpsests because of something vaguely to do with asteroid HR-6984 – and that it was something that I put them up to.

'Really? Any idea what?'

'None at all. Lunch? I'm meeting Landen at the Happy Wok at one and it's only in Wanborough. I've got a Blyton fundamentalist stuck to me like glue, so she'll probably come too.'

'Mrs Hilly?'

'Met her?'

'She's been leaving messages on my phone. The Blyton Modernists apparently took umbrage at Mrs Hilly's demand that females in the books should be seen doing more cooking and cleaning, and threatened to "rough her up".'

'Then you've got something to talk about.'

'Gee, thanks.'

We walked out of the Adelphi, and Mrs Hilly pulled up in her Austin-Maserati. I introduced them to one another.

'Can I leave my car here and drive yours?' asked Phoebe with an eager gleam in her eye.

We made it to the Happy Wok in record time. Phoebe's driving was as fast as Mrs Hilly's, but a little less terrifying.

25

Wednesday: Blyton

> 'The Office For Ultimate Risk is one of the many departments within the Ministry of National Statistics, originally an "experimental" department. The statisticians at Ultimate Risk proved their worth by predicting the entire results of three football World Cups in succession, a finding that led to football being discontinued as a game, and the results being calculated instead. The Asteroid Strike Likelihood Committee is based within the department, and take thousands of factors into account when calculating the risk factor.'
>
> Dr S. A. Orbiter – *The Earthcrossers*

'Have you seen the news?' asked Landen when we were all seated about twenty minutes later, the three of us smelling of hot exhaust and burned rubber. I read the news story he had indicated on page four, sandwiched between an article suggesting which obscure illness would be most fashionable in the spring, and the best way to achieve the 'Neanderthal Look' then very much in vogue. It was about HR-6984: the Asteroid Strike Likelihood Committee had recalculated the possibility of a cataclysmic impact as up from 34 to 68 per cent, which was the first time it had gone above a 50:50 chance in ninety years.

'Was this to do with the ChronoGuard Destiny-Aware meeting last night?' I asked. 'I saw Mr Chowdry of the ASLC.'

'It seems so.'

'But none of the ex-potential employees were stated as actually dying *during* the strike,' I said, 'only *before* it – accident, murder, but none during the strike itself.'

'Good job too. If a single one *had* been killed by the asteroid, then the likelihood would have jumped even higher – perhaps to as much as ninety-eight per cent.'

'Has there been much panic over the figures?' I asked.

'I've been listening to the radio, but not much. Anyone over forty isn't worried because they'll probably be dead anyway by 2041, and to anyone under twenty, thirty-seven years is a time too long to comprehend. The middle group are jittery, but sanguine – after all, sixty-eight per cent is still a thirty-two per cent chance it won't happen, and as we've seen before, wishful thinking and being easily distracted are powerful evolutionary survival tools. Ooooh, look,' he added, his eyes scanning the menu, 'they've got a special on crispy duck.'

'Have you talked to Friday about the new figures?' I asked. 'After all, it's those blasted Letters of Destiny that have caused our chances to drop.'

'He says it all looks very dodgy, and not just from a mathematical point of view. I think he wants you to go with him to the old Kemble Timepark this afternoon.'

'Any idea why?'

'He said something about "inferring a narrative" from the Destiny-Aware letters, and no, I have no idea what it means either – but he seems very intent about it. He resigned his job this morning on the basis that he'll be in custody from Friday morning anyway.'

'Because he's going to murder Gavin Watkins?'

'Right. He thinks HR-6984 might have something to do with it, and how the potential future him was going to tackle the asteroid strike.'

'Ah.'

This was something that had been bothering Friday for a while. He knew vaguely that he would have saved the world numerous times from the various meetings he had with his future self over the years, but it was only when his summarisation papers arrived that he knew HR-6984's aversion would have been the first. His big test, so to speak – the apocalypse avoidance that made his name.

'Were you right to bring along Mrs Hilly?' asked Landen, indicating where Phoebe and Mrs Hilly were having an animated conversation on whether Noddy books could be viewed as 'classics' in the same way that *Huckleberry Finn* could be seen as a classic, and if so, whether it meant a 'Grade II Protected Book' status could be enforced.

'I had no choice,' I said, 'I needed a lift.'

'Ah. Do you want to share a crispy duck with me?'

'Yes, so long as you don't hog all the hoi sin.'

I told him about Jack's appearance that morning, and what had happened; about Jack having a day player of his own, about the palimpsests in St Zvlkx, that I'd be seeing Bunty Fairweather after lunch to see what 'Smote Solutions' was all about, and most importantly of all, about Krantz and how he was actually *helping* us, not trying to do us harm.

'Explain that again,' said Landen.

'Jack told me Krantz was a traitor to Goliath – but since no one can blab owing to an explosive brain implant, he instead brought five day players to Swindon in order to help me halt Goliath's plan – whatever that happens to be.'

'I get it,' said Landen, 'so where are we on the whole day player tally?'

'Krantz brought five with him, and there have been two of me and one of him. Two left. Him, me – not sure.'

We sat in silence for a moment, digesting what had happened. I took a sip of tea and asked Landen whether there was any news of Tuesday.

'She was sent home this morning for pulling Penny Smedley's hair and using "inappropriate" language to describe Mr Biggs, the games master. I asked her specifically whether she had been flashing for cash again and she said "no" in the sort of way that meant "yes", and then vanished into her laboratory.'

'So no breakthrough in understanding the Unentanglement Constant U_c?'

'None.'

'Blast.'

The meal arrived. Mrs Hilly had gone for the Swindon/Szechuan fusion menu, and had steak and chips dim sum followed by hot Fanta in a teapot. She took a small bite, and in the silence occasioned upon the table by our eating, launched into a carefully prepared diatribe.

'Enid Blyton was writing very much of her time,' she began, 'a time of sandwiches, fizzy drinks, English supremacy, endless summers, cranberry jelly and a firmly entrenched and highly workable class system that was the envy of the world.'

I stole a look at Phoebe, who shrugged.

'Everything was a lot simpler in those days,' continued Mrs Hilly, 'and the twisted and corrupting morals we see in modern life are but an aberration that we Blytonians aim to put right. By returning the books to their original and unsullied state before the heinous hand of political correctness trampled their true and guiding spirit, we will build a new England. One that smells of freshly baked bread and echoes with the sprightly call of rosy-cheeked farmer's wives, dispensing fresh milk from churns to children dressed in corduroy and summer dresses.'

She was in full flow by now. We had all stopped eating, and were staring at her. I think she mistook our shock as agreement, so carried on with even more gusto:

'To deny modern children the historical context of an age in which most foreigners were untrustworthy and women were useful only in the kitchen denies our children a realistic window into a bygone era that we should be promoting as an ideal to be cherished rather than a past to be improved and airbrushed.'

She stopped and smiled, then began to distribute leaflets that defined in more detail her Blyton-based political ideology.

It was true that Blyton books had been extensively revised over the years to accommodate shifting opinions, and it was also true that her books had been unfairly marked out as being a lot more offensive than they were – owing probably to a certain degree of intellectual snobbery and a fundamental misunderstanding of why they were written. The argument had raged for decades on either side, and culminated in the so-called 'Noddy Riots' of 1990, when the warring factions clashed on the streets of Canterbury, inflicting almost £6 million worth of damage and leaving six dead – not even the Marlowe/Shakespeare riots of 1967 had been that fierce.

'Let me get this totally straight,' I said. 'You don't want to just stop any more changes – you want to *return* the books to their pre-revisionist state and use them as a template for your view of a new and better England?'

'I couldn't have put it better myself,' she replied, beaming happily. 'A woman's place is definitely in the home, England functioned better when the working class knew their place, and foreigners are incorrigibly suspect. What do you think "fundamentalist" means in "Blyton fundamentalist"? In fact,' she went on, now in something of a lather, 'we aim to *reinterpret* and *enhance* the texts to more subtly export our own ultra-English worldview, and have even written a series of commentaries as to what Our Blyton *truly* meant when she penned her great works. It is our intention to run the nation according to this new and radicalised Word of Blyton – we will insist that England is returned to a world of perpetual summers, simplistic politics and the explusion of anyone who looks even vaguely foreign, and make the sacred words "gosh", "crikey" and "wizzo" a compulsory part of the English lexicon.'

Landen leaned towards me and whispered in my ear.

'What's Chinese for "fetch me a straitjacket"?

'Ssh. Well,' I began, 'here's my view as head of the Wessex All You Can Eat at Fatso's Drink Not Included Library Services: Enid Blyton's work is a force for good in children's literature because of its simple readability and exciting fundamental concepts of adventure and independence and the incontrovertible notion that adults are pretty useless and good only for supplying meals and calling the police. Yes, the books should be revised and modernised to more fully embrace modern society, and yes, they have shortcomings – but the fundamental truth about Blyton is that they get children into the habit of reading – and reading is a habit worth having. I utterly reject your proposals and your politics, and what's more, I think you're dangerously insane.'

The smiled dropped from Mrs Hilly's face.

'Modern life is not perfect,' I went on, 'but at least it attempts to reflect the tolerance of diversity and social inclusiveness that much of fifties England lacked. I will battle your every attempt to malign the books to suit your own twisted ideology.'

There was silence. We all stared at Mrs Hilly to see what she would say, and I saw Phoebe's hand move towards her pistol. When it came to fundamentalism, stakes were high.

'It's like that, is it?' said Mrs Hilly, standing up.

'Yes it is.'

'The Chief Librarian's role is non-political,' she warned me. 'We will petition Commander Hicks to have you removed at the soonest opportunity.'

'You may try,' I replied coolly, 'but his negative views on literary extremism are well known.'

We stared at one another for a few seconds.

'Then we have no more to say,' she said in a haughty tone of voice. 'You haven't heard the last of *me*. Good day.'

And she threw her napkin on the table.

'You haven't finished your dim sum,' said Landen.

And with an almighty 'hurrumph!' that rattled the windows and is still spoken of down at the Happy Wok, she was gone.

'That was a shame,' said Phoebe.

'I don't think it was a shame at all,' I said. 'Perverting the texts for their own political ends. I've a mind to make the Blyton fundamentalists a "banned association" within library boundaries, along with the paramilitary arm of the Anti-Farquitt Brigade and those idiots who like to dress as Zharkian stormtroopers.'

'No,' said Phoebe, 'I mean it was a shame because I was hoping for another go in her Austin-Maserati. I haven't had so much fun since I took my brother's Reliant-Bugatti Veyrobin for a burn up the M4 – great fun, although that single wheel at the front wobbles something dreadful when you hit 180 mph.'

'Wouldn't it have been more stable with the single wheel at the back?' I asked.

'One of the planet's greatest mysteries,' replied Phoebe. 'Mind you,' she added, 'I'd be wary of outlawing any group, especially Blyton fundamentalists. The "Make England a jolly sight more Blyton than Blyton" movement has several million members, and some of the Regional Library Authorities are sympathetic to their cause.'

'Do you want that hoi sin?' Landen asked me.

'No, you have it.'

My mobile buzzed in my pocket. It was Duffy, and I walked out of the restaurant, as etiquette dictated. They'd found my Daimler – or what was left of it, anyhow. It had been dumped outside a disused factory unit in Blunsdon and set on fire.

'They discovered two bodies inside,' he said, 'burned beyond recognition and smelling of hot nougat.'

It explained why Jack had been back in his own body so quickly.

I thanked him, then called Stig to tell him to get his Neanderthal butt over to the Daimler as soon as possible. They'd be very obviously synthetics, and I needed him to take possession before the police made them vanish as soon as they were cool enough to touch.

'News?' asked Phoebe when I got back in.

I told her what had happened, and she pulled a face.

'I knew Goliath were tricky,' she said, 'but not quite how tricky.'

'They're tricky squared,' I said, looking at my watch. 'Can we drop you back in town?'

Landen dropped Phoebe at the Adelphi to pick up her car, and we drove back into town in silence. I was relieved that this time I needed no help in forgetting to visit the tattooist – Landen forgot too.

26

Wednesday: Smote Solutions

> 'Early attempts to discharge the Stupidity Surplus were of a "theoretical" nature whereby dumb and idiotic parliamentary bills were enacted with little or no chance of being implemented owing to their self-apparent uselessness. Annoyingly, some were embraced by a citizenry who turned out to be "dumber than expected". The "Longitude Self-determination" bill was one example – it allowed individual regions to cede from cartographic convention and publish maps with their own meridian for local use. Sadly, this also permitted regions to insist on their own time zones as well.'
>
> *The Commonsense Party Stupidity Surplus Policy Explained*

Duffy looked at me nervously as I limped into the office. He had already replaced the sofa cover, and you wouldn't have known that only this morning an unlicensed non-evolutionary life-form had been dispatched in a violent manner.

'The only person I want to see is Bunty Fairweather,' I said as I walked in, 'and put the banning of the Blyton fundamentalists on the agenda for the Board of Governors' next meeting.'

Duffy coughed politely.

'There is no Board of Governors, Chief Librarian.'

'There isn't?'

'No – you wield absolute librarying power here in Wessex.'

'In that case: I ban Blyton fundamentalists from all Wessex library property.'

'Are you *totally* sure that's wise?' asked Duffy. 'They're a powerful lobby.'

I glared at him before sitting down at my desk.

'Very good,' said Duffy with obvious approval of my stance. 'Shall I send Miss Fairweather in straight away or wait a couple of minutes?'

'Straight away.'

Bunty Fairweather was a tall woman, for whom the words 'willowy' and 'pale' might have been invented. I knew her quite well, although we hadn't spoken for over a decade, when she was on the SpecOps complaints committee. It was a job in which she could have been difficult and vindictive, but she always played fair.

'Hello, Thursday,' she said brightly as we shook hands and I offered her a seat, 'congratulations on your appointment. Fed up with the carpet business?'

'I was attracted back to the literary world by the bright lights and good pay. You've done well for yourself. Last time we met you were adjudicating complaints against the department.'

'I've been at the council for almost eight years,' replied Bunty jovially. 'After my SpecOps liaison work, they thought I'd be best placed to deal with the mildly odder aspects of council work. At present I'm negotiating with the Swindon Meridian Society to try and stop them insisting on implementing a city-wide Swindon time zone.'

'I heard about that.'

This particularly fatuous idea had been in the news a lot recently, and would require everyone to set their watches seven minutes back when going into Swindon, then seven minutes forward when they came out. Luckily, the chief sponsors of the bill all lived in Liddington just outside Swindon, so they were given their own time zone in order to shut them up.

'It would cause chaos at Clary-Lamarr,' said Bunty, 'and set a dangerous precedent around the nation. So, what can I do for you? There's a limit to what we can discuss ahead of the budget meeting tomorrow. You do know I'm on Swindon City Council's Fiscal Planning Committee?'

'Yes – but I wanted to talk about Smote Solutions.'

She nodded her head approvingly.

'Good,' she replied, 'for there is much to discuss. I am also head of the city's Smiting Avoidance Team. It is my responsibility to ensure that people and property are safe from the mysterious yet destructive ways of our creator.'

'Do you want some coffee?'

'No thanks. The nation had been hoping the Anti-Smiting Defence Shield would offer some kind of defence by now but I understand there have been a few overruns.'

'She said it would take eight years,' I replied defensively, 'it's only been three so far.'

'No one's blaming your daughter, Thursday. We have to work with what we've got.'

'It's possible she may crack the software issue in time,' I said. 'The only stumbling block is finding a value for the Madeupion Unentanglement Constant.'

'What does that mean?'

'Something about acorns in Hertfordshire,' I said, thinking hard.

'Well, if she manages it then so much the better – Swindon would be a fine place for the Defence Shield to have its first success. But we can't leave it to chance. Now, Swindon's strike will be the tenth around the globe, and the previous nine have given Smote Solutions Inc. valuable experience in what to expect.'

I rubbed my leg.

'Do you mind if I walk around?' I said. 'I get the most excruciating pins and needles if I sit still for too long.'

'Not at all,' said Bunty, continuing from where she was perched on the sofa as I paced around the office.

'So let me get this straight,' I said, 'Smote Solutions is a company?'

'One backed by one of the pre-eminent tech companies in the world.'

'The Goliath Corporation?'

'Who else?'

'Go on.'

Bunty cleared her throat and launched into the subject using her best presentation voice.

'The nature of a smiting is pedantically identical on every occasion,' she said. 'A ground burst of a circular nature precisely fifteen hundred ancient cubits or half a mile in diameter, and centred on the biggest place of worship within the target area.'

'The cathedral?'

'No – the Bank of Goliath's fifty-seven storey Greed Tower.'

I looked out of the window to where we could easily see the glassy tower, framed between the traditional wonky spire of the cathedral and the Skylon.

She passed me a map with a circle drawn showing the area of potential destruction.

'As you can see, the "Absolute Zone of Smiting" takes in three of the skyscrapers in the financial centre, most of the cathedral, part of the croquet stadium, a four-hundred-yard section of railway track, two complete neighbourhoods, the sports centre, six shops, a launderette and a motorcycle dealership.'

'But the SpecOps building and the library are well outside the zone, yes?'

'Absolutely. Not even the Brunel Centre will be touched.'

I'd never seen a smiting but it was quite a show, apparently. Everyone would be watching it from a nearby hill. The parting of the clouds is an impressive precursor to the main event – a pillar of pulsating orange light the colour of a setting sun, and with sparkly bits firing off inside the column of fire. It's especially spectacular if it's raining: the water vaporises with faint popping noises like bubble-wrap, and you can get up to nine rainbows at once – all in different directions.

'Okay,' I said, 'so what's the plan? Evacuation?'

'*Total* evacuation within the zone of destruction, and for a hundred yards beyond it.'

This explained the lack of any large-scale evacuation plans from the council. A smiting was both hideously destructive but peculiarly precise – the Smiting Zone ends so abruptly that houses – people even – have been known to have been sliced clean in half.

'So we're going to lose the financial centre?'

'Not if we can help it,' said Bunty with a faint smile. 'The technicians at Smote Solutions have offered us an alternative to losing anything at all. They have a novel and proven method of luring a smiting *away* from a city.'

I stopped pacing around the room and stared at her. She was looking straight ahead, unwilling to catch my eye.

'What's the plan?'

'I'm not fully aware of the technique,' she said quietly, 'I am only here to organise evacuation policy in the city and I must respectfully demand that library staff be evacuated from the building an hour either side of the time of smiting. We're extending the evacuation zone.'

'Why?' I asked.

'As a precautionary measure.'

She gave me a memo outlining when we should evacuate the building, and where to. It was less rigorous than for the Smiting Zone downtown, but still quite large.

'You're not going to tell me any more, are you?' I asked.

'I'm sorry. The less people that know the better.'

'Fewer,' I said, 'the *fewer* people that know the better.'

'Right,' she said, 'well, I'll be off then.'

'How much?' I asked as she hurried out.

'How much what?'

'For Smote Solutions to fix the problem.'

'It's no secret,' she said, '£100 million. Considering the potential damage to property, it's a snip.'

'Goliath are like that,' I said sarcastically, 'magnanimous and generous to a fault.'

'If you were in our shoes you'd do the same, Thursday. They offer a solution, and we take it.'

'You can't trust them,' I said.

'We don't have a choice,' she replied pointedly, and she was right. I'd do exactly the same.

I saw her to the door and then walked through to Duffy's office where they all abruptly sat down. Like all good assistants, they had been listening at the door.

'Right,' I said, looking at the large map of Swindon stuck to the wall in their office, 'let's see what Bunty and Smote Solutions are up to.'

Duffy, Geraldine and I plotted the places that were listed on the memo's distribution list. There were about sixty in total, and it looked as though she was visiting companies and private residences in a swathe a half-mile wide leading from the financial centre towards Wroughton, a few miles south-south-east of the city. It looked like a corridor of sorts – and if Smote Solutions planned on luring the smiting away, it had to be drawn away to *somewhere*.

I tapped the map at the disused airfield at Wroughton.

'Something's going on here,' I muttered.

'Any idea what?' asked Duffy.

'None – but I aim to find out.'

'Chief Librarian?' said Lucy, the other assistant.

'Yes?'

'Your son is waiting in reception. About a trip to the Kemble Timepark.'

I told her to tell him I'd be straight down, then asked Duffy to cancel all appointments for the rest of the day. He looked faintly annoyed, but agreed – and then reiterated how important the budget meeting was the following morning.

'That's the one where we learn by how much our budget is cut?'

He nodded.

'Wouldn't miss it for anything.'

27

Wednesday: Wroughton

> 'The decidedly unsporty Griffin Sportina, like all cars built in the Welsh Socialist Republic, had a projected design life of a century, or five million miles. With a chassis designed for a dumper truck and bodywork of heavy-gauge steel, the car was almost indestructible – and heavy to drive. Newcomers to Sportina driving were excused for thinking there was steering lock on when there wasn't, and an hour of clutch and gearshift selection exceeded the Surgeon General's minimum daily exercise recommendations for a week.'
>
> Euan Lloyd – *Griffin Motors: Cars for Eternity*

'So why are heading up here?' asked Friday as we drove up and out of Wroughton village and towards the disused airfield.

'Goliath have a company named Smote Solutions, and I don't like the sound of them. We'll have a quick look and then do your thing over at the timepark. Is there something wrong with the gearbox? It's making a lot of noise.'

'It has to,' he said, 'or you'd be annoyed by the incessant whirring coming out of the back axle.'

Friday drove a Welsh-built 1967 Griffin Sportina. He loved it despite its many strange idiosyncrasies, such as a better drag coefficient when in rain, and the 'Pencoed' V8 engine that could run on anything from high-quality aviation spirit to powdered anthracite. Although the car had done over five hundred thousand miles, it was only just considered run in.

We topped the hill and came within site of the deserted airfield. I sank lower in my seat.

'Drive past the gates, slowly the first time.'

Friday did as I asked and I looked out of the window in a bored fashion so as to not attract attention. The front entrance of the disused airfield, usually just chained and padlocked, was being guarded by two Goliath security personnel. I tried to see what was happening on the airfield itself, but the land rose ahead of the runway, and it was difficult to see anything.

'Turn round and go past again,' I said.

'I'd prefer to find a roundabout,' he murmured. 'Only body-builders and former tank drivers attempt three-point turns in a Griffin.'

'Tank drivers? Then let me try, you great big soft baby, you.'

'You drove armoured personnel carriers,' said Friday, smiling, 'hardly the same thing.'

'It had tracks and a V12,' I said, 'so do as you're told or I'll stop doing your washing.'

'Okay, turning round.'

He didn't need to do a three-point as it turned out, as a gate was open to a field, and he drove in and began to turn the Sportina around in a large arc.

'Isn't that—?' I said, pointing to a car hidden from the road inside a clump of birch trees.

'Yes it is,' said Friday, 'Uncle Miles.'

We parked the Sportina next to Miles' car and climbed out. Initially, he seemed surprised to see us, but soon realised that if there was any Goliath mischief kicking around, then I'd doubtless be involved somewhere.

Miles Hawke had worked in SpecOps Tactical Support after a brief career in professional croquet. His midair roquet in the 1984 Superhoop was the high point of his career as he succumbed to a knee injury soon after. He and my brother Joffy hooked up in 1986 and were married two years later. He had resigned from SO-14 to help Joffy raise the Church of the Global Standard Deity from an obscure religious group to the world-dominating force it is today. Of course, this didn't mean that Miles was involved in the day-to-day running of GSD – he wasn't – he was simply support for Joffy, and looked after his partner's spiritual and emotional well-being. And on occasions like this, it seemed, he also did a bit of hands-on surveillance. SO-14 training can be useful.

We greeted Miles, and after exchanging pleasantries and the almost mandatory short conversation about the weather, I asked him how Smote Solutions intended to lure the smiting from Swindon.

He pointed at a camera that was attached to a tree branch high above us.

'I have an eye in the sky,' he said, 'take a look.'

He was holding a miniature flat-screen TV in his hand, and the camera above gave us a good view of the airfield. A good but *unremarkable* view of the airfield. Even when he remotely zoomed the camera it was quite unexciting – just a large marquee which had been set up right in the middle of the main runway.

'That's it?' I said.

'You don't actually need a marquee,' said Miles, 'but Goliath know full well that not even the *supremely* sinful will wait to be scoured from the face of the earth by a flash of energy without at least a choice of drink and a sports channel to watch.'

Friday understood first.

'Are you telling me,' he said, 'that Goliath aim to *divert* the smiting by having a few immoral people collected together?'

'It's precisely what they intend,' said Miles. 'When He has decided to undertake a smiting, it is only ever for one reason – to rid the earth of sin, and cleanse the land so the meek and righteous can walk free and unfettered by the dark shadows of the wayward. In technical terms, what this means is that the pillar of all-consuming fire can be swayed from its course by a point source of concentrated sinfulness. A television tube works on the same principle, but instead of having a beam of photons shifted by an electromagnet, you have a pillar of fire moved ever so slightly by an unrepentant axe murderer.'

'A single axe murderer is going to shift an entire pillar of fire?'

'No, you'll need more sinners than that – and we're not talking simply immoral people or even questionable thought crimes such as ox-coveting. No, we're talking about the big ones: murder, thievery and sadistic violence. And only in those who are evil beyond measure. The sort of people who are so twisted and degenerate they can *never* find redemption for their crimes.'

Miles spread a map of the local area out on the bonnet of his car. He had already drawn several circles and lines upon it, plus some simple geometry.

He pointed at his calculations.

'Since smitings originate at 100,000 feet, they need to deviate the ground burst by a little over four miles, or 13.2 degrees of arc. That will probably require eighteen mass murderers, six stranglers, five poisoners, sixteen conmen and eight career bank robbers.'

I stared at the screen again.

'Does England even have that many?'

'I think we're short on poisoners,' replied Miles, 'but France has a few they'll let Smote Solutions use, and I think "The Butcher of Naples" is being imported from Italy to make up the shortfall of axe murderers. Since Goliath run the prison service, they shouldn't have a problem getting them all together.'

'Do they know they're going to be vaporised in a sudden flash of God's wrath?' asked Friday.

'I don't think they'd take to it that kindly,' replied Miles. 'No, my guess is they're being brought here on the pretext of "outdoor rehabilitation" or "fresh air therapy" or some nonsense like that.'

'But that's . . . *murder*,' said Friday. 'They're in custody – doing time. They can't just be used as smiting bait.'

'I know,' said Miles, starting to pack his stuff up, 'it's wholly immoral, despite their crimes. Which really leaves us with only three options. One, Tuesday figures out the Unentanglement Constant between now and midday Friday and the anti-smiting shield functions as normal – the City Council save £100 million and the searing heat of His unbridled frustration at His creation's inability to stop its morally questionable behaviour is transferred into a useful 22.6 megawatts of electricity.'

'And option two?'

'We let Smote Solutions do their thing, and fifty-three irredeemable felons are vaporised for cash.'

Friday and I exchanged glances. No one likes axe murderers – not even their mothers, *if* they have survived – but as Friday had pointed out, the sinful were in custody. It would be like killing POWs. Murder.

'The third option is that we nobble Smote Solutions' plans, and allow much of downtown Swindon to be laid to waste.'

'It would be a shame to lose the cathedral,' I said, 'but it's less than fifteen years old and we could always build another. With almost six billion followers of varying enthusiasm, the GSD has certainly got some cash. And Goliath can certainly afford to rebuild the Greed Tower.'

'That's what we thought,' said Miles, as he folded up the map, 'and to be honest, we never liked the cathedral much anyway – too gloomy, and no provision for a canteen or wifi.'

'How *do* you nobble Smote Solutions?' asked Friday as Miles placed the TV screen, remote control and maps in the boot of his car.

'Simple,' he said, 'with a strategically placed Righteous Man.'

'A Righteous Man?'

'Or woman. It doesn't matter which. Find one of those and place them near the sinful and bingo – the Lord cannot smite the righteous on a matter of principle, so Goliath can kiss our arse and downtown gets a serious smiting instead.'

He looked at us both in turn.

'You don't know of any, do you? Righteous people, I mean. We've got a few pencilled in, but it never hurts to have a few more in reserve.'

'I know some *self-righteous* ones,' I said.

'That's not really the same thing at all.'

'What about you or Joffy?' I suggested. 'I don't know anyone more selfless than you two.'

'You're very gracious,' said Miles, 'but I killed two people when I was SO-14, and although Joffy is good and just and wise, I think he actually *enjoys* the possibility of having a round table with God to discuss the Ultimate Question of Existence.'

'The sin of pride?'

'Right. And he'll hide chocolate in the back of the fridge so only he can find it – something that a truly righteous man would never do. Besides, the Righteous Man has to be good in *all* known dimensions, since the Almighty is pan-dimensional. If our Righteous Man put a cat in a wheelie bin in Dimension FX-39, then His Great Omniscience would see it and *know*. And the problem with Joffy and me is that there are at least seventy-eight dimensions where our relationship is seen in the eyes of some to be a heinous sin almost as bad as murder.'

'You're kidding. Why?'

'Not a clue. But there are some seriously weird dimensions out there. Did you hear that Henshaw[F76+] had two heads?'

'Argued with himself, I heard.'

'Me too.'

'Where do you usually find Righteous Men?' asked Friday.

'There are a few professionals about, but Smote Solutions are smart – they've booked them for other jobs at the same time as the smiting: helping a lady across the road, being with someone at a difficult moment, reminding someone of the path, that sort of thing. Trivial, one might think, and easily cancelled for this job. Trouble is, a Righteous Man would never back out on an agreed appearance – and you can't offer them more money, because they won't take it.'

'And if they did, they wouldn't be righteous.'

'Exactly.'

I should have known there would be one or two snags.

'So as you can see, we should have a few subs in case of mishaps, just in case. But they're tricky to find as they don't draw attention to themselves, and would never volunteer themselves as righteous because they would never see themselves as such. Plus we have the usual problem of being swamped with volunteers, eager to promote themselves as righteous.'

'And all of whom can be instantly rejected for that very same reason.'

'Right.'

'Luckily for us, we've got a *seriously* righteous man lined up. He's a real pip – not even a shred of malice, ego or selfishness. Even a whiff of him will be enough to divert the stream of destruction away from the sinful.'

'Don't let Goliath find out,' I said.

'Don't worry,' he said with a smile, 'we've got him in a safe house where he is being looked after by semi-righteous people – who are in turn being protected by people who are quite happy to be not righteous at all when it comes to protecting the main guy.'

He gave a smile and climbed into his car, slammed the door and wound down the window.

'Give my love to Landen and Tuesday, won't you?' he said. 'And although I don't want to add any pressure, if Tuesday could find the value of U_c before midday on Friday, it would save a whole lot of uncertainty – and we can keep our Righteous Man in reserve for another time.'

'She's doing her best,' I said, 'but she *is* only sixteen. Most scientists don't start achieving this level of success before they are old, grey, cantankerous, forgetful and smelly.'

'I know,' said Miles, 'the planet's lucky to have her. Cheerio!'

He started the engine, and we waved as he drove off.

'So, Mum,' said Friday, 'the timepark?'

'The timepark.'

28

Wednesday: Kemble Timepark

> 'The C-90-F "Reverse Fluxgate" Time Engines, despite being shown to not work, still maintained a residual capacity to bend space-time and exhibit time dilation phenomena. Physicists had argued long and hard over the apparent contradictions, and concluded that time travel *might* exist in an entangled intermediate state of working and not working, with no apparent contradiction. In that respect time is very like a tiresome soap star: wayward, petulant and unpredictable.'
>
> Norman Scrunge, *time industry historian*

Kemble was situated about twelve miles to the north-west of Swindon. The 720-acre facility had been home to the Main Temporal Transport Device ever since the service was inaugurated in 1932 and had seen six different engines built on the site. The last ones had been the C-90-Fs, which had been used for only three years before being decommissioned. Since then, they had remained empty and abandoned, the massive seven-storey containment domes dominating the surroundings. The interior of the base was designated a no-go zone, but trespassing wasn't a problem. The hazardous nature of the timepark was well known, even to idiots with mischief on their minds.

'So,' I said as soon as we had made our way back on to the A419 and were heading north, 'why am I missing the Wingco's pizza evening to take a trip to visit the Kemble Timepark?'

'Here,' he said, handing me a folder. 'Shazza and I have been doing some research. We set up a bulletin board for anyone else who was now Destiny-Aware to make contact. Do you know how many people have done so?'

'First things first: how are you getting along with Shazza?'

Friday thought for a moment.

'Not *brilliantly*, but we're working on it. Trying to pre-kindle a spark that will make us inseparable soul mates in two decades' time is proving a bit tricky. I think she's a whiny foul-mouth with a victim mentality, while she thinks I'm an arrogant middle-class ponce with an attitude so patronising she would throttle me if it weren't illegal. We tried sex to see if that would cement the relationship, but it didn't help: she told me she'd "had better" and I told her that yelling out the titles of Tom Hanks movies was, well, *distracting*.'

'So not going too well?'

'No. And with less than forty-eight hours before I'm arrested, it's not likely to improve.'

'That might not happen. Besides, people have different needs at eighteen to when they're forty. And if those needs diverge, it can cause serious conflict. Probably accounts for break-ups. Your father and I didn't hook up properly until ten years after first going out. If we'd stayed together, we might not have survived. As it is, we're still very—'

'Mum, I'm going to stop you before you start getting all smushy about Dad.'

'All right,' I said with a smile, 'have it your own way. Do you want me to tell you how much I love you all too?'

'*Definitely* not. Look at the folder.'

'Okay. What were you saying?'

'I said that Shazza and I had set up a bulletin board for anyone else who had received career summaries from the Union of Federated Timeworkers. Do you know how many people have got in contact?'

'A thousand?' I suggested.

'One,' replied Friday, 'and he only missed the meeting because his car had a flat – he lived over in Bedwyn, on the other side of the Savernake.'

'That's unusual,' I said. 'The ChronoGuard must have employed several thousand from around here alone. What does it mean?'

'It means that only those timeworkers who were living in the Wessex area have received Letters of Destiny – more specifically, only those in the Swindon branch of the Timeworkers Union. But this is what's strange. It's a shitty thing to do. If I were my future self I wouldn't send myself a Letter of Destiny. So then I got to thinking that maybe there was another reason I did it.'

I looked at the folder he had given me. There were copies of all the letters. Two each per ex-potential worker – one of how it might have turned out, and one of how it would. There were copies of the envelopes, too, and several maps, cuttings and news reports about the disbanding of the ChronoGuard – it was big news when it happened two years before.

'What's on your mind?'

'Let me explain the scenario. You're head of the ChronoGuard, and entering your seventy-sixth year, one year from retirement. You can gaze happily back upon a long career maintaining the Standard History Eventline. You've defended its manipulation by the unscrupulous, and altered it to protect the citizens from mischief, asteroid collision and innumerable other menaces. You are happy that you have done what you could to keep the world safe, and that when you hand over the ropes to the next chief, the department will be in good shape.'

'Okay, I can see that.'

'Good. So this is what happens: everything, but *everything*, you've worked for is to be undone. Time travel is suddenly not possible, and owing to the demands of a failure in the reverse deficit engineering principle, all the Time Engines have to be switched off. It wouldn't be so bad if it was going to happen in 2062, the time of your retirement – but it's not. The switch-off will be retrospective from 2002. This is a worry, because the most dangerous event of all, the one that made your career, is slated for February of 2041.'

'HR-6984.'

'*Precisely*. Everything you would have been, everything you would have done, everything that made you what you were, will be erased. The Eventline is frozen. You're not allowed to send yourself a message, and worst of all, the disaster that made you is now going to happen because you weren't there to stop it. A single event with a potential seven billion lives at risk, all on your shoulders. What would you do?'

'Yell? Kick some furniture? Get seriously shit-faced?'

'Mum, I'm serious.'

'Sorry.'

'Yes, to begin with you could do all those things. But then, I got to thinking: what if there *was* a way to help the young me change the Eventline? How could I find a way to deliver a purposefully obscure message so I could do something about HR-6984?'

I smiled at my future son's resourcefulness.

'Let me guess: you made totally outrageous union demands.'

He nodded.

'I'm assuming this is the way it went: as chairman of the Swindon branch of the Federated Union of Timeworkers, I *insisted* on the Letters of Destiny. I probably had to pout a lot, get annoyed and chuck stuff around – even threaten strike action – but I got my way. The Eventlines were compared, the letters compiled and arrangements made for them to be sent.'

'Even if true,' I said, 'what were you trying to tell yourself?'

'I don't know, but none of us live beyond the asteroid strike. Of the fifteen who die, seven are definitely murdered, five meet with accidents that might be murder, and only three die of natural causes. Someone is disposing of ex-ChronoGuard *before* the strike.'

I stared at the list of murders. The first one wasn't to happen until 2040, almost thirty-six years from now.

'Makes it tricky to solve, doesn't it?' said Friday with a sigh. 'Crimes that haven't happened, motives that aren't yet apparent and perpetrators who may have no idea they're going to do it.'

'So what *do* you know?'

'I know three things for certain: I kill Gavin Watkins on Friday morning and a cold-blooded killer is murdering ex-ChronoGuard thirty-six years from now. We know nothing about him except that he might be driving a Vauxhall KP-16, a car which hasn't been designed yet, and is handy with a baseball bat.'

'And the third?'

Friday smiled.

'I know that someone posted these letters from a Kemble postbox only recently. Why wait until now to send the letters? The thing is, *someone* sent these letters – and whoever that might be could have an idea about what's going on.'

'Okay,' I said, 'I kind of understood that.'

Which was unusual, given the complex nature of the time industry.

We passed the 'Bad Time' warning signs seven miles from Kemble Timepark and drove slowly into the 'Mild Distortion' zone, where a certain temporal lumpiness punctuated the countryside. For the most part everything appeared normal, but the odd hot-spot of temporal fallout showed up as a patch of spring foliage when the rest was late summer, and even, on occasion, an isolated patch of snow. We noted that in several places the road had been diverted around hastily fenced-off anomalies. The hot-spots were quite obvious to the time-savvy – the shadows cast by the sun were bent either forward or back, depending on whether the anomaly was running fast or slow. We also noticed that the land within the zone was cultivated, but in a unique way: the emerging science of Agritemporal farming used the dilation gradients to ensure a rolling supply of ripe produce, as well as non-seasonal growth. In one field we saw a farmer driving a tractor while wearing a clumsy gravity suit. We waved, and he waved back seven seconds later.

We entered the village of Kemble soon afterwards. The township was neat and tidy, but several abandoned houses suggested that living here was not without its risks and frustration. The school had long since been closed and fenced off, the children now bussed to Cirencester, when a particularly steep gradient had seeped into the school one Friday afternoon, extending Mrs Auberge's French lesson from forty minutes to six days.

We stopped at the main gates of the abandoned facility. A small group of a dozen or so campaigners were camped out with several shabby-looking caravans, and placards had been tied to the fence. The first read 'Please would it be too much trouble to ask you to clean up our town' and the next: 'Villagers want assurances over real time if that's okay with you'. I'd seen these guys before, and knew of the protest. It was by local middle-class residents – hence the polite placards – who, despite assurances that the decommissioned Time Engines were 'perfectly safe within the broad definitions of "safe" as outlined by the Environmental Agency', had been collecting evidence of their own to the contrary. We parked the Sportina and climbed out.

We greeted the protesters, who were friendly and unthreatening, and listened to their complaints with interest. It seemed that the engines were leaking flux at an increasing rate and that 'no one was interested in doing anything about it'.

'What time do you have?' asked one of the group.

I told him and he showed me his watch. It was six minutes slow.

Five others showed me their watches too, and they all displayed errors between two minutes and six hours.

'Have you spoken to the decommissioning agents?' I asked.

'They ignore us,' he replied, 'or tacitly suggest that we should be grateful for living longer according to an outside observer.'

The account of other grievances was long and tedious – mostly about a little-understood phenomenon called *dilation lag* that prevented mobile phones and other transmission signals from being able to mesh.

'If we want to watch TV,' grumbled one, 'we have to go to Oaksey. The only radio stations we can pick up are those on AM, and the pitch of that is noticeably high.'

'Yes,' said another, 'I know for a fact that they're thinking of moving the Stroud–Swindon rail line six miles to the east. I understand that the train is now *always* three minutes late – they have to slow down when travelling past here to stay on schedule.'

'And house prices are tumbling,' said another. 'If I wanted to sell I'd have to accept half of what I paid for it.'

'And what did you pay for it?' I asked. 'Just out of interest.'

'A hundred pounds. They're dirt cheap because no one wants to live here.'

'We get occasional backflashes too,' said the fourth.

'And what did you pay for it?' I asked. 'Just out of interest.'

'A hundred pounds. They're cheap because no one wants to live here.'

'We get occasional backflashes too,' said the fourth, 'but we only know that from external observers. Ooh, look,' he added, pointing to a woman standing two hundred yards away who was waving a red flag, 'Lori says we've just had one.'

Most of their problems could be solved by simply moving away. None of the protesters were the original residents, who had all been compensated generously and had wisely moved out or taken up Agritemporal farming. We listened to them for just long enough to get their respect, but not so long that our ears started bleeding.

'Does anyone know who posted these?' asked Friday, holding up the fifteen envelopes when there was a lull in the conversation.

'Let me see,' said the one who seemed to be in charge. He examined the postmarks and passed them to a second man, who looked at them, nodded, then passed them back.

'That would have been the Manchild,' he said, nodding his head towards the disused facility. 'He made a rare appearance to post them.'

'Do you know why?'

'You'd have to ask him.'

'George!' said the first. 'You can't encourage people to go . . . in *there*.'

There followed an argument in which the more moderate members of the group thought it insane that anyone would go any closer than the thousand yards away we were at present, and some other members who thought we should do as we wanted, and then a third part of the group who didn't know what they wanted, but just liked to argue.

'Hang on,' said another, who had just noticed that Lori two hundred yards away was frantically waving a yellow flag. 'Gravity wave coming our way.'

And we hurriedly moved to the other side of the road as the wave moved past, bending the shadows cast by the fence as it went and drawing dirt and debris from the road closer to the fence.

'You don't want to meet the Manchild,' said one protester, whose name was Ken, 'he's—'

'Everyone should know what has happened here,' interrupted another. 'If you see him, take a picture so we can use his suffering to advance our own agenda – no, hang on, what I meant was: so we can get him the help he deserves.'

The arguing continued with increased vitriol until Friday said: 'I would have become the fifth Director General of ChronoGuard.'

The protesters all fell silent, and looked at one another nervously. When the leader spoke again it was in a quiet, respectful tone.

'You're going to need gravity suits.'

29

Wednesday: The Manchild

> 'The D-H87-B Mobile Localised Temporal Field Generator, colloquially known as a "gravity suit", was developed and built by Dover-Percival Aerospace, one of the main contractors for ancillary equipment to the time industry. The first suits were introduced in 1938 but were prone to leaks and malfunctions. They could only function at a limit of Dilation .32, and had a limited range owing to their clockwork mechanism. Later suits greatly improved upon this, and the D-H114 of 1978 was the last improvement upon the line and could increase the variable mass substrate to a staggering D=.88.'
>
> Norman Scrunge, *time industry historian*

They kept the gravity suits in the abandoned school, and we were measured precisely for size as an ill-fitting suit could give you 'old feet', which was not recommended. After we were weighed, had our density checked and then our centre of balance ascertained by lying on a tilting bed, we were helped into the hardshell suits after first removing anything of greater than bone density from our pockets. I'd worn a gravity suit once before, but a long time ago. It was when Dad was still at the ChronoGuard, before the regrettable Sarah Wade stretching incident brought the SO-12 'Bring a child to work' days to a rapid end.

The suits looked old and worn on the outside, but almost brand new on the inside, which was at least some comfort. Friday pointed out that the suits had been built in 1992 and had long surpassed their four-thousand-year design limit, but I simply shrugged. The Dilation level inside the facility was a life-frittering D=.31, and if we didn't wear gravity suits, we'd be lucky to get out within ten months. Once the suits were latched and tested for leaks, the helmets were secured in place and the power supply and life support units placed on our backs.

'Comfortable?' yelled the protester named George.

'Not at all,' I yelled back. 'Bloody heavy, in fact – I can hardly move.'

'Totally normal – it'll weigh less than nothing when they power up. Don't forget the Tachytalk™ intercom has a range of only forty-seven seconds, so don't stray too far from one another. The batteries will give you an hour's suit time at anything up to D=.5. Skirt any hot-spots and you'll get longer, but don't venture inside the main Engine Room – we think it's at D=.82 in there. You'll need these.'

He handed us each a whiteboard the size of a legal pad, and a marker pen.

'Okay?'

'Sort of.'

'Good. You'll feel a slight thump when you flip the switch, but wait until we get to a safe distance, won't you? Gravity suits have an eight per cent chance of explosive fragmentation on start-up.'

'Nice to know,' I murmured.

Friday and I exchanged glances, and smiled nervously at each other.

'Ready?' I asked.

'Ready,' he replied, and I turned my backpack towards him so he could switch it on.

The thump was anything but slight – more like seven idiots hitting you repeatedly all over the body with three-day-old baguettes. I felt the suit creak and flex as the variable mass substrate started to increase its unidirectional mass to offset any Dilation gradient outside the suit. Inside the helmet were a few gauges – one that

'Gravity suits have an eight per cent chance of explosive fragmentation on start-up.'

listed battery power, a second that was marked 'External Flux', which was broken, two that just blinked annoyingly, and an analogue clock with two second hands – a normal one, and one that rotated the dial once a second. There was an identical clock mounted *outside* the suit, and as soon as we powered up the clocks started to run out of synch. I gave a thumbs-up to the protesters and was delighted to find I could move a lot more easily in the suit than I could outside it, which was something of a relief as I wouldn't need my stick.

We waved to our new friends and walked across the road to the chain-link fence. We pushed open the gates and climbed aboard an electric crew cart designed for gravity suit use. The old car park was covered in dead leaves and other detritus, and as we trundled towards the administrative buildings almost a mile away, the asphalt became older as the Dilation gradient became more apparent. The closer we approached the source of the leaking flux, the older the surroundings became. As we moved in, the trees grew and the building decayed until by the time we reached the front entrance the paintwork was mottled and cracked, woodwork had rotted away and the internal steel within the concrete had begun to rust, spall and fracture, leaving large areas where the concrete had fallen away from the wall. As we stepped off the electric buggy, it almost corroded to dust beneath us.

'The building was only abandoned two years ago,' murmured Friday, sounding a lot like Jane Horrocks, one of the unavoidable consequences of the Tachytalk™ communication system. 'It looks like five decades have passed.'

We walked cautiously past a warning sign marked 'Warning: Steep T-Gradient' and the sun suddenly moved faster across the sky.

'I don't get it,' said Friday, 'are we in the future now?'

'Yes and no,' I replied, once more reinforcing the strange duality of time. 'If you equalise your suit,' I explained, pointing to the big red button marked PURGE on his chest, 'you'll stay at the out-suit time. If you walk back up the temporal gradient, we'll stay on in-suit time. Watch this.'

I stopped, turned round and took a few paces back in the direction we had come. There was a shuddering in the suit and my skin prickled as I walked back up the gradient. I turned back to Friday and asked whether he was okay.

He said he was, but I could see that his mouth wasn't moving when he spoke. I was talking to him as he was now, but *seeing* him as he would be in about thirty seconds. Conversely, he was hearing what I said now, but seeing me as I had been half a minute ago. As I watched, he drew a picture on his slate and then showed it to me. It was of an elephant.

'Want to see a neat trick?' I asked.

'Go on, then.'

'Draw something on your slate but don't show me what it is.'

'Okay.'

I waited a few seconds.

'It's an elephant,' I said.

'Okay,' he said, 'that was weird. How did you know?'

I walked back to him and as I drew closer I could hear his speech once more creep back into synch with his mouth.

'It's a simple demonstration of instantaneous communication across a Dilation gradient. A lot of the ChronoGuard's work was done using that very effect. I *saw* the picture of the elephant *after* you drew it, but spoke to you before you had.'

We stepped inside the main admin block as the sun set and the internal lights flickered on in the rapidly gathering dusk. Two years before there had been a staff of over six thousand working here, and everything had been left as it was when the building was abandoned – in one room we saw a map of Stalingrad, and in another were a pile of ancient Egyptian artefacts. Everything was old, decayed, dusty and corroded.

We pushed open some swing doors marked 'Maintenance' and entered a vast hangar full of large machine parts with overhead cranes. I'd seen something similar in a power station. The C-90 Time Engines had been a major engineering project.

'I know the time industry was shut down because it was deemed impossible,' said Friday as he looked around at the long-abandoned building, 'but it seems pretty credible from where I'm standing right now.'

'I don't think anyone ever truly understood it,' I replied. 'What's all this furniture doing here?'

A large section of the maintenance hangar was filled with old furniture loaded on to pallets. We walked on and came across about two dozen motor cars, all vintage, and all ageing quickly. The paint was beginning to crackle, and light corrosion marks were appearing on the chrome. As we stood there we saw a strange, misshapen figure stand momentarily in front of us, shaking and buzzing like one of those accelerated films of a plant growing. The next moment, I felt a tug at my sleeve and my whiteboard was suddenly propped on a reproduction Regency sideboard close by. It had writing on it:

What are you doing here?

I saw the odd-looking person flit past us and one of the cars vanished, only to be replaced by another. I rubbed the board clean and wrote:

Can we talk about stuff?

In an instant the whiteboard had been wiped and replaced by another message:

I'll be with you in twenty minutes.

And we saw the figure dash off again.

'He's running about four times faster than us,' said Friday, 'so about five minutes.'

'How did you figure that?' I asked. 'Comparing clocks, or an extrapolation of the Dilation gradient?'

'Neither,' he replied, 'he just looks like the VCR at home running at "4x" shuttle feature.'

'Very technical.'

But Friday was right. In a little over four minutes the Manchild appeared again, but this time he had brought a chair and sat patiently still so we could get a good look at him. He was indeed a Manchild – the left side of him was a boy of no more than ten, while the right side of him was a man approaching middle age. The two flowed into one another like hot wax, and his features were stretched sideways across his face, with one shoulder considerably lower than the other. To walk, his younger leg had a extension on the base of his shoe, which gave him a lilting gait.

'I was working here before we shut down the engines,' he explained in a voice that sounded like a speed-faulty tape player, 'as part of SO-12's legal team. I was down here to view the new C-90 engines when I tore my suit and suffered what's termed a "Progressive Negative Bilateral Aggregation". I was going to have a hard time explaining this, even *with* a new career history, so I decided to stay.'

'Will you be all right once the left side catches up?' asked Friday.

'You're going to have to speak quicker,' he said, 'I can't understand you.'

So Friday repeated himself as fast as he could, and the Manchild gave an odd sideways smile and chuckled.

'No,' he said, touching the child side of his head with his older hand, 'this side is getting *younger*. The left side of my mind is gradually reverting to that of a child's.'

'I'm sorry to hear that.'

He shrugged.

'Accidents happen. I'm just glad I didn't have what happened to Sarah Wade – and besides, being able to laugh in an uninhibited manner about poo and wee is really very liberating.'

'You sound vaguely normal,' said Friday, again as fast as he could, 'yet we're running four times slower than you.'

'I'm speaking very slowly for your benefit,' he said with a faint smile. 'I don't get many visitors. What do you think of our little enterprise?'

He made a jerky gesture in the direction of the hundreds of pieces of furniture.

'The craze for shabby chic,' he went on. 'People like stuff that looks old, but don't have the time to wait, and "distressed" stuff just doesn't look right, don't you think? I have a business called Age-Fast which specialises in making things old. It's the same with those sports cars. All those idiots who restored their cars to factory condition now realise that they've stolen their very soul – but down here I can put sixty years back on them in a little under a week. Nice patina although I do have to keep them rotated to avoid over-ageing one side. We have over a million bottles of whisky, too – twelve years in only three weeks. Vintage Chateau La Tour in six months? No problem. Wine, whisky, counterfeit Vermeers – we do the lot down here. I've seen the future, and it's old.'

'So the core really is running close to D=.82?' I asked.

'Two minutes in there is almost four months,' he said, 'and the gradient is getting steeper by the second. In thirty-seven years it should be about ready to pop.'

And he gave a soft, knowing chuckle.

'Who are you, anyway?' he asked.

'Thursday Next,' I said, 'and this is my son, Friday.'

'Ah,' he said, 'you must have come about the Letters of Destiny.'

Friday and I exchanged looks, and he asked the Manchild what he knew about them. It was, it transpired, just one of several jobs he had been asked to do after he had stayed on, but he didn't know why. All he had was a timescale to stick to, and instructions to pass them on if he became old, incapacitated or dead.

'There must be something you can tell us,' said Friday. 'I'm going to kill someone for no reason on Friday morning, and I need to know why.'

The Manchild blinked his mismatched eyes at him and thought for a few seconds.

'I saw you drawing an elephant earlier,' he said. 'Your mother was demonstrating a simple cause and effect reversal, yes?'

'Yes?'

'Okay, tell me this: who made the decision to make it an elephant? Thursday because she saw you draw it, or you, because you *did* draw it?'

We said nothing; there didn't seem to be an answer.

'The truth is that you both did, and neither of you did – which leaves only the drawn elephant, who seized an opportunity to exist through a chink in the tightly enmeshed cause and effect paradigm.'

'A drawn elephant has a desire to exist?'

'Certainly. All of everything came into existence simply because it wanted to be. The Big Bang wasn't so much a Big Bang but a hasty dash towards an opportunity to trade nothingness for somethingness. The main contributory factor to the entire universe was a momentary effect in need of a cause. And in that split second, everything that wanted to have existence – which is everything – came dashing through in one huge hot mass. They've been trying to sort themselves out ever since.'

'Kind of like a Harrods sale?' I suggested. 'When the doors suddenly open?'

'*Exactly* like that – only with six quintillion shoppers all trying to get to the knock-down perfume counter in a trillionth of a second – and through a garden hose.'

'I'm sure this is going somewhere,' said Friday, 'but I'm not sure where.'

'It's about cause and effect, and how the two can be separated and even entangled. Often it can become tricky to see which cause leads to which effect, or even which effect leads to which cause. And in cases like that, you need to let go, and do as your spirit guides you.'

'That's pretty deep,' said Friday.

'I have a lot of time to think,' said the Manchild, 'and a unique brain that can understand the complexity of the very simple. Oh-oh,' he sniggered, 'fart. *And* it'll be a stinky one.'

And after cracking one off in a childish manner, he giggled about it for several minutes.

'Right,' I said when he had recovered his composure, 'so Friday will kill Gavin?'

'He will and he won't. It'll work out, you'll see. You must have faith and remain true to the guiding principles within you. You didn't get to be the Director General of the ChronoGuard by luck – it was on account of your sense of justice, selflessness – and ability to gauge cause simply by viewing the effect. Not one in a trillion can do that.'

'I don't understand,' said Friday.

The Manchild rested his child's hand on his visor.

'You will, if only fleetingly. Sometimes we do our best work without even knowing it.'

'We've got to go,' I said, glancing at the battery indicator in my suit.

'I need to know more,' said Friday. 'How does this have anything to do with averting HR-6984?'

'*Everything*. You'll figure it out. Take a bottle of fourteen-year-old whisky with you and don't worry too much about prison – the alternative is unthinkable. The other fourteen will thank you – or won't, as it turns out. Oh well,' he added, 'time waits for no man, as they say.'

And he hobbled rapidly off. We watched him walk faster and faster as he moved past the cars and down the T-Gradient towards where the main Time Engines were located, before vanishing through some double doors.

We turned our backs and plodded painfully back towards the exit. I had badly underestimated the extra effort required to walk back up the Dilation gradient, and even with Friday helping me, it was slow going. We'd only got halfway across the car park when the power packs finally failed. We purged the suits and found ourselves five hours away. It took us only ten minutes to walk to the main gate and the demonstrators, but we lost another forty minutes in the process – it was now past ten o'clock at night. I was sweating buckets and had to be helped out of the suit, trying hard not to scream with the pain.

'How was the Manchild?' asked George.

'Good for another ten years – his time,' I said.

They all looked solemn.

'He said he wanted to be buried in the churchyard next to his mother,' said another of the villagers in a respectful tone. 'I'd best book a funeral for the spring.'

I called Landen on the landline to tell him we were okay, which was just as well as he was beginning to worry, and he reported that another St Zvlkx book had been vandalised in a private collection in Guildford. There had been two Special Library Service guards on duty supplied by the Surrey Bentalls Centre for All Your Shopping Needs Library Service, and they were now both in hospital – one on the critical list.

Friday and I recovered with tea and some especially baked scones, kindly prepared for us by the townsfolk, and we then headed back towards town.

'What did he mean,' said Friday after we had driven along in silence for ten minutes, 'about "sometimes we do our best work without even knowing it"?'

'I don't know, Sweetpea,' I said, already beginning to drift off to sleep. 'Why not sleep on it? I know I'm going to.'

I leaned my head against the door pillar, my leg feeling as though it were on fire. I tried to gather my thoughts about what had happened but it was too much effort and in an instant I was in deep, grateful slumber.

30

Wednesday: Dodo Buffer

> 'The first dodo to be brought back to life was in 1966, and this was the official start of the home cloning revolution. "Dodo 1A" lived a year before being dismantled for inspection, and the second dodo wasn't sequenced until 1971, as a precursor to the popular home cloning kit. A Dodo V1.2 made from a Genome Dynamics kit in early 1978 is the earliest still living, and the model has been steadily improving since then. The latest GD-V10 is a huge improvement upon early marks, and is able to undertake basic double-entry bookkeeping, and can be updated wirelessly through a home network.'
>
> *Haynes Dodo Manual*

I arrived home having slept for almost the entire journey in a hunched-up position, and was so stiff when I awoke that Friday had to heave me out of the passenger seat. He helped me for the first few steps until my leg had loosened up sufficiently for me to walk on my own. I noticed that one of the SLS troopers was standing on guard outside and the lights were still on in Tuesday's laboratory.

'How did it go?' asked Landen.

'Truly weird,' I said, 'but I could do with wearing a gravity suit more often. You can almost dance in them.'

I had something to eat and talked to Landen about the afternoon's fun at the timepark, and just how Smote Solutions planned to avert the cleansing. Landen already knew about this, as Miles had dropped around earlier in the evening to explain that, despite protracted negotiations and last-minute submissions by Joffy's team of top-class theologians and ethicists, God's winged tribunes had confirmed that the smiting would go ahead as planned. Joffy had apparently grown quite angry at this and announced that he would elect to remain in his cathedral during the smiting, there to be incinerated as a protest against the Lord's intransigence.

'You're kidding me,' I said, my heart falling.

'I'm afraid not,' said Landen, resting his hand on mine, 'but it could be a bluff.'

'It's not,' I said, taking a deep breath and rubbing my eyes wearily, 'it's not possible to bluff an all-seeing deity.'

'Well, it's put a cat among the pigeons. The Lord's people are all in a lather about it, and pleading with Joffy not to question His Will and Judgement.'

It didn't sound good, but then there were other possible outcomes to the event. Smote Solutions – and as an outside bet, Tuesday and her shield.

On the other hand, there had been some news about Aornis. Millon and the Wingco had traced the Alfa-Morris Spyder that Aornis got the lift from at Agutter Services. They had traced the car on motorway cameras all the way back to Swindon. Landen had asked them what she could have been up to and no one had a good answer.

'Does she have any family left in the city?' I asked.

'None that I know of. All the others are in prison or have moved away, and the Hades Family Mansion was given to the City Council to be used as a hospital.'

'She must be hiding *somewhere*. Somewhere we wouldn't think to look for her.'

'I know where she is!' said Landen quite suddenly.

'Where?'

'I had it for a moment,' he said, looking mildly confused, 'but it's gone.'

'Senior moment?'

He nodded.

'How did you get that bruise on your face?'

'I don't know,' he said, touching a purple area above his eye. 'I've got some cuts on my knuckles too. Did you drop into the tattooist's?'

'Forgot again.'

'Damn,' he said, 'we need to find out why you've got the tattoo on your hand, when it should be on Tuesday's.'

I stopped what I was doing suddenly.

'*What did you just say?*'

He repeated himself, and I felt a sense of rising panic. But then there was a thump outside the door, and when I investigated, a vase was lying on the carpet. I didn't believe in poltergeists, but just recently we'd been having all the hallmarks of one – things moving around, doors swinging open, that sort of thing. When I got back to Landen, he asked me whether anything was up, as I had looked alarmed when he told me about Tuesday's Mindworm.

'Nothing of any importance,' I said quietly, while having the oddest feeling that I was missing something very important; that there was something I hadn't seen, something vital just out of reach.

'But you're right,' I added, 'I did forget. *And* I passed the tattooist's three times today.'

And we sat there for a while in silence, mildly annoyed.

'You're back,' said the Wingco, who had popped his head round the door. 'I made some progress into my Dark Reading Matter project. Do you want to hear about it?'

'Are you distracting Tuesday from calculating the Unentanglement Constant? I've got a brother in line to be barbecued that I'm really not happy about.'

The Wingco had to admit that he might have – but that Tuesday often said that going away from a problem often made her fresher on her return, so it wasn't as much of a distraction as we thought.

'Go on, then,' I said, getting to my feet and walking with him down the hall to Tuesday's laboratory. 'Did the dodo idea work?'

'Quite well, actually – and don't worry, we didn't use Pickwick. We obtained a V3.2 called Daphne that was at a knock-down price at Pete and Dave's Dodo Emporium. The V10s are just in, so they're getting a few pre-owned in for part exchange.'

'I'm not sure I like the idea of pre-owned classic dodos being used for experimentation.'

'There are risks in everything,' said the Wingco with a shrug, 'and the Dark Reading Matter *is* important.'

We walked into Tuesday's laboratory to find her dozing in her armchair. She'd been working hard, and it was late. We were going to sneak back out but she jumped awake.

'Mum,' she said, 'it *worked*!'

I sat down in front of the screen as the Wingco told me what they had done.

'One of my Imaginary Childhood Friends was about to leave for the DRM as his host and creator was in the Daniel Street Home for the Almost Gone. The ICF was called Joey, and I convinced him to take Daphne with him when he went across.'

'Okay, let me get this straight in my mind. Imaginary Childhood Friends go to the DRM because they're like living fiction?'

'That's about it,' said the Wingco, 'but we think that *everything* that has been unrecorded within a deceased person's mind also transfers to the Dark Reading Matter. I think that's why the Dark Reading Matter is so big. It's not just books that have been destroyed, but is packed with *memories*. In fact, with seventy or so billion people having already died, the fabric of the DRM might be composed almost entirely of lost moments.'

'Lost moments? How many?'

'Lots – and I think they're packed quite tight.'

'Okay,' I said, somewhat dubiously, 'so where do we go from here?'

'Right,' said Tuesday, who was getting more excited, 'we took the Encephalovision to the Home for the Almost Gone and made sure it was tuned into Daphne the Dodo's cerebral buffer. At half past nine we got what we were after. The Imaginary Childhood Friend's host died, and Joey moved across, taking Daphne the dodo with him.'

'In the same way that I could once jump into the BookWorld with someone holding on to me?'

'Pretty much.'

'And?' I asked.

'We waited for a minute but . . . nothing. The Encephalovision simply showed static. But then, Daphne suffered an overload of sensory input, and her buffer started to fill. We started receiving pictures a minute after that. *These are the first images ever of the Dark Reading Matter!*'

Tuesday flipped a switch, and the playback began. At first it was it difficult to make out anything at all, but soon shapes started to form on the screen. Strange creatures that looked a lot like pepper pots with bumps all over their lower body, a domed head and a sink plunger sticking out in front.

'What are they?' I asked.

'We think they're Daleks,' said Tuesday, 'an early type.'

'You're saying the Dark Reading Matter is populated by Daleks?'

'No – we believe this might be a lost *Doctor Who* episode, from one of the master tapes wiped in the seventies.'

'Wiped because they didn't have room to store it?'

'Probably because it wasn't very good,' said the Wingco. 'It's possible the Dark Reading Matter might contain all forms of lost or discarded storytelling endeavour.'

'Or Daphne has a Dalek fixation. You know how obsessive dodos can be.'

'All too well,' said Tuesday, looking across at Pickwick, who was on the floor attempting to sort dust particles into their various colours, 'but it wasn't only Daleks. Watch the rest.'

So I did, and in those seven minutes of buffered dodo thoughts we observed what appeared to be several half-completed buildings, and then a woman hunting tortoises, apparently alone on an island. But just as it was getting interesting, the vision feed cut off and the images were gone.

'That's it,' said the Wingco, 'we won't get any more.'

'It's not conclusive,' I said, 'but the reference to the tortoise hunting sounds like Melville's *Norfolk Isle and the Chola Widow*.'

'That's not lost,' observed the Wingco.

'No, but *The Isle of the Cross* is most definitely lost, and it was often assumed the survivor might have been a reworking of the lost original. It's not a hundred per cent proof, but it's the closest so far to establishing that the Dark Reading Matter exists. Write it all up and get a report over to Commander Bradshaw as soon as you can.'

It was an interesting development, but I had too much on my mind to be either excited or worried about it, and saw it simply as an ongoing part of my continued interest in the BookWorld, even though I hadn't been able to read myself into the BookWorld since my accident. It wasn't simply being physically well enough to cross the barrier between the real and the read, but the mental concentration required.

I ordered Tuesday to her room to get some sleep, kissed her goodnight and then walked upstairs to my bedroom.

'I wonder if I could read myself into the BookWorld while a day player?' I mused as I brushed my hair.

'With a brain like that, I'd be seriously surprised if you couldn't.'

* * *

I read until I fell asleep and slept soundly until I woke quite suddenly at four in the morning, thinking I had heard a noise. I went downstairs to find the TV and the lights on, then made myself a sandwich and some hot chocolate and watched a rerun of *The Streets of Wootton Bassett*, which was every bit as bad as I remembered.

But the odd thing was, even though I'd made myself a sandwich and a hot chocolate, I couldn't remember consuming them, yet they were gone – so I made myself some more.

I didn't sleep after that, and was still awake when *The Early Breakfast Show with Adrian Lush* came on at 5 a.m. I threw my shoe at the television, but missed.

31

Thursday: Budget

> 'Budget meetings have never been interesting, ever, despite numerous attempts over the years to try to josh them up. Notable uplifting techniques involved the use of fire-eaters and performing elephants, but it didn't work. The dry proceedings are well known to bring on a form of tired lethargy that can stay for the rest of the week, and "Budget Therapy" was used with great success in the treatment of patients suffering an excess of good-natured perkiness.'
>
> Randolph Moles – *Modern Living*

'You don't look very well,' said Duffy.

I was sitting at my desk, head down on the cool walnut surface, my temples throbbing as though fit to burst. I was tired, annoyed, frustrated, and my leg hurt badly.

'I don't *feel* very well,' I answered.

'Can I get you anything?' he asked. 'Painkillers or something?'

'It won't work. I've got so many patches stuck on my arse my cheeks look like a couple of shrink-wrapped turkeys.'

I was silent for a moment.

'Duffy,' I said, face still resting on the cool desktop, 'I need someone to go and score me some stronger painkillers. Not the stuff you get in chemists' or from doctors – the sort you buy in a pub car park at night from a guy named Nobby who pretends he's your best mate.'

Duffy gave a polite cough.

'Commander Hicks is here, ma'am.'

I looked up to see that, yes, Braxton *was* here, and presumably must have heard my attempt to coerce my subordinates into scoring illegal patches on my behalf.

'It's the pain talking,' I said quickly, 'I wasn't serious. What I really need is a new body – and that's not as daft as you might imagine. Are you here for the meeting?'

He nodded and placed a copy of his budget proposal on my desk. It looked suspiciously thin.

'How's the job going, Thursday?' he asked, somewhat ominously.

'I got shot at yesterday morning. Mrs Hilly of the Blyton Fundamentalist Movement has made death threats, and Colonel Wexler of the SLS is none too pleased that I won't sanction dawn raids for overdue books.'

'Librarying is a harder profession than the public realise,' he said. 'People think it's all rubber stamps, knowing that Dewey 521 is Celestial Mechanics and saying: "Try looking under fiction" sixty-eight times a day.'

'I was an assistant librarian when at uni,' I told him. 'The Dewey system stays with you *forever*.'

'Listen,' said Braxton, suddenly becoming more serious, 'I want you to know that despite what happens in there, I'm on your side.'

This sounded even more ominous.

'What *is* going to happen in there?'

'I'm on your side,' he repeated, 'just remember that. See you in there.'

He left to go through to the boardroom and I heaved myself to my feet, wincing badly.

'Want a hand?' said Duffy, who was at my side.

'I'll be fine. The muscles work, it's the ragged nerve endings that are giving me hell.'

'What did Braxton mean by him "being on your side"?'

'Don't know. Now, let's kick some budget butt.'

* * *

The boardroom was down the corridor from my office, and I was stopped just outside by Phoebe, who looked agitated.

'Can I have a word?' she said. 'It's important.'

'Okay.'

I told Duffy I'd only be a moment and moved a little way up the corridor.

'So what's up?'

Phoebe looked left and right and lowered her voice.

'I'm thinking of killing Jack Schitt during the budget meeting.'

'We favour reasoned debate.'

'It's not about the budget. It's about Judith. Judith Trask.'

'*Who?*'

'The name I gave Jack when he asked me at the Adelphi. Judith Trask.'

'You mean it *wasn't* a fake name?'

'No,' said Phoebe, her eyes wide with shock and the enormity of what had happened. I felt my heart fall, too.

'He killed her?'

'*Someone* did. Judith's name was the first that popped into my head. She's not even an active SpecOps agent – simply a logistics officer at SO-31. An accountant. Someone took her out at the junction of Goddard and Mill. She was married and had two children.'

'Okay,' I said, having come across this sort of thing before, 'firstly, that might not be Jack Schitt in there. Secondly, when you want to take on Goliath, you play the long game. Promise me you'll do nothing.'

She looked at me.

'But—'

'Promise me. If you want to be like me, this is one thing you have to do.'

Her shoulders slumped.

'I promise.'

'Good. We'll talk later.'

I patted her arm and walked into the boardroom.

It was a large room with one wall entirely glazed so there was a somewhat precipitous view to the main lending floor five storeys below. Settled neatly in a recessed alcove at one end of the room was a bust of Andrew Carnegie, and at the other end of the room was another of Sir Thomas Bodley. Everyone was there when I arrived, but was yet to be seated. Jack Schitt caught my eye immediately and we stared at each other. I was wondering whether he was real or synthetic, and he was doubtless wondering the same about me.

'Good morning,' I said as I lumbered to my seat. 'I'm Thursday Parke-Laine-Next, the new Wessex Region Chief Librarian. We'll run around the room briefly for anyone unfamiliar with who is present. On my left, Regional SpecOps Commander Braxton Hicks.'

He nodded a greeting to the room, but everyone knew who he was.

'Next to him is the newly appointed Divisional Chief of SO-27, Phoebe Smalls.'

She nodded a greeting and ignored Jack's patronising stare.

'Next to Miss Smalls is Mr Jack Schitt, who is representing Goliath while Mr Lupton Cornball is on . . . other duties. Just what are those duties, Mr Schitt?'

Jack Schitt looked at me and smiled, then addressed the room.

'Mr Cornball is currently liaising with the City Council and Goliath subsidiary company Smote Solutions to spare Swindon's downtown from the scheduled smiting tomorrow.'

'And how do they plan to do that, Mr Schitt?'

He stared at me for a moment. Using convicted felons to avert a smiting would not be popular, even if they were axe murderers. It would be a sorry return to those dark, barbaric days when nations actually executed their own citizens. Jack looked at me and smiled.

'We have engaged the services of convicted felons, who have agreed to be vaporised in order that property be saved. Their considerable fee – over a million pounds per man – will be paid to their dependants and families as well as victims, if any are living. I would like to stress that this is entirely voluntary, and we will be erecting a marble tablet for those who sacrificed everything to bring about the saving of Swindon's valuable architectural heritage.'

That didn't go *quite* how I planned it. Miles hadn't said they were volunteers. I looked around the table, and everyone nodded sagely at the felons' selfless sacrifice. One of the city councillors wiped her eyes with a handkerchief.

'Right,' I said, 'sitting next to Mr Schitt is Mrs Bunty Fairweather of the City Council, and her assistant, Mr Banerjee. Next to them is the Wessex Library Services' chief accountant Conrad Spoons, and Colonel Wexler of the SLS is sitting next to him.'

I had the six others introduce themselves as I wasn't sure who they were, then ended by explaining that Geraldine would be taking the minutes, and that we could drop the 'Fatso's' part of the Wessex Library Services title, as we needed to be done by midday.

First up was Conrad Spoons, and he outlined in a drab monotone the annual budget of the Wessex Library Services, beginning with the current and projected running costs, and then outlining his plans for capital expenditure. I was quite glad when Duffy sneaked into the room to whisper in my ear that Miles wanted to have a quick word.

'Carry on,' I said, making for the door, 'I'll be back soon.'

I found Miles in the corridor.

'Is Jack Schitt in there?' he asked.

'Maybe yes, maybe no. I haven't made up my mind yet.'

'Eh?'

'Never mind. Did you hear the felons up at Wroughton actually *agreed* to be vaporised in exchange for some cash for their victims and family?'

'That's a lie,' said Miles. 'Goliath don't give money to anyone, *especially* axe murderers. Besides, such an act of self-sacrifice would show considerable empathy and remorse, and that could engender a limited form of absolution – they would hardly be effective at all in drawing the fire from Swindon.'

Miles' argument rang true – *never* believe anything Goliath say.

'What are you here for anyway?' I asked. 'I'm in a really boring budget meeting but it's kind of important.'

'*They nobbled him!*'

'Nobbled who? Joffy?'

'No – our Righteous Man. Goliath managed to infiltrate our defences and after forty minutes of careful argument, succeeded in persuading our man to pursue a life of hedonistic self-destruction. He's currently down at a lap-dancing bar getting plastered and running up gambling debts while eating delicacies made from panda's ears.'

'That was quick work.'

'Smote Solutions have a team of dedicated debasers, specially trained to darken and pervert even the purest mind. If someone has a weakness, they'll find it. Our man's weakness was liquorice, and once they knew that, it was a short hop to a life of immoral excess.'

'So what do we do now?' I asked.

Miles looked around and lowered his voice.

'We thought this might happen, so we kept a Righteous Man in reserve – just in case. But since we've obviously got a mole at the GSD blabbing stuff to Goliath, we need someone we can trust to bring him in. Someone with guile, cunning and resourcefulness.'

'You want *me* to bring him in?'

'No, we wanted you to ask Phoebe Smalls for us. Just kidding. Yes, of *course* we want you to do it.'

I tried to tell him I was in no fit state to do anything, and he said that all I would have to do was escort the Righteous Man up to Wroughton and get him to within twenty yards of the felons at midday on Friday. It seemed easy enough, so I agreed. He then said he would contact me tomorrow morning with an address, and left.

I was about to go back in when Duffy stopped me.

'Lucy got this from a guy loitering near the bins.'

It was a sticky patch about the size of a Post-it, upon which was printed a smiley face.

'Nice work,' I said, pulling up my shirt so he could stick it on my lower back. 'Not a word to Braxton about this.'

'Sorry about that,' I said as I walked back into the boardroom. 'Where have we got to?'

'We were just talking about the Special Library Service's budgetary requirements for next year,' said Colonel Wexler, 'and extra staffing levels if we are to implement dawn raids for overdue books.'

'Is there a legal framework for that?' I asked.

'Indeed there is,' said Conrad Spoons. 'The Library Act of 1923 specifically states that a library may do everything in its power to retrieve its property.'

'And I'll need funding for an indoor water cannon,' continued Wexler. 'The riot over Mr Colwyn Baye's new book nearly got out of hand.'

'The SLS should be under the jurisdiction of SO-27,' said Phoebe Smalls, 'so their budget should be transferred across to me. That is, of course, unless you have any objection?'

'Not at all,' said Colonel Wexler. 'My duties will remain the same, yes?'

'Pretty much.'

'Will I be able to lead dawn raids for overdue books?'

'Dawn raids, certainly. Not sure about overdue books – that will be outside our mandate.'

'Oh,' said Wexler, mildly disappointed.

Braxton confirmed that switching the Special Library Service to SO-27 made a lot of sense, and also that this was a good time to outline just how much of the Wessex Library budget should be transferred to SO-27, and he suggested as a starting point £50 million, about a third of our current budget. I looked at Conrad Spoons and he nodded. Without the policing budget, we could concentrate on core library activities, such as lending, the pursuit of knowledge and Finisterre's antiquarian book section.

While this had been going on I had been looking occasionally at Jack Schitt. Something about him seemed different, and since I knew that if he was a synthetic he'd have lightning reactions, I slipped off my shoe and lobbed it at him.

'Ow!' he said as it hit him a glancing blow on the forehead.

'Thursday, what on earth are you doing?' said Braxton.

'I thought I saw a mouse,' I said somewhat stupidly, and apologised to Jack, who seemed himself after all. He glared at me and I shrugged. After my shoe had been returned, the meeting continued.

'Perhaps,' said Conrad Spoons, 'we could ask the City Council whether any extra cash will be given to the Wessex Library Services in order to fund the additional collections of books made available to us from the closure of the Lobsterhood?'

'Well,' said Bunty, 'this is an *excellent* opportunity for us to go through what we think is correct for the fiscal year 2004/05, and at the same time peg the funding for the next ten years.'

'Yes?' I said, for Duffy had walked in again and moved to whisper in my ear.

'Your son is on the phone.'

'What? Tell him I'll call him back.'

'He says it's *most* urgent.'

'Sorry,' I said, getting to my feet again, 'another emergency. Family or something.'

Duffy told me the call had come through to my office, so I went through to take it. It meant I could stretch my legs, too.

'This had better be good,' I said into the phone, 'I'm right in the middle of a budget meeting.'

'Sorry, Mum, but it's about something the Manchild said. I didn't give it much thought at the time, and it doesn't make sense.'

'*Nothing* he said made sense. Which part? About the beginning of the existence, or who first thought about the elephant?'

'Neither. He told me not to worry about prison and the other fourteen will thank me – *or won't as it turns out*. Do you see?'

'No.'

'They won't thank me because their murders won't happen and no one will ever know they were going to happen. I'm going to change all their futures. Don't you see? Gavin's the killer, but has no idea he will be. I murder him, and everyone gets to live normal lives.'

'Hmm,' I said, 'it's kind of a stretch – and besides, you can't kill him for something he won't even *think* about doing for another thirty-six years, no matter how unpleasant he is.'

'There's something in what you say.'

'Wait a minute,' I said, 'the Manchild told you that "the other fourteen will thank you"?'

'Yes?'

'But it's not fourteen, is it? With Gavin dead and you not thanking yourself, only *thirteen* could thank you. The Manchild sent the letters so he must have known how many there were, and that means—'

'There were *sixteen* letters sent, not fifteen,' said Friday.

'Right,' I replied, 'there's someone else Destiny-Aware in Swindon, and they've decided not to come forward. Don't kill anyone or anything until you find out who they are.'

'Hang on,' he said, 'I'm just writing myself a note. Don't . . . kill . . . anyone. Got it.'

He told me he was going to see the Manchild again, and I told him to be very careful, adding that if he *insisted* on going to the timepark he should take one of Landen's home-made Cheddars and get the Manchild to age it for a year.

I returned to the boardroom and sat down.

'My apologies,' I said, 'teenage sons and their problems. Tch! What are we to do? Why are you all staring at me?'

'You'd better tell her,' said Phoebe to Conrad Spoons.

'Why me?' said Conrad.

'Because you're our accountant?' I said.

He stood up, took a deep breath, and began.

'The City Council has reallocated to SO-27 *more* than Miss Smalls asked for,' said Conrad. 'Funding has been reduced across the board and includes – but is not limited to – a cut on new books, staffing, maintenance, research and staff perks.'

'We could always lose the Michelin-starred chef, I suppose,' I said. 'What are the numbers?'

'Hang on,' said Spoons, going through his hastily written calculations. 'Okay, here it is: this year's Wessex Library budget was £156 million, *all* of which goes to SO-27. The Wessex Library operating budget for next year will be . . . £321.67.'

I stared at him for a moment.

'That *must* be a mistake.'

Spoons looked at the figures again.

'Sorry,' he said, 'you're right. It's £322.67.'

It wasn't quite the level of mistake I was hoping for. At this rate I'd have to ask a hundred million times to make a difference, and I didn't think that was going to happen. I looked around the table. Jack Schitt had a supercilious half-grin on his face, and Braxton and Phoebe were looking elsewhere. Colonel Wexler was unconcerned, since her budget had not been affected in any way. Mrs Fairweather was the only one returning my stare.

'That's ridiculous,' I said, 'you can't stop all funding. That's just, well, *insane*.'

'Not insane,' said Mrs Fairweather, '*stupid*. There's a big difference, and Swindon City Council are taking the stupidity deficit issue very seriously – we have to meet our stupidity targets just like any other, and cutting all funding to the Wessex Library Services is an act of such astonishing idiocy that we need commit no additional dumb acts for at least five years. You should be honoured that your department is discharging the surplus for the rest of us. It's going to be hard, and we're all in this together.'

'Commander,' I said, addressing Braxton, 'you told me when I took this job I had an operating budget of £156 million. Okay, I understand SO-27 will have to take some of that as we relinquish security duties, but—'

'I didn't lie,' said Braxton, 'you do have that for this year – it's *next* year we're seeing reductions.'

I suddenly had a nasty thought.

'When does the new financial year begin?'

'Midnight on Sunday,' replied Spoons, 'four days away.'

'That figures,' I said, glancing at Jack Schitt, 'and how long will £322.67 keep us going?'

'I thought you might ask,' said Conrad, checking his notepad. 'If we assume a £100 million budget *without* Colonel Wexler and the SLS, £322 equates to about one minute and forty-two seconds. If we cut everything to the bone and only buy seven books next year, we might stretch that same £322 to last eight minutes and nine seconds.'

'What about if we lose the Michelin-starred chef?'

He checked his notes.

'Eight minutes and *twelve* seconds.'

'So let me get this straight,' I said, 'come Monday morning there won't be any libraries open in Wessex at all?'

'Not a single one,' said Mrs Fairweather, 'but don't take it personally. To make this even more idiotic, you'll receive a final salary pension after less than a week's work, and a hefty bonus for surpassing your own Stupidity Target.'

There was silence in the room. I asked whether there was anything I could do about this, and was told there wasn't. This was a done deal, probably agreed well before any of us had entered the room, and with Goliath's connivance.

'Okay,' I said slowly, 'any other business?'

Astonishingly, there wasn't.

'Then I call this meeting adjourned.'

Everyone got up and left. Phoebe and Braxton apologised to me and said that they didn't like it either, but it was out of their hands. Conrad Spoons shrugged at me across the table and said he was off to the jobcentre and would be back in an hour if there was nothing suitable available.

'I'll be here Monday,' said Duffy, 'and every day you need me until I collapse from starvation.'

'Me too,' added Geraldine, 'although I'll probably last longer than Mr Duffy as I'm carrying a little extra weight at the moment.'

I gathered them closer so the others couldn't hear.

'I appreciate the loyalty, guys. Does the library have anything to sell? Spare books or Finisterre's Tiltrotor or a private airship or something?'

'The books are owned by the nation,' said Duffy, 'but we'll have a look at everything else. What are you thinking of? A garage sale?'

'Pretty much. For breathing space. See what you can find.'

They told me they would and filed out, leaving only myself and Jack Schitt in the room.

'Well,' I said, 'did that meet all your expectations?'

'Surpassed them, old girl,' he said. 'I wonder what the press will make of your generous pension and bonus?'

'This is all your doing, isn't it?'

'Of course! Do you think for one moment I would pass up on an opportunity to cause trouble for you?'

'Protocol 451 really has been cancelled, hasn't it?'

'Most definitely. Call this partial payback for the trouble you've caused us over the years. I hate to kick an old dog when they're down, but we knew you'd have blunted teeth one day. I'm just glad I lived long enough to see it.'

'I'm glad to see you've lost none of your charm, Jack. But these teeth aren't as blunt as you think.'

'Look at you,' he sneered, 'a shambling wreck, sent out to grass as a librarian. Believe me, my girl, you are well and truly blunted.'

I stared at him, my anger rising. Not because of his taunts, but because he was probably *right*.

'Now,' he continued, 'I want you to take me downstairs to see your friend Finisterre. I need to look at some St Zvlkx books, and as Chief Librarian, you have access to the vaults.'

I felt my heart sink.

'You're another day player, aren't you?'

'I could have ducked the shoe,' he said with a smile, 'but I purposely chose not to in the quarter of a second it took to leave your hand and arrive at my head. I love being a better me. So strong, so smart, so *perfect*. Do you know the cube root of seventeen?'

'It must have slipped my mind.'

'I do. It's 2.57128159. Do you want the next seventy-two decimal places?'

But I had more important things on my mind.

'Why did you have Judith Trask killed?' I asked. 'She was innocent of everything.'

'To show your youthful protégée that lying to a Top One Hundred is not to be tolerated, and that actions have consequences. Phoebe Smalls has trouble stamped all over her. Now, take me downstairs to the vaults.'

'I'll not help you, Jack.'

'I think you will. If you don't, I will pick you up and throw you through that window.'

He indicated the glass panel that led to a five-storey drop on to the main lending floor.

'You'd land somewhere between the books of Helen Fielding and that author with the beard whose name I can never remember.'

'I have problems with his name too. Think you can get out of the building without being seen?'

'Already taken care of, girl. Look there.'

He pointed at a figure dressed in identical clothes walking towards the exit. The figure stopped for a moment and looked up. It was Jack Schitt – or a copy, at any rate.

'The real you?'

'No, I'm in a coma at present, that was just a standard Mk. Va "Alibi" model. By the time anyone got up here following your fatal fall, I would have zipped myself up in a body bag and hidden in the roof space just behind the water tank. I'd probably not be discovered for years. The point is that with the "through the window" plan you'd be dead, and I'd be in the clear to try another method to get to the vaults. From my position it's win-half-win, and from yours it's lose-lose. So think again.'

I did. In fact, I *desperately* tried to think up a plan of action. I would probably be able to get to my gun since he was on the other side of the room, but then I realised with a sinking heart that he probably already had it. He guessed my thoughts and showed me the revolver he had lifted from me earlier.

'I took it from you when you entered. And don't even *think* about going for the Beretta on your ankle. I can have you through the window before you get even halfway there.'

He was doubtless right, and the situation was looking increasingly desperate. But just at that moment, I suddenly felt *different*. My leg was no longer hurting me – in fact, I felt no pain at all, and a warm feeling of euphoria swept over me. I felt better, stronger and fitter, and even some of those feelings for Landen, too. I must have been replaced during one of the two interludes out of the boardroom – probably when on the phone to Friday. Knowing that changed the game plan. I would be as fast as Jack and get at least three shots off before he'd even touched me – and all the shots would make the same entry hole, even if he was moving. I was *that* good.

I made a swift lunge for the Beretta in my ankle holster.

It didn't quite work out the way I'd planned. The limited mobility in my back and leg stopped my hand four inches from the pistol, and I misjudged the position of the table on the way down, and hit my forehead. Momentarily off balance, I grabbed the chair behind me, which had castors and slid away from me, causing me to lose my balance completely and collapse in an undignified heap on the floor.

'Shit,' I said, glancing at the Mindworm tattoo on the back of my hand for confirmation, 'I'm still me.'

Jack had watched the pathetic spectacle and simply walked up, took the Beretta from my ankle and then dragged me to my feet by the scruff of the neck and pressed my face hard against the glass.

'Are you an idiot or something?' he demanded angrily, his sickly-sweet breath hot on my face. 'Why are you taking such foolhardy risks in the face of such overwhelming odds?'

I didn't know either, until everything started to change colour and I heard birds singing.

'Oops,' I said, 'my PA gave me an illegal patch from some guy loitering near the bins.'

'You are a sad, pathetic little creature,' said Jack, 'and I pity you. Now: we're going to the vaults. If you don't, I'll make sure that it's not just you who suffers, but your family too – even the imaginary ones.'

'Hang on,' I said, trying to reach my smiley patch to pull it off, but failing since they're buggers to get off when you've just stuck one on, 'would you mind?'

He ripped it off but it didn't hurt. Nothing did, in fact.

'My hands have gone numb,' I said with a giggle, 'and my tongue feels too big.'

'Come on,' he said as he handed me my stick and pushed me to the door, 'and make it convincing if anyone talks to us.'

We met Duffy in the corridor outside, although I had to *assume* it was Duffy as his head looked more like a jack-o'-lantern.

'I've got a list of things we could possibly sell,' he said, 'and your husband is on the line to remind you not to miss Tuesday's keynote address at MadCon 2004 at two.'

'I'll call him back,' I said. 'Mr Schitt is being shown the antiquarian section.'

I was going to add some semi-ambiguous statement that would alert Duffy to what was going on so he would in turn alert Colonel Wexler, but it was difficult to concentrate with a Haysi Fantayzee track going around in my head full volume, and in a moment Duffy was gone.

'Which way?' said Jack.

'That way,' I said, pointing down the corridor, 'first left after the lizards.'

32

Thursday: Finisterre

> 'The Brotherhood of Perpetual Defenestration were a small order of pious monks who threw themselves out of their abbey window twice a day following prayers. The reason for this curious custom is not recorded, but the order supplied stuntmen to the theatre and film industry for over seven decades. A popular tourist attraction for over three centuries, the brotherhood might be with us still but for a poorly conceived move to the eighth storey of a town building, and the order was extinguished in under an hour.'
>
> Fairfax Rearwind – *Vanished Religious Orders of the British Archipelago*

We took the elevator to the sub-basement and stepped out into the same small security cubicle I had visited two days ago with Finisterre. A different guard was staring at us from behind the glass, and he smiled when he saw me.

'Good morning, Chief Librarian.'

'Shiny shiny,' I muttered, 'bad times behind me.'

'I'm sorry?'

Jack tightened his grip on my arm, which, while not actually painful, made me at least realise he was serious, and sobered me up. The patch was gone, but its effects would be with me for a while.

'Nothing.'

I licked my finger and placed it in the DNA tester. The green light flashed and the door swung open.

'So easy, isn't it?' said Jack as we walked down the corridor. 'I always say it's not what you know, but who you know . . . you can bully.'

We walked down the corridor, past the glazed display cases I had seen earlier, and into the main conservation room. Finisterre was there, but no one else. I could sense Jack's suspicions.

'Where is everyone?'

'It's lunch,' I said, then giggled out loud.

'Are you okay?' asked James.

'Yes,' I replied as soberly as I could. 'I've got something odd in my bloodstream that generates inappropriate responses. This is Jack Schitt, the Goliath rep. He wants to vandalise our St Zvlkx codices.'

James looked at Jack, who stared back impassively. Finisterre wouldn't be armed, but day player Jack would know that already from the way James's clothes hung on his body.

'He was the guy at the Lobsterhood on Tuesday?' asked Finisterre, still staring at Jack but addressing me.

'In a manner of speaking. He's ruthless,' I added, 'and has no fear of death or pain. I recommend you do as he asks.'

'These are my children,' replied Finisterre, indicating the shelves of old books, 'and I would die to protect them.'

'Noble,' replied Jack, 'but in war as in literature, we have to sacrifice our babies.'

There was a pause, and I noticed Finisterre's eyes flick to something behind us. Jack saw it too, and drew and fired in one smooth movement *without looking or turning around*. The guard didn't even make a sound as he fell, and I looked at Finisterre, who swallowed nervously. He *did* love his books, but after due consideration was decidedly *not* willing to die for them.

'Which book are you after?' he asked.

'It was a thirteenth-century bestseller,' replied Jack. '*Zvlkx's Brothels of Dorset on Sixpence a Day*.'

Finisterre looked momentarily confused.

'You'd kill someone for *that*?'

'I'd kill someone for fun, Mr Finisterre.'

'Well, you're going to have to be disappointed. We haven't got a copy.'

'It's awaiting cataloguing,' replied Jack confidently, 'from the library of the now-extinct Brotherhood of Perpetual Defenestration. I have good intelligence.'

Neither Finisterre nor I moved. I could feel my head clearing, and my hands were a little less numb. In five minutes I'd be useless, and not *utterly* useless as I was at present.

'Listen,' said Jack, taking a pair of cutters from his pocket, 'it's very, very simple. I'll remove your fingers one joint at a time until I get what I want. How many fingers and how much pain do you think a Zvlkx codex is worth?'

He was right, in an odd sort of way. *Brothels of Dorset on Sixpence a Day* was not rare; it could be bought in any antiquarian bookstore for about £500, more if it had salacious margin notes and 'interesting' staining.

'Take it,' I said, 'and leave.'

'I'm so glad you're seeing it my way at last,' he said. 'Mr Finisterre, lead the way.'

We walked over to the other side of the room, where the books awaited cataloguing. The Brotherhood of Perpetual Defenestration's small collection was lying in a cardboard box on one side of the copying table, and as soon as Jack saw this, his mood changed abruptly.

'What is this?' he demanded, indicating the flatbed scanner used by the library to copy all works.

'We copy all books,' said Finisterre while rummaging in the cardboard box for the book. He found it, eventually – a sad, tired and very well-thumbed book, the racier pages darkened by seven centuries of surreptitious titillation. This would be a copy that would barely make £200, even on eBay.

'Has it been copied?' asked Jack, and I looked at the records.

'Yes,' I replied, 'this morning.'

'Where would the copy be?' he asked angrily.

'Uploaded to our server, two floors down.'

'Anywhere else?'

'Zurich,' I replied. 'Our servers are backed up every hour.'

'Son of a bitch,' he muttered, 'that was a waste of time.'

He took a deep breath.

'Then again,' he added, 'I could kill the pair of you – at least then the morning wouldn't be a total loss.'

I think he would have done it, too, but just as he raised his gun arm there was a sound like a melon exploding and James and myself were spattered with the contents of the day player's head.

We stood in silence for some moments, and I picked off a scrap of bone fragment that had landed on my upper lip.

'That,' said Phoebe, who had appeared at the other end of the vault, 'was for Judith Trask.'

She walked up and tapped the headless corpse. Those old top-break revolvers carry a fearsome punch. She handed me her gun and badge.

'Arrest me, Thursday – I should stand trial for murder.'

'You didn't murder anyone,' I told her. 'It'll take more than that to avenge Trask. But I'll tell you this now, I'm grateful you did what you did.'

They both looked at me, then at the corpse, which was starting to ooze an unnatural yellowish liquid from the top of its spine.

'What in hell's name is that?' said Finisterre.

'It's a kind of temporary satellite consciousness,' I said in a soft voice as I felt a tingling return to my leg. 'Let me explain.'

I told them what a day player was, and how Jack Schitt would be back at his suite at the Adelphi right now. Phoebe apologised for disbelieving me, and after we had discussed it at length, I called

Stig to alert him that we had another non-evolved life-form for collection. And while the colonel secured the scene, Finisterre and I cleaned ourselves as best as we could with a box of wet-wipes.

'So why did he lose interest once he knew *Brothels of Dorset on Sixpence a Day* had been copied?' asked Phoebe when we had explained to her what had happened.

'No idea.'

Finisterre was busy looking through the small volume.

'What palimpsest was he after?' I asked.

'We can find out,' said James, 'by using multispectral filming, and by superimposing the images we should be able to view each palimpsest and identify the source of every single reused page in the book. Some recycled pages will have been well washed and scraped, others less so. And the comparing of the palimpsests with known works that Zvlkx bought in bulk will take some time. I suggest dismembering the book and having several teams working on it until we find something.'

'Like what?'

'Something we don't expect to find. I'm thinking perhaps a book of peculiar rarity and importance made it into Zvlkx's rebinding factory – and that those pages made their way into random copies of his books.'

'Then we should get started right now,' murmured Phoebe, who seemed relieved that she wasn't going to be arrested for murder after all.

I told them to call me when they had *anything*, and left them to it.

John Duffy was waiting for me back up in my office. I borrowed some spare clothes from the lost property bin and went to have a shower to emerge refreshed twenty minutes later wearing a tweed skirt, mismatched socks and a large Swindon Mallets sweatshirt, something that Conrad Spoons found unaccountably funny when I returned to the office.

They were busy inventorying what the Wessex Library Services actually owned, and had found about £2.4 million worth of cars, vans, two Tiltrotors and 40,000 date stamps that had been ordered in error.

'How much time will £2.4 million buy us?' I asked.

'About a week.'

'It's a start. Anything to give us some breathing space. Duffy?'

I beckoned him over and he asked me what I needed.

'Keep this quiet, but did Lucy score any more of those patches?'

'Ten, I think – she was thinking of selling them around the office and making enough profit to buy a new car.'

'Get me another one and a pair of scissors, will you? I think a half might be just about perfect.'

'Are you certain?'

'Never been more so.'

Duffy did as I asked, and a few minutes later I headed off for MadCon 2004.

33

Thursday: MadCon 2004

'MadCon is a contraction of the ironically titled 'Mad Scientists' Convention', so named because of the derision which heralded the inaugural event in 1931. The co-founder of MadCon was Mycroft Next, who attended every meeting in the Swindon Convention Centre that now bears his name, and eventually won the prestigious Lifetime Achievement Award in 1988. The event caters for those interested in outlandish scientific ideas, and despite being shunned by the conventional scientific community, MadCon continues to deliver top-class science to the world.'

Francine Grooper – *On the Edges of Science*

The Mycroft Next Convention Centre main hall was huge, noisy, and filled with people. But despite this being MadCon, it was populated not just by insane scientists working on the very edge of accepted rules of physics and mathematics, but also journalists, industrialists, private equity firms and conventional scientists in disguise, all eager to see what the deranged geniuses among the scientific community were up to. There were many trade stands, too, manned by both oddball and respected scientific foundations that wanted to help bring bizarre and seemingly impossible ideas to the marketplace.

There was an hour to go before Tuesday's keynote speech, so I made my way slowly towards the stage at the far end of the Convention Centre. The Anti-Smiting Strategic Defence Shield Corporation was here in force, hoping to sell the technology to other nations that might also have cause to attract the Lord's ire owing to some misdemeanour of their own. I passed by the large Goliath stand, which was this year promoting the idea of home-grown donor organs with zips for easy transplanting, or, for the more budget conscious, externally worn organs that could be used on a 'timeshare' basis. Beyond Goliath was someone peddling intelligent string to wrap up parcels unaided, and for self-tying shoelaces. After that there was the stand of a tech firm that had designed a joke compression standard which would allow gags to be encoded digitally, stored and then played back with no loss of nuance, subtlety or humour – even after thousands of years.

'Once we can successfully synthesise gags,' said one of their reps as I stopped for a moment, 'we'll have found another industry that the digital revolution can destroy for no reason other than it can. We're calling the compression standard "JAPEG".'

He passed me a sheet of paper. It read:

```
20<run joke/chestnut/musichall/dog_no_nose.jok>
30<jokeclass=setup><pete> 'I say I say I say,
  My dog's got no nose'</setup></pete>
40<jokeclass=retort><dave> 'How does he Smell?'
  </retort></dave>
45<IF recipient=humour (ODD) GOTO 55 if
  recipient=humour(CONVENTIONAL), GOTO 50>
50<jokeclass=punchline><pete> 'Terrible.'
  </punchline></pete>
52<GOTO 60>
55<jokeclass=Alt Punchline><pete> 'He can't
  smell <pause=.8 sec> he has no nose.' </
  punchline></pete>
60<IF laughter=1 GOTO <joke/chestnut/musichall/
  wife/westindies.jok> IF laughter=0 GOTO 65>
65<end joke>
```

A few stands farther on was a tech start-up company hoping to solve all our energy problems by inducing power from the sun's magnetic field via a 100,000-mile tether being towed behind a space station anchored gravitationally at Lagrange One. The power would then be transported to Earth by a high-powered laser with a transfer efficiency of 1.3 per cent – not impressive, but still powerful enough to cater for three-fifths of the Earth's electrical needs.

'Would you like to take a leaflet?' asked an eager young man. I told him 'no thanks' and walked next to a group of tech companies that were adapting ancillary time technologies to assist modern living. I noted that Age-Fast had a trade stand here with one of their perfectly weathered Jaguar XK120s in pride of place.

Next door to them, and still on the same theme, was a company marketing the *Dilatorvator*, a fridge that kept food fresh by simply slowing down time.

'The interior of the storage unit will age only two seconds every week,' explained the promoter. 'A fresh steak will last four centuries – and at room temperature. Food storage problems are finally solved for ever. And when our Photon Dilatorvator is perfected, we really mean for ever.'

I hurried on, trying not to be distracted, and had almost reached the stage when I came across a stand that was manned by someone of more immediate interest – Mr Chowdry, Swindon's Asteroid Strike Likelihood Committee rep.

I walked up and introduced myself to Mr Chowdry, who was a tall man with a kindly manner and a soft voice that sounded like the E string on a double bass.

'Tell me,' I said, 'how do you calculate the Ultimate Risk Factor for events like HR-6984?'

'I have little to do with the *actual* calculation,' admitted Mr Chowdry. 'I simply feed in relevant details. Longevity projections of the Destiny-Aware were of huge assistance. Since we have no one who lives past February of 2041, the destruction looks more and more likely. In fact,' he added, 'we've just updated our forecast this morning. The likelihood of a fiery end has jumped from yesterday's sixty-eight to eighty-one per cent.'

'Why?'

'Several reasons. Pension applications have dropped off, and there has been a significant jump in the number of endowment policies planned to mature one year before the strike.'

It looked as if people were beginning to get worried after all, but then they usually did when the Likelihood Index rose. I suddenly had a thought.

'But surely,' I ventured, as maths was not my strong point, 'the fact that people are making provision for our end can't actually raise the possibility itself?'

'*Classical* probability theory would exclude human expectation from the result,' said Mr Chowdry in a quiet voice, 'but *Expectation Influenced Probability Theory* postulates that the observer can and will affect the outcome of events purely by the weight of their own expectations. If enough people believe that HR-6984 will miss, then the Eventline will bend to ensure that it does – similarly, if we all believe that we're going to die in a fiery cataclysmic event, we shall.'

I stared at him for a moment. The notion seemed, well, counter-intuitive.

'I know the Eventline *can* be changed,' I said, 'but I always thought our intervention was limited to things we could physically alter thanks to choice and free will – not a chunk of rock the size of the Isle of Wight travelling through space at 42,000 mph.'

Mr Chowdry thought for a moment.

'Take your brother Joffy and the Church of the Global Standard Deity as a case in point. For the past thousand years the existence or non-existence of God has bobbed around the thirty-two per cent mark, given the multitude faith dilution. Once all the major religions were joined together the likelihood of His existence jumped to over eighty per cent – and what happened?'

'He revealed himself,' I said in a quiet voice.

'Right,' said Chowdry, 'and once all the atheists were on board He began all this smiting. Without faith He is nothing. But with faith, He is *everything*, and in this context "everything" means real, dangerous, vengeful – and unknowable.'

'Is this proven?' I asked.

'Not at all,' replied Mr Chowdry, 'Expectation Influenced Probability Theory is right on the edge of accepted mathematics. You should get over to the stage if you want to hear your daughter talk.'

I thanked Mr Chowdry for his candour and walked away. If I had understood it correctly, the asteroid wouldn't hit if we didn't think it would. The trouble was, we thought very much that it would. To turn around the 81 per cent we needed something to change people's minds – like some sort of proof, or failing that, *doubt*.

I pushed these thoughts to the back of my mind and headed towards the stage, where I could see Landen standing at the side with Tuesday chewing her nails. Most of the five hundred seats had now been filled, and those unlucky enough to have been having a quick sandwich or a pee or something were standing at the back.

'You made it, Mum!' said Tuesday, giving me a joyfully nervous hug. 'But where's Jenny? Dad said she'd be with you.'

I thought quickly.

'She's with Gran and Polly.'

'They said they wouldn't be here.'

'They changed their minds. I was just talking to Mr Chowdry about Expectation Influenced Probability Theory. Does that make any sense to you?'

'It should do,' she replied, 'I invented it. It's a sweet theory because it's obligingly self-proving and fits in nicely with the human psyche. It will prove itself correct, because we want it to. Why are you dressed like that?'

'I got covered in . . . actually, it doesn't matter. You look terrific. Ready?'

She pulled a face and crossed both fingers. She looked more like a schoolgirl about to give her first flute solo, rather than the twenty-sixth finest mind on the planet about to address her peers.

'Good afternoon, ladies and gentlemen,' said the compere, who had just walked on to the stage, 'and welcome to Day One of MadCon 2004.'

There was a burst of applause and the compere went on to welcome everyone to the conference, then there was five minutes of boring stuff about where the fire exits were in case someone tried to blow something up, or create a white hole or a Small Bang or something, and then a list of the high points of the conference, such as tomorrow's demonstration of AA-size 'Duraspin' Kinetic Batteries, a new form of copperless copper and how earthquakes could be harnessed to prevent earthquakes. He started to ramble after this and I lost interest. I was pondering Jack Schitt's curious behaviour regarding the copied Zvlkx book when the compere suddenly announced:

'Ladies and gentlemen, it gives me great pleasure to call on . . . Tuesday Next!'

There was more applause and Tuesday walked nervously on to the stage.

'It is a great honour to be here,' she began, 'speaking at a conference that my great-uncle loved so much and devoted so much energy to. I'd like first to thank the staff of MadCon, and the board of trustees for their generous help in . . .'

I moved closer to Landen and grasped his hand, and he squeezed mine in return. Despite other events – the smiting, Goliath, HR-6984 – all I could think of was how much I loved my children and how proud I was. I like to think I'm pretty resilient, but listening to Tuesday talk I felt my eyes water and my chest tighten. I remembered what a small baby she had been; how she had walked late, talked early. Of her first Meccano set at two, her first long-chain polymer at four, and of learning Latin at five, so she could better understand the *Principia Mathematica*. I remembered her first day at nursery school and how the teachers said how much they'd learned, her first patent application for an improved alphabet with only eighteen letters and going up to collect her doctorate in mathematics aged eight.

But through all that she had been our little girl, and despite her dazzling intellect, we had endeavoured to bring her up as normally as possible. And while I watched her fluff her lines with the nervousness of a normal person rather than the detached and mechanical tone of her contemporaries, we knew at least that we had succeeded in making her as human as she was brilliant, and with that, we trusted, came an ability to see beyond pure science and the application of knowledge, and to be able to make a distinction between what science could do, and what it *should* do.

'Makes you proud, doesn't it?' whispered Landen.

We listened to the rest of her speech, but it had become increasingly technical, and by the end we could understand only one word in seventeen. But we were delighted to be on the list of people she thanked at the end, in particular for showing her 'the value of normality'.

'That was really good,' said Landen as she came off the stage to thunderous applause. She hugged us both, then was whisked off to do a press conference, leaving us standing quite alone. We wouldn't be telling her to go to school any more. As far as we were concerned, our job was done.

'Well,' I said to Landen, 'how are things with you?'

He looked at the tattoo on my hand and said that he was fine, that Friday wouldn't be back until late given our last trip in to see the Manchild, and that we were parentally redundant.

'I suppose that's what we should be striving for,' I said, 'which reminds me, did you get into Image Ink this morning?'

'I forgot again.'

'Me too. Twice. Hang on,' I added, 'what's Gavin Watkins doing here?'

I had seen him through the crowds, sitting quite alone at a small trade stand. We walked over.

'Hello, Gavin,' I said, using a conciliatory tone of voice.

'Oh,' he said, glancing up dismissively, 'it's you. The tart's mother.'

It wasn't a good start.

'Okay,' I said, 'we need to talk. You don't want to be killed, and we don't want to have to visit Friday in prison for the next three decades. Do you want some tea?'

He gave a resigned shrug.

'All right.'

34

Thursday: Gavin Watkins

'The content and use of slow-release patches was once totally deregulated, in order to allow those to whom drugs have an unavoidable lure a safer method of ingestion. The concept was simple in that it was thought impossible to overdose from a patch – but human ingenuity and stupidity know no bounds, and after two people were found dead covered in patches from head to toe in a steam room, the illegality of non-approved patches was reconfirmed. They remain, of course, hugely popular.'

Julia Scrott – *The Nonsense of Prohibition*

We bought Gavin a cup of tea and a cupcake and sat in the canteen while a *Nemicolopterus syntheticus* flapped around above us, part of a project to revitalise the ailing home cloning industry. The tearooms were filled with mad scientists of one sort or another, many of whom had the unkempt 'wild hair' and mismatched clothes look that seemed never to go out of fashion. Some sat quietly, too shy to order or too unaware to know it was self-service, while others could not stop themselves and insisted on regaling the staff with logical methods by which they could serve more efficiently.

Gavin sat slumped idly in his chair, his slovenly manner, ill temper and foul mouth endearing him to no one. But he knew as well as we that if he was going to survive the next twenty-four hours, we were going to have to at least pretend to get along.

'So if I'm *not* murdered I turn out to be a serial killer in thirty-six years' time?' he said once we'd explained just what we'd found out. 'But why do I kill those useless and boring people? Without that dumb meeting on Tuesday night, I'd not even know them – and moreover, not even *want* to know them. Worse, I end up buying a Vauxhall. I'd *never* buy a Vauxhall. Not even to kill someone with.'

He took a deep breath.

'Okay,' he added, 'I admit it, I can be a bit intolerant towards the mendacious savages I call my fellow men, but there's a big jump between that and serial killing. And if I *were* to survive your moronic son tomorrow, why would I wait until I'm fifty-six to start a rampage? What suddenly changes me?'

'We don't know,' said Landen, 'it could be anything: death of a loved one, passed over for promotion, brain abnormality, a bet, boredom. The list is long. And yes, Vauxhalls might be shit now, but in three decades they could be like Volkswagens are today.'

'You mean driven by smug, self-important middle-class idiots with hideously spoiled children?'

'It's possible, yes.'

He thought about this for a moment.

'But if those other ex-potential ChronoGuard are *already* dead in *this* future, how will killing me change that?'

'Because at this precise moment in time,' I explained, 'you're still around to kill them.'

'But I'm not,' he insisted. 'If both those events represent this timeline, killing me has no effect – if they were alive right now, then *not* killing me would guarantee their deaths.'

'There is something in what he says,' said Landen.

'But both those events do not represent one timeline.' I added, 'I can only think that we are seeing two timelines at once, with all events. Your murder is in *their* timeline, and *their* murder is in your timeline. Once a timeline is taken out, all will revert to as it should be.'

'Wow,' said Landen, clearly impressed with my explanation.

'Smart girls give me the horn too,' said Gavin sadly, 'but they always ignore me. Tuesday ignores me.'

'Maybe you should try washing,' I said, 'and keeping a civil tongue in your head.'

'Will that work?'

'Probably not in your case, but it's certainly worth a try.'

He nodded reflectively. He responded well to straight talking, so I tried a different approach.

'Gavin, how did you turn out to be such a nasty piece of work?'

He shrugged.

'I could blame my parents but that's just whiny victim bullshit. Some people are just naturally unpleasant. I've known for a long time that I'm something of a shit. I tried for years to hide it, but it never worked, so in the end I decided to just go with it, and see where it led me. What's your excuse?'

This time we just laughed at his impertinence, and surprisingly, he laughed too.

'Okay,' he said, 'what's the deal tomorrow? Do I conveniently reveal my soft underbelly for that toerag Friday to gut, or do I run?'

'We don't know,' said Landen, 'but Friday is at this moment attempting to find out more. He thinks there might have been *sixteen* Destiny-Aware ex-timeworkers and not fifteen.'

'How will that make a difference?'

'Someone may know something that we don't. For it to be murder, then there has to be a *motive*. Without that, he can't kill you.'

'So I should do nothing?'

'If you can.'

There was a pause.

'Why are you here anyway?' asked Landen. 'Shouldn't you be in school or breaking windows or pushing over grannies or something?'

'I'm a freelance mathematician,' he said loftily, 'offering my unique services to those either too stupid or lazy to work it out for themselves. Do you want to see something seriously batshit cool?'

'Okay.'

He took a grubby piece of paper from his pocket and unfolded it to reveal a three-digit number. Landen and I stared at it for a moment.

'It's an *even* prime number,' he announced. 'It's been lying there unnoticed since the dawn of maths, and I found it. Archimedes, Euclid, Gauss, Fermat, Newton – they all missed it. How dumb were they?'

Landen and I were staring at the number. The thing was, now he mentioned it, he was right – the number *was* prime, and *was* even.

'That's incredible,' I murmured. 'Does anyone else know about this?'

He folded up the paper and put it back in his pocket.

'No. I'm still studying the implications, since it renders two of Euclid's axioms entirely fallacious – much of the planet's mathematics will have to be *completely* restructured.'

'Then you're good? *Really* good?' asked Landen.

'Good? I'm the *best*. Euclidean, Riemannian, polytrop, differential, 27-dimension mapping, advanced Nextian geometry and even Expectation Influenced Probability. Tuesday did the groundwork, but I took it farther.'

Landen and I exchanged glances. This sounded hopeful.

'What about a value for U_c?' I asked.

'Ah!' he said with a smile. 'The ever-illusive Unentanglement Constant. I've been doing some initial work that looks promising, but I was distracted by the need to expand and catalogue my collection of pornographic magazines.'

'How long would it take?' asked Landen.

'Alphabetically, about a week. If I do it by my favourites, then a lot longer.'

'Not the porn, the Unentanglement Constant.'

'Oh. A workable solution to U_c? About a month.'

Landen and I got to our feet.

'We don't have a month. We don't even have twenty-four hours. Come with us if you want to work with Tuesday.'

After some hunting, we found Tuesday at the Anti-Smiting stand, where she was chatting to some Spaniards who were keen on buying the system, owing to one or two smitings that they'd so far managed to disguise as 'another fire fiesta that got out of hand'.

'Gavin?' said Tuesday, looking at him and then us in a quizzical manner. 'What's going on?'

I quickly explained what Gavin had told us, and how he might possibly have the answer to the U_c. Tuesday looked doubtful.

'Listen,' she said, 'only six people on the planet claim to understand Madeupion Quantum Unentanglement Theory, and five of them are mistaken.'

'Oh yeah?' said Gavin. 'It's between 6.4 and 6.6 quintillionths of a second, right?'

'I never had it *that* accurate,' she replied, looking at him suspiciously, 'and I've been working on the problem for two years.'

'Yes, but you're a donkey,' remarked Gavin. 'Look here, it's obvious.'

He brought out a copy of *Big and Bouncy* from his jacket and started to write a long equation on the cover in felt tip. Landen and I stared at one another, unable to understand what was going on, as Tuesday and Gavin were talking in an odd language full of Greek words and out-of-context nouns and adjectives. Tuesday was wary at first, expecting this to be one of Gavin's tricks. But the explanation continued on to the next page, and the next, and soon the letters to the editor, several trade adverts for odd-looking devices, a lengthy dissertation on friction coefficients and most of '*Readers' Spouses*' were covered in Gavin's spidery algebraic notation. He and Tuesday argued at length, with Gavin often lapsing into insults and Tuesday hitting him hard on the side of the head when he did so. While this was going on, I, Landen and one of the Anti-Smiting reps simply stood there and talked quietly about the weather, and the Defence Shield, and how Smiting Solution's 'Sin Magnet' was so stupendously brilliant in every single way – except for the bit regarding murder.

We had to wait forty minutes before Gavin finally declaimed with a flourish:

'You see? Obvious!'

Tuesday stared at him, then at the notation, then at us, then at the mock-up of the smiting tower.

'That's . . . *brilliant*,' she breathed, and gave Gavin one of those sixteen-year-old dreamy girl looks that can spell big trouble. She grasped him by the ears, pulled him towards her and started to kiss him, right there in front of us and thirty or forty MadCon delegates. We all looked away, hoping they would stop, but they didn't, and after Landen had suggested a bucket of water and I had glared at him and mouthed 'do something', he tapped Gavin quite hard on the shoulder and told him to 'cut it out'.

They disengaged and Gavin turned to Landen with a scowl on his face.

'What is your *problem*, man?'

'My problem? My problem is this: an unwashed lout with a foul mouth and an unhealthy porn obsession is snogging my daughter, *that's* what.'

'And . . . ?'

I almost thumped him, but it was Tuesday who intervened.

'Oh, Dad!' she said. 'Don't be so hideously old fashioned. Gavin is a *genius*. Do you know how lonely it is on this planet if you have an IQ of 240?'

'Yeah,' agreed Gavin, 'so back off, dorkwad.'

'Steady, Angelcake,' said Tuesday, laying an affectionate hand on Gavin's cheek. 'You will apologise to my parents. If you don't, I will never speak to you again – genius or no genius.'

Gavin thought about it for a moment, then hung his head and mumbled:

'Sorry, Mr and Mrs Parke-Laine.'

We told him it would be okay but to 'mind his mouth', and Tuesday told us that she and 'Gav' could probably sort out the U_c problem by morning. We gave them money for a cab and they trotted off excitedly, Tuesday hanging on to Gavin's hand and telling him how he would eventually meet her sister Jenny.

'She's really funny, you'll like her.'

'Is she an . . . elder sister? The sort that takes a bath quite often and who never locks the door?'

'Not at all,' she said, giving him a thump, 'she's my younger sister.'

'Blast.'

'If he carries on as he is,' said Landen under his breath, 'I may have to kill him myself.'

'Don't even think about it. The world needs Gavin – or his intellect, anyway – and Tuesday seems to be fond of him in an unfathomable sort of way. Besides, if they *can* figure out how to make the shield work, Joffy in the cathedral and the felons up at Wroughton don't get fried, Swindon gets to keep the £100 million from Smote Solutions and the library gets some funding. Best of all, I don't have to transport a Righteous Man around all tomorrow morning. You know how tiresome they can be.'

'You're right,' he said, 'children first.'

We stood there in silence for a while, contemplating the unusual turn of events, and the mixed feelings they engendered. We were glad that Tuesday finally had a boyfriend, just disappointed it had to be Gavin.

'What now?' asked Landen.

'I need to get back to the office. Duffy and Spoons will be organising a garage sale to try and fund the library service.'

Landen said he would drop me there on his way home – I could use my official car to get home, or a taxi.

'We can drop into Image Ink on the way,' he added.

'Okay – but let's not forget this time.'

35

Thursday: Evening

'John de Hepburn's Eleanor of Aquitaine tell-all of 1209, *Bonkeing Kinges for Pleasure and Profite*, was the first true celebrity bio. Despite receiving rave reviews and a massive two-figure advance for a sequel, the book did not find favour with King John, Eleanor's son, and de Hepburn was found dead the following winter having apparently "*Atempted to swim, with dire foolishness, the river Cherwell while disporting himself chained to an anvile*".'

James Finisterre – *Genres in Classical Literature*

I spent the rest of the day at the library, attempting to change the large quantity of saleable equipment that Duffy and Spoons had earmarked into cash. The difficulty was not in finding a buyer – there was a lot of good stuff there – but persuading the banks to agree to a line of credit ahead of the sales. They wouldn't be working tomorrow since the financial centre was to be evacuated as a precaution owing to the upcoming smiting, so it was imperative that this was sorted before the end of the day. If it wasn't, by the time the banks reopened on Monday morning, the Wessex All You Can Eat at Fatso's Drink Not Included Library Services would be bankrupt and closed, the rubber stamps would have fallen silent, and all chance of retrieving overdue books gone for ever.

I'd called home several times to see how Friday was getting on at the timepark. Millon had gone with him to keep us advised of progress, but other than a call on the landline to say that Friday had donned a gravity suit and gone in, there was no news. If he had to go 'deep slow' at the timepark to find the Manchild, he might not be out for hours.

Twice during the afternoon I had my hand on the red phone and the emergency hotline to Nancy at the World League of Librarians, but each time Duffy laid his hand on mine, telling me this was not anywhere near a serious enough emergency, leaving me wondering just what *was*. But he was right. By the time early evening had rolled around, I had negotiated a half-million-pound overdraft. We now had two whole days in which to figure out our financial problems.

I dropped down to the sub-basement as soon as I was done to see how Finisterre and Phoebe Smalls were doing with the palimpsests.

'We're working through the pages of *Brothels of Dorset on Sixpence a Day* one leaf at a time,' replied James, whose eyes were looking tired from comparing hundreds of pictures, 'and we've managed to source where the manuscripts he reused might have come from – mostly mass-copied cookery books and celebrity bios.'

Phoebe held up a scan of one of the palimpsests, the old writing running under the new.

'This was originally a page from the thirteenth-century bestseller *Parsnipe Cooking with Olive of Jamestown*, which was the first cook-book to have a production run of over two figures.'

James held up another example of lost and recovered writing.

'And this was originally from an edition of John de Hepburn's scurrilous Eleanor of Aquitaine tell-all *Bonkeing Kinges for Pleasure and Profite*.'

'Yes, yes,' I said, 'all very fascinating, but anything *unusual*?'

'There's only this,' said Phoebe, holding up a picture of a grubby page with the palimpsest highlighted behind it. 'It's not from the Respected Keith's *Evadum*, nor, as we suspected, an early treatise on *Dry Rot & Other Cankers of the Joiste* by Howard de Winforton. In fact, we can't find out what it is.'

'But what does it *look* like?' I asked.

She thought for a moment.

'It bears something of a similarity to the style and spelling idiosyncrasies of the Venerable Bede, but strays far from his usual subject matter. Bede generally wrote boring ecclesiastical histories and translated biblical tracts, but this looks more like . . . *comedy*.'

'I didn't know the Venerable Bede did comedy.'

'He didn't. What's stranger is that this comedy does not seem eighth-century in taste or style. Not so much wenching, farting and jokes with dead animals, but more gentle and lyrical – more in keeping with the storytelling tradition known collectively as "Homer".'

'What are you saying?'

'We're not sure. We've called Bowden in to have a look as he's more into Homeric verse than us, so we should know more then. He might recognise it, or at least give us an indication of what might be going on.'

I told them to call me the instant they had something, and then took a cab home, deep in thought about the week's events, and the possibilities that might face me the following day. Friday had still to kill Gavin but for no good reason that we could see, and the possibility of avoiding going to prison was looking pretty faint. Tuesday still had to find the answer to U_c, something that would allow the smiting to impact harmlessly on the Anti-Smiting Defence Shield. If she and Gavin *couldn't* find the Unentanglement Constant in time, then twenty or so hardened felons were to get fried. *Unless* I could get a Righteous Man in place, in time – and then Joffy got fried. I didn't much care for any of my options.

As soon as I got home, I went and changed my patch for another one of the smiley-faced illegal varieties that Lucy had scored for me. It was working better than a Dizuperadol, but I reduced the dose to a third of a patch rather than a half, as I was still a bit giggly at inappropriate moments.

'How are things?' asked Landen from the doorway of the bathroom.

'Pretty crappy,' I told him, outlining what I had to do tomorrow.

'You'd really fry Joffy?' he asked.

'*I'm* not frying anyone,' I said, 'and I'm hoping it won't come to that. Gavin looks like he knows what he's talking about.'

'Joffy has family to miss him,' said Landen quietly, 'billions look to him for guidance. He has good work still to do on the planet. Theological unification is just one step on a greater journey.'

'That's true,' I murmured, hitching up my skirt once the patch was on, 'but the murderers have family that'll miss them too, won't they?'

'No, actually, they won't,' said Landen, following me down the upstairs corridor. 'I checked and they killed most of them. Some of them even killed other families that *reminded* them of their real families. What I'm saying is that Joffy is worth fifty of them.'

'He wouldn't agree with that sentiment.'

'No, but if you were to "accidentally" drive the Righteous Man to the wrong airfield or were delayed or took a wrong turning or something, no one would ever think badly of you for it.'

'Don't think I haven't thought of it,' I said with a deep sigh as we walked into the kitchen, 'but Miles made me promise. Maybe Joffy is the price we have to pay in order to find the answer to the meaning and purpose of existence.'

'It'll be a waste of a good Joffy. I don't think God has any more idea than you or I about what's going on.'

Landen had made this point before. He called it the 'Nihilist Deity Viewpoint by Proxy' approach. I filled the kettle.

'Perhaps He is just a part of the riddle of existence. Perhaps we all are.'

'Tea or coffee?'

'Tea. Think of it this way: a single brain cell has no intelligence but in company it can do extraordinary things. Perhaps the entirety of existence is the true, unifying intelligence that drives what occurs – for a reason that is quite beyond our understanding – or even to a higher plane where the concept of understanding is laughably redundant.'

It was an interesting concept. Mycroft had often theorised that the whole of existence was so large and hideously complex that it must be sentient. And if this was so, then it must have a truly warped sense of humour and have an abiding love of maths and hydrogen – and a deep loathing for order.

We stood in the kitchen for a few minutes in silence.

'Any word from Millon or Friday?' I asked.

'On their way back. It didn't sound as if they had much luck. Our maths geniuses are hard at work. There was a panic earlier when Tuesday took Gavin to meet Jenny, then found she wasn't there. I made up some story about Jenny being off at a sleepover.'

It was one of our standard excuses.

'She does a lot of sleepovers.'

'I know. Damn that Aornis.'

I looked down at my tattoo, then noticed that I had a plaster on the back of my hand – a new one, next to the tattoo. I frowned, then lifted up the corner of the plaster, read part of the words beneath and stuck the plaster down again. I looked at the clock. It was just past six.

'Landen,' I said quietly, 'we should have a family meeting, here in the kitchen at *exactly* eight o'clock – and bring the cordless drill and some screws.'

'Why?'

'I can't say.'

'You can tell me.'

'No, I can't say because . . . I don't know.'

36

Thursday: Aornis

> 'The Hades family when I knew them comprised, in order of age: Acheron, Styx, Phlegethon, Cocytus, Lethe and the only girl, Aornis. Once described by Vlad the Impaler as "unspeakably repellent", the Hades family drew strength from deviancy and committing every sort of horror that they could. Some with panache, some with half-hearted seriousness. In time, I was to defeat three of them.'
>
> Thursday Next – *A Life in SpecOps*

Friday got back at seven, very tired and none the wiser. He had met the Manchild again, who had confirmed that there *had* been sixteen letters, but he had no idea who the sixteenth might have been. He was simply told to dump them in a postbox at the correct time, which he had done. The only thing he did mention was that two of the envelopes might have been opened and then resealed – but for what reason, again, he had no idea.

Millon had gone down to his hermitage to practise thinking deep thoughts to himself and swot up for his upcoming hermiting exam, and Gavin had nipped out to speak to the Professor of Mathematics at the Swindon Best Deals for Used Cars at Fish Brothers University, who while an 'oaf with so little knowledge it saddens me' could nonetheless offer a few pointers regarding knot theory, which might open a potentially exciting new line of enquiry regarding the U_c.

I had just finished a call from Phoebe when Landen walked into the kitchen at quarter to eight with the cordless drill and some screws, and I told him what she had said: that Bowden had been up to the library and identified the mystery palimpsest as being a lost work of

Homer's entitled *Margites*, and that it was probably translated by the Venerable Bede, which was not only one coup, but two. Phoebe was working on the theory that this lost epic poem of Homer's had accidentally found its way into St Zvlkx's recycling pile along with mostly eleventh- to thirteenth-century dross, and that the book had then been spread around Zvlkx's mass-copied publications – and Jack Schitt had been going around hunting them down to destroy them.

'Why destroy them?' asked Landen.

'I don't know,' I said. 'Perhaps to give another copy greater value, a little like the plot of *Goldfinger*, but given the risk involved, it hardly seemed worth it. Besides, Jack Schitt was a high-level operative with a Top One Hundred Ladder number – why would he waste his time on a lost work of Homer's?'

'And why *didn't* he want the Defenestrator's copy when he'd found it had already been catalogued?'

There was no good answer to this either. But at that moment Tuesday walked in, and the matter was quickly dropped in lieu of something that I *thought* was more pressing, although I still didn't know what it was.

'Okay,' said Landen, 'we're all here and it's almost eight o'clock. What's this all about, hon?'

'I can't remember.'

Landen raised an eyebrow.

'Aornis?'

I said nothing, and after handing the cordless drill to Friday, told him to secure the three doors that led into the kitchen.

'Through the door frame?' he asked, since the doors were all Regency period doors with architraves.

'Do it now.'

So he did, and the wood screws bit deep, splintering the wood and looking shockingly untidy. I could only hope that we weren't due a visit by English Heritage's militant wing any time soon.

'What now?'

I told them all to sit down, and explained to Tuesday that Jenny didn't exist – never had done, in fact, that she was just a Mindworm created by Aornis Hades in order to mess with our heads.

'That's crazy,' said Tuesday. 'She came into my lab to say hello to Gavin not half an hour ago.'

'No, you only *remember* seeing her. Like all the other memories you have of her.'

'So I didn't rescue her when she got into trouble swimming on that holiday on Rhum?'

'None of it happened. Jenny is an implanted memory. A Mindworm.'

Tuesday thought for a moment.

'Okay, let's just say that's real. I can see that. But now I know she's a Mindworm, I can deal with it.'

'You can't because you'll *forget* that you have a Mindworm. That's part of the Mindworm. In many ways it's a burden on us, not you. Here,' I said, 'write it on the back of your hand.'

I passed across a pen and she wrote 'Jenny is a Mindworm' on the back of her hand. I handed a sheet of paper to Friday.

'You're taking minutes. A rough idea of what's happened, with the time. All pertinent points listed.'

'Okay,' he said, 'so where does screwing the doors closed come into this?'

'I don't know. But something doesn't add up, which begins with the obvious question: why Tuesday? Wouldn't the Mindworm be *more* effective on me or Landen? I then got to thinking that maybe it once was – which would explain why I have a tattoo on the back of my hand, and no one else.'

I showed them the tattoo.

'I had this done two weeks ago, and the only plausible explanation is that I was then the one with the Mindworm. And if Aornis is still in Swindon, then it's entirely possible she might be living under our very noses. In the house, perhaps.'

They were all silent and looked at one another.

'You have evidence for that?' asked Friday.

'None – but there is quite often stuff left out, fridge left open, doors closed when they should be opened, and the booze levels fall a bit more quickly than they should. It's the obvious place to hide. Where better than in plain sight?'

'But what can we do about it?' asked Tuesday. 'I mean, if she's in the house and can change our memories retrospectively, who's to say we will even remember this?'

'There's been a development,' I said. 'For the past few days I've been meaning to go into Image Ink and find out why I had this tattoo put on my hand. I forgot every time.'

'Senior moments,' opined Landen.

'Maybe not,' I said. 'What if I *did* go in all those times, and every time I went in there I'm met by an exasperated tattooist who has told me the same thing all week? And how annoyed do you think I would be once I knew I'd know nothing about it after leaving the tattooist's?'

'I'd imagine you'd be pretty annoyed.'

'Me too. So annoyed, in fact, that I'd try and do something about it. In fact, I probably have been doing something about it all week. I woke up with a black eye and skinned knuckles on Tuesday.'

'One of my motorbikes had mud all over the wheels this morning,' said Friday, who was still writing the minutes furiously. 'Someone was chasing all over the estate on Wednesday night. The thing is, no one knows how to start that bike but me.'

'Then *you* were the one riding it. Chasing Aornis, I presume. You may even have caught her. But then she got to you. You forgot you had captured her, and she slunk away.'

'I had a bruise above my eye and skinned knuckles when I woke up this morning,' said Landen.

'I think we've all been battling Aornis all week – but just have no memory of it. *We may even have had meetings like this.* All attempts to capture her have failed. We may even have made the same mistakes again and again because, without any recall, we can never learn.'

'Okay,' said Tuesday, 'that sounds totally whacked, but yes, I sometimes get the feeling I'm being watched, and the clothes in my cupboard get moved and smell of Organza when I don't use scent. The thing is, how do we capture someone like that?'

'Back at Image Ink I probably asked myself the same question. I may even have been making preparations. I found this an hour ago.'

I held up my hand and peeled off the plaster. There, in small letters, was tattooed:

`Secure family in kitchen for 8 p.m.`

'You had that written?'

'I think so. I have no idea what's going to happen, but what I do know is this: what is happening right now is not a memory. The only reliable course of action is one that we take instantly. We have to act compulsively, and without mercy.'

'Can we be sure Aornis isn't in here now?' asked Tuesday, looking around. 'I mean, what if she's making us forget her almost the same instant that we see her?'

There was no simple answer to this, and we all looked around nervously. Landen even opened the broom cupboard.

'If that is the case,' he added unhelpfully, 'anything we said at the beginning of this conversation might not actually be what we said at all.'

'The minutes reflect pretty much my memory of what's happened,' said Friday, scanning the handwritten sheet carefully.

'We're safe in here,' I said, 'or at least, for the time being.'

Tuesday picked up the cordless drill and stood up.

'What are you doing?'

'Letting Jenny in.'

We exchanged glances.

'There is no Jenny, Tuesday.'

'Bullshit. She's been crying outside the door to be let in for the past ten minutes, and you've been telling her to piss off for as long.'

'Is she talking now?'

'No.'

'How long since she stopped?'

'Ten seconds. What's the problem?'

'Look at your hand, Tuesday.'

She did, and there was 'Jenny is a Mindworm' written in her own handwriting.

'Now look at the minutes Friday has been jotting down.'

She did, and there was nothing about Jenny listed at all. She sat back in her chair, thoroughly confused.

I beckoned everyone closer and lowered my voice.

'The reason you can't hear her now is because she's only in your memory. Jenny's not outside, Aornis is.'

'But what this tells us,' said Landen, 'is that her power through a closed door is limited to the person with the Mindworm. If she could get to us all at once, we would have opened the door by now, Friday's minutes would have been destroyed, and all of this forgotten.'

'Right,' said Friday, 'and ten seconds must be about the limit of her manipulative horizon.'

We heard the boards creak outside, and we exchanged nervous glances.

'Aornis?' I called out, my voice sounding less confident than I might have wished. 'We know what you're up to.'

'You have no idea what I'm up to,' came a familiar voice from just outside the door. It was Aornis. 'You've figured me out sixteen times already in the two years I've been living here, but I always win. Whoever controls the past controls the present, Thursday. Screwed the doors shut, eh? Good move. The last time you locked the doors, but the keys are all missing now, aren't they?'

'We'll defeat you,' I called out.

'From inside a locked room? No. I'll get to you all eventually. Pretty soon you'll all start remembering the holiday on Rhum, the one where Tuesday rescued Jenny from drowning. The only reason you've noticed me around this time is that I've been moving the worm around before cementing it permanently in all of you. After that, my power over the whole family will be complete, and we can enter a new, joyous era of me as your unpaying guest, and you all as my compliant servants.'

'Not this time, Aornis,' I said.

'I'm getting memories of Jenny,' said Landen, 'small, and giggly, and on that holiday.'

'Me too,' said Friday, logging the occurrence on the sheet of paper in front of him. I too was getting them, now – not just holiday memories, but old ones, of a painful birth. It seemed real, but I knew it wasn't – but it would doubtless become so.

'I'm getting the birth now,' said Landen. 'You?'

I nodded, and a phone started ringing. It wasn't our phone, it was a mobile phone somewhere, and I glanced at the clock – it was eight o'clock precisely.

'Not mine,' said Friday, patting his pockets.

'Yours,' said Landen, and I searched through the pockets of my jacket where it was hanging on the back of the door. I found nothing, but the ringing was *definitely* from there, so I searched the jacket until I found it – a vibrating lump sewn into the lining.

I slit the lining open and a mobile phone dropped out. I quickly pressed the answer button and put the instrument to my ear.

'Hello, Thursday,' came a voice I didn't recognise. 'Do you know who is speaking right now?'

'Not a clue.'

'She's more powerful than I imagined,' said the voice. 'We've spoken six times in the past week. I'm the Cleaning Lady. Does that ring a bell?'

'No.'

'Listen carefully. I'm outside the main gates. You have to let me in and then keep Aornis occupied in any way you can. She can delete on a ten-second horizon, so you cannot let her out of your sight for that long or she'll be gone for good. Even if you've forgotten the plans we made earlier, you will still be able to access those erased memories by acting on impulse. Let your instincts take over.'

She then gave me some hurried instructions, told me not to fail, wished us good luck and the phone clicked dead. I turned to look at everyone as the memories of Jenny learning to walk came creeping back.

'Was that the Cleaning Lady?' came Aornis's voice from outside in the hall. I ignored her and beckoned Friday and Tuesday closer.

'I need you two to open the security gates,' I whispered, 'so remind each other within a ten-second time frame. This is all you have to do, and if you feel the urge to do something random on instinct, then go with it – they'll be forgotten recalls. Okay?'

'Okay.'

'Landen, you're to cause disorder in Aornis's mind. Mnemonomorphs are highly attuned to recall, so I want you to just lose yourself in your memories. It's only when we are forming new memories that she has a pathway in. On constant recall you'll be nothing but a distracting buzz in her head, and she can't get to you. Do that from here.'

'I'm getting Jenny's eighth birthday,' he said.

'We booked her a magician.'

'Who turned up drunk.'

'It seems so real.'

'It might as well be.'

'Where's your pistol?' I asked.

'I don't remember.'

'Blast,' I muttered, for Aornis was already putting a few safeguards in place. I handed Friday the cordless drill.

'Fed up with this. Let's deal with Aornis for good.'

Friday, Tuesday and myself positioned ourselves at the door. I turned back to look at Landen, who had his head in his hands and was thinking hard, deep in his own thoughts. I listened at the door for a moment, and when I couldn't hear anything, I signalled to Friday, who unscrewed the door, and as soon as it was open they both dashed out.

'Open the security gate no matter what,' said Friday, 'and repeat this order.'

'Open the security gate no matter what,' repeated Tuesday, 'and repeat this order.'

'Open the gate no matter what,' continued Friday as they ran down the corridor, 'and repeat this order.'

I trod quietly into the hall, then into the living room. There was no sign of life – nothing. I could feel the memories of Jenny coming back, and already a sense of confusion was rising at the edge of my conscious mind, the sort of feeling you get when waking from a deep slumber and you're not sure where you are – mixed with having a word on the tip of your tongue, and that odd empty feeling when you walk into a room not knowing what you're doing there.

I walked to the fireplace simply because I thought I should, and touched the cold marble. I picked up a vase and turned it upside down. A note fluttered out. My fingers might have been trembling slightly as I unfolded it. I already knew who it was from.

I've been in New Zealand for the past six months [the note read], *so no, I'm not in the house. Everything that has just happened to you – the Cleaning Lady, the sealing of the kitchen – are merely memories; a time-released gift from me to make you realise the futility of even considering you can rid your mind of me. I'll let you savour this frustration for the next half-minute and then it will fade. The joy of all this is that I can mess with you and your family as many times as I want and you'll just never get it.*

It was signed: 'Aornis'.

'Hello, Mum,' said Tuesday as she walked in, 'what are you doing?'

'Did you open the security gates?'

'You told us never to do that unless for a good reason.'

'I don't suppose it matters now.' I sighed, sitting on one of the arms of the sofa in a dejected mood. The whole thing had been staged. And I had only half a minute to ponder my own hopelessness before losing it altogether. I stared at the note again and prodded absently at the handwriting. I stopped, for the ink had smudged. I hobbled to the writing desk. A blue biro was lying on the desk, the stack of notepaper still with the impression of Aornis's note upon it.

'Shit,' I said, 'she's still in here.'

'Who?' asked Tuesday.

'Aornis. Open the security gates . . . *Now!*'

She scurried off and I looked around. Aornis couldn't instantly delete herself from my memory, and I still had twenty seconds left. I could feel my concentration lapsing as I tried to concentrate on what I was meant to be doing, the same way as when battling fatigue, and fighting off sleep. The house was too large to search in the time available, so I looked around in desperation. And then I saw it. The pull-cord from the curtains across the large bay windows was rocking. It would only be doing that if someone had recently touched it, and the only way that might have happened was if someone were hiding behind the sofa.

I looked around for a weapon while outside I could see the security gates swing slowly open. I wondered why this was happening and cursed myself for being distracted as my mind struggled to keep my concentration on the task in hand. *There was someone behind the sofa, and they were dangerous, and they shouldn't be there.* I limped across as quietly as I could with my stick raised but in my enfeebled state I knocked against the bureau and the figure behind the sofa jumped up like a jack-in-the-box. It was Aornis Hades.

'Aornis!' I exclaimed, for I hadn't seen her since her trial and enloopment. 'What in hell's name are you doing in my front room?'

She was still under forty and was an attractive woman, well dressed and with a misleadingly affable demeanour. I knew vaguely of her powers of memory manipulation, but had never considered for one moment that she might have tried any of it on me – or indeed, was still doing it to anyone. Which made it even stranger that she was in my front room.

'I was looking for my contact lenses,' she said in a friendly tone. 'Would you have a look? Your eyesight's better than mine.'

'Sure,' I said, then stopped and frowned.

'What were you doing in here?'

She leaned closer.

'I need to talk to you about my elder sister Phlegethon,' she said in a conspiratorial whisper. 'She's *completely* out of control. Remember that incident this morning, when someone tried to kidnap Jenny?'

'When?'

'You remember . . . this morning.'

'I . . . no, yes, wait – that was her in the blue car?'

'She wants vengeance because you killed her brother. You saw her face clearly, didn't you?'

I stared at her, my temples throbbing.

'Didn't you?' she asked, this time louder.

'Yes, I saw her face clearly,' I said slowly, 'I'd know her anywhere. But why would she wait eighteen years for revenge?'

'She dithers. It used to drive Mum nuts. But the thing is, she's dangerous. *Really* dangerous. So dangerous you might have to shoot her dead on sight.'

'I thought Phlegethon was your brother?'

'He changes sex as the mood takes her. But you remember what she said she'd do to Jenny? Can you really let someone like that live?'

'Are you sure it was this morning?' I asked, trying to recall the events. For a fleeting moment the attempted kidnap had been clear, but now I was having trouble figuring out even where it happened, and it might have been a black car, not a blue one. My doubt had a visible effect on Aornis, who suddenly looked worried, stopped, and looked around.

'Where's Landen?'

'Conducting a recallathon.'

'A *what*?'

'I don't know,' I said with a shrug. 'The word just popped into my head.'

We heard the front door open and Tuesday say: 'Can I help you?'

'Remember,' said Aornis, 'Phlegethon is dangerous. You can't let him live.'

'Her.'

'What?'

'Her. You said Phlegethon was a woman at the moment.'

'Silly me,' she said, 'see how confusing it can be? But she's dangerous, and you know what she looks like, and she should be shot on sight. Now, I must find my contact lens.'

And with a cheery smile she ducked behind the sofa again, leaving me standing in the middle of the large room.

It seemed strange to be standing there all alone in the living room, wondering . . . quite what I was doing there. I knew I had come into the room to do something important. I sat down on the arm of the sofa and my mind clicked over, trying to connect the trail of events that led me there. We were talking in the kitchen, and Landen was still there. He was doing something. Something *important*. Maybe something about Phlegethon's attempt to kidnap Jenny that morning.

And that was when the door opened, and Tuesday came in.

'There's a cleaning lady here wanting to know if you need any cleaning done.'

'We have Georgina and she comes Tuesdays and Fridays.'

'That's what I told her.'

'Where's your father? He can deal with it.'

'He's mumbling to himself in the kitchen and won't be distracted.'

'Really?'

The door was pushed open wider and a middle-aged woman walked in. My heart thumped and in an instant my pistol was pointed at her. I flicked off the safety and Tuesday stepped hurriedly aside.

'Mum?'

'It's her. Phlegethon. She tried to kidnap Jenny this morning.'

'When?'

'On the school run.'

'You never mentioned it,' said Tuesday, 'and anyway, Phlegethon is a man.'

'He changes sex as the mood takes him.'

'I'm not sure that's possible.'

'I'm not Phlegethon,' said the woman, 'I'm the Cleaning Lady, and you're going to have to put the gun down. Rely on nothing your memory tells you. You've been led astray by Aornis Hades and her memory tricks.'

'I haven't seen Aornis for years.'

'You saw her less than a minute ago. She's somewhere in this house.'

My finger tightened on the trigger.

'Impossible! Don't try anything. You fired three shots into our car this morning. You tried to kill us.'

'If that's so, then why can't you remember the police interviewing you afterwards?'

I looked and there was nothing. Just an isolated event – her, a blue car, several shots and Jenny screaming. But it seemed to lack depth and detail, as though I had seen the highlights on a bad TV screen, and only once.

'She's making the memories up right now so you will kill me. She hasn't had the time to put in the detail, but she will.'

My temples ached and a stab of pain hit my head.

'She's right, Mum,' said Tuesday. 'I had lunch with Jenny and she was fine – you know what a chatterbox she is, and she would have been talking about nothing else. I don't think it happened.'

'*Shit!*' I yelled as loud as I could. 'She's in my head. I can feel it, like a spider, crawling over my subconscious, her feet leaving false memory trails like water on a bathroom floor!'

'Where is she?' demanded the Cleaning Lady. 'It's a big house and we need to find her before she starts *really* doing some damage.'

'I don't know!' I yelled angrily. 'I knew once but it's gone. It's like a hole in my head, a dark space spreading. It's like . . . *my mind is going!*'

'Aornis's whereabouts are in there,' said the Cleaning Lady, 'and can be accessed only through instinct – the subconscious working with forgotten recalls. Act now. Do or say the first thing that comes into your head. No matter how strange.'

I was angry now.

'What kind of shit is this?' I said, taking two paces forward, still with the gun pointing at the woman. 'Do anything? No matter how strange? You're crazier than Aornis, you know that? And what if you *are* Phlegethon?'

'Just let go, Thursday.'

'Let go? Let go? I'll show you how I can let go!'

And so saying, I fired four shots into the sofa without looking or aiming.

'Happy now?' I yelled, my face only inches from hers.

'I'm sorry?' she said. 'My ears are ringing.'

'What was that?' said Landen, bursting through the door. He looked at me, then at Tuesday, then at the newcomer.

'Are you the Cleaning Lady?' he said. 'The one who called Thursday ten minutes ago?'

'I'm getting confused,' I said. 'She called me when?'

'Gunshots in a small space are *loud*,' said the Cleaning Lady, waggling a finger in her ear. 'Hello, Landen.'

'Do we know each other?'

'You helped me sew the mobile phone into Thursday's coat at Image Ink this morning. It's been a rough week for all of us.'

'What were those shots?' said Friday, running into the room.

'Mum shot the sofa,' said Tuesday.

'Again?'

'It's stopped,' I said suddenly, 'the kidnapping that didn't happen. It's halted half remembered.'

We all stood there for a moment, attempting to figure out what was going on. My mind was no longer falling in on itself. It felt clear – confused, but clear.

'Aornis has gone,' I said, 'or at least for the moment. Will she be coming back?'

'No,' said the Cleaning Lady, as she looked across at the sofa. 'I don't think she's coming back.'

Landen cottoned on first, and walked over to look behind the sofa.

'Straight through the eye,' he said, 'well done.'

'I didn't mean to kill her,' I said, 'or at least, I didn't *consciously* mean to kill her.'

'I'd better call SO-5,' said Landen. 'They'll be well pissed off that you got her before they did, but pleased at least the job was done.'

I turned to look at the Cleaning Lady, who had sat herself in one of the armchairs.

'Who *are* you?' I asked.

She never told us her name. A brief search of the house revealed that Aornis had taken over the attic above the east wing, and used it as the base of operations for a global network of criminal activities that ranged from securities fraud to counterfeiting, human trafficking and arms sales. SO-5 could hardly believe their eyes when they started delving into her filing cabinets, all of which contained a host of useful information – contacts, front companies – the lot. According to the records they found she was worth in excess of £350 million but didn't seem to be spending very much, if anything. She was in it only for the misery – she was, after all, a Hades.

SO-5 took the body, cleaned up after them and were gone in a couple of hours with the advice that this 'was so not worth worrying the cops over'.

We agreed wholeheartedly, and while Aornis's death was certainly no reason to shed any tears, I felt unfulfilled over the whole episode for two reasons. First, that she didn't stand trial, and secondly, that even though I now knew Jenny wasn't real, Aornis had left me in a trans-memory moment where I would think of Jenny, then realise she wasn't real, then muse upon the loss of a daughter, and all that this entailed. I could tell the others felt the same way, too. We invited the Cleaning Lady to supper, which, given all that she had done, was the least we could do. Without her guiding influence, Aornis would still be living undetected in the attic.

She was, of course, also a mnemonomorph, and she told us all the wide and varied adventures her sort had undertaken. From the first great erasure in the Middle Ages to the more recent retellings of recent history, some of which was still going on.

'Some things humans can't and shouldn't remember,' she said, having outlined one particular incident that was now only sporadically recalled, and then only by fringe groups who no one believed anyway.

'Who decides what's to be globally forgotten?' asked Tuesday.

'There's a six-person cabal,' she explained matter-of-factly. 'We meet four times a year to discuss whether there is anything pressing that would be better off forgotten, but we also spend a lot of time tidying up after our more criminally minded brethren.'

'People like Aornis must give mnemonomorphs a bad name,' observed Tuesday.

The Cleaning Lady patted her hand and smiled.

'The stories we could tell, the things no one ever remembers. It could make your head spin. But if you've had that strange feeling that you're in a room and you don't know why, or felt that you should be doing something but can't remember what, you can be pretty sure you've just had something erased. It doesn't have to be big or anything, sometimes just a small part of a larger puzzle.'

We were all silent around the table. We all knew we had heard too much, and that led to only one possible outcome for the evening.

'We're not going to remember any of this, are we?' said Friday.

'Maybe when you're older small shreds of Aornis's death will filter up from the deep subconscious, but they will be indistinct, no more real than half-forgotten dreams.'

'What about Jenny?' I asked. 'What will happen to her? She's so strong in my mind I can smell her. I can't imagine her not being here any more than I can imagine Friday or Tuesday or Landen not being here.'

'You'll never know she was ever there,' said the Cleaning Lady. 'There was only ever one Jenny, and she wasn't yours.'

'Aornis had a daughter?' asked Tuesday, who was sharp enough to pick up this stuff two minutes before the rest of us.

'No one ever created a *Homo mnemonicus* without an intimately known and intimately lost person as a subject. I think Aornis missed Jenny dreadfully, and wanted her to live on. The more she created her for you, the more Jenny became alive. But it's not important. We can remove every single part of her so all you will retain is a fondness for people named Jenny.'

'You're that good?' asked Tuesday.

'I'm the second best there's ever been.'

'It's a great plan,' said Landen, clapping his hands, 'and we all need to get an early night. Big day tomorrow.'

'I was about to say the same thing,' said the Cleaning Lady, glancing at the clock. 'It will take a couple of hours, and I have a serious eradication tomorrow – and the trains are not that regular to Whitby these days. Now, if you can simply relax and all hold hands it will make things easier, and none of this will have happened. And don't worry about the tattoo,' she added. 'You'll go into Swindon on Monday and have it removed. You'll think the scar was a scald that you got three years ago when the handle broke off a pan of water. So if you'll just empty your minds, Jenny and I can be out of your hair for good and—'

'Wait.'

The Cleaning Lady raised an eyebrow and stared at me.

'I want to keep her.'

'*What?*' exclaimed Landen.

'I want to keep her. You might as well tell me you were going to scrub Friday.'

'Mum,' said Tuesday, 'she's not your daughter and never was. Just a notion designed by Aornis – based on the daughter she had and lost.'

I looked fixedly at Tuesday.

'Can you remember her?'

'Yes.'

'And those memories are good?'

'It's irrelevant, Mum. Sure, she was a hoot and great fun to have around, but I know she's not real. Besides, by tomorrow you won't even know she was once here.'

'But I know about it *now*, and it's the wrong decision.'

'But you won't even know about your wrong decision,' said Friday in an exasperated tone, 'if it's wrong at all – which I doubt.'

'All my decisions will be forgotten eventually,' I said quietly, 'but it doesn't mean I shouldn't make the right ones. I'm going to keep her. Can I?'

'It would be a lot easier,' said the Cleaning Lady, 'and with less risk of peripheral memory loss.'

'I think you're nuts, Mum,' said Tuesday.

'I want to keep her too,' said Landen, reaching out to hold my hand. 'You'll not be the only one in the house who has fond memories of a child with existence issues.'

There was silence for a moment.

'I'm in too,' said Friday. 'Sis?'

'Okay, fine,' said Tuesday. 'She always made me laugh, the little scamp.'

'All righty,' said the Cleaning Lady. 'Looks like I'm going to make that train to Whitby after all.'

She pulled a mobile phone from her pocket and pressed a couple of buttons. 'Remember that ten-seater Tiltrotor that came down near Barnstaple two years ago owing to a gearbox failure?'

'Yes?' I said.

'Jenny would have been on that, en route to visiting a pen pal in Liskeard.'

Landen and I looked at one another. I held his hand and he blinked away a tear.

'Graham?' said the Cleaning Lady into the mobile. 'You were right. They're going to keep her. Get on to the Falsification Department and tell them we need a memorial stone in Aldbourne cemetery.'

She looked at me.

'Jennifer Houson Parke-Laine-Next,' I said, tears welling up in my eyes, '1990–2002.'

'Under the yew,' added Landen. 'The dappled shade during the summer will make it a peaceful spot.'

I gave out a choke of grief and Landen got up to give me a hug. I had seen her not half an hour ago, and soon she would be gone for good. But we'd remember the good times, even if they'd never happened – or at least, not to us.

'Don't start blubbing, Mum,' said Friday, wiping his eyes, 'you'll start us all off.'

But it was too late.

'All set,' said the Cleaning Lady, snapping the mobile shut. 'I'll bid you goodbye. You might hear from me again, and if you do, you'll do me a favour but never know why. We often need favours. Right,' she said, cracking her knuckles, 'let's put everything to rights.'

'Can I ask a question before we lose all this?' asked Landen.

'Of course.'

'Has something like this happened before? A daughter like Jenny, a family like us?'

'Many times.'

'And do they always opt to keep them?'

She smiled, and laid a hand on his shoulder.

'Always.'

37

Friday: Morning

> 'The GSD has a fairly elastic set of rules, as it endeavours to cater for all faith tastes, from those who enjoy the dressing up and high theatre, to those who rarely, if ever, attend church. The GSD's ten *Bastions* are the central pillars of the church, and it is prescribed that everyone undertake "at least four" of the Bastions every day. How you undertake this is a matter of personal choice. The Third Bastion, "Pause and Consider", can last less than a second or over an hour, depending upon taste. The Seventh Bastion, "Moment of Levity", is often considered one of the most important.'
>
> David Twiglet – *The Unification of Man*

My eyes flickered open and I rolled over. I was lying in bed and could feel Landen's warm body beside me. I glanced at the clock. It was just past six, and I'd not slept better for weeks. The room was dark, and outside I could hear the faint hooting of an immature tawny owl. Beyond this was the distant murmur of the M4, and as I stared into the darkness I heard the distinctive hum of the induction motors as a Skyrail car moved through the village below, doubtless taking early risers into work. I looked across at Landen and put out an exploratory hand. He rolled over, placed his hand on my stomach, moved it up, then down . . . and was out of bed within about an eighth of a second with a shriek of alarm.

'What the . . . ?' I cried, and then realised. I didn't know what a tawny owl would have sounded like, and I'd have to have superhuman hearing to detect the hum of a Skyrail a mile away. But then I wasn't me. I lifted the sheets and had a look. Something was missing. I'd been replaced again.

'I thought I was feeling a little too good,' I said in a resigned manner, jumping out of bed and looking around the bedroom.

'You won't find what you're missing by looking around,' said Landen, rolling a sock on to his stump and reaching for his leg.

'I'm not looking for *that*,' I said, 'I'm looking for me.'

I checked the closet, the en suite, then the upstairs corridor, the linen cupboard, and eventually found myself in the master guest bedroom, tucked up snug and warm with a sandwich and glass of water in case I was hungry or thirsty when my tenure in this body was up. I'd seen myself like this before, up at Booktastic, but this time there was more time to stare. I looked different to how I imagined, not simply because I usually saw myself reversed in a mirror, but because there was something ineffably alien about seeing yourself directly.

'I look kind of peaceful, don't I?'

'Very,' said Landen, who had been assisting in the search, 'but then I'm used to seeing you like this.'

'Asleep?'

'No – out of your head.'

He laughed.

'Very funny.'

'In all seriousness,' he said, 'you're not going to kill me or anything, are you?'

'If I'd wanted to I'd have done it already,' I replied, 'as you slept. No, Krantz is delivering these day players to help us defeat Jack.'

'Glad to hear it. Defeat him doing what, exactly?'

'Okay, find out what he's doing and *then* defeat him.'

We stared for a few moments more at the real me.

'I'm going to make some breakfast,' said Landen. 'I know you don't eat, but do you drink?'

'Aside from respiration,' I said, not knowing how I knew, 'I'm totally self-contained.'

'Well, I'm not,' said Landen, and went downstairs to make some coffee.

I told him I needed to 'check something out' and walked outside, then down the gravel path in the early-morning light. There wasn't a breath of wind in the air. Everything seemed somehow peaceful, even though the day did not portend well for a number of reasons, an inevitable murder being one of them, and a cleansing pillar of fire the other.

I made my way through the grounds to the yew walk, the tropical hothouse and then the walled garden, and thence to the cascade and lake. I wasn't expecting to see Millon as he rarely appeared before eleven, but I was curious to know how my day player had got past our security system, and I had found a small piece of what looked like the bark of the European beech, or *Fagus sylvatica*, under my fingernail. I followed the high close-mesh security fence towards the bottom field, took a right into the beech wood, and there, parked about fifty yards outside our high perimeter fence, was a large box-van. I chose the most likely-looking tree, quickly climbed to the higher boughs, swung twice on a handy branch and leaped clean across the fence, doing a closed triple forward somersault simply because I could. I caught the bough I was aiming for and dropped noiselessly to the soft forest floor.

I found Krantz still sitting in the cab of the rented box-van. He was purple and puffy and both his eyes were open, although one was looking upwards and a small amount of blood had leaked from his ear and nose. On his lap was a pad of paper on which he had been writing when he died. I twisted the pad from his stiff fingers and read:

Use yourself well, my friend. Protect the dark world we love from all would do her harm. I have been twice dead, so once more makes little difference. Here's what's been happening: I was asked to

I stared at his words for a moment until the meaning suddenly became clear. A 'past best' day player was probably not a terrific thing to be once the organs started to shut down one by one, and he'd wanted out. Goliath's Whistleblower had done for him. Jack had been right. Day players of Goliath staff also had them fitted.

I opened the back of the van to find the same sort of medical paraphernalia we had found at the Finis Hotel. But aside from the discarded Tupperware coffin lying outside the van, there was only a single sarcophagus remaining, the seals unbroken and marked 'T. Next MkVII – activate within one hour if seal broken'. I peered through the semi-translucent polyethylene and could see a figure inside. I quickly added up the day players on the manifest, and how many we'd seen. One more go at this and I'd be back to single me again.

I gently heaved Krantz into the passenger seat and drove the van around to the front of the house, keyed in the security numbers and went to the coach house to deposit the sealed sarcophagus in a disused stable. Next, I carried Krantz to the rose garden to bury him in one of the beds, despite the 'recycle responsibly' mark I found on his forearm. It wasn't a human body, so I wasn't breaking any laws and could have put him out with the trash quite legally, but it was the last vestige of Krantz, even if whatever had made Krantz Krantz left the real Krantz a week ago. It seemed the least I could do.

'Morning, Mum,' said Friday as I walked into the kitchen, 'you look . . . *different*.'

'And you seem very perky for a potential murderer. What gives?'

He shrugged.

'I've kind of resigned myself to it. The Manchild told me that the future me was pretty smart, and I should have more confidence in my own future abilities. The truth of the matter is that this afternoon, at 2.02 p.m. and two seconds, Gavin will be dead by my hand and there's nothing anyone can do about it.'

I gave him a hug but he sensed something wasn't right and pulled away.

'Mum . . . ?'

'It's me and it's not,' I said, and explained what I was. Once Friday had told me it was 'pretty weird, even for Mum' and Landen had agreed but added loyally 'It's still your mother – kind of', Friday accepted it, but I saw him looking at me strangely for the rest of breakfast.

Gavin appeared soon afterwards, yawning and scratching.

'Hey, Friday,' he said, 'still going to kill me this afternoon?'

'I guess.'

'D'you know why?'

'I can think of a number of reasons, why I *might*,' he said, 'but none as to why I *should*.'

'Any luck with the Unentanglement Constant?' I asked Gavin.

'None at all,' he said, pouring himself some Shreddies. 'We went down a dead end until four a.m. last night, and restarted the calculations in a different direction at six. I'll be honest, it's not looking good.'

'Shit,' I said to myself. If Gavin and Tuesday failed it meant Smote Solutions would be the first line of defence against the smiting, and I'd have to swap twenty seasoned felons for Joffy, always supposing I could deliver the Righteous Man on time, and in the right place.

'Gavin?' said Landen.

'Yes?'

'It's not good manners to come to breakfast dressed in only a T-shirt.'

Gavin stared at him.

'It's worse manners to murder a guest. Your son is going to kill me and you're worrying that I'm half-dressed?'

Landen fell silent at this. Gavin was right. It didn't make much sense.

Tuesday walked in, hair damp from a shower. She knew instantly that something was wrong about me. But she was less freaked out than Friday, and peered closely at my skin and eyes, then asked several probing questions about metabolic functions until I felt like a frog on a dissecting table.

'What am I,' I said, 'your science project?'

'Oh boy, if *only*,' said Tuesday admiringly. 'Where's Mum if you're not her and you're here?'

I told her I was upstairs, and asked her about the U_c, but she gave the same answer as Gavin.

'We've only been working on it since yesterday,' said Tuesday, helping herself to some orange juice. 'These things generally take a lifetime. If we work *really* hard we might get a small amount of preparatory work done before Gavvers bites the bullet.'

She laid a hand on Friday's arm.

'I know that this is a whole destiny thing, but if there's any way to avoid his early demise, I'd really appreciate it.'

They stood there together in silence for a few moments until Gavin belched, then got up to get some coffee from the machine.

'Oh, for all that is good and decent,' muttered Tuesday angrily, 'put some trousers on, Gav – no one here wants to see your arse.'

And she took him by the hand and led him out of the door, telling him he should have a shower – if for nothing than to be at least clean for his own autopsy.

'She's taking it quite well, isn't she?' said Landen.

'Resigned to it, I guess,' I replied. 'It must be her scientific mind. Once she feels something is inevitable, then worrying is a waste of time. Mycroft was the same.'

'I wish I could feel the same way,' grumbled Friday.

My mobile rang. It was Joffy. I paused for a moment, unwilling to answer it. I'd not spoken to Joffy since Miles told me he was going to be vaporised along with his cathedral, and I wasn't sure what I could say, given that my actions might assist his demise. But I wasn't going to *not* answer it. I flipped open the phone to hear him laughing.

'Hello?' I said, but the laughing continued for a moment until he came on the line.

'Hi, Thursday?'

I told him it was me, and asked him with rising hope if the smiting had been cancelled.

'Sadly, no,' he answered. 'We were just running through the ten Bastions of the GSD and had got to Moment of Levity.'

He asked me whether there was a chance that the anti-smiting shield would be up and running by midday and I had to admit that I wasn't that hopeful, even though 'our best minds were working on it'. I then asked him whether he would reconsider leaving the Smiting Zone.

'It's complicated,' he said, 'but the bottom line is this: unless we at least get an *indication* of when talks might begin as to seeking the Ultimate Question of Existence, this flock might have to look for another shepherd who is more willing to listen to our requests.'

It was a dramatic disclosure, and presumably, given His omniscience, would already be known to Him.

'You're threatening to switch allegiances?' I asked incredulously.

'Nothing's off the table,' he replied. 'We thought Diana the Huntress might make a good alternative. Strong, a good looker, and more feminist in her outlook. Smiting would be off the agenda, and we might tip the current gender imbalance away from the male-centric.'

It was a radical notion, and not one that I thought God would accept without some degree of anger, *especially* as it flagrantly contravened Article One. I suggested this, but Joffy was well ahead of me.

'According to Expectation Influenced Probability, if we stop believing in Him, He will cease to exist. It's a last resort, of course, so He has to know we are serious, and my sacrifice would do it.'

'I'm not sure I follow.'

'Me neither, but He's big on self-sacrifice, martyrdom and extreme signs of loyalty. Put it this way,' added Joffy, 'I've run out of ideas, and this seems the best bet.'

'Joffy . . . ?'

He guessed what I was thinking.

'I know I'm asking you to do a lot,' he said, 'but I can't have Smote Solutions use the sinful as a smite magnet. You're going to have to do your best work with this Righteous Man. We asked you to do it for a reason. Well,' he added with an air of finality, 'I guess this is goodbye.'

'The hell it is,' I responded. 'I'll figure something out.'

He laughed, told me he loved me, that I was a good sister, none better and that Miles would call me nearer the time to tell me where to find the Righteous Man – but that if I positioned myself near Chiseldon from eleven, it might help.

I said I would, and he hung up.

I snapped the mobile shut and looked at Landen.

'He's serious, isn't he?'

I nodded and called Phoebe. Chiseldon was about ten minutes' drive from Wroughton airfield, and I'd doubtless have to fight every step of the way. Goliath would be taking no chances.

'Hey,' I said, 'it's Thursday. Do you have access to a sniper rifle?'

'Of course. What Swindon girl doesn't?'

'I'm serious.'

'So am I.'

'Oh – right. Well, I need someone to cover my back.'

'Is it illegal?'

'Quite possibly.'

'Might I have to kill someone?'

'I'm hoping not,' I said, 'but can't guarantee it.'

There was a pause, and I could sense her reticence. The last time I asked her for help, we had – technically speaking at least – sexually assaulted a Goliath Top One Hundred at gunpoint, as a consequence of which, Judith Trask had been murdered.

'It will involve causing a serious amount of grief for Goliath,' I said, 'not to mention humiliation, and a potential £100 million loss.'

'Ah!' said Phoebe in a happier tone. 'I'm in.'

I told her where to position herself, but after that there was little to do but wait, so after checking Gavin and Tuesday were working on U_c – they were, I was relieved to find – I made myself a coffee out of habit, then realised I couldn't drink it, so smelled it instead. I was amused, in an abstract kind of way, to discover that I could tell not just which country the coffee came from, but the probable region, and year of cultivation. I then tuned the wireless to Toad-AM and listened to Lydia Startright's live broadcasting from just outside the Smiting Zone. Little seemed to have changed – Lupton Cornball of Goliath came on air to reiterate the lie that the murderers were all willing participants in their own destruction, and after that I listened to a spokesperson for the GSD, who confirmed that Joffy would indeed be in the cathedral at the Time of Smiting, and that a last-minute cancellation of the smiting had been refused owing to issues regarding infallibility.

I paced around the kitchen for the next hour and a half, variously interrupted by either Millon, who was still cramming for his hermiting certificate, and who wanted testing on logical positivism, or the Wingco, who, despite their expectations, had been receiving sporadic images all morning from the Dark Reading Matter through Daphne the dodo's buffer, which was still transmitting.

I told him I had a moment, so he showed Landen and me the images that had been sent back. The pictures were again fuzzy and indistinct, and difficult to interpret. I could see what I *thought* were mountains and streams and clouds and a unicorn or two, and then explosions and large tracked vehicles.

'Do those look like battle tanks to you?' said Landen.

'I've been watching glimpses of conflict all morning,' replied the Wingco. 'Things don't look good in there.'

'Can we get another dodo inside to see some more?'

'Interesting point. I spoke to the Swindon Dodo Fanciers club, who tell me that pre-V2 dodos have almost four times the sensory bit-rate, and a larger buffer. If we could get a Version Two or lower in there, we might get some better images – and sound.'

'You wouldn't get a Version Two in any condition these days for less than half a million,' I replied, a comment which reflected the greatly increasing value of early home-builds.

'It was just an idea,' replied the Wingco, 'but a sound one – I would even volunteer to take it myself.'

'How would you enter the DRM?' I asked. He gave a few instances of how it might be done, and I froze as a sudden thought struck me. Jack Schitt's inexplicable behaviour of late – in having an assistant destroy the pages with the lost works of Homer written beneath the later, crappier works – might not be so inexplicable after all; and might just explain why the pro-literature Krantz was so willing to help us by supplying day players on a regular basis.

'By the gods,' I murmured, 'I think I know what Jack Schitt and Goliath are up to.'

The Wingco and Landen looked at me.

'Krantz worked for decades on the Book Project at Goliath, and it was his love of literature and the written word that set him on his self-destructive course.'

'I hope you're not going to do one of those bullshit "I'll tell you more when I know for sure" deals,' said Landen. 'That could be a *serious* annoyance.'

'Not at all,' I replied. 'As the Wingco will tell you, travel to the Dark Reading Matter is a one-way journey. You can *never* get back. Unless you have one of these.'

I pointed to myself.

'A left breast?' said Landen.

'No, *clot*, a day player. What I'm walking around in here might have been designed to be a twenty-four-hour disposable office worker or soldier, but it's also the perfect way of getting into the Dark Reading Matter.'

I paused for a moment, waiting for this to filter in.

'Nope,' said Landen, 'not getting this at all.'

'Okay, let's start with his apparent escape from the Lobsterhood. He didn't fast-descend to escape and he didn't base jump. *He read his way into the lost work on the palimpsest.* He then had his confederate destroy the pages. It was the only copy, so once destroyed the now deleted work entered the Dark Reading Matter, *with Jack in it.*'

They stood and stared at me in silence.

'Jack could read himself into a book?' said Landen. 'I thought that was something only you could do.'

'A day player can do almost anything. I'd say we were almost *designed* to be able to cross the transfictional border. Jack could stay for as long as his day player holds out, then die or be killed – and come straight back out of the DRM and into the real world, memories and consciousness intact.'

'I think you might be right,' said Landen, 'but why Krantz?'

'He spent fifteen years on the Book Project ostensibly because he loved literature. I guess he didn't want to see mankind's lost works defiled and exploited.'

There was a long pause while we all thought about what this might mean. The Wingco broke the silence.

'What are they up to in there?'

'I'm only guessing here,' I said, 'but past experience might indicate there is a seriously large pot of cash involved. They've probably been infiltrating the BookWorld for months. All those tanks we saw could well be Goliath – attempting to subjugate the residents of the Dark Reading Matter. I'll find out more the next time I meet Jack Schitt.'

'I need to report this to Commander Bradshaw,' said the Wingco. 'We may have to start sending troops in on a one-way journey. I don't think it'll be considered a suicide mission any longer – just a permanent reassignment.'

'And I've got to go,' I said, glancing at the clock. 'Joffy told me I should be ready and waiting at Chiseldon from eleven.'

Landen asked me whether I was going to be okay, which seemed a bit daft, to be honest. The only thing to fear was the failure of my set task – the good thing about being a day player was that death was downgraded from a vexatious lack of existence to merely a temporary inconvenience.

'If the worst comes to the worst,' I said, 'you'll know about it because I'll be yelling for a cup of tea from the guest room.'

I kissed Landen, checked both my pistols were fully loaded and took spare clips from the gun safe, slipped a dagger into my sock and then popped my head around the door of Tuesday's lab. To my silent question she simply shook her head, and once back in the kitchen I asked Friday whether I could borrow the Sportina.

'Why?'

'It's the closest thing we have to a tank, and I could really do with one of those right now.'

'Game on, Mum,' he said, tossing me the keys.

'Thanks – and don't do any murdering until I get back. Promise?'

'Promise.'

38

Friday: The Righteous Man

> 'The size of the Righteous Person sector within the population is difficult to estimate, but calculations extrapolated from charity work, donations and the "Samaritan Index" might indicate an occurrence of about 11 per 100,000 population. Of these, perhaps only 2 per cent might be considered *truly* righteous, wholly selfless and without a shred of sin – a total of about 100 people living in England today. Who they might be, it is difficult to say. They don't advertise the fact.'
>
> James Hidden – *The Good among Us*

As I headed towards Chiseldon I could now see the hillsides surrounding Swindon were filled with spectators, eager to see the smiting at first hand, as no broadcast images could ever do justice to the terrifying beauty of a pillar of fire descending from on high. Many people had tried to describe it adequately, but usually without success. My favourite description was: 'The sort of spectacle that married the bold elegance of a solar eclipse with the visceral thrills of bare-knuckle croquet.'

Chiseldon is a small village on the Swindon–Marlborough road comprising a few houses, a petrol station, a shop and a railway station. There had been a basic training camp for Crimean conscripts near by, to which I had myself been assigned before moving to Salisbury Plain for vehicle training. The camp had reverted to farmland once the Crimean War had ended, but the iron gates were still present, along with a large bronze statue of Colonel 'Trigger' Dellalio, now covered with ivy and graffiti.

I stopped at the deserted petrol station and climbed out of the car to have a look around. I walked to the road and looked up and down the dead-straight highway. There was traffic, but it was all heading into town, presumably latecomers wanting to indulge in what had been sniffily dubbed 'Smote tourism'. Even though there was an hour to go, the clouds had begun to heap high above the Swindon financial centre. Smote Solutions' 'honeypot' of hardened criminals would theoretically attract the pillar of fire as it descended in a sinuous curve, similar to the twisting nature of a waterspout.

I checked my watch again and nodded to Phoebe, who was parked in the entranceway to the abandoned Chiseldon camp three hundred yards off. The clock ticked by until it was eleven, then 11.15. The traffic died down as presumably everyone was in place to watch the spectacle, and even the staff in the petrol station closed down the shop to go and watch. Within a few minutes I was completely alone.

As I stood there I noticed a large Pontiac driving down the road in a slower than normal fashion. It pulled into the petrol forecourt and stopped, just the other side of the pumps. I walked cautiously towards it and noticed that the engine was still running, and that the windows were tinted.

I knocked on the driver's window. There was a pause, and the window wound down. A tanned man with a military-style haircut was sitting in the driving seat, and out of the window there came the faint waft of gun oil, coffee and body odour. There were four of them. They were armed, bored, and had been for some time.

'Yes?' said the man.

'You know who I am and why I'm here,' I said softly, 'and I want you to turn the car around and leave.'

He looked at me curiously and gave a slight smile.

'And why would I do something like that?'

'Because I don't want to kill you, and you don't want to be dead.'

The smile dropped from his face.

'I don't respond well to threats,' he said. 'There are four of us, Miss Next. How many of us do you think you can take down before we kill you?'

I stared at him, then at his passenger, who had his hand beneath a newspaper on his lap, presumably hiding a weapon of some sort.

'I can take three of you down for certain, four possibly. But it needn't come to that. You're not Goliath. You're mercenaries. So aside from the cash, you've got no real reason to show any loyalty.'

'We think a lot of you, Miss Next,' replied the young man, 'and we don't actually want to hurt anyone. It's messy, the paperwork is a headache, lawsuits frequent and the clients don't like it. Our instructions are clear: take the Righteous Man into custody until after midday. But if anyone stands in our way we are required to take whatever action is deemed appropriate. Do I make myself clear?'

'Perfectly. Now just go home and we'll forget this ever happened.'

He shook his head, and I head two faint clicks from the back seat as safeties were released.

'We can't do that. We have reputations to consider. Do you know how oversubscribed the menacing business is these days? Gigs are hard to come by, and one failure can lose you clients as easily as blinking, and what's worse, slash the daily rate in half.'

And that was when I heard a mild squeak on the adjacent railway line. It was a faint noise, but one that unmistakably heralded an approaching train from the south at a distance of five hundred yards. I could sense the speed it was going, too, and given that it was slowing at a progressive rate, my day player mind calculated I had a little over thirty-one seconds to get rid of these idiots before the

11.36 from Marlborough pulled into Chiseldon station. The Righteous Man was arriving by train.

'Reputation, huh?' I said. 'Ever heard of the Special Library Service?'

They had. *Everyone* had. Ex-SLS could get a job in security anywhere in the world. Half of President-for-Life Vera Lynn's bodyguard had been SLS at one time. The driver looked momentarily worried, and there were some mumblings between the two in the back seat.

'The SLS have no interest in Righteous Men,' said the driver, 'or people like you.'

'Wrong,' I said. 'I'm the Chief Librarian of Wessex. The SLS care very much what happens to me, and right now you're surrounded by a half-dozen SLS. Make a wrong move and you'll have more holes in you than a lump of Emmental.'

The driver and the front-seat passenger looked around. They couldn't see them, of course, for the simple reason that they weren't there. I wasn't here on library business, and had no right to ask the SLS to risk their lives. It rattled the mercenaries in the car, though.

'Bullshit,' said the driver at last.

'Okay,' I said, 'watch.'

I pointed at one of the many lamp standards that were dotted around the periphery of the forecourt. I had to just hope that Phoebe had seen the car pull in and had positioned herself well. She had. The lamp fitting on the standard exploded into fragments from a well-placed shot from her sniper rifle.

'So,' I said as the train heaved into sight along the tracks, 'you're going to leave now, aren't you?'

The driver didn't answer and instead drove out of the forecourt a lot faster than he had come in, and was soon lost to view.

I gave Phoebe a cheery wave, wherever she might have been

hidden, then walked across to the station and pushed open the gate to the platform.

The train pulled in, paused for a moment, then pulled away again. I thought for a moment that I had been mistaken as no one had alighted, but as the carriages moved out, they revealed a middle-aged man standing on the platform opposite the single-track line. He had a beard, a kindly face and was wearing a brown suit and carrying a small suitcase.

'Hello,' he called across cheerily, 'you must be Joffy's sister.'

'Thursday,' I said, and beckoned him to the crossing point so I could take his case and escort him to the car. I learned that his name was Tim, and he had only managed to fit this job in because there had been a late cancellation.

'All requests are treated equally,' he explained. 'No one person is more important than another. What's the job?'

'See that?' I said, pointing to the sky, where the clouds were swirling in a circular pattern above the city. 'There's going to be a smiting, and a group of sinful men have been gathered in order to attract the pillar of fire away from the town.'

'There must be a lot of them,' he said, being something of an expert. 'That's almost four miles away.'

'Twenty convicts, I believe.'

'Poor things,' he said, 'they must be terribly frightened.'

'I don't think they know anything about it at all. All we need is to place you near them to shift the smiting back to the city.'

'No problemo,' replied Tim cheerfully. 'Goodness! A Sportina. I haven't ridden in one of these for years.'

I started the engine and took the back road to the airfield. The time was 11.42, and the sky darkened as a circular void began to open in the centre of the swirling mass. There'd be some hail most likely, then a ripple of thunder.

We sped along the back roads to avoid Wroughton town, and

although I was a day player and more able to think clearly under stress, I could feel my heart beat faster and an odd sense of nervousness that was not positioned in my stomach, but was wholly in the mind. I was driving faster than was necessary in the narrow lanes, while at the same time keeping a careful lookout for the distinctive glint of a rifle barrel. We were vulnerable in the open countryside, and I'd be a fool to think that the mercenaries were the only people employed to stop me. The Righteous Man, for his part, just chatted amiably about things in general. If he felt any danger, he didn't show it.

I looked in the rear-view mirror for perhaps the umpteenth time and noted with relief that Phoebe's red Mini was now behind us at a distance of perhaps two hundred yards. The relief was short lived, however, as a car pulled out of a side road and blocked her way. I put my foot down, we picked up more speed, then turned a corner – and were greeted by the sight of two cars parked end to end, blocking the road. Since the smiting was intended to be here, there was an exclusion zone around the airfield. Smote Solutions might not care two hoots about the sinful, but it certainly cared about civilian collateral damage – it would be bad for business.

I didn't pause or lift my foot off the throttle and we thumped our way through the roadblock, sending the two cars flying into the ditch – this was the reason I'd brought the Sportina, after all. We carried on, this time with cars in pursuit, and with the harsh ring of bullet-hits striking – but not puncturing – the heavy steel of the Sportina. The manufacturers of the car had worked not only to a longevity criterion, but to a military one. All Griffin motor cars could withstand a standard-velocity round from fifty yards.

'Should we stop and see what they want?' asked the Righteous Man. 'Those gentlemen seem very upset about something.'

'"Should we stop and see what they want?" asked the Righteous Man. "Those gentlemen seem very upset about something."'

'They've been paid to kill us,' I said, negotiating a tight corner. 'I don't think talking is high on their agenda – or skill base.'

'Oh dear,' said the Righteous Man, 'how frightfully disagreeable – but I forgive them. Probably the result of an unhappy childhood.'

The cars behind had been gaining on us, then abruptly stopped as we passed a pole with an amber flag attached to it. I wasn't sure why this was so until we passed a red flag a few hundred yards on, and the reason they'd stopped became apparent. We were now in the Smiting Zone of complete destruction, and there was less than thirteen minutes to go. As far as any of the guards were concerned, we were dead meat, and they were too if they followed us in. I didn't stop, took a left through a gate, bumped across a field and then found a particularly dilapidated section of the perimeter fence and drove through it, the broken wire clawing long scratches in the paintwork.

The large marquee that contained the sinful was in the centre of the deserted runway, and we pulled up outside the tent with nine minutes left. The sky had darkened more by now, and the brightest part was the circular hole in the clouds through which a beam of sunlight was shining vertically downwards, illuminating the centre of Swindon as a graphic precursor of what was to happen next.

'Do I have to do anything?' asked Tim.

I told him he just had to be himself, then jumped out of the car to make sure I hadn't been hoodwinked. I hadn't. Through a gap in the tent I could see a group of dangerous-looking men, all in their own perspex cells watching TV and seemingly unaware of the fate that until recently had been about to befall them. There was a sudden shower of hail and I looked up. The hole in the clouds had widened, and the clouds around it were beginning to rotate faster.

Despite the success of my mission, my heart fell. Most of the financial district of Swindon would be annihilated, along with the cathedral and, worst of all, Joffy.

'So long, Joff,' I said under my breath. It didn't seem right, but I was at least glad, if that is the right word, that family had helped him be the agent of his chosen end, and that somehow the GSD would benefit from his sacrifice.

I felt a lump in my throat, but no tears came. I was a synthetic, and tear ducts in day players don't reflect emotion.

'It's impressive, isn't it?' said Tim, who had climbed out of the car and was staring at the strange cloud formation. We could see the air suddenly soften with another localised hail shower and a bolt of lightning plunged to earth somewhere near the M4. Another minute ticked by, but all I could think of was Joffy. The stuff we'd done, the stuff we'd never do.

'You're going to lose someone, aren't you?' asked the Righteous Man, who had been watching me.

'Yes,' I said, 'but I won't be able to weep for him until I'm back in my own body.'

'I'm not sure I under—'

'Hang on,' I said, for I'd just noticed a distant smudge on the low horizon. It was an aircraft of some description, and it seemed to be moving towards us at a good speed. As it grew closer I heard the distinctive *thup-thup-thup* of a Tiltrotor, and I suddenly grew suspicious that perhaps this was *not* quite the end of it. The small craft orbited twice, then touched down not fifty feet away. The engines continued running, and the passenger door opened. I could tell by the laboured way in which the passenger clambered out that this was no copy, no day player, but an original – in all their obnoxious glory.

It was Jack Schitt.

39

Friday: The Smiting

> 'Of the six smitings (to date) since the Oswestry event in 2002, the scientific community has gathered much relevant data, allowing leading smiting researchers to conclude that past unexplained phenomena around the planet might actually have been divine. It is now believed that the unexplained and violent Tunguska event of 1908 was likely a "practice smiting", undertaken by a deity who thought no one would be watching in an empty region of the planet.'
>
> Charles Fang – *Mankind and the Modern Smiting*

'Well, well,' said Jack as he walked up, 'so Joffy found a Righteous Man after all? And there we were, making sure they were all either fully booked, dead or defiled. Goes to show: the unworthy can *always* trust the righteous to louse things up.'

Jack made a move to his coat and I pulled out my pistol, only to see my forearm explode as a high-velocity round passed straight through it. The hand, with the gun still in it, went cartwheeling off past the Righteous Man. It didn't hurt, and the day player military self-sealing design parameters had the blood flow stopped in less than two seconds. In an instant I went for my second pistol, but stopped when I saw Jack pointing his weapon at the Righteous Man.

'Thanks for that,' I said in as sarcastic manner as I could, the somewhat distant relationship I had with my disposable body still surprising me.

'My pleasure,' said Jack with a smile. 'Always useful to have a sniper covering your back, isn't it? Crabbe,' he said, addressing his henchman, 'would you?'

The Goliath agent I had last seen at the Lobsterhood divested me of my ankle Beretta and my dagger, and handcuffed me by my ankle to one of the marquee poles. He took my left hand and placed my pistol in it, then held my arm tight in the direction of the Righteous Man, who looked impassively at us both. I tried to move my arm, but I think Crabbe was a day player too, and his two arms were more than a match for my one.

'Smiting minus six minutes,' said Crabbe.

Jack lowered his weapon and walked up to me with a supercilious grin.

'It's over, Thursday. The unrighteous will be destroyed, and you with them.'

'I'm a day player,' I told him, 'as you well know.'

'Indeed.'

He held the mobile phone he had been carrying to his ear.

'Are you in place? Good.'

He turned back to me.

'I have one of my people in your house at the moment with a weapon pressed against the head of the real you. This is what's going to happen: the Righteous Man will be killed in order that the sinful may continue to attract the pillar of fire away from Swindon. I could kill the Righteous Man myself, but I thought: Hey! Wouldn't it be more fun if it were Thursday?'

'Go to hell.'

'Undoubtedly. Two choices. Option A: you kill the Righteous Man and we let the sleeping Thursday live, or Option B: I kill the Righteous Man myself, and the real you is no more. Either way he's dead, but using Option A you get to survive. What will it be?'

'Do you get some kind of weird kick out of all this?' I asked.

Jack Schitt smiled.

'I do, actually. Like having Judith Trask killed. Unnecessary, but with a certain *virtuosity* in the baseness of the act, don't you think?'

'So,' I said, 'what didn't you understand about "go to hell"?'

He laughed again.

'Smiting minus four minutes,' muttered Crabbe, this time with a hint of nervousness.

'Really, Thursday,' said Jack, 'it's a no-brainer. Him and you, or just him.'

'I think you should kill me,' said the Righteous Man. 'Joffy always spoke well of you, and you have earned this one small transgression in an otherwise blameless life.'

'You see?' said Jack Schitt. 'Even the Righteous Man wants you to kill him. Count of three.'

I glared at Jack, then struggled to be free without success.

'One,' said Jack.

'I know all about the palimpsests.'

'Two.'

'And I know about you travelling to the Dark Reading Matter. We'll fight you every step of the way.'

'Three.'

And without pausing, he shot the Righteous Man twice in the chest. He slumped to the ground without a sound.

'Bastard!'

'Correct,' smiled Jack, 'both literally and metaphorically.'

Crabbe took the gun out of my hand and headed back to the Tiltrotor. Jack lifted the mobile to his mouth, said 'Kill the bitch', then tossed it aside.

'Mr Schitt, sir!' called out Crabbe from the Tiltrotor. 'Smiting minus three minutes!'

'We've big plans for the Dark Reading Matter,' said Jack. 'A pristine land ripe for domination – and what's more, independent of humans. It will be the perfect lifeboat when HR-6984 strikes. Just imagine: seven billion inhabitants all looking for a new home ahead of the collision, and Goliath able to offer them one in the

Dark Reading Matter – and on a sliding scale of payment. Five-star hotels, so-so apartments, fetid slums – or standing room.'

'You'd be able to transport everyone across?'

'Each survivor who can afford it. Each will be given a synthetic to inhabit, then read into an original work which is destroyed to take them into the DRM. But these synthetics won't be day players. They'll be fully functional models, or at least, they will be if you can afford one. Kind of an ironic finish, isn't it? Mankind surviving the end of the world by retreating into the forgotten thoughts of our forefathers. The current residents of the Dark Reading Matter aren't taking it too well, but they'll come across.'

'I should have killed you long ago.'

'Yes, it was most remiss of you. There! At least we agree on *something* – good to end on a positive note, don't you think? Here.'

He dug the key to the handcuffs out of his pocket.

'If you run *really* quickly you can make it out of the Smiting Zone. But don't forget, the real you is dead. I'm giving you this opportunity to say goodbye to your family before you're slowly poisoned by your own waste products. Day players are named day players for a very good reason. Goodbye, Thursday. You've been a worthy adversary, but it's time to move on.'

He tossed me the handcuff keys, then quickly boarded the Tiltrotor, which spooled up to full power, lifted into the hover and sped away.

I looked up at the clouds, which were now circling ever faster. The sky had become darker and a sharp wind had whipped up, throwing clouds of dust and dirt into the air. I picked up the handcuff key and released myself, then ran across to the Righteous Man, who opened one eye.

'Well,' said Tim, 'he wasn't very nice, was he?'

'You're alive?'

'Of course! I'm righteous, not stupid.'

He opened his jacket to reveal a thick padded Kevlar breastplate that was snugly fitted around his chest. There were two slugs lodged in the padding.

'Makes me less than truly righteous, doesn't it?' said Tim with a smile. 'The sin of suspicion?'

'Shit,' I said as I realised something, 'now you're alive the smiting will move back to Swindon, and my brother will be vaporised.'

'No chance of that,' said Tim cheerfully. 'I'm not nearly righteous enough to move a smiting any appreciable distance. My sin is not just suspicion, but vengeance, and calculation.'

'So . . . we're about to get smitten here and now with all the axe murderers?'

The Righteous Man divested himself of the breastplate, murmured that he thought he might have a broken rib, then stood up and looked around.

'Where is that nasty piece of work right now?'

I pointed to where the Tiltrotor had positioned itself about two miles away, static in the hover, presumably to watch Smiting Solution's success, and the £100 million price tag that went with it.

'Ooh,' said Tim, looking up. 'Impressive, don't you think?'

I followed his gaze. The hole in the centre of the swirling clouds was now bright white, and with a deep rumbling sound, tendrils of a plasma-like substance began to descend. The tendrils grouped, then fused, and were soon a dense tongue of fire. As we watched, the pillar of fulminating power moved sideways and headed towards us. I made to run, but the Righteous Man held my arm.

'Wait a moment,' he said. 'Few get to see something like this at such close range.'

The pillar of fire moved towards us and the air became warmer. The wind dropped and we heard a noise like the soft crackle of burning pine needles. The concentrated wrath gathered speed and a high-pitched whine filled the air. The smiting was almost upon us when it abruptly shifted direction and with a sound like a tornado moved rapidly towards the most evil, unjust, debased and sinful person within the immediate vicinity. Not 'Mad Axeman McGraw' or the 'Butcher of Naples' and not even the infamous 'Toe-cutter of Southend'. No, the pillar of all-consuming fiery vengeance was seeking to punish the transgressions of just one man: Jack Schitt.

I think Jack might have realised what was happening, as the Tiltrotor suddenly dipped towards us and became larger, the noise of the rotor increasing as they tried to outrun the long and fiery arm of punishing redemption. The small craft was almost overhead when the smiting caught it, and the machine exploded into a bright ball of fire that evaporated into nothing, leaving only softly cascading specks of glowing embers that fell about us like snow. Almost immediately the pillar of fire vanished like smoke, the clouds high above closed with a distant rumble, and we heard the applause from the gathered spectators in the far distance. A moment or two later the sun came out, and I blinked and stared at the Righteous Man.

'Wow,' I said.

'I never get bored of those,' he said with a smile. 'Like twenty Bonfire Night displays all squeezed into one. Well done, Thursday.'

'I didn't do anything.'

He placed a hand on my arm and smiled.

'Don't undersell yourself. I'm moderately righteous, but I can't divert a twenty-felon smiting, even with someone as bad as Jack near by. No, the reason it worked was because of your selfless adherence to what was right and just and true. You were willing to sacrifice yourself and your brother rather than kill an innocent man. With you and me pushing the smiting away and Jack pulling, it was a cinch. Teamwork – and they're right. He does work in mysterious ways.'

He nodded towards where the murderers were incarcerated.

'They won't thank you, though. Welcome to being righteous.'

'Who are you?'

He smiled again.

'Let's just say I'm someone who wouldn't want to see any harm come to you or your brother. The GSD has a large and committed flock, and we sometimes make . . . plans in the background.'

'But I *did* come to harm,' I said with a sinking heart. 'I was killed by Jack's assassin at home. I've got about sixteen hours left to live.'

'I took the liberty of calling your husband earlier. The assassin got no farther than the back door. That was the Wingco responding on Jack's mobile. And Joffy was never in any danger, either. You just had to think he was for this to work.'

'You planned all this?'

'Righteousness is a tricksy beast,' he replied with a shrug, 'and has to be helped sometimes. But you came out with flying colours. Can you drop me at the station?'

So we drove quietly off the airfield, and past the cordon, now manned by confused-looking Goliath security personnel. We found Phoebe where she had been released, next to the wreckage of her Mini. I thanked her for watching my back earlier, and she climbed into the back of the Sportina.

'Where's your arm?' she asked.

'Long story. This is Tim. He's a Righteous Man.'

'Hello,' said Phoebe. 'Got any advice for someone who has caused the death of another?'

'You need to contact Judith's husband and explain. It will not be easy, but you can and will find forgiveness.'

'You know about Trask?' asked Phoebe.

'He knows things,' I said. 'I'm not sure asking questions actually helps.'

'Right,' said Phoebe.

We left Tim at the railway station. I told Phoebe all about Jack Schitt and the day players and the palimpsests and the Dark Reading Matter and HR-6984 and everything else he had been up to – and that Goliath would doubtless continue on this course without him.

'There are many more like Jack at Goliath,' I said.

'If he was Ladder number ninety-one,' said Phoebe, 'then there are probably about ninety worse than him. With Jack dead, the object of my hatred has moved to Goliath. What would you say to a merger of our departments? Your funding would be restored; we can recruit from within the library service and then really start to hit Goliath where it hurts.'

'Let's see: run the Wessex Library Services, assist at the new SO-27 *and* kick some Goliath butt?'

'How about it?' asked Phoebe.

I smiled.

'I am so *totally* on board.'

I gave her my hand to shake and she squeezed it gratefully.

We drove back to my house in silence and I let her take the Sportina into town. Phoebe, I reflected, was a good sort, reliable in a scrap, driven, and she disliked big business and all that it stood for – particularly Goliath. We'd make a good team.

I pushed open the doors to be greeted by Landen and the others. My erstwhile assassin was being carted off by the local police.

'What happened to your arm?' asked Landen.

'Long story.'

I related the day's events over lunch, and described as best I could what it was like to be within spitting distance when a truly sinful man is vaporised by the all-consuming wrath of God.

'Cool,' said Gavin once I'd finished the story, 'so all's well that ends well?'

'Not *precisely*,' I replied, glancing at the clock. 'It's now 1.30 p.m. Destiny is heading towards you and Friday, and will be with you in thirty-two minutes and four seconds. If it can be sidestepped, so much the better.'

'How do you sidestep destiny?'

'It depends what sort of mood she's in – warm and forgiving, or cold and immovable.'

'How do we tell?'

'We can't – until afterwards.'

Gavin's face fell.

'Bummer.'

40

Friday: Destiny

> 'Of all the implausible notions with which the unconventional scientist has to battle, destiny is the one which gives the most trouble. The notion of predestination, that the future might be already fixed irrespective of the billions of random interactions that precede it, sits poorly within the laws of physics and probability. But from a spiritual point of view, destiny sits very comfortably and in some cases, is the sole guide to a sentient being. A beacon to follow, a guiding light in an otherwise empty existence.'
>
> Millon de Floss – 'Intelligent-sounding stuff to spout', from *The Hermiting Manual*, 2nd ed.

'Okay,' I said, once everyone had gathered in Tuesday's lab, only because it was conveniently large, 'let's just talk this through point by point. Friday, you're not due to kill Gavin for . . .'

I looked at my watch.

'. . . another twenty-six minutes.'

'I think I might stand in front of him if you try,' said Tuesday.

'And I think I might let you,' said Gavin, who was clearly eager to add 'coward' to his long list of personal failings.

'It won't help,' I said. 'Both your Letters of Destiny say this *will* happen.'

'Agreed,' replied Friday, 'so let's talk out the problem. First, some evidence.'

He opened a briefcase and produced a plastic wallet that contained some yellowed scraps of paper.

'This is what the Manchild unearthed up at the Kemble Timepark yesterday. Despite the murders not happening for another thirty-six years, part of the investigation records survive.'

'You have records for things that haven't happened yet?' asked Tuesday.

'Certainly. There had to be something from which to compose the Letters of Destiny. But annoyingly for us, the records were kept near the engines. The leaking flux has aged them almost three and a half thousand years.'

He placed some of the aged documents on the table.

'What we have offers compelling evidence for what we've suspected – that Gavin will definitely be behind the murders. We have the remains of witness statements, a security camera image of the Vauxhall KP-16 that kills Shazza, and a registration document with Gavin's name on it. On the remains of the interview logs, we see that Gavin would have worked for the Goliath Corporation, and as Ladder number 2789 – pretty high up.'

'I'd never work for those losers,' said Gavin, 'in the same way as I'd never own a Vauxhall.'

'We all do things we never thought we'd do,' said Landen, 'people change.'

'Not me,' said Gavin cheerfully. 'I'm a tosser for life – however long or short that might be.'

There was silence for a moment.

'My guess is that the motive for the murders is nothing to do with the people concerned, but everything to do with how long they live,' I said. 'If Mr Chowdry is correct and HR-6984 will strike us only because we are expecting it to, then evidence of life beyond 2041 will lower expectation to zero and we'll survive. If Gavin killed these people at Goliath's behest, then Goliath are plotting the destruction of the planet and everyone on it.'

'Hang on,' said Landen, who was always the slowest when it came to this sort of thing. 'Goliath want the Earth *destroyed*? For what possible reason? They'd be destroyed too.'

'The Goliath Corporation,' I said, 'are trying to use the Dark Reading Matter as some sort of a lifeboat – a Brave New World to be run by them and them alone. It won't be ideal for mankind, but will at last fulfil Goliath's mission statement: to own everything, and control everybody.'

We all thought about this for a moment.

'So let me get this straight,' said Friday, 'I've got to kill you to stop you killing the others, so that everyone can see they live beyond 2041, and thus avert a strike by a rogue asteroid which could be influenced by human expectation?'

'That's Expectation Influenced Probability Theory in a nutshell,' said Tuesday.

'Sodding hell,' said Friday.

'What?'

'I'm on a total, *total* loser here. I kill Gavin, the murders won't happen, the ChronoGuard operators will live long and healthy lives, and the probability of an asteroid strike will drop to almost zero.'

'That's a total loser?' said Tuesday. 'Aside from the murder bit, you'll be a hero. Listen, I'd kill Gavin if it meant saving seven billion lives.'

'And that's the shitty bit,' said Friday. 'As soon as I pull this trigger, the Eventline changes to include the shooting and *no one will ever know why I killed Gavin.*'

We stood in silence for a moment, trying to get our heads around this. We weren't sure, but I think he was right – Shazza had suggested the same thing back during the support group meeting. The Letters of Destiny might have changed several times during the past ten minutes.

'You'll never know why I did it,' he continued, 'I'll never know why I did it, and the seven billion or so lives I save will never know it either. I'm going to rot in a prison cell for the rest of my life still believing my function is unfulfilled, and having no idea why I killed Gavin.'

'I'm not sure I buy that,' said Tuesday.

'It has a precedent,' said Landen quietly. 'Almost every single lone gunman who has assassinated notable figures was never sure why they did it – and neither was anyone else. Maybe that's what they all were. Eventline crimes, for which there can never be any absolution, no matter how strong and noble the motive.'

Tears had welled up in my eyes at this stage, and both myself and Tuesday rushed to give Friday a hug.

'*Oh, stop,*' said Gavin. 'What about me getting a hug? I'm the one about to die. Boy oh boy,' he said to himself at the thought of it, 'mother *and* daughter, hugging me and pressing their breasts upon me, *together*.'

'You're disgusting,' said Tuesday.

'Ah yes,' he admitted, 'but at least I'm consistent. Can you say the same for the rest of the serial liars who deign to call themselves civilised?'

We ignored him. This had been future Friday's plan all along. The last-ditch effort to save the planet. The Destiny-Aware letters as part of the union agreement, the faith that his young self would figure it out and have the selflessness to give up his freedom to help those he had sworn to protect. And it meant Friday had the one thing he had been wishing for: a function. All he had to do was kill Gavin.

So we said our goodbyes, and Tuesday gave Gavin another one of those long kisses that was just a little bit too uncomfortable to behold, and I gave Gavin a hug in which he pulled me a little too close for comfort, and even Landen shook his hand and said that he had his thanks.

'There's still a teensy-weensy problem,' said Friday. 'Motive.'

'Aren't his future crimes the reason you kill him?' I said.

'Seems a bit cold blooded,' replied Friday. 'Besides, once the Eventline has changed, they'll be no motive at all, and I'm not sure the Eventline can tolerate stuff like that. It has to fit together at least a little bit.'

'I know why,' said Gavin. 'Because you think I'm a shit and it's possible I might have got your sister pregnant.'

There was a sudden icy silence.

'Tuesday?' I said in my extra-stern voice. '*You had sex with Gavin?*'

'Might have done,' she said in an offhand manner.

'Tell me you used protection.'

'Well, Mum,' she said, staring at her hands absently, 'we were kind of caught up in the moment.'

'And it was a *terrific* moment,' mused Gavin, rolling his eyes, 'hubba hubba.'

And we set to squabbling after that, mostly about young people not being responsible, and that 'being dead in under an hour' is no excuse for anything, and that Gavin should jolly well be more careful because he wouldn't be around, and then Tuesday said that she wanted something to remember him by and if that was a child with superior intellect and his nose – which was quite good, as it happened – then she jolly well *would*, and besides, she was sixteen, and lots of people she knew got pregnant at sixteen, and didn't we want her to have a normal life and be a normal person and do dumb teenage things so she was a real person and so on and so forth until Landen yelled:

'*STOP!*'

And we did.

'Have you seen the time?'

'Shit,' said Gavin, staring at the home-made atomic clock on Tuesday's wall, 'I'm not dead. How did that happen?'

He was right. It was 14.02 and twenty-six seconds. Destiny had not been fulfilled. We all looked at each other, confused.

'What happens now?' asked Gavin. 'Shoot me dead and apologise to destiny for being late?'

'No,' replied Friday, 'it hasn't happened because it wasn't meant to happen – and if we don't fix this right now, it will *never* happen and Gavin will murder those agents in the future and Goliath will succeed in coercing HR-6984 into our path.'

It was Landen who broke the empty confused silence.

'I've an idea,' he said. 'What if everything we know right now is entirely consistent with the Eventline? Gavin is killed *and* Friday goes to prison *and* the ChronoGuard serial killer is still active thirty-seven years from now? That the Letters of Destiny will happen *exactly* as stated.'

'Great Scott,' said Friday, looking at us all with a shocked expression, 'Gavin and I *have been set up*. I was being tricked into killing him: I kill Gavin, I go to prison, the ChronoGuard are still murdered, and the whole plan carries on as normal. They relied on me to fulfil my destiny and that I would do it without question. The whole thing makes total sense. Even if I had killed Gavin, nothing would have changed – because that slimy piece of shit over there is the *wrong Gavin*!'

'There's another Gavin Watkins?' asked Landen.

'Probably dozens. But there's only one other who would have been ChronoGuard, and he's the sixteenth man. All they had to do was swap over the Letters of Destiny.'

He held up a copy of Gavin's summary.

'This isn't you. You're not going to die, and I'm not going to kill you.'

Gavin looked triumphant.

'I told you I'd never buy a Vauxhall.'

'*Exactly*. But killing you would have fulfilled my destiny. All that remained after that was for Goliath to train up the other Gavin Watkins. Brainwash him, pay him off, coerce him – whatever it takes – to murder all those ChronoGuard. My future self was leaving provision to save everyone, and the future Goliath was doing all they could to thwart me. And they almost succeeded.'

There was a pause.

'Okay,' I said, 'just supposing this all does make sense, where is the other Gavin Watkins? And how can you kill him three minutes ago?'

'Given the timescale,' said Friday, 'only one possible place.'

'Liddington,' I murmured.

'Right,' said Friday, 'all that "Swindon Time Zone" nonsense means that only Liddington is running on Swindon time – and that's seven minutes *behind* Greenwich. I've got . . .'

He looked at his watch.

'. . . three minutes and eight seconds to find him. And you know what? I will. It's my destiny – and his. Tuesday? We need an address.'

He ran out the door and I ran with him, and within a minute we were on the road back into town. Tuesday rang me with an address as we drove past the signs declaiming Cartographic Independence on the edge of the village, and I gave Friday the directions. A few moments later we screeched to a halt outside an ordinary-looking house. Friday jumped out, ran up the garden path and opened the front door with me close behind. We found a young man of no more than eighteen, standing in the hallway reading his mail. There was a suitcase on the floor; it looked as though he had just returned from a trip.

'Gavin Watkins?' said Friday, glancing at his watch. I checked too. There was one minute and twenty-six seconds to go.

'Yes?'

'My name's Friday Next, and I'm going to kill you.'

'Ah,' said Liddington-Gavin, showing us his freshly opened Letter of Destiny, 'I've just been reading about you. Why has that woman only got one arm?'

'It's a long story,' I said.

Friday explained what he had to do, and why he had to do it as the other Gavin Watkins listened quietly. Friday told him about murders that Gavin would commit, and that Friday was sacrificing his own freedom, but saving the murdered ChronoGuard, seven billion people and an agreeably pleasant yet somewhat taken-for-granted blue planet. When he had stopped there was a pause. Gavin looked at Friday, then at the gun he was pointing at him, then at the clock.

'But you can't and won't,' he said with a smile, waving his Life Summary at us, 'according to *this*, I marry your sister and have three children with her. We go on to do great work together – *seriously* good science – and I become one of the greatest mathematicians of my generation. I don't die now – I die in my sleep aged ninety-four in 2082.'

'Sure you do,' said Friday. 'Good at maths, are you?'

Gavin frowned.

'Actually, no.'

Friday first pointed at the letter, then indicated the pistol.

'You've got the wrong destiny. You actually turn out to be a murderous thug, a lackey of Goliath and complicit in the destruction of the planet.'

Gavin looked at the summary again.

'This isn't me?'

Friday shook his head.

Gavin's lower lip trembled as the realisation of his impending fate sunk in.

'You can't kill me for something I haven't yet done!' he said, his voice rising.

'But I will,' replied Friday, his voice now with a mild tremor, 'it is my function.'

He spoke to me next, but without taking his eye off Gavin.

'As soon as I pull this trigger, the Eventline will change, Mum. The whole future will be remapped. I won't know why I did this. You won't know why I did this.'

'But we know why right *now*,' I said. 'Better to have discovered your purpose even for the most fleeting of moments than never knowing at all. In an odd kind of way I'm proud of you. It's just—'

'Just what?'

'You're better than this.'

'What do you mean?'

'I mean that this is a blunt way to change the Eventline. I'm thinking perhaps you can do this better. Some way whereby you won't have the burden of guilt for the rest of your life. Sure you save a planet, but killing someone in cold blood isn't what your future self would have wanted. And besides . . .'

'Besides what?'

'You're a Next. And we don't murder people. Not even for future crimes.'

'Mum, I have to kill him to be certain!'

He was confused now, and I shouldn't have raised any doubts, but I couldn't see my son become a murderer. It was too late. We were out of time. I saw a tear well up in Friday's eye, and as Gavin's clock clicked over to 2.02 p.m. and four seconds, Friday pulled the trigger.

41

Monday: End

> 'When the Asteroid Strike Likelihood Index was solely mathematically derived, there was a 73% chance of HR-6984 striking the Earth. Once the six Letters of Destiny were received in 2004 from the now-defunct ChronoGuard, the likelihood dropped to 1.3%, where it has remained ever since. Of the sixteen ex-ChronoGuard listed in the summaries, seven survived beyond 2041, one by as much as twenty-six years.'
>
> Dr A. Chowdry – *Asteroid Collision Risk Calculation*

So there we were: my husband Landen and I, sitting in the comfort of a Skyrail car, gliding effortlessly above the North Wessex countryside, heading back from Swindon. We'd just listened to the judge remand Friday in custody: 'irrespective of his previous good character and his family's high standing in the community'. Our lawyer had suggested he might do two years if we could plea the charge down to 'accidental wounding' from 'grievous bodily harm', plus another six years for firearms offences. He'd be out in three, with good behaviour. It might have been worse. Any gunshot wound is potentially fatal, and if Gavin had died, Friday could have been in for life. He'd take the plea and do the time: after all, three years in hokey was *exactly* as Friday's Letter of Destiny had predicted.

That's pretty much how it all took place. A week that began with a trip into Swindon with Landen and ended with a pillar of fire cleansing the world of an evil it could well do without, and with my daughter Tuesday with a husband and soul mate, and the knowledge they would both live a long and eventful life with three kids. We also knew from his summary that Gavin remained constant and true despite his tiresomely vulgar demeanour. We'd probably get to like him in our own way, so long as we never invited him to dinner with other people present. Or if we did, we'd make sure they were fully briefed, and supplied with earplugs.

'I still don't know how he came to shoot the other Gavin by mistake,' said Landen, 'or even how he knew there was another Gavin.'

'Friday doesn't know either. A moment of inexplicable madness. So let's just move on.'

My mobile rang. It was John Duffy. He spoke a few words, I thanked him and snapped the mobile shut.

'News from the hospital: Gavin in Liddington lost his leg above the knee. The bullet did too much damage as it passed through for him to keep it.'

'Poor bastard,' said Landen. 'Do I have to start this foundation for people with missing limbs? I've never really had a problem losing mine.'

'Yes,' I said sarcastically, 'you never complained. Not once. One-legged Gavin will run it when he's well enough. His Letter of Destiny says so.'

'I'm glad someone found a function out of this fiasco.'

'Friday will find his,' I said, laying my hand on Landen's. 'He'll just not be able to start looking for another three years.'

'I have the oddest feeling he might already have done so,' said Landen. 'Something about all those Letters of Destiny just doesn't ring true. If your future self could send your younger self a message telling you how it would all turn out, would you?'

'Not in a million years.'

'No,' said Landen, 'neither would I. But I have an idea that the shadowy potential future Friday might still have some surprises in store for us – kind of looking after his younger self, y'know?'

'I hope you're right.'

The Skyrail car sped over the M4 as it headed towards Aldbourne, and home.

I took a deep breath.

'Landen?'

'Yes?'

'Would you be really annoyed if I did some . . . *exploration* in my spare time?'

'What, like in Tierra del Fuego? Someone said there might be an undiscovered continent somewhere around the theoretical South Pole.'

'No, somewhere farther, deeper – into things lost and forgotten.'

'You want to take the last day player into the Dark Reading Matter, don't you?'

'The DRM's in trouble. God only knows what Goliath are up to in there – and besides, I need to get Pickwick back.'

The absence of our pet dodo had confused us until Tuesday's Encephalovision started to send back images of giant marshmallows and more scenes from *The Dukes of Hazzard*, interspersed with the best pictures we'd so far seen of the Dark Reading Matter. Pickwick went across the night before the shooting. The Wingco put forward the theory that an Imaginary Friend might have moved across about that time, and taken Pickwick with her.

We questioned the Wingco closely as he seemed to know something we didn't, but if he knew anything, he wasn't being very forthcoming.

'The DRM is the new frontier,' I said. 'When you're talking human imagination, there are really no limits. I'll take the last day player and be back in twenty-four hours.'

'Well,' he said, 'you'll probably need a torch, and a length of rope – but I won't bother with a packed lunch.'

I laid my hand on his arm, and we sat in silence for a while until the Skyrail car passed Aldbourne's church, and the yew tree with the warm sunny spot beneath it, and a memorial stone.

'Do you ever think of Jenny?' I asked, staring out of the window.

'All the time.'

'Me too.'

Thursday Next returns in TN8: *Dark Reading Matter*

Acknowledgements

I am indebted to Penguin and Hodder for taking (once more) late delivery of manuscript with good humour. Carolyn Mays and the team at Hodder, and Josh Kendall at Penguin, whose company and assistance I have greatly enjoyed over what turned out to be an all-too-short association.

The illustrations in the book were drawn by Dylan Meconis and Bill Mudron, of Portland, Oregon, whose work gets better and better each year, and whose ability to work to brief in a short time is nothing short of remarkable. More of their work can be found at their respective websites: www.billmudron.com and www.dylanmeconis.com. They welcome commissions.

Back after a short absence to the illustrating team are Maggy and Stewart Roberts, and my thanks to them for designing some of the postcards. Maggy's work can be viewed at www.thepaintednet.com.

New to the illustrating team is Phillip Colling-Blackman, who drew 'Beacons' and 'Smote' at the back of the book, and another illustration that will be one of the giveaway postcards. His work can be seen at www.biro-art.com, and he too will take commissions.

My thanks to John Wooten as Nextian science advisor, who told me that the Madeupion and 'Unentanglement field theory' were closer than I realised, but that Ninjas probably won't help science much, although they are fun.

Thanks go to my extraordinarily understanding wife Mari, our two daughters for being there and Jordan for being a cracking big brother to them both. Maggy and Stewart are also owed my thanks for all around support – especially taking care of the family when I had to work through our holidays. Oops.

My thanks go to Claire and Will and Rebecca and Kirsty and Tim and Jessie at Janklow's for their tireless help and support.

I'd also like to thank the Van Allen belts for protecting us from the harmful solar wind, and the earth for being just the right distance from the sun to be conducive to life, and for the ability of water atoms to clump so efficiently, for pretty much the same reason. Finally, I'd like to thank every single one of my forbears for surviving long enough in this hostile world to procreate. Without any one of you, this book would not have been possible.

Jasper Fforde

Wales, 2012.

P.S. Regular readers of my acknowledgments will be glad to hear that we finally have a new dog. His name's Ozzy.

AGE-FAST™

ADDS YEARS IN SECONDS

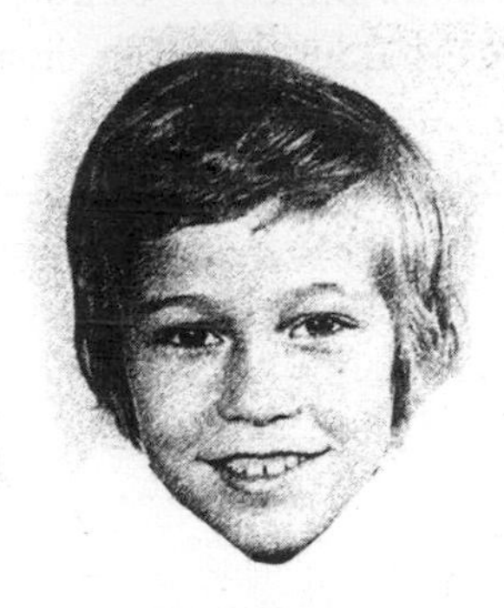

BEFORE

AFTER

I wanted people not to treat me like a kid, so I had thirty-seven years added on in nine minutes. People still treat me like a kid, but luckily my childish mind and infantile sense of humour have assisted in a career as a writer of fantasy novels - thank you, Age-Fast!

- Mr F. of Hay on Wye, Wales.

AGE-FAST™ BE THE FUTURE. NOW.

CALL YOUR NEAREST AGENT FOR AN INFORMATION PACK

TAKE YOUR HOLIDAYS IN THE

SOCIALIST REPUBLIC OF WALES

BRECON BEACONS

not always raining

See your tourist office for details

For 2002 try the proven 1985 model

Griffin Sportina

Now with tyres as standard!

Manufactured in the Socialist Republic of Wales

SMOTE SOLUTIONS INCORPORATED

Modern Solutions To Ancient Problems

A GOLIATH COMPANY

Do you wish this wasn't the end?
Join us at www.hodder.co.uk, or follow us on Twitter @hodderbooks to be a part of our community of people who love the very best in books and reading.
Whether you want to discover more about a book or an author, watch trailers and interviews, have the chance to win early limited editions, or simply browse our expert readers' selection of the very best books, we think you'll find what you're looking for.
And if you don't, that's the place to tell us what's missing.
We love what we do, and we'd love you to be part of it.
www.hodder.co.uk
@hodderbooks
HodderBooks
HodderBooks